★
**Where
You
Goin,
Girlie?**
★

★

Novels by Josephine Carson

Where You Goin, Girlie?
First Man, Last Man
Drives My Green Age

★

Nonfiction

Silent Voices

★

Where You Goin, Girlie?

★

Josephine Carson

★
The Dial Press
New York
1975
★

Library of Congress Cataloging in Publication Data

Carson, Josephine
  Where you goin, girlie?
  I. Title.
PZ4.C3215Wh [PZ3553.A768] 813'.5'4 75-5849
ISBN 0-8037-9815-6

Manufactured in the United States of America

First printing

Book design by Paulette Nenner

★

In memory of T.L.C.

And for Betty, Ross Peter, Brooke, Bruce and Diane

★
With special thanks to

The Yaddo Corporation
The MacDowell Colony
Ossabaw Island Project
Virginia Center for the Creative Arts

"Simply the thing I am Shall make me live."

—All's Well That Ends Well,
William Shakespeare

★

**The Great Depression of the Thirties
never came to an end. It merely disappeared in
the great mobilization of the Forties.**

—John Kenneth Galbraith
★

I HAVE WANTED TO BE A GREAT PAINTER IN OILS.
AS SOON AS I HAVE CARRIED OUT MY PROGRAM FOR
GERMANY,
I SHALL TAKE UP MY PAINTING.

—Adolph Hitler

That the commanding officers
had failed was evident enough, but why?
Part of the answer may lie in the fact
that Americans, for complex reasons that include
racial chauvinism, had never taken
the Japanese people seriously.

—*The Glory and the Dream,*
William Manchester

**What more could we ask than
the Atlantic Ocean on the east
and the Pacific on the west?**

—Charles Lindbergh

**But history itself
is nothing but the activity of men
pursuing their purposes.**

—Karl Marx

PROLOGUE

Renfro

Renfro hadn't planned it but had slept halfway across the state and not opened his eyes until the smell of the refinery, rich, heavy, impounded in the sensual memory, began to rip past the open boxcar door and then to fill the car. He staggered up. The bum who had started out with him in Phoenix the day before had jumped somewhere along the way. He stood at the door, the wind flapping his shirttails, that familiar burnt-out summer wind off the thick mast of the rocky oak-studded land, a smell of those days just after school started in the fall and all the fiddling of summer was quickly folded back down in the dreams again—a smell of chance. That was it. First day in school. First day at the refinery —the *shuup shuup* of the pumps, the hum . . . couldn't have been more than ten miles away. He hardly thought twice, he just jumped, rolling down the gravel bank, skimming the bellies of his forearms. And the freight rolled on past him and out of sight.

And then, sitting stunned on the bank, he realized he had left his sack in the car. But except for his other socks and a ragged sweater, it held little that was essential to him—a stale cinnamon roll, half a box of dried-up raisins. He could find more of that.

Home. Dropped off home by accident. He imagined trying to tell it to someone the way the men had told one another what they had wanted to hear themselves say—all those stories-of-my-life in the jungles of litter and snapping fires in the old metal drums, end-of-the-world fires in the hobo camps and city dumps. Here he was, dropped off home, rid of it all suddenly. Magic. Pitched back home again out of an empty boxcar. Crazy!

He scrambled up the gravel bank and crossed the tracks, watching her off into the rising eastern light, her rear end like that of a cross old bear swaying along—*ticklty-tacklty-ticklty*—clattering down the rails. That was his grown-man lullaby now, well printed on the brain. He lifted his nose like a hound and caught it again on the still air—crude oil.

He leaped across the ditch and climbed the low hill the other side of the tracks, heading into the underbrush and toward the timber. When he reached the trees he turned back and there it was below him—buildings and pipes, the blue and white and red tanks. They had gussied the old place up. There it was. An early shift was beginning—must be seven A.M. then—and a slow procession of cars was winding off the west side of the bridge, around the hill out of sight briefly and then along the drive up to the refinery gate, stopping and starting, showing pass cards. Lots of them. He had heard somewhere about the new hiring. It had come across the air to reach him and the others in the camps, on the trains. Many of them hadn't believed it. As many more hadn't cared. He himself had thought, Too late. But he watched now, fascinated to see the refinery going full blast again after the partial shutdown of ten years ago. A slow, patient train of insects winding into oblivion, it looked to him. A sense of freakish escape hit him. The order and so-called sanity of returning to work eight hours a day, checking in, putting on the gray cotton shop jacket . . . He shook his head. Death! *You wouldn't believe, you wouldn't understand what's happened to some of us.* He thought it out to some boss somewhere.

He sat down suddenly, staring down at the cars which began now to thin out. Idiots! Strikes, exploitation, sucking up to the foreman, promotions. God!

After the shutdown, Alda had supported him, supported all four of them, in fact. For two years! All that sitting around. Playing solitaire and Russian bank with Julia, her hair rolled up in those vicious little metal curlers all day, waiting for some poor penniless sixteen-year-old drugstore delivery boy to call her up, buy her a Coke, bring over two Baby Ruths! His jaws shot a poisonous nostalgia of spit into his mouth and he swallowed it.

Well, his going had been neat at least. The refinery had given him two weeks' notice. He gave Alda two hours. Take what you can get, he told her. Marry Vic now, don't make him wait. Doesn't matter where you live or what you do, just marry him. Take your life in your hands, for chrissake!

Don't go, Weldon, she had said simply. An older sister is more intimate than a mother. He tried to recall that special weary twang of her voice. They'll start up the refinery again, she said. Mother'll feel like you were driven out. As long as the schools are open, I'll have work.

But he had gone, and in anger to make it easier for himself. Left a note for his mother, didn't even see her. God! He had been young then, twenty-one going on sixteen. He went west. There were so many. Like living trash discarded from a mythical winged passage across the country, some terrible pregnant bird of death that dropped its progeny every few miles, a scattered, driven humanity that either made it to the jumping-off place or fell in the dirt. He could hardly remember the feeling of it, only the acts, the doing, and the sense of guilt and freedom. He had stayed clear of other men at first. He took on no human baggage. He remembered that light terrified feeling as if his life had never meant anything before that moment of going. Hit the rods—grease monkey, picker, dishwasher, pusher and peddler and punk, free windy vagrant, barely man, unfettered, invisible. At first, in that alarmed way, he had relished every hour of his days, including the desperation. Finally his only distinction from the other flotsam that drifted with him was sobriety. No booze. That became, after a drunken year and the loss of half his teeth and half his memory, his only rule—no booze. It might have been anything, he saw now, any rule. One made a new primitive order. Any child would do it, make a simple law and cleave to it.

So now, as he always suspected it would, something in his going and doing had tricked him and thrust him off here. He could have ridden right on through, hiding in the car, of course. But the freight stopped in town right in the station. Imagine being locked in there! It wasn't a mile from the house. Were they still in it? Ten years. Probably sold it. Or lost it. Alda, sweating it out all those years. Maybe Julia got work. Or married. And Mother? Or had they failed? Been sacrificed? Or was he the real lamb and could he get back his . . . whatever it was?

He chewed on a twig and watched the refinery gobble up the last man out of the last car, ants all, into the steaming hole, and didn't want any of that, didn't think of it as related to him and his salt and bone in any way. And yet it fascinated him.

He stood up finally, thinking of the dried cinnamon roll and the hard little mouse-turd raisins he had left in the boxcar. He meandered through the scrub oak and underbrush, on the crackle of late summer ground, thinking it out, his brain as if flooded over with all that had been imbedded below the surface of his life all this time—ten neat dropped years—and thought, *maybe this is my time, maybe it has come round or something and I ought to hear this for what it is.* Because he had lost time a long time ago and now it seemed possible to pick up the beat again. Queer thing.

And then, stumbling vaguely around, he suddenly stopped on a slope at an open place and saw, on the bark of a hickory, down low, animal-back height, a tuft of something. He moved near it, pulled it away gingerly, it was so *alive!*—a fine shred of sheep's wool caught there as a packed herd had moved through rubbing against these trees. All that was left of their passing, grazing for slaughter. He held it. He had left even less. Jesus! He was home.

★
**Where
You
Goin,
Girlie?**
★

3

The civilized world, Pom said one night at our table, is coming to an end.

"Wow!" said I, because that meant something was happening, and in Deliria, USA, 1941, how could you be sure there really was a world out there? Pom had said it before but never with that simple conviction. His expressing doubt gave me pause and raised a new regard for him in my heart.

He wiped his mouth then in those tidy civilized zigzags of his with the big monogrammed linen napkin (not our initials) that we reserved for him, and I looked at Sarah who made her predictable comment—

"Aw, Hon, that awful old Hitler! Why don't the Germans just get rid of him, Hon? He's one of their people."

I knew the question was crazy but it was one I couldn't contest because I knew the Germans couldn't or wouldn't get rid of him. And Pom flushed up around the ears as always when she frustrated him. That sudden drenching red and the quick disappearance of it were all we had ever seen of his anger, and I doubted that Sarah noticed even that. He mumbled something polite about its being too late for the Germans and I was relieved. We'll be in it soon enough, God willing, he would often say. Since the fall of France he had changed. He was gloomy and restless, often in a kind of remote peeve and much preoccupied. His world was always falling these days, a world that to me had always seemed like something out of a movie—ships and foreign cities and theaters. But nobody cabled anymore, nobody sailed. Thank you Adolph Hitler. Pom often said he was glad that Lou (his actress wife) was not still alive to see it all.

"You really think civilization is coming to an end, Pom?" I asked, leaning toward him attentively the way Bette Davis did, taking men so seriously. I didn't want him to know how ignorant I was.

He began his sermon then. If Britain falls . . . And Sarah sighed, grimaced and declared Oh Law, and My Stars, Hon, why that's awful!, sincerely playing the good audience the way she did with her clients. Pom's talk was really all for her and not me. He knew he hadn't reached me with his civilization and he should have known the same about Sarah. He informed her regularly, which was rather like blowing up a balloon that had a tiny prick it its side. It would all have leaked out by morning. I had once believed in opéra and cabaret and château-whatever-it-is, all the Louis and Medicis and Rhônes and Rhines, the Tristans and Misérables of Pom's civilization. But my life seemed to have remained the same old doggy number it had always been and I took a certain secret satisfaction in that. If he had been so eager to civilize me he might have bought me a ticket to somewhere, I was thinking just then.

He grumbled on—the Donets Basin, the Caucasus . . .

"*Basin*, Hon?" Sarah queried with a little chuckle and a sly look at me. Ah, between us we could have leveled civilization in half an hour—one of her giggles, one of my sighs, her *Aw Hon*, my highly refined raspberry. But we loved Pom and respected his fear for the world. And he fit into our lives just fine.

Yes, the Donets Basin and the Kronstadt Fortress. "We've got to get over the idea we're invulnerable" he said. And Sarah chuckled again, fondly, and raised her eyebrows. When had she or I ever entertained any notion of invulnerability in our whole windy hand-to-mouth lives?

I stared at Pom's profile. He had that firm fine clear flesh that makes a person look young forever, but he was in his late sixties, I calculated. I stared, musing over him. It hit me smartly just then that all summer I had been wanting to kiss him. Not in the old kid way but differently. I wasn't kissing anything those days but the wall by my bed. I shrank back, furious with myself.

Sarah suddenly said, "Well, I wonder what he hates so much about the Jews, Hon? My Stars, look at that old sweet Abe Dietler. Why how could anybody . . ."

Abe was a friend of Pom's. "Oh, Abe's been an American for ages," I said.

Pom reflected that Abe still had cousins in Austria somewhere. "He's been trying to find them and get them out for two years. If he'd realized earlier— You see, that's just the point. . . ." He shook his head and then helped himself to the tomatoes like a careful surgeon. He's too clean, I told myself for the hundredth time, but you could kiss him anywhere. Wow!

"Right out of Ruby's garden, Hon," Sarah said of the tomatoes. She watched him and then turned to help me to asparagus.

"Just one, thanks. I'm full."

She laughed, forking it onto my plate. "One asparagus, Hon? Why—let's see. That'd be . . . asparagum! Asparagum asparagas asparagat! Heh . . ."

I let out a hoot and Pom shook with half-choked laughter. Sarah blushed as always, peachy, rosy, something by Renoir, Pom used to say. We howled and she batted her eyes, foolishly pleased. She, who could speak all afternoon in Latin if she chose, was obviously the real enemy of civilization around here. She made a farce of things, I reminded myself. Me, for instance. Or take Higgens, for example. Who was Higgens, really? He loomed up that way sometimes in my head. They had just met somehow down there in Shreveport when Sarah was on vacation and bang! —here I was twenty years later. God! Why hadn't she told him about me? I never asked it anymore. *Law, Hon, he was a travelin man. He went all over. You couldn't live a life like that.*

"It's worse," said Pom, "than their letting us know. The Russian invasion puts a whole new slant on the thing anyway. If they get their hands on that Caucasian oil . . ." He sighed and sipped his iced tea like a woman. Then he took out a hankie and patted his brow. His world fell around us in remote crashes and howls. That, and the heat, wearied us. Sarah fanned herself with her napkin.

"Well, Hon, I can't quite understand how the world can let a man get away with all that. My Stars!"

"He's insane, My Dear," Pom said finally. Ah! A summary. I always knew I could expect it from Pom if I were patient. Hitler was becoming more interesting. "It's too simple to be grasped by most people," he went on. "The world tends to accept the power-is-virtue equation, anyway. Especially Americans. But even the British were duped this time. Except for Churchill, of course. It takes a military man to spot a classic enemy." He laughed softly. "Some of them wait a lifetime for a devil like Hitler to appear."

We laughed too then, relieved.

"They'll float in on a sea of oil again, like last time," he surmised. "Think of it—*one hundred and eighty-two tankers* on the bottom of the ocean! What an irony! These thieving oil men will only get richer. Ha! Have to include myself in that, I suppose." He shrugged, helplessly rich.

"Aw, Hon!" Sarah said.

So Pom had cast his gloom, and finally, when Ruby brought dessert, he leaned back and smoked a cigarette as if to seal a pact. Then he asked about us. But by that time we were both wrung out. I told him the everyday lie I usually told Sarah—that I was looking for a job. But not an office job. I didn't want him to find me one.

"Law, Hon," Sarah said. "I don't know how you can even *think* about work in this old heat." She picked up the Japanese fan some client had given her a year ago and plied it as if to swipe away Pom's war exhaust. It *was* hot, even at nine o'clock. Ruby had the electric fan in the kitchen. I wondered why we hadn't bought another one. A sodden orange moon hung near the lease and the house, seeming to cast its own heat. Pom could have paid for ten fans to cool our house if he'd thought of it. I sighed. There was something ironic in his feeling ironic about the war making him even richer. He just couldn't lose money. Even the crash had only temporarily disabled Pom. He had driven out tonight in his pigskin-covered Stutz Bearcat, a gift from a rich oil man long before the crash. He kept it in good shape and drove it only on special occasions or when some whim of excess seemed to hit him. Otherwise he used his Packard. No, he hadn't lost much.

"How about a ride?" he asked Sarah later. She went and I helped Ruby clean up.

★

Afterward I went to lie on my bed. There wasn't much else to do. I flipped through a few books and went back to *For Whom the Bell Tolls*, which was driving me mad with envy and excitement. I didn't know whether I was Pilar or Robert. And then all at once my eye fell on the *Biography of Enid McCleod*, my life work, and it hit me why Pom had been so moody at supper. It was the eighth anniversary of the murder and this was the first year I had let it creep up on me that way. No wonder he was gloomy. Murder. His own son shot by Aunt Enid. In the head. Temporary Insanity. Acquittal, if you can believe it, for popping a bullet in your own husband's head, from the back even, while he was reading a paper in an armchair. I opened the Biography. It sickened and thrilled me—what I had written, what I remembered. Eight years ago. My last entry said—

In the summer of 1941, on a warm night on the porch at her sister Sarah McCleod's house, Enid said of the war—"Let them all kill each other (meaning men). They deserve it, the fools!"

Acquittal, even after eight years, had not improved her opinion of man.

She had said that one night in June when she and Cousin Beasley had come out to supper. Enid had arrived sober and stayed that way all evening. I shuddered. It made the Spanish Civil War and the bell tolling seem like a fairy tale. That one shot—and George Raft couldn't have done a neater job—ran in all our heads like an old always-exploding dream. I wrote—

The Eighth Anniversary passed. Enid spent it at home lying as usual in the dark of her bedroom, sipping bootleg wine and listening to police calls on the radio.

The moon was low now, retreating in the south. I could hear Ruby out back talking to someone. Horace, probably. Wishbone, her steady, was out of town. Horace was her extra. I liked and despised that low flat music of their talk.

But what to do? I listened for the world. The lease was so far from town, and town—Deliria—so far from the real world, that I could have been living on the moon itself. I heard a truck out on the highway; ever so faintly it passed. The crickets seemed to have spent themselves. The soft silence dazzled and terrified me. I had to do something to make my life move. Maybe I ought to get up right now, I thought, and take the electric to town and go to the Creole by myself for a change. Usually I picked Beasley up and took him along. If I went alone maybe someone would dance with me and take me out in the car and all the rest. I didn't know how to make it happen but as long as I had Beas with me I doubted that it would. But I couldn't go alone.

I flounced over on my side and turned out the lamp, lying in the dark. They mumbled on in the yard and now and then a smack broke through the air, someone slapping mosquitoes. I felt like howling. At least Ruby had her men and all that thrashing around she did with them. I wondered if Beas realized this was the anniversary of the night when he heard that shot and came out of his room and saw his father's head blown half away and his mother holding a smoking gun exactly as in a movie with Joan Bennett and James Cagney. What to do? I wasn't civilized. That was it, of course: Pom's civilized world always had something to do—the sound of ice in glasses, music and people milling, they were always milling or kissing or taking trains or writing letters or shooting guns. . . .

Ah well. I turned on the lamp again and opened the book. Maybe *The Bell* was tolling for me somewhere. I read for a few minutes, thinking through the words. Yes, I ought to have taken the electric and gone into town. By myself. Pom ought to have sent me to college and then to New York. I would have met a gangster. Maybe I would have become a great doctor, with emergencies and all. I knew I was feeling six-years-oldish but I couldn't help it. Finally, just when I decided to get up and go, I heard the Stutz in the lane and Sarah and Pom coming through the back gate. They brought a cold watermelon with them. It seemed to me they often defeated my plans that way, by doing something that involved me in their pleasure.

"Look at this lovely thing, Hon. Shall we call Ruby in?"

"Wasn't she in the yard?"

"I didn't see her, Hon."

I did not say that in that case Ruby was in the quarters in bed with Horace. Screwing was as familiar and unfathomable to me as Ruby herself. She had several people to do it with and seemed to know how and I had never had more of it than a front-row seat at her great performances on the cot in the moonlight with one of them.

"Don't bother her. I think they took a walk," I said.

"It's a beautiful night, Hon. You should have gone with us." They hadn't asked me, of course. "You wouldn't believe there was anything wrong in the whole world," she said. "But we saw a carload of those Army fliers from the flight school out there."

We sat at the kitchen table drooling over the watermelon. Pom salted his and cut into it with a fork, beginning at one end and working toward the other. I tore into the middle of mine.

"Thank God," he said, "Beas won't be drafted. The lab has been declared an essential defense industry, and by the time the draft gets to him *he'll* be essential to the *lab*."

I almost laughed. Beas wasn't even eighteen. He worked after school at the labs owned by Abe Dietler's family.

"Law, Hon, it don't seem possible that he'll be eighteen this winter. That old sweet child. I know Enid's proud of him."

Pom froze and then patted his mouth with a napkin and continued to eat. Enid's name hung like an invisible shroud in the air around us. Pom looked up and our gazes locked. Yes, he did remember this anniversary. Why not? We all did. I had been silly to think anyone could forget.

Later, when he was gone, Sarah and I listened to Guy Lombardo and I thought that if I had it to do over I'd have exploited Pom's passion for dispensing culture and told him I wanted to see the world and become educated and famous. I would really have liked a quick little chance, even that, at his civilization. If I didn't get up and get out of Deliria soon, I told my sodden self, if I didn't discover sex and men and cities, I'd never know whether civilization had been worth all the agony it seemed to have cost. But I just knew I was going to get into the world too late. I could see myself, tardy, strolling the burnt-out cavernous former civilized world looking for some of that rich living Pom had known. He had seen Paris before there were automobiles there. He had picked up his wife, Lou, at the theater in a horse and carriage after her first European performance. And he even took his son, mean old murdered Jack Russell, to France and Italy as a boy, and in Italy, so the stories went, they said Jack looked like Lord Byron.

"I never cared much for August, Hon," Sarah said when we were about to go to bed. We stood in the hall where she tried to unbutton her dress at the back. I helped her.

"Neither did I," I said, hoping the murder would come to life and flame up between us. We had never discussed it, *never!*

But she only sighed and yawned. "Law, I think we should've invited them over tonight, Sugar." Meaning Enid and Beasley.

Ah yes, she remembered. Enid was our wound and our secret. What we knew together was her crime. And her life plagued ours because it was more a death than any of us could bear to consider.

The next afternoon I lay naked, played over by muggy air from a sixty-nine-cent electric fan, fuming through a nap I had recently decided was not mine. It wasn't Ruby's either although she too took it, lying out there under the peach tree on her old Army cot with an aplomb that infuriated me. Now and then she would get up to slosh her body with water from the old cistern, dress and all, although Sarah had been warning her for years that the water was contaminated.

No, the nap wasn't ours, it was Sarah's. Ruby and I had both somehow developed this lazy habit of waiting for Sarah to wake up and give that little chirp that announced the beginning of evening. She would go padding down the hall then to the bathroom to emit what I had decided was the Lacrima Christi of her bladder. That was how Pom and his civilization and his wine cellar had stricken my life.

Sarah was oversleeping. She had had a rash of unexpected clients all morning and was worn out. They'd probably be the last to pay, as usual. These emergencies never seemed to notice that we were poor.

I dipped my hand into the bucket of icewater by my bed and flipped the drops like little knife stabs over my belly. *For Whom the Bell Tolls* slid off my flattened lap and to the floor. No, our holdings weren't much. We were lucky these days if a client paid even two bits in cash and no cloisonné cigarette boxes, ironstone pitchers or old velvet hats. Sarah listened to their agonies all morning—treacherous husbands, ungrateful children, thieving maids, vicious hairdressers, incompetent parents—she listened in her cubicle off the kitchen behind the paisley curtain and they paid with a reticule of old lace collars. Ruby used to say of them before she became jaded—Ooooo, those ladies is gonna kill that woman someday with all that blabbin. They all be's worryin where they oughta be doin some kinda job work. Thass they trouble.

Yes, Sarah earned her nap. It was an inextricable part of her whole secret rhythm and the inviolable nature and drift of her existence which just happened to be crazy. She could not be altered nor influenced. She was crazy, as I figured it, and perfect. Civilization was nothing when compared to the mystery of our existence, I told myself. Let it fall.

The phone rang and got her up early. I staggered up and went to wash my face. Enid was on the phone. The anniversary had passed and she was still in the world. I didn't see how she could keep up her dreary life another year. I tied back my hair with a shoelace and threw on a pair of shorts and a halter. Sarah was in the kitchen pouring out her May wine by the time I got there. Her bare arms were mottled and purplish sometimes, worse, it seemed, on that day. She had always had questionable circulation.

"Law, Hon, this heat! Enid called. She says she's getting air conditioning for her room." She laughed at herself. "I could hardly get myself up." She'd probably chuckle when she saw the lid of her coffin closing.

I fussed with my mint tea, stabbing at the ice with a blunt pick. Immediately, and I marveled at this, I assumed in her presence the huge scab of family personality below which, if she had ever bothered to peel it back, she would have discovered everything I was, writhing away under there.

Her white billow of hair had been hastily repinned at the back but was slightly askew like the hat of a woman at a year-end sale. Her puffy angelic face broke open affectionately at me. Yeah, she was perfect. How could a person survive without malice? She had never heard of it.

"You overslept," I grumbled.

"Law, Hon, I know it and Hattie Finch is coming over in a few minutes. She called me this morning. She's got an emergency."

"Oh, no!" She seemed to be breaking the rules a lot lately, letting clients come in the afternoon. "Pom's right," I grumbled. "The world's falling apart." And she laughed and so I laughed because I was her monkey on a string. "What did Enid want?"

She hesitated and then said, "Nothing much, Hon. Sometimes . . . she calls like that . . . you know."

I knew. Sarah kept Enid going. I hated to think how it hurt Sarah—Enid's life, all that drinking, lying in bed half the days of the week and all the evenings unless she came out to see us or Iantha Abernathy took her to dinner, or Pom took her to the country club. Usually she preferred to come to us and she never asked us back. She wasn't going to change although Sarah seemed to think that somehow she would. She'd been waiting for eight years for Enid to get on her feet and take up a life. It was crazy. Enid's house was like a morgue, that place she called her "sweet little bungalow over on Madison Terrace." She had decorated it and then never used it. Beas spent his evenings in his chemistry lab in the basement of that little bungalow, making up unfathomable concoctions that sometimes exploded and blew out the window, blackened the walls and singed off his soft golden bangs and his whitish eyebrows. He would come upstairs afterward all sheepish and amazed and even proud of the minor error which, if it had been a major one, would have blown the bungalow and the two of them to smithereens.

"Why can't Hattie wait till morning?"

"Aw, Hon. Bradley ran off to the Canadian Royal Air Force and she's all upset about it. Her only boy."

She opened the back screen for me and I nipped out carrying my mint tea and Ruby's root beer. "She oughta be glad to be rid of him." I remembered my childhood peer Bradley Finch, whose most courageous acts had been to hang cats or run sticks through the spokes of children's bicycles as they rode by.

Out back Ruby had turned on the sprinkler and drawn her old cot near to the lawn furniture we had received recently from Mavis Travis for a year's consolation.

"Take a chair, Hon. Mercy!" Sarah had been saying that to Ruby for six years. But Ruby never took a chair. She only dragged that splitting cot around with her like some miserable tail. If Sarah knew what she did on that thing at night with Wishbone Watson, I was thinking, or Horace, or even with Gifford if nobody else was around, she'd find it hard to mention the cot.

I fell into the glider and Sarah took the chaise. It was a marvel of comfort, this furniture. But Sarah had earned it. Mavis would have thrown herself under a train, she often said, if it hadn't been for Sarah's commiserations, her Aw Hons, every morning all that year.

I sipped my tea and began to swing a little. Ruby sucked up her root beer and rammed her fabulous red-hot tongue down into the glass to chase the ice, gurgling like a drowning dog. Ruby Rubio Rubissimus. You mustn't decline Ruby, Hon, Sarah had told me when I was ten years old. Because she's colored, I had decided. A fascination. I did it even now, at nineteen, in secret. Ruby had a dozen nasty names for me and predicted my going to hell at least once a day, but I never messed around with her name aloud.

Sarah suddenly held up a hand to the sound of a quail, or maybe it was a rat or a rabbit in the woods beyond the yard. We froze. Our P.M. music was beginning. She sighed then and rattled on again about Hattie Finch and Bradley's enlistment. I half listened. Ruby rattled her ice, nodding. She seemed to listen to Sarah's merest chirp as if it were the word of Jesus. Her mind was as literal as a wall. I let my own mind out on a string like a kite. It, at least, could be allowed freedom even if my body was stuck here. God! It was all the fault of my virginity, I was thinking as usual, and

Sarah was in some way to blame for my virginity, it seemed. I couldn't have explained it but felt it to be true.

There was the four-oh-nine whistle. We listened. The train clattered into hearing over the trestle two miles away and then trailed off.

"Law, Hon, he's early. 'Blow, let us hear the purple glens replying.' Heh . . ."

I smiled and Ruby ducked her head. You never knew what you'd tune in on if you weren't a steady listener around here.

"Don't do that one," I said. "Do 'The Owl.' "

"Whass the matta with 'The Bugle'?" said Rube. "I likes it bess."

But Sarah was too hot and tired today to do more than dribble little lines like pennies cast to the poor. Sometimes, on command, she might stand, smooth her skirt, clasp her hands and without the merest guile deliver a dozen stanzas, clarion, lyrical, passionate, every line true. Then she would laugh, bow and say "Aw, Hon!" as if to apologize for "The Lady of Shalott" or "The Goose" or "The Bugle." "I think that's my favorite," she would always say, no matter which it had been. She knew Tennyson the way I knew certain phone numbers.

It's Pavlovian, Pom would say. A train whistle might blow, an owl cry, a thrush flute, a dog howl, a truck pass in the distance or someone might merely open a door and she would let it loose—"When merry milkmaids click the latch . . ."

Once I dressed up in her clothes and entered her room to announce myself an old wife lean and poor and Sarah laughed for two hours. I smiled to recall it. I took another look now to see if she were flesh.

"Jess do the lass few lines of 'The Bugle,' " Ruby said. She waited, knowing she would get her way. She smashed a few mosquitoes on her arm as if indifferently.

" 'Our echoes roll from soul to soul,' " Sarah began.

I leaned back in the glider. Maybe she had a purpose to which I should cleave. I pondered her, blocking out the poem.

"I likes that one bess," Rube declared. "I tried to tell Wishbo that thing but I cain't get it right. He gots to hear you do it someday."

They babbled on. I stared. Yes, maybe she had a purpose. Maybe I should leap up, I thought, and shout, "*Cast me loose!*" She'd have understood that, having taken elocution lessons. She was back on Hattie Finch's son now.

". . . just don't seem to know what he wants. He goes from one thing to another, that poor boy."

"Well," I offered, opting for reason, "I hope he'll stay away. Hattie will get over it. And at least she's been known to pay in cash. That's more than we can say for the rest of them."

She laughed. "Well, Hon, heh . . . she was just askin me if we could use a case of canned salmon. Her brother caught it up at the Columbia River and had it canned up with his name on the label and all."

"Canned salmon? God! How many cans to a case?"

She opened her mouth. "Why . . ."

"They's twinny-fo cans to a grocery case. I knows that," said Rube.

"Twenty-four cans? But she's been coming for over *six months*! That's not even one can per session! What a cheapskate!"

Ruby gagged and spilled root beer foam out over her chin, where it clung in soft bubbles for a moment like lace.

"I doan know zackly what that sawmen is, innyways. What is it?"

"It's that pinkish fish in the tall cans, Rube. They call it sockeye or something. Ha! Sock-in-the-eye salmon from Hattie the Finch."

Ruby spat again, leaning over her knees, hanging her dark arms down and swinging her head. "Shhhhttt! Girl! You somethin awful!"

Sarah laughed, giddy, her chest trembling and flushing.

We giggled there helplessly for a while and then we sighed. Here we were, that was all. This, I told myself, was our ramble scramble niddly-noodling P.M. oddity and idiocy. Our saga. And I had to get out of it and make them accept my going. But there lay my loins on Mavis Travis's glider, perfectly comfortable. If I had jumped up and shouted, *Look at me!* Sarah would have answered merely, *Aw, Hon, it's just this awful old heat a-makin us all nervous.* Us, you notice. Not me, not you. Sarah did not know my limb-for-limb separateness from her own body, I could have sworn it. She hardly knew of the stranger's separateness, in fact. The catechism of this household, if there was one, concerned only them—humanity—for whom we seemed to be in some nebulous way responsible, whose pains caused us to suffer, or ought to have, we being something divinely more and foolishly less than human ourselves.

Sarah rattled on—Hattie Finch, Bradley, Mavis, Edna, Louise, Bridget Waldemeyer whose husband had thrown the colored girl down in the backyard seven years before and had yet to be forgiven. Pom was going to Washington to an oil council and might even meet the President. But about the salmon, Hon . . .

"Oh, let's take the dumb stuff!" I said. "What the hell. I'll eat it for breakfast. Jews do that. They eat fish and creamed cheese and dark bread for breakfast. It's healthy."

And Sarah said, Aw, Hon, don't curse. And Ruby said:

"What you talkin bout Jews? That lady Lucille work fo is a Jew lady and she nevah had no fish fo breakfass. You plumb crazy!"

Oh God oh God oh God oh Zeus oh Civilization come and get me! Couldn't they see I was going mad? Couldn't they see I needed simple cash—twenty dollars or something? Couldn't they see I had this excruciating body to which nothing whatever on earth was happening? Couldn't they see I was hugging the pillows and kissing the wall? I began to writhe. And then Sarah went inside and Ruby said to me—

"You ain't nevah gonna git shet o that ressless messin roun till you gits you some kinda job work. What you doin sleepin all day and drinkin beer all night down at that Creole outfit is what I like to know. You needs to work."

"I'm getting a job when the plant starts hiring again. In September. And it's none of your business anyway."

"Hit be's my biznez whin I grows the food an my frins brings half the suppa ova heah. Horace done brang us two rabbits agin lass night."

Ha! So it *had* been Horace.

"I hate rabbit," I scowled. "I don't believe in killing rabbits. Besides, he caught them on our land. That makes them ours anyway."

She spewed out her Shhttt at me, that fine oath, that unfathomable scorn. "You blieves in eatin, though, I seen that all right."

I sighed. I had learned to change the subject. "You going out tonight?"

"Mebbe I is an mebbe I isn."

"Who with, Wishbone?"

She pulled a basket of fresh corn out from under her cot and dumped it on the grass. "Heah. Gimme a han with this stuff."

Her long tobacco arms rippled slightly with the action, lifting now and then to swipe halfheartedly at her ears where the mosquitoes sang and hovered. I bashed at my head violently against them, shucking two ears to her one even so. Her dark lean hands pulled and peeled it back in a dragging rhythm that wouldn't let the world move at all. Ah, the dull patience! I marveled at those long fingers like wands with their big, faded, apricot-colored rectangular nails. What did they know, those hands? They were mute and patient, if not resigned. Some Miss Ann down in Arkansas had taught them how and why to iron white people's linens (and I wouldn't let her iron mine; I liked those rough dry wind-smelling sheets to chastise me, some rashy kin to my soul's discomfort) and had taught her to grow food, to preserve, to save butter papers, to wring a chicken's neck, to cut the throat of a hog and dig out the entrails of a catfish quick as a wink. To gather and scour and pick and scrub. And taught that mouth to say Yes Ma'am when company came. Enid got that treatment from her. Pom got it unfailingly. *Mista Pom be's a gennaman. Doan you sass him none.*

We hadn't taught Rube anything. She had just come by one day on an old truck that a month before had taken our maid Ada off to the Arkansas bottoms to pick cotton. Ruby had gotten off at our back gate explaining that Cousin Ada was quitting and had sent her along to do the work. She was fourteen then. I was nine.

Old Rube. I remembered how she stood there with those long blackish scaly knees and that hair pulled behind her head as if snatched back, leaving her face surprised. We paced each other off and finally I gave her a hollyhock doll I had made that day. She gave me a genuine animal tooth on a string. I gave her an old battered copy of *Nancy Drew and the Case of the Missing Necklace.* She gave me a tiny red-and-green potholder made by a blind colored woman in Memphis.

She stayed, moving into the quarters among Ada's meager trappings, and became our keeper, or Sarah's anyway. She was more like tormentor to me but she would have handed over her life for Sarah as if it were a sneeze. But who wouldn't have?

I had been trying lately to find a new tack with Ruby, but we bickered on. We shucked the corn and she told me I had ruined my cousin Beasley with all that beer drinking down at the Creole, and I told her it was nicer than those jooks where she went with Wishbone and somebody always got cut up. And she said that Wishbone was a man and not a boy under age, and I said Yeah! remembering Wishbone's bare shiney brown rump which I knew better than I did his face, due to all that thrashing around on the cot he and Ruby had done on the hot nights of the last five summers. And then she said I had better get my *li*cent to drive that *lec*tric car or the *po*lice were gonna git me and I said the *po*lice weren't interested in a car that went only thirty per and she retreated to her old predictions—

"Oooooo, you somethin awful! You goan to hell *so* fass, you know that?"

Was that a life? I used to stare at her, or at Sarah, or Enid. Any of them. Were they living? Sarah with her clients all morning, naps and sips and babble. And Pom's war worries and dying civilization, and Enid drunk and prone in that shadowy house. Was all that living? What was Pom's civilization if we had lived through it on these mere peanuts?

And should I then get up, I wondered, merely to find a job in some aircraft plant so I could come home to Ruby's rabbit suppers, bringing to Sarah my cash earnings which she would stash away in the ice bag under the towels that had someone else's initials on them and probably forget? I'd work and they'd have my slippers waiting as if for a man. I'd never get away. The clients would stop bringing even napkin rings when they found out I had a job. Sometimes I heard Sarah tell old Iantha Abernathy, who meddled in our business, "When they start hiring again, Hon. She's waiting to hear. Only last week, Hon, she worked for Miss Nina Brosky on that refugee program for the British children. Law, that lovely big house and all. They had *caviar* for lunch, Katie said. My Stars! She'll do all right. Don't worry about Katie." With that apologetic wondering laughter which always took care of my reputation for another week. In what way, I wondered, would I do all right?

Should I keep these windy lives going? Or should I run from Somnambula Junction, from Deliria, Assinopolis, Idiotsville, USA on a Greyhound bus to New York City to become a moll, or a junior reporter, a girl Friday, or a star packed in sequins and feathers on the top tier, a Rockette, a mistress? I asked it but the fates were silent.

Back in the house that evening, I consulted the mirror again to find the same flawless mute answer. Ruby was right when she said, catching me at these musings once, "What you lookin fo, Girl, hit ain't in the mirra."

Later, when she was cooking, I asked her again, "Well, is Wishbone coming or not?"

And she told me, old punch-line Ruby—

"Wishbone done gone down to Awkinsaw to say good-bye to his people down theah."

"Good-bye? Where're they going?"

"*They* ain't goin no place. Wishbone the one goin."

"Huh? Where?"

She could just have told me right out, the fiend. I always regretted asking her a simple question. She loved this bargaining for information.

"Wishbone done joint the Army lass week. He commencin to be a soldier."

"*What?* What'd he do *that* for?"

She shrugged, turning on the steaming sink water to rinse her hands, scalding them as if they were numb.

"Well, he cain't git no job work . . ."

"But those plants are hiring . . . everybody."

She shot me a low look. "Then how come you ain't out there workin?"

"I didn't apply yet."

"Well, he say that draft bizness git him innyways. Might as well go now. He git all his food and laundry and quatahs in that army. An some money fo his po ole motha, besides. An twinny-one dollahs a month cash. Hit ain't bad."

But soldiers and war and guns? Killing? *Wishbone?* All at once I felt her feel his going. She couldn't imagine the map of the world —I had tested her. He was just going away.

"I don't think anybody should go. Why don't all these guys just refuse to fight?"

"Well, then who goan to stop that fella Hitla that coming to git us all?"

I stared. She was infected like the rest of us. Even Rube.

I continued to sweat out August working in secret on my masterpiece.

★
The Biography
of Enid
★
Notes

Born Cambridge, Mass., before Kevin McCleod came west and made himself mayor of several towns, one after the other, in Indian Territory, then finally settled, built the McCleod building. Where there were no schools he opened schools and always found a young man who could teach his daughters. Sarah attended them but Enid, younger, a shy child who clung to her father's coattails the way most children cling to a mother's skirts, insisted upon being taught at home. Old photographs of Enid on her father's knee with a book. In schools around the Territory, Sarah learned Latin and geography and history and mythology. Enid learned to read. She read indifferently a great many books, most of which she forgot. Doing things, walks and shopping trips, rides in the surrey, the old family tales said, seemed to be her preference. Events somebody else created. She took walks with her father, holding up her long skirts. On her first date with a young man, her father followed behind with his shotgun. Indian boys riding by on their ponies splashed mud on her dresses. She cast glances back at her father, demure, gently commanding glances. He obeyed her. Her sister Sarah told of it—

"Law, Hon, she had Papa under her thumb from the day she was born. Especially since her illness."

Diphtheria. Age eleven. Kevin McCleod locked himself in her room and nursed her. Wouldn't let his wife near the child. He received food for the two of them through a little panel cut into the door which he locked afterward, handing back spoons and dishes that he demanded be sterilized immediately. He slept on the floor on a pallet at the foot of her bed like a darkie and wouldn't let the doctor be summoned. He never believed a real doctor would come out to Indian Territory when he could be living comfortably in St. Louis or back east somewhere. Only escaped criminal doctors or shyster doctors would practice in the Territory, he said. And when Henry Killeen opened his practice there, Kevin waited until he had delivered a hundred babies and performed a hundred operations.

"Daddy always thought he understood medicine better than any doctor," Enid said. "He probably did, in fact. You know how he got me well? He talked me into it. I was dying. I didn't care at all, I felt so low and exhausted with all that choking. He sat there night after night and talked to me. 'Try hard now, Baby. Breathe slowly.' What a saint he was!!" And she laughed ironically to think of the waste of such a man. "Sarah's just like him. All that sweetness, no discrimination at all. Except against doctors and lawyers, and maybe the drummers who used to come through."

"Oh, and gypsies, Hon. Law, Daddy hated the sight of a gypsy."

There was a tintype of him as a young man at Harvard.

"Law, Hon," Sarah said, "it's hard to think of Daddy as a *young* man. Such a fatherly fellow."

★
Where
You
Goin,
Girlie?
★
17

And Enid, swinging her crossed leg and smoking with the long black ivory-inlaid cigarette holder that once had belonged to her mother-in-law, Lou Foray, said, "Men of his generation were that way. More fatherly, even when they were young. They knew how to treat women. Lou was lucky to have a man like Pom, even if he was younger than she."

She had hardly known her actress mother-in-law, who had died when Enid McCleod and Jack Russell were adolescents and who had, in any case, rarely been in town. She recalled the glamorous actress who was always catching trains and for whom Pom had bought that special railroad car with the gold fittings and the marble bath. "God!" she would say, "what's happened to the world? Nobody lives with style anymore."

Yes, all that time, even when she was a child, the plan was being laid, fitted together, in which she would admire the mother of a little boy named Jack Russell whom she would later marry, hoping perhaps to find some germ of that grand life in his nature (and did not)—yes, whom she would marry and then kill. All that time, the future was fitting itself together that way.

It was difficult to find any deep difference in Enid after the shooting. She seemed perhaps more idle, more silent, more wry and bitter, but not markedly. She still stayed in bed four or five days a week, sipping. The violent world rattled on out there. She listened to its echoes silently, cloistered, the same as when she lay dying in that dusky room where her father had bewitched her into life again. It made a kind of sense that shuttered rooms, dusky light and emergencies—dying, killing, calls for help—should be the motifs of her life.

Sometimes it seemed her mind was clear and almost empty, that it made no deductions. A memory or an idea might float up into speech, the way a feather catches an updraft in a still garden, surprisingly, a meaningless show of action. But that was rare.

The judge demanded one year of psychiatric treatment, six months of which she got at Menninger and six at home with a Dr. Duberman who later moved away. There had been vague rumors of an infatuation—hers for him—nothing concrete. But once Iantha Abernathy took Enid on a little trip to Fayetteville, where he had moved. At that time Beasley was at Foxe Hills Military Academy. They stopped there to see Beas on their way home, but the attention Enid got offended her and Beasley, and she never returned. Beasley came home instead on vacations and they spent much of that time at her sister Sarah's.

Yes, a memory or an idea would float up suddenly and she might say something quite intimate or revealing to whomever was present—

"That thing you're knitting, Iantha, reminds me of Rowena Pratt, that funny crazy woman I liked so much up at the sanitarium. She used to knit giant-sized stockings and give them to the men patients at Christmas. She was always madly in love with some doctor or one of the patients, poor thing, she looked like a hippopotamus. Once she knitted a bright red codpiece for Dr. Swallow! She told me his genitals were the size of her arm!"

And the sour shriek of Iantha's laughter made the place a madhouse itself. And Sarah, who sputtered and chuckled apologetically, said "Aw, Hon, My Stars! Maybe he had a disease!" which sent them all howling away and Enid crying, "Oh, my God! Isn't she the most divine idiot that ever lived! She was *crazy*, Sarah, for the love of God! She never saw his *genitals!*"

And at that moment Katie, Enid's niece, somewhat late to grasp the meaning of genitals, suddenly got the point and let out a hoot from her hiding place that set them laughing again. For even as a child she knew of her own mother Sarah's literal mind.

But Enid's laughter was always tarnished, unbelieving, a laugh as much at the deceit of the sayer as at the wit or absurdity of the thing said. She assumed that most utterances were lies or misconceptions.

Note: Enid as killer. Sitting among her family, a broken gift, their wound, a scab, not a scar, always available to reopening somehow.

Note: Their shielding her for the reason that she seemed to presume that killing did not kill the killer, maimed but did not kill. And her presumption that small talk was all life need afford. She would sit, swinging a long leg with that abstract irritability, manipulating the long cigarette holder, inhaling deeply and spewing smoke, her head back, with that same rue and scorn which marked her talk.

Note: The peculiar languid vigor of her limbs. How her long, bony, muscleless yet well-turned forearms lay so still and smooth as if dully waxed, a flat, dulled honey color, on the arms of the wicker chair. How undeclarative they were, how patient and perfect, convinced that they need not act, need not achieve, as if they had done, already, the ultimate act and were, thus, wise.

Those rare mentions of her wrecked life—her childhood, her patient days at Menninger—had an innocence and modesty, a casualness that shocked the listener.

And her niece, Katie, hiding, spying, listening, groping for the truth of the horror of murder and survival and acquittal and a meaningless mounting of days all alike in that woman's life, and in other women's lives (not in men's, never in men's, not even Pom Russell's although he paced the floor like an overbred animal in a cage)—her niece submitted to the validity of this greater-than-real person, this killer woman who obliterated for her all other heroic figures—Joan of Arc, D'Artagnan, Jason, Billy the Kid, Jesse James—fixed herself to an idea of some huge truth to be found in Enid, a logic worth a life's pursuit.

And she became royal biographer.

Notes: July, 1935

Beasley, wanting to come home after two years at Foxe Hills Military Academy, bought his mother a canary in a beautiful old cage. It sang for her, to her, for six months, bravely alone against the silence of that house. She tried to tell of it with pride but that had a false sound in her voice. She hated the bird. She muttered once to Sarah that it was driving her crazy, that silly carrying-on all day. Katie felt that like a slap in her own face, her body being half Cousin Beasley's, half her own.

How Enid forgot to get bird food.

How she let the cage become dirty. How she then rushed to clean it, in a kind of slow fury.

How, a few days before Beasley returned from military school for good, Enid announced that the canary had disappeared. Her cleaning girl had stolen it, perhaps. The cage was empty. How Sarah, with her genius for shifting the subject of an idea, said, "Law, Hon, maybe she was lonesome." And Enid said, "Who was lonesome?" And Sarah said, "Why, the cleaning girl, Hon," as if the discussion had been concerned with the cleaning girl and not the bird, thus somehow deflecting the importance of the bird's fate to the greater problem of the loneliness of the cleaning girl.

Motives occurred to Sarah as remedies did, as if inspired and shot directly from the mad jumble of odds and ends that composed her own life and her memory, without benefit of the mind's censorship. She would make some wild loose connection and reveal to them its spark as if she had fused two incompatible wires, not for current but for explosion. If there was a way not to get the point, Sarah would find it.

Thus Enid could always laugh at her sister.

Thus Sarah could apologize lovingly, mirthfully, and remain foolish.

Thus life was absurd as witnessed by biographer Kate.

Katie's thirteen-year-old mind closed down on the truth of the life of a bird of singing joy from a young boy to his mother who had killed his father.

Note: Beas never mentioned the bird, never looked at the cage. He never mentioned his father, either. When they passed the old house in a car, Beasley turned his eyes away.

★

It had taken me a year to write that and I wasn't sure if I meant or believed any of it.

Renfro

Didn't go home. Went to the Salvation Army and asked for a bed, got some clothes, unironed bleached-out cotton pants and a well-mended old shirt. The uniform of the purified, of St. Julian. But he wanted no more of the leper. If he could write, he'd tell the leper's side of things and send Julian back where he came from. Saving souls, healing lepers was suspect. Give them bleached-out Salvation Army shirts to cover their sores. This was quite a practical organization, regardless of their intentions upon his soul, which they seemed to pursue casually enough.

He listened to the Gospel from a skinny preacher whose Adam's apple quaked with zeal—

If I have wounded any soul today
If I have caused one foot to go astray . . .

He sang along and followed afterward into the huge echoing vault of the old warehouse loft and ate his soup with idiot pleasure. He slept like a lead sinker amid the tomcat swill of a hundred sleepers.

They moved, these men, like lizards. He hardly saw them at first but then, fed and chastened and rested, he singled himself out from them and began to see. *Some men my age have never worked a day in their lives.* Exotic idea—work. Not jobs but work, the abstract. Why so necessary? There was no way of indifference to it. Even in the seediest head there was some cell of the work-or-not-work disease.

They gave him a cigarette. After the soup. He smoked it as a sacrament. Work was holy, maybe. Something was holy. Not love. Maybe work. He sucked it down to its fire and dropped the ash into a cracked saucer. The glazed eyes across from him watched indifferently. Some sat chewing their lips. The remote shout inside him was thrown at them as a mere sliding look of reproof. He sat. And then he rose and went to the dormitory and lay on the cot. And then he rose again to stand at the window and stare out over the roofs of town.

And finally it began to overtake him, the reality of being here at this moment looking out over these streets—Boston Avenue, Rialto Lane, Cincinnati, his own street, Detroit, St. Louis, like rail stops—streets of his boyhood. He was *home*, gathering up a fever for exploring it again, invisible as he now was. Who would recognize this sorry half-toothed mug? He could do it. All his moving had made of him a mover. He shuffled his feet at the window. He took out a butt he had picked up from the gutter the night before and lighted it. He inhaled and his eyes cleared, his head.

Why had he never killed himself? A hundred chances, a thousand reasons. But chance and reason weren't the requirements. Something in the cast of mind and body was. Look at these poor bastards dragging between bed and shower and table, who had lived through it and emerged on the windy other side of it.

He swallowed hard and turned away with a small pain of near elation. Oh, yes. He walked springingly, fabulously empty, across to the door of the latrine. Yes, that was hope that had flown through him just then. *Hope.* He peed, handling himself very respectfully. The pants they had given him had no zipper but only faded blue buttons. He fussed with them patiently. He went back to the window.

Below on the street two men, one of them colored, were unloading a large truck of cartons into a warehouse. He looked down on their heads. Earnest, rhythmic, exaggerating the sweeping motions of lift turn rise reach, lift turn rise. . . . Because that was what they were doing. Enough. Because the same lift and turn, the same remote elation, worked in their limbs and opened their ribs; a sort of chemical hope.

Labor. Motion. Grace. Yes.

★

Out across the sharp outlines of roofs beyond were the red clay hills, the white tower of the refinery, the new white and blue and red tanks. Closer was the new bank, whale-colored and tall, a somber testament to the new economic rise. And there was the Sooner Hotel sign and the old hotel itself—he remembered the sounds of its insides from his delivery-boy days, glass clinking, carpets, elevator swoosh and men, their growl. It was all comprehensible, this boomtown coming to life again, this *home.* He saw what a town was all at once, that particular rhythm. And what had to be done in a town. Work.

The spire of the Methodist church sparked like frozen flame, silvery under the thin acid sun. He had climbed it during construction. Ten years old, maybe eleven. And Alda had come running along below like a bug calling his name out across the air—a trailed ribbon of dream sound. It had floated thinly up to him then, he remembered the exact sound now. *W e l d o n !* strung out, the sound separating as it rose until it became—*Well done!* And he had called down to her in a panic, suddenly convinced that he couldn't get down, couldn't even remember how he had climbed up.

How the devil did I get down finally?

He drew his gaze in closer. To the right, just north, was the penthouse of the McCleod building where that rich Pomeroy Russell had once lived. Used to be a regular garden up there. He had delivered from Schwartzkopf's Gourmet Grocery to Mr. Russell, maybe once a week, usually in summer, long after Mrs. Russell had died. They had traveled all over the world. Always in the newspaper. Some scandal in that family later . . .

Early autumn haze buffed the distant contours now, dulling the river. Beyond the din of warehousing somewhere he could hear, with that trained ear, the dread marvel of shuttling trains, the slam of coupling cars, then the slow build of departing engines. He let it wreck his musing. It sickened him with fear and excitement. He was off them for good. For good, remember. Could have gotten off a year ago for that matter. Queer how he had sensed before opening the door of the car that he was here. And it was time.

He was going to stay in a town now. Incredible how a life can take up again. War plants hiring now, someone had said. Work. But listen to those trains. Still a few empties in spite of defense shipping. He could hear out an empty anywhere, how fast it moved, gaining or losing speed, the light clatter.

But forget it. Let them run through his other mind, his back mind, if they must—and they would, he knew it—but with his clear frontal seeing mind he would shut them out.

He turned around. The dormitory was full of men now. Near the shower door was a full-length mirror before which a sad sack of at least sixty stood, vaguely pressing down his wrinkled clothes and spying his ruined face. What the hell did they see, these worn-out hunks? Didn't their rough rashy greasy faces remind them, warn them? Didn't their bitter mouths? He laughed to think of his own mouth. He went to sit on his cot and lecture himself. All his molars were gone and two bicuspids. He would have to remember to keep his mouth fairly tight out at that plant when he applied for work. And even after, if they hired him. He had to nibble his food at the front. Later he could find a dentist, but for now, Christ, he couldn't even so much as talk to a woman. Jesus Christ! What the hell was a woman to him now? He could think only of Alda and Julia, of his mother. He wondered if they were still here, if they sensed his nearness somehow. Was there such a thing as telepathy?

He shook himself and went out for a walk. If someone stopped him and said, Say, aren't you Weldon Renfro? he could say Hell no without a qualm, turn his back and walk away. At least he had that.

He walked through the warehouse district and toward the river, fingering the sheep's wool he had put in the Salvation Army pants pocket. Salvation pockets, he said, his hands in them. Salvation pants and salvation soap, a lye smell that the air made fresh on him now. Sterilized salvation style, thin and light as a twig, walking like an acrobat come awake after a great fall. But he wasn't sure where to go. He only knew where not to go—home or to the railyards. So he headed for the river.

Finally it rained. The cityish smell of steaming asphalt thrilled me. I thought I could smell New York City. I went to three movies in one week with Beas, sitting through each one twice. He slept through *Girl's Dormitory*, but I shook with bliss every time Herbert Marshall opened his mouth. Di Finlayson had once told me that he was a pervert of some kind and had a wooden leg, but she didn't realize that those things only raised his stock with me. I practiced pouting like Simone Simon for two hours one evening when there was nothing to do. Somewhere in the world maybe a certain exotic man was moving through his life toward me. The idea, which I conjured occasionally, shook my bones. Prepare! I commanded myself. But how?

I wandered the lease alone—dark heavy moon, those vast flat late summer skies. I was drawn up into them. I became religious again at nineteen as I had been as a child. I had always prayed ardently when small, usually out-of-doors. Now I apologized to God for myself. I didn't seem to be able to settle myself. I vowed to be pure, to strive toward Sarah's kind of tranquility and innocence of heart, to forgive without question the way she did. But I couldn't throw myself into it. After a short limpid sensation and a feeling of having been drawn up into the Silence, I lost the need. I started reading the lives of the saints again, treasuring my loneliness. If not St. Julian then St. Jerome. With that lion and all, what a life, alone in the desert!

A nun! Maybe that was the answer. That would shock them! But could I keep it up? Probably not, but it might start my life moving. Or a nurse? No. A poet or a writer or a singer or an aviatrix, in that order. Or a dancer.

Everything had changed for me. My old and only boyfriend and

Beas and I had been a tight society of three bock-beer and red-whizzer drinkers for two years. I was crazy now. Summer maddened me with simian cravings. All I could do was run, as if I were ten years old, run it off, run it out of me whatever it was. If God couldn't take me, maybe nature could—the animals, the woods.

Enid came out several times suddenly toward the end of August. Iantha Abernathy brought her and sometimes Beas, and while Beas listened to "Information Please" or Jack Benny, the women gabbed on the sun porch and Enid tried on some chic clothes once that Sarah had gotten from a client, stuff with important labels like Chez Ninon and Bergdorf Goodman. Enid took her pick as they were all too exotic for Iantha, but Iantha got the labels, which she sold for a quarter apiece to women who put them in their own homemade clothes.

I paced the hall that night whistling "The Muskrat Ramble" until Beas was tired of the radio. They rattled on out on the porch, all the usual old hash—Clay Danbo, Iantha related for the fiftieth time, still carried a torch for Jane Skidmore who had refused to marry him because she feared one of them might break wind at the wrong time and ruin the whole thing. And after all those years it occurred to me that I had never been sure whether Jane Skidmore meant during the wedding or during their whole married life. Not one fart allowed? That was Deliria for you.

But you never know when the time in the core of your life changes, I had always told myself. Thus, Beas said to me on that late August evening—

"I ran into Eric Witcher in the barbershop this week," sounding very much like his grandfather, Pom. He peeled back the wrapper of a Butterfinger and offered me the first bite as usual. I shook my head. Eric Witcher, with whom I had gone through high school, for some reason had always made me blush and shake.

"He's joined the Navy. Going for officer's training. He says if you get in now you can get the deal you want, but if you wait to be drafted, you're just cannon fodder."

I shrugged. "Well, the Navy is welcome to Eric Witcher."

Beas gave me an astonished look. "Why, I thought you liked him. You always dance when he asks you."

How could I tell my seventeen-year-old boy-wonder virgin cousin that I danced with Eric Witcher because he got me excited and you had to get excited a lot first, I reasoned, before you could go the limit. You had to be so desperate for a long period of time that no matter when or where or with whom, when the moment struck, you were ready.

"Oh, I dance with him because he's a good dancer. I doubt if he has any brains."

He stared at me. "You're as practical as a scientist." His eyebrows stayed up while he ate the Butterfinger. "He was accepted into Dartmouth College. He can't be so dumb. But anyway . . . I told him we'd be at the Creole tonight. Maybe I shouldn't have said so."

I told him it didn't matter, but it did. What use to get all het up dancing with Eric Witcher and then go home and maybe have to lie listening to Ruby and somebody on that cot in the yard? If someone would just force me, I thought, then the whole thing would be taken care of. I didn't know how to get the message to them. You necked and necked till you were crazy and then they apologized and rushed you home.

We drove Enid home and went to the Creole as planned. When she disappeared inside the house, I felt again that pang I often got when we left her alone in her sweet little bungalow that she took the trouble to fix up and never really lived in. They never had a guest unless we dropped by uninvited with a mess of hot tamales, Enid's favorite food and the only vulgar thing of which she was capable, according to Iantha. And I wondered if she would accept if Beas and I invited her along. I tried to visualize her sitting coolly in the Creole, that dump where her son had been drinking beer since he was fifteen and once, on the night he read about that chemist Kekulé, who was one of his heroes, had carved on our table there the formula for benzene—C_6H_6—and a diagram of its circular chain of molecules.

She'd faint, I told myself. But nothing could reduce her much further. In the Biography I had told about Enid's sweet little bungalow over on Madison Terrace—its French blue and champagne colors; its velveteen and Chinese silk; its miniatures and crystal and pewter and tiny tortoiseshell picture frames; its silver and ivory. Slowly over the years it had become sterile, partly through neglect and partly through the loss of many of those treasures. She had traded them to Robert Swan, her fairy decorator friend who bootlegged on the side, for wine or whiskey, mainly wine. I remembered her before she shot Uncle Jack, standing in the middle of the room in her dark-red velvet dressing gown one morning, her long shimmering flaxen braid down her back like a rope of pulled taffy, saying to Swan, "Now, Bob, if you're going to try to Jew me down . . ." and his saying—

"Sweetheart, you don't seem to see what's happening. Nobody's buying, everybody's selling. You know what I got Winny Herndon's crystal chandelier for this morning? Just take a guess."

But she stared him down and got her price as usual. Her price, witness murder, was high. Iantha Abernathy said Enid was just naturally chic and superior, born that way, and nothing could change her. Meaning of course that neither drunkenness, loss, murder nor court trials could change her.

Well, that sweet little bungalow spelled her life. It depressed me with its dead-flower smell, its dusk and the passing of my favorite human in the world, Beasley, through its chilly unaffectionate chic little rooms while his mother lay half drunk in her silky bed, the ghostly urgency in the air from her radio police calls. If I could have roamed through the house with a movie camera, I would not have had to *write* the Biography at all. It was all there somewhere, hanging, waiting.

So. That August was the eighth anniversary of a day on which we all changed forever and Enid became our wound and our alibi.

I still wondered at her beautiful thoughtful hands holding and firing a gun! Usually those hands lay in her lap passively. Did they regret?

There was a grave at Rosewood Cemetery modestly marked

JOHN BEASLEY RUSSELL
1894–1933

a grave Enid had never visited. In the Biography it was written—

The acquitted murderer always leaves a trial more guilty than before. Because murder, unlike acquittal, has nothing to do with reason or motive. It disdains logic and is pure and friendless.

That statement was my ultimate. I could read it and get, any old time, that quick zing in the head and chest by which I recognized my rarest thoughts. I read it many times, not certain what exactly I meant by it nor if I had even actually written it. The whole Biography, in fact (which was handwritten in an old red leather record book from a client of Sarah's), had that queer life of its own which seemed not to have come from me at all. It was automatic writing. Sarah, if she had known of it, would easily have accepted the idea of my being a medium.

Well, Enid was condemned forever by a murder for which she had been acquitted. Temporary Insanity. I thought that was crazy. Everybody I knew was temporarily insane all the time. She had expected punishment, a sentence, I was sure of it.

She perpetuates the trial [so the Biography went] in secret in her cloistered shuttered bedroom. Those bony fingers of hers sometimes come together, all ten of them, in an attitude of supplication. They act autonomously. She does not seem to know what they do now any more than she did then. They seem chaste and preoccupied. They finger meditatively everything they touch as if to examine and blindly learn again a world which they once destroyed by lifting from a drawer a small pistol and aiming it at the back of a human head.

Etc. Building her life. And her nature. It was no longer necessary for me to read the old yellowed newpaper clippings of the trial that Sarah kept in a hatbox on her closet shelf. I knew them word for word, and the thing they didn't contain was that which she had not offered up at the trial—her reason. When I got that I'd write the last paragraph.

I had known Uncle Jack as a red-faced bully with black curls and a nose like a small rubber ball. Beasley knew him as father and developed by living with that mean man the same sort of deadly patience which I had learned living out Sarah's nap and her rhythms there in Deliria. Children, I learned, are the patients of time. Beas and I shared that. And Beas was at least half me, anyway.

Eric was standing in a group around Nina Brosky's table. She drew men like gnats. She could have held court in a Greyhound bus. When she was in high school she had, so Iantha claimed, something called a salon in the back booth of Solomon's, the only delicatessen in town. But that was twenty years before our time. Her head tilted back now with that black silky hair that would frizz up in the damp weather into a dark filmy halo around her face, and she let out a rich laugh that I knew but couldn't hear through the din of that moment. She had hired me the previous spring a few times as flunky on her program for British refugee children. I had earned enough money from her to buy a one-way bus ticket to New York, but sloth, I told myself, spineless confusion and virginity kept me from going.

Nina had been a singer, semiprofessional. She was rich and fat and sexy and gorgeous. When that oil man Red Southwell had ditched her right before their wedding, she had more or less moved into the Creole and set up a new salon and public mourning. I had gotten that and a lot more dirt on her from Iantha, to whom I pretended not to listen, beaky old bitch that she was. Pom called Iantha Witness on Tap (which when uttered by Pom had the ring of Always a Bridesmaid) because she had waited to testify at Enid's trial and never been called.

Well, there was Nina with a dozen men hanging over her, a lot of laughter, that rich syrup of her voice laving them. The sight of it stung me with envy and admiration. Beas and I dived into our corner and ordered beer. It was crowded and rowdy and smelled like all beer joints. When Eric spotted us I had had three beers and Beas was extravagantly sober, his usual mildly drunk state. He half rose off the seat to take Eric's handshake. He wouldn't initiate a shake himself but liked it to be thrust upon him. He was staring with a fix at Eric.

"Where's your uniform?"

Eric ignored him. "Hiya, Kid" He slipped a long finger into my palm and I drew back my hand. "Where you been keeping yourself?"

I blushed and shrugged. We filled his glass from our pitcher. He was all shiney and foxy like Mr. Hyde. Only handsome. But like a BVD ad. He had always gone with what was called a fast crowd, rich kids like his girlfriend Ann Coolidge. But he wasn't rich himself. Finally he condescended to answer Beas.

"I don't wanta go around here in that outfit. I'll be in officer's training soon enough. I'm not ordered to duty yet."

So. He was too vain to put on a sailor suit.

Beas understood, nodding at him soberly. "Isn't that Nina Brosky over there?" he asked.

Eric nodded. "Really packs them in, doesn't she?"

"I like her," said Beas, like a child. "She's so big and . . . generous looking."

We laughed. "Got a big heart, that woman," Eric said. And then he slid me a look. Ah, hatred! I whipped it up against him.

"Where you been, Katie? Didn't know I'm a sailor now, did you?"

"Beas told me." When he looked at me that way I lost my smart tongue.

"When do you report?" Beas asked him. And Eric resigned himself to Beas for a few minutes, patiently and with a kindness that infuriated me. He couldn't help condescending, I thought. It was just the nature of the superior beast. When they began their war talk, I got up to weave back to the john.

"Hurry back. I wanta dance with you."

On the wall of the john at eye level for the seated it said FUCK HITLER. It had always been you or me and now it was Hitler. It also said RANDALL ZAVITZ HAS A TEN-INCH POLE, very long, I supposed. And it said BONNY AND ZEKE, SEVEN TIMES A DAY. Whoever they were. I was obviously the only Delirian who was not doing it. It all sounded pretty rough. But my virginity must have shown in my face, I thought. I checked the mirror where Ruby said it ain't, holding my hair up in a pile at the back like Nina's. The difference was shocking. Nina looked like her beautiful Russian mother who had fainted when she put her foot down on American soil for the first time; fainted when her husband first kissed her; fainted when she heard she was the mother of a girl and fainted when Nina came home from high school one day with pierced ears and little gold loops. For this, she had cried out, women were emancipated! Might as well be through your nose! Nina spoke of her mother with great passion when I was there one day working. Her father had been a small quiet refugee from the Russian Revolution whose little chicken farm across the river from Deliria had been discovered to be floating on an oil pool. He had kept the mineral rights after selling it and made a fortune which, when he fully realized it, had caused him to fall down dead.

For this, Nina said that day, he escaped the pogroms of Europe. To die of riches!

Back at the table, Beas was saying, "Grandfather says within six months."

"I say that's conservative," Eric said.

"I say let's talk about life and not death," said I. And Eric broke out his big jackal-toothed smile and dragged me off to dance on the six-foot-square floor. He dropped his nickel in and got "Tuxedo Junction."

He asked all about me, breathing and whispering into my ear and bending me against his hard, jived-up body. I gasped and lied to him about work and all that. I could feel the time of my own secret history jamming up against me, in my veins. I was going to break out. Everything was going to happen to me too late if I didn't. If it happened at all. I clung to Eric and danced so well it made him laugh.

When he left us again for Nina's table, we both drooped. We got drunk together then, Beas and I. His sunshine-yellow bangs lay like cornsilk over his brow. His celestial eyes, those startled blues, were drowsy. He drew molecular patterns on the table, dulling his fountain-pen point and then dropping it listlessly.

"Come on. Let's go." I stumbled up and he followed me. When we passed Nina's table she called me. She wanted me to work again, she said, and I beamed gratefully. She must have thought I was a slob. She laughed and looked at Eric. "Honey, take these kids out of here before they both fall down." Eric, *Honey*, was exactly my age. Exactly! I could have stabbed her. I had thought that somehow she would be in league with all women against all men after what Red Southwell did to her.

Eric asked us to take him home and we clicked off in the electric like three short circuits.

★

Beas staggered up the walk to his house, looking very small.

"Think we oughta wait? See if he can make it?" Eric said.

I laughed at old Beas. "Oh, he can take care of himself. He may leave the door open though." I started to tell him I had found it open one Sunday morning and two strange dogs wandering the silk-and-velvet living room, but changed my mind. Gossip about Enid and her house was rampant enough even eight years after the *fact.*

Beas disappeared. We waited.

"Shall I go close it?"

"Wait a minute more," I told him, tremblingly. I was alone in the car with Mr. Foxy-Loxy, Mr. Hyde, a kind of elongated George Raft. I was breathing hard.

All at once Beas came back and slammed the door with a thundering crash which sent us off into hoots of laughter. But through it I felt a single shaft of sorrow. Because that slam was a kind of statement to Enid, I knew it, something he could never say with mere words.

★

I let him drive. And that, I told Luise Rainer in a little Russian tearoom somewhere in the world, was my undoing.

"Where you going? I thought you lived on the North Side."

"Got a view I wanta show you. It'll only take a minute. I bet you've never seen it."

"There's nothing in Deliria," I said, "that I haven't seen."

And he laughed at that and said you nut and then he lighted two cigarettes and handed me one. I didn't tell him I didn't smoke. I threw back my head and spewed out the smoke before it got near my throat, doing a kind of Carole Lombard. But he didn't notice. I cautioned myself. He had kissed Nina good-bye on the cheek; she had called him Honey; he was engaged to Ann Coolidge and he looked like a BVD ad.

"It's getting late," I tried.

"Just take a minute." He put an arm vaguely at my back. His fingers wandered at the back of my neck, spidery. I goose-bumped all over. He laughed. "Christ! It takes this thing forever to go a block. But I kinda like it. It's like being in a room."

"It's my house," I cried.

"Ha! You're a funny kid."

I bit my tongue. The electric was beginning to smell like burning wires, he was working it so hard. But we crossed the river and ground up Blue Mountain to his secret spot. We were unearthly quiet, knowing.

We took the old patchwork quilt out of the back seat and doubled it on the ground under a tree. There below us was Deliria, the whole spangled skyline of it to the north across the river, peaked by the Methodist church spire. The buildings hung as if made of scraps and suspended from the sky, delicate and sketchy.

"Wow!"

"Like it?"

"Yeah." I didn't know how to act and was beginning to lose control of my face muscles. I had practiced even, but nothing fixed there. "I didn't know Assinopolis could look so beautiful."

Well, I could make him laugh anyway. He let out a shout and pulled me against him, sniffing at my neck and chuckling.

"You smell like a baby."

"I washed my hair."

He sniffed around my neck and I shuddered and felt my mouth go dry. My lips were numb. He'd find out the worst about me first and that would be that. And anyway, what about Ann Coolidge?

"Out on the lease we don't have a view. It's all flat . . ."

He hovered over my mouth and then we shot together and fell backward. My head hit the roots of the tree and I saw stars. He tasted like Doublemint and cigarettes. His hands were all over! He was a better kisser than anyone. I was going blind. He moved fast.

"Wait! Take it easy."

He stopped, breathing like a werewolf, and then sat up and lighted two cigarettes again and I smoked, lying back, because I intended to start. Egyptians. Like Nina.

"You spend a lot of time at the Creole these days," I said.

He grinned at me in the dark. I pulled my blouse together a little. I felt like something poured over the ground and slowly seeping downhill.

"Not as much as you do," he laughed. "Nina says she sees you in there every weekend and some week nights besides."

They discussed me! "Where else can you go? Beas doesn't dance . . ." I was telling too much about myself.

"How about George's?" That was a bootlegger whose place was outside the city limits. Josh, my old boyfriend, and Beas and I had gone there one summer to sit on the old broken porch furniture and drink red whizzers.

I sat up. "How do you know so much about me?"

"I've got my spies out." He laughed and leaned over. "You're not like other women."

Women, Kid, what the hell did he think I was and what the hell was I?

"Ever been on a ship at night?" He was staring up, leaning against my side, radiating intense heat. "Night skies at sea are really spectacular. Ever read Conrad?"

"A little."

"I always knew," he said, "when I read him first that I'd go to sea someday."

"I'd go too if I were a man."

He blew a big smoke ring and then put the cigarette out and came after me again, pulling me against his hard body cave, forcing me slowly carefully back, drowning me in his big toothy kisses. I was losing everything, everything. Maybe this was it! He raised his hips and pulled away his trousers. Oh God! He took my skirt, how did he? and felt me everywhere oh God this was *it!*

"Oh!"

"Relax, Baby."

I went blind. "My eyes!"

He pulled away. "Your eyes?"

"They're crossing or something."

He laughed and kissed me on the neck and then undid my blouse again. I heard it tear somewhere. Oh God! Into my mouth again and then raising himself up, hovering there over me, moving . . .

"Oh! Ow!"

"What's the matter?"

"You put your elbow down on my hair!"

He waited, looking at me through the dark. "Oh. Sorry."

He stalled. I twisted slightly. We went on, all that rolling and moving, kissing, slipping away and down and he found everything oh God taking away all my clothes stroking and then pressing down with his oh God his huge his big oh! This was going to be IT.

"Oh!"

"Just relax. . . ."

He drove against me.

"Oh! Ow! Oh! Stop. No. Wait. Stop. Oh! It gives me pains . . ."

He jerked away. "Pains? I hardly started."

"In the bottom of my feet!"

"The bottom of your *feet!*" He pulled back roughly. "Jesus Christ! You're like a bad wiring job or something."

I was hysterical. "Maybe I'm just a specially *good* wiring job."

He fell over on his back and sighed. There was his big his huge right out in the moonlight!

"What I know, Kid, is," he let out a little desperate laugh, "you talk too much. You and Josh do all this talking?"

"*Josh?* We didn't do it. Never."

"What? Whadda you mean? You never . . . ?"

"We never did it, that's all." I stared up at the sky. This was my fate. Let it fall on me and kill me.

He was quiet. Then he touched my side but what was the use? It was over. Well, I thought, take it like a man.

"Jeez, I thought you and Josh . . ."

"Please don't keep bringing him up! I haven't even seen him for six months. Anyway, we never did it."

He leaned near, kissing my cheek, searching me with those big black pruny eyes. "What've I got here, Kid—a virgin on my hands?"

I nodded.

"No kidding?"

"Yep."

The End.

He thought a minute and then he snuggled me up suddenly. "Well. I don't know about this. I don't have anything with me. . . ."

"Oh, forget it."

He was quiet now. He kissed my forehead like someone's father. I thought of his big pole which was shrinking down curiously. I hadn't realized they got so big and so hard nor that they shrank up so much, but I couldn't get a good look. I wanted to feel it a little to get the idea of it. Beasley's seven-year-old button was all I knew.

Oh *life*! I thought. He'd never like me again now. I should have let old Josh do it, or found someone stupid to teach me.

"Listen. You talk to Nina and she'll tell you what to get. A diaphragm or something, and I'll . . . Shit! I don't know why I didn't bring some Sheiks with me."

"It's okay. Forget it. I don't know why you're doing this with me anyway. I thought you and Ann Coolidge . . ."

"Naw, we quit. She wants to get married and I can't see marrying when I'm on my way into the service. Maybe even war. And anyway, we were breaking up."

War. Back where we started. I sighed. "It's hard for me to think about . . . people I know going to war and all."

"Well, you'd better get used to it. They'll get all of us before long. Maybe even women."

"Ha! They'll never get me."

He laughed. Then he sighed and pulled up his pants. The mosquitoes had found us and we began to slap ourselves madly, laughing. He slapped me then, carefully, as if to test me.

"I knew a girl once who couldn't get hot unless you smacked her ass a few times." And then he looked at me quickly. "But that was a long time ago. C'mon, let's go before they eat us up."

Back in the electric he said, "No kidding, talk to Nina."

I bit my lips. He must have thought I was six years old.

"I like you a lot," he said, snooping at my neck again. "I'll show you. I'll call you real soon."

I turned away. "I better go home. Sarah will be calling all over town for me."

What a lie! She had never tracked me down in my life.

★

A bad wiring job was more likely than a good one. I lay on my dais swollen and throbbing, my rear end lumpy with raging bites, and heard Rube come through the gate with someone. I raised myself and watched them highstep over the grass quietly—Horace or maybe Gifford, I couldn't tell for sure as both were taller than

Wishbone and lean as trees. She seemed to like that type better, but Wishbone had been her first. They slipped through the milky moonlight into her quarters. And she was wearing my clothes as she sometimes did, the fiend! My peasant skirt and the white ruffled blouse she liked that she always claimed was down in the basement waiting to be ironed. There they were ironed to a fare-thee-well and about to be torn from her body by her lover in that big swinging bed of hers. She took on a man the way you catch a falling balloon. If she knew what a failure I was, she'd never let me live it down.

I fell back on my bed. I was jealous of Rube at times. Sometimes she would walk a mile out to the railroad tracks to meet Horace in the early evening when Wishbone was away, and wait for him to come by in that little handcar that was driven by some white man. It didn't stop entirely but only slowed down for Horace, who would jump off laughing and wave back. Tall long gourdhead Horace. I liked him, maybe even better than Wishbone, who continued to let himself be cheated. But if he really knew about Horace, surely he'd stab him to the heart with an icepick or slash him with a knife, though none of that sounded exactly like Wishbone. He and Ruby had had one fight that I knew of and that time, early summer, she had raised a dozen knots on his head by throwing little hard green peaches off our tree at him while he flopped around the yard drunk.

Shhhhtt! Rube, one way or another, had managed to keep me awake and feeling guilty or jealous ever since she came here. She was writhing away on that cot all spring and summer with Wishbone or somebody by the time she was *fifteen*! At fifteen I was still monkey-running around the lease, digging caves and hanging by my knees from the pecan trees. Even at thirteen I had had to be told, by Enid naturally, to keep my legs out of the air now, quit hanging by my knees and all. Yeah, Rube had it all over me. She had been sent by the Devil to prod me to further idiocy.

I grabbed the pillow and wrapped myself around it. I wasn't much of a sleeper. I was bored when I slept. He had said I like you, I'll show you. I recreated the voice—*I like you I'll show you.* But he wouldn't. He was just giving me his line which was famous. I was even glad I hadn't gone the limit. But even so I was dying to get a look at his big firecracker.

I vowed to get up, to get a life, virginity or not. I was buried under the clients and their junk, under Ruby and her men and her cautioning, under Sarah even and her Aw, Hons and her commiserations that wouldn't allow anyone to be tough. Pity. That was what she had for the world. If she knew how pitiful I was with my rear bitten half off and my virginity intact, she'd devote the rest of her commiserating days to me and my soul.

I fell into a dopey sleep. He wouldn't call, I reminded myself. Somebody else would do it to me. Just as well. But my mind had hold of him like an owl with a mouse, awake or asleep.

Enid

His usual step on the basement stair. If she calls he may answer, may not. Not often anymore. Beasley waits for necessity. His sneaker steps in the hall. Does he still powder his socks? Probably. Military school does that for them, and sex training. Order. Manliness. Growing up, shaves every few weeks, comes in later and later. Katie's influence.

"Beasley, that you, Honey?"

He is very nearby, little animal. Used to be an odor of warm bread and grass about him. Now chemicals. His fingers blue or brown stained. Singed half his hair off that time in an explosion. She can feel-smell him animal near. He lives in her head, anyway, silent, arrested in some vestibule of her consciousness; a statue erected to that moment when she will say one word, *the* word that has not been said ever . . . yet. Everything that ever was remains and is eternal. The mind a graveyard of markers, frozen events, eternally paused creatures, names . . . names . . .

"Beas?"

"Yeah?"

"C'mere a minna, Honey."

At her door.

"What?"

"Gessum money outa the phone drawer and go up to the Grille for dinner. I don't quite feel like cooking . . . have a lil headache." The slur, she knows, drifts over him like a veil of nettles. She can hear it herself. But none of that matters anymore. Her mind works perfectly well.

"Okay." Turning away. Alone. Darkness. Streets.

"Be careful, Honey. Take your bike . . . take plennya money."

"Okay."

"Get a steak."

"Okay."

She lies arched. The radio says RAF bombers set fires in Berlin . . . Krupp armaments works at Essen. Roosevelt and Churchill at sea. She laughs dry-mouthed scorn. At sea is right. Last month Pom called to say he was having Beas deferred. The lab had had itself declared essential defense industry. They *do* need him, said Pom. But he's nowhere near twenty-one, she said. And Pom said, But they'll lower the age limit soon enough.

Oh, men! *Men!*

She turns the dial and hunts. Too early for police calls.

The front door slams. A siren streaks through her brain. A killing pain through her chest. His bicycle sounds in the driveway, turning, rubber on hot cement. The back of his head is like a five-year-old's. Too innocent to be in this world. She falls back into herself and the bed. Eight years ago her arm went out. Of its own volition her hand took aim. Does he know yesterday was the date? Do they remember such things or is it only Sarah who keeps it all in her head?

And so, Mrs. Russell, following the argument . . .

There was no argument.

Excuse me. I will rephrase the question. Following the striking of your son Beasley by his father, Jack Russell, the deceased . . .

Eight years. Time—a drip, a tick, a bubble forming. But the words and acts and the very air of it have always floated loosely about in her head's universe, fragments. Why select out particulars now?

Guests that time on Jack's birthday, in the back garden. A lot of drinking. Too early. Jack's ears and neck red. Little Beas naked, running across the grass with naked Katie. Their tiny behinds. How Beas saw the strangers suddenly and took up a cup from the table and held it over his genitals that way, playing all afternoon with one hand, the other holding the cup. Jack taking it away from him finally. Roughly? Maybe. When did the violence begin? How he put pants on Beas then. And how patient Beas always was at being handled. Trusting. What and whom did he trust? Not Jack. Oh, children!

She turns the dial.

. . . probably for the first time in the history of America's modern communications, the public of this country has not been informed of the whereabouts of the President for more than four days . . .

Turns it again. Music.

We'll build a stairway to the stars . . .

After a while, she is thinking, lowering the volume, I'll get up and fix myself a little bite of supper. Floating, rocking inwardly to some thin pulse. Hungry maybe. Seven P.M. *At just about this hour . . .* rolling the dial—

I'm in the mood for love, simply because . . .

. . . sailed today, even so, from Los Angeles to Vladivostok with ninety-five thousand barrels of aviation gasoline . . .

And now here he is, Ladies and Gentlemen—Eddie Cantor!

Back to I'm in the mood for love oh the music goes round and round she goes and where she stops nobody knows the trouble I've seen.

Dark. Alone. Pedaling uphill. He will order steak. Those mute small tidy hands, stained, holding the fork down close to the tines, stabbing at his food as a baby does. *Baby!* Or order a hamburger and keep the rest of the money for lab supplies. Pom said, That's one place I won't stint. Let him have a charge account at the supply house. The cost of a few chemicals and beakers isn't going to break me.

Up on an elbow fishing for the bag, opening the bottle for two scalding swallows. Better than wine, quicker. It drives through her veins, pleasant warming paralysis.

Oh, if Mother had not died, if she had not grown old and if I had not left and married and we had not had Pom's money to rescue us all the time. Always money there . . . but when Mother did die and Sarah kissed her bare feet they were already dead and Sarah never cried before that day. God! Once I was a little girl . . . my hair . . .

Enid McCleod Russell, daughter of City founder the late Kevin McCleod and the late Adela Beasley McCleod, went on trial for murder today in Superior Court . . .

Following the striking of your son Beasley by his father, you state that you attempted to console your son but that he went to his room and locked himself in before you could speak with him and that the deceased, Jack Russell, then sat down in a chair in the living room and began to read the paper. Now, Mrs. Russell, at that point when your son locked himself in his room and you could not persuade him to open the door, when you turned away and saw that Jack Russell, your husband and father of the boy, had sat down in a chair . . .

That was his style. He pretended to read the paper after being violent with one of us.

She had never intended to talk at all. She had always before the trial believed she could just sit and stare at them, knowing they'd never understand anyway, any of it, the not-logical thing, the inevitability; but suddenly finding herself talking that way, explaining things, intimate things, the ordinary intimacies that never need be mentioned. *That was his style!* Even Jack ought to have been protected from that discussion. Even he deserved his privacy.

She had suddenly wanted to defend Jack from the trial, Jack the victim. Right then was when she had thought she might be going mad, considering defending the privacy of a murdered man, her own victim. She would close inward then, away from them, having realized how much talk they had gotten from her. And for days she would withhold and sulk, oh, she knew she was sulking and that they had that terrible legal masculine patience to wait for her to talk again, and she always did, finally.

I see. And at that point, having taken note that the deceased was reading the paper, what did you do at that moment?

I've already said I went to bed.

But she could never resist them, not for long.

Had you been in bed already, Mrs. Russell, before this incident?
Yes.

. . . leaning closer, tapping with that pencil of his . . . Gerald Pitts, State's Attorney.

And what time was it then?
It was just growing dark so it must have been a little before eight.
And so you had been in bed for some undetermined time before *the striking incident occurred and you got up upon hearing it to go* . . .
I've answered all these questions before.

Before. Again. Put it away.

Last week. Sarah saying thank God things are a-pickin up, Hon. These old plants, I know they're just makin bombers and guns and all, but at least the men do have work.

Rest assured, my dear, he will be deferred. He will never have to go. Never!

Oh, men! Once she laughed after the trial, telling them about attorney Gerald Pitts cheating in the ninth grade, how she had often done his math homework for him. And Pom gave her a pained look, apologetically appalled at the lack of decorum. That was it—her laughing after the trial had been in bad taste!

She laughs, even now. *Fools!*

Beasley

Still hot, even at seven o'clock. And the sun still burning on his back, and the rubber grips on the handlebars sticky. He pivots and rolls over the grass which he forgot to cut, bouncing over the curb. Maybe he should have taken more than two dollars. Maybe with a little extra he could have chili, a Spencer or even a New York, some pie and still enough left to get some ether at Sharpe's pharmacy. Crazy to run out of ether that way. But maybe she wanted him to bring something back. But usually she said so if she wanted to eat. But how can you go without so many meals? It's stupid. No wonder your head aches. Even if you were sober your head would ache if you were hungry. But wine and whiskey have calories. But maybe people don't really need all this food. Takes up so much time. She's right, why fix it *every* day. It's a bother. Maybe one big meal. But Chester at the lab says man's metabolism is really different from a dog's altogether. And besides, we don't do all that lying around. Humans burn up so much, working, thinking, worrying. She doesn't . . . but thinking maybe or worrying. But . . . Of course Fine, Katie's old dog, always got two meals a day. Katie said one wasn't enough. She gave him real meat even if she didn't have any herself. But he slept mostly. But run! Oh, he could! Like a shot . . . into the lease woods after rabbits. They're supposed to be skinny. We too? Looking down at his thigh which is not skinny, not fat. Never thought about his own body. What is it?

Pumps up Sycamore Avenue to the boulevard, turns and rolls into the big corner parking lot of the Cinema Grille. Streets are quiet—a pause before the relief of sundown, pause before the big sigh. He has noticed that pause in all the rhythms—morning and noon rhythms, evening music of talk, fragments, traces of passing minerals, minerals of antiquity; old ores of earth; old ghost gasses murmuring together, haunting the world. The hair stands up on the back of his neck. He loves that—the intricate connection and pulse of all matter.

Across the street the Park Cinema. *Rebecca.* He winces. Movies have to be about men to be good; the only argument he has with Katie, and he *knows* that she knows it's true, she's just too stubborn to say so, and she wants women to be more . . . whatever it is. But in movies they aren't. Except if brave. Pioneer women are pretty good. But for women he prefers large and soft like Aunt Sarah. Tender. Jolly. And what's that they call it? Oh, yeah— vulgar. Maybe even vulgar. Not hard but like a large friendly colored lady. Laughter. The idea strikes into his groin. You'd put it in one of them and sink, disappear!

He locks the chain and goes into the Grille.

"Well well well! Beas! How ya, Sport?"

"Okay, Fred. How're you?"

"Pretty good. Pretty horny but too hot to do anything about it. Keeekeeekeee!"

He bites the grin but it breaks through. Old Fred.

"You still down to that lab? Haven't seen ya in quite a while. Thought they might of caught you in the draft."

"Nope. I still go there after school. I'm going to be deferred, I guess. But I'm not of age yet." He fiddles with the menu, not quite looking at Fred.

"Well . . . what'll ya have?"

"You got Spencers?"

"You bet. I'll fix you up a nice special. Got a big juicy one. With a plate of fries and salad?"

"Okay. I'll have that. And chili first. And milk."

Fred laughs, showing crude squarish teeth and spaces; a face like a grate. Talk talk. Well, let him.

He gorges the chili, feeling a peculiar gratitude. Something warms in him as Fred turns his back. It's not bad in here, a long clean green-and-white diner. If Fred were a woman, big . . . He empties the bowl, wipes his mouth, stains the milk a little even so as his lips touch it. He wipes his milky lip. He eats the steak with a steady thoughtful rhythm and then the pie.

Some people have come in. He hurries.

"Gee. I forgot. Lemme see if I have enough money."

"Fergit it. You kin bring it up later in the week."

He finds the wrinkled bills in his shirt pocket. While Fred serves the others down the counter, he folds the paper napkin into an airplane but restrains his arm from sailing it across the counter. In Leonardo's notebooks—a gift from Grandfather

To my Grandson Beasley

The inventive genius of man renders the highest form of love.

From Pomeroy Russell
Christmas 1939

—is a drawing of a fantastic flying vehicle, looks like an insect. A glider. No engines in those days. And Columbus, coming all the way here with sails! He reaches for Fred's pencil and begins to doodle. It's all balance, stress—wings wide enough to carry, even overwhelm, the body without breaking it. Formulae. Everything the same. The balance, once it's off, too much stress on an adjacent part which is also a formula of elements balanced, all joined, yielding to design, once you shatter that . . .

It was eight years ago last night. Does she realize that? Probably she does. A shattering human skull, slivers and red pieces, the design broken . . .

Her prone being hangs in him, dead center. Go home now. Take the long delaying cruise through thick dark, in the core of the leafy blocks. Yeah . . . His crotch stirs. Outdoors is a better place to do it than in the lab at home. It is hot hot hot and then explosion. And then tired, that wonderful flattening tired, everything streaming like a river inside his arms and legs. But it's better outside.

He stands up. If they knew how big it was on him now, they'd pass out. Into some girl, they have hair there and soft . . . juice . . . and ram ram . . . He has to do it soon and not alone anymore.

"One forty-five, Beas. See, you got some change left over. Git yer girl a box a candy! Keeekeekee!"

The smart ring of the cash register. It is funny and nice in here, homey, but he lunges out to his bike. On the bike you can almost do it without touching it but then there's a mess. Happened that way once not on purpose. Shoot it right onto a tree is better, or into a bottle the way Brad Finch used to do, but it's too big for bottles now, even the wide-necks Brad used to use. Call up Cynthia Gillespie and just tell her to be down at Kellogg Park in ten minutes with no pants on.

Rolling through the leafed dark, the green smell night cool, and in rooms in all the blocks the naked swaying moaning women who are, yes, people, but not the same as men children girls. Large women. Soft. Find one. But how? It takes talk.

Brad said how she grabbed his balls and damn near tore them off. Oh Cynthia Gillespie, ball grabber, bring your mouse to Kellogg Park! Ah, it is huge up in the night absolutely longer than the bike bar right out there on Eleventh and Sycamore where in their windows they drink lemonade and play Monopoly with no pants on under the card table. But if you ride all the way to the

Willows, some colored lady (it's bright pink sometimes, said Brad) might let you sock it in for fifty cents and there's fifty-five in the pocket but how to ask them and are they dirty and anyway it's too late too late . . . ah . . . ah . . .

If he lay on the parking in the grass and someone came by he could say he had fallen from the bike and was stunned. And catch a rest that way. You need to lie down afterward, and nothing is as perfect as that. Except during, at that moment when it is going to happen no matter what you do or who comes along. But you have to get a woman sooner or later. Someone kind and wet. *Don't get a tightass,* said Brad. *They're dry.* But how can you tell at first? What *is* a tight ass? He should have asked Brad a few things instead of just listening and listening with a slow stiff coming on.

Semen under the microscope is a disappointment. Jissom, said Brad, drives them *crazy!* But how? Why? He doesn't know *anything* but he has to get a woman and find it all out soon or he'll never be real and he'll never get away. He might just go find a colored lady who would take him over and do everything necessary. Once a long time ago that colored girl, when she gave him a bath, rubbed it and rubbed it and said, *Looky there! Blue!* and then pulled it till it hurt, rolling it finally between her fingers and laughing loudly. She oughtn't to have done that to a little child. And stern Katie in the garage behind some crates, feeling it—This belongs to you and me, Beas. Don't let anybody else get hold of it. Ever! But did he agree? Did he promise anything?

God! What is he even thinking about Katie for? What does she have to do with it? She has her own monkey business which, he suddenly realizes, he has never seen.

Renfro

Stared at the river. Could easily walk in and swim to the current. There were strong whirlpools, he remembered. He had been cautioned many times as a child. No one would know. Body found at the Gulf somewhere. Or never found.

He saw his drowned chaste body lying on some mud bank somewhere amid storm debris. It would decompose, rot.

God! What a morbid son of a bitch he had become. He walked along fingering the sheep's wool. Stranger than any migrating animal. *They* had a destination, at least that. He had to stop thinking of it. He would go home after he had work and strength, new teeth and new clothes, a respectable exterior and some kind of new tough hide to cover the deformed interior.

He turned to walk back up the bank and saw a nickel lying in the mud. He picked it up, laughing. It seemed like a sign. Buffalo. The plains. The West. A token.

He walked back into the center of town. He went into the

entrance of the McCleod building and bought a package of Life Savers. The smell of the building—cigars and men, marble floors, spittoons, business—thrilled and disgusted him. He went out quickly. He wanted to get it straight with himself about work— that this McCleod-building world of oil and legal offices was not what he meant. No offices. Unless they were those of foremen, construction bosses, something like that. No business. He imagined some kind of work with a pencil. He went to the corner, chewing the mints two at a time. He imagined drawing the buildings carefully and showing them to someone—some man from Mars who had no idea what they were, explaining them to him. Maybe he ought to have been a teacher like Alda. No. Not children. He remembered feeling a quick pang of desire to teach and help and civilize an old coot he had shared some white lightning with somewhere, in a field. While he was living in those packing cases. That was it. The guy had been intelligent. He himself had found a water-soaked copy of Baedeker's *Guide to Rome* on a rubbish heap somewhere. Oh, yes. It was coming back to him. He had examined those beautiful fine drawings of St. Peter's, the Forum . . . yes. And the fellow had found some hooch somewhere and given him half. That was when he had decided to stop, that week. But how that old guy had quizzed him! Rome. He had found himself telling the poor coot *what* Rome was, not *where*. Where had been out of the question. *What is Rome?*

He laughed. He passed the Walgreen's on the corner and a blast of chilly air swept out. He wished he could go in and sit at the counter and drink a cherry phosphate or a lemon Coke and talk to the soda jerk, in the cool, in the Walgreen's smell which was fabulously safe somehow. Scented and clean, all the supplies with which to keep the old hide from rotting away . . .

He longed to belong to the simplest part of this world. He longed quickly—it made him breathless—for the linoleum on his mother's floors. The linoleum that had always offended Alda. And the little spitting gas stoves in the fireplaces. And the net curtains. The chain on the toilet. The tassels on the arms of the sofa. He yearned for a long snoop through a house. Yeah. A house.

He didn't go back to the Salvation Army until dusk. He realized when he went up to his bunk that he had learned to despise men by living so long alone with them. He knew them too well now. They amounted to zero, that was all. Even the smart or the brave or the cunning. They were zero unless they had houses to live in. They were junk. He was junk. He thought again of the river. The sun set against the smeared panes of the dormitory windows, burning away the western sky. He stared until he had spots before his eyes.

He ought to have slipped quietly into the river and let himself be drawn down, drowned, and washed to sea. He always realized too late what he ought to have done.

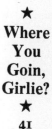

★
**Where
You
Goin,
Girlie?**
★
41

No Eric.

Sarah was pale. She took a longer nap. We took her nap with scalding patience. I couldn't sleep at all, day or night. I dozed and thrashed and waited. Ruby hummed and lay out there poking at her teeth with a broom straw. At least she had Wishbone who had something happening to him. And some substitutes besides.

Oh hot! Restless! Burning! Waiting! The telephone died. *Keep the shades down, Hon. Law, this is the worst I've seen it in years.* Maybe, I told myself, it is only a preamble to hell.

Her breathing was heavy. Her plump arms mottled purple. The clients continued to come and go, though, bringing ginger ale and opera glasses and offers to take us up to the Grand River for a weekend. But I said no. I thought of the ring of the telephone and said that Sarah should go alone. But she didn't care to move. Yeah, ginger ale and opera glasses and silver gravy ladles. Pom had said early in summer, You ought to call that fairy decorator of Enid's [he knew Robert Swan's name perfectly well] and get him out here to buy some of this stuff. You need cash! He laughed as if he would weep when he saw the opera glasses. Good Christ! What're you going to do with *these*!

Watch civilization die, I did not say. Watch for clients and bolt the doors against them.

Clients—our rhythm. Myrtle Bishop in the dark hall at midday, wiping her eyes with her dead husband's hankie, smelling faintly of onions and talcum. Everybody has a history, don't forget, I cautioned myself. Oh, those sad women bungling down the hall-way! Sometimes one of them would seize me and give me a terrible hug. Women seemed to want to crush someone to them all the time, except for Enid and Sarah, of course. But nobody wanted to be crushed to them. It was terrible. They suffered so much. Sarah hadn't one male client. But she helped them; she endured them; she believed them.

Aw, poor Myrtle. It helps them, Hon. Some things they're just not a-gonna say to the doctor and the preacher.

Some things! I'd say *most* things!

Myrtle Bishop once paid us in cough drops and Band-Aids and aspirin, of which we used practically none (except that Ruby liked those Ludens), because her husband had a drugstore. Only three years ago, I mused, buried back in Sarah's nap again, a sexual failure, a dreamer. So, I tried to keep my mind on Myrtle and Phil Bishop.

Phil Bishop, druggist, Rotarian, Third-Degree Mason, couldn't make it work. Tried letting the soda-fountain boy go. Tried adding magazines, stationery, a new line of cosmetics. Tried two cents more on all common prescriptions. Shorter hours, closed forty minutes at lunch. *Saves on lights, for chrissake!*

Tried and tried, always small things. Then borrowed. Then stayed away, and then—

Went to the roof of the building at nine P.M. over the sign that hadn't been lighted for a year. *Those lights cost more than the rent, goddammit. . . . What else can a man do . . . what's left? Oh Myrtle! Oh Phyllis! Oh Sonny! Oh God!* and went off headfirst (to be certain) after a heavy dose of something-or-other, leaving a widow, one daughter, one son. . . .

A widow. Wiping her eyes with a dead man's hankie in a hallway in August in Deliria, USA. Nineteen hundred and forty-one.

Damn! Pom had said. In another six months, a year at the most, business would have doubled for the poor devil. They'd have put his pharmacy right in the new bank building.

But a year is forever, Mr. Pomeroy Russell. Forever. Even an afternoon is forever.

★

So, pity. Sarah was right.

In the hall the smears and shadows of past wounds; out of the paisley womb, delivered by Madame Zuma McCleod, pay-as-you-come-and-go, pay-as-you-will-and-can—doodads and promises, they're all good for something. Hand over the foolish trifle of your existence, your pain. Sarah, I realized slowly, had never *asked* them for mere cash. She kept thinking we didn't need anything.

The clients continued, therefore, to talk and weep and pay with a mildewed steamer trunk.

"Don't you get tired of them? They're all so fascinated with their own troubles."

"Well, Hon, heh! They *are* kinda fascinating, you know."

But that junkery, that graveyard of monogrammed castaways we called *home*! Nobody in the world had our initials! BLZ, KRA, SOH like tombstones on everything we owned in that rambling piece of nowhere in the year of our Lord. . . .

I leaped up. She was still sleeping. I stood, indecisive, but erect. Yes, it would drift that way. I knew it. She would be too old finally to work, to see clients anymore. Ruby would stay like the furniture. And I would work.

I stood there dripping, not bothering with the mirror. I wished a little bit, therefore, that I were a man. Just a little. They knew how.

I dressed and ran out the back past Ruby, who shot me a look of scornful amazement. I unplugged the electric and went up to Nina's an hour early.

Enid

I don't like their closeness. All that running around in cars, beer. That trashy Creole place. He's just a child still. Katie's been fooling with him since he was a baby. *Baby!* That feeling. Little hands and feet. Cutting those tiny nails. I did that so easily, as if he were part of myself. Holding him. Keeping him from Jack. Always did that. Jack! Nobody has said his name in eight years. Hardly remember. What would it feel like now? The first time we did. The queer surprise of it—being entered. Almost too natural. More for an animal than for a human. I was not natural enough for it. As if some of us should never have heard of it nor felt it. Had to drink a little wine first always, to relax. Jack used to say, No hurry no hurry Honey. But then if he had too much to drink himself it was a waste. Became impotent so soon. Why? Not much of a father, no pride in it. He was domestic but like a sulky cowardly ten-year-old boy hanging around the kitchen door. No mother and too much mammy. I know, I know.

I said Henry, I want to talk to you about Jack and me. I've got to tell someone.

And he said, Oh, Enid. Find a nice old family doctor. I'm really just an eternally embarrassed intern. Never got over the shock of medical school. Besides, you know how I've always felt about you.

No. How?

But he wouldn't go on with it. I would have. They all adored him and he never married. Old Iantha, half choking to death like that over him. Good God! What fools we all are! I should have seduced him and married him. I was always a coward.

If war would break out. Clear the air. Stop the talk and speculation. Pom's everlasting predictions. If something *had* to be done —I'd get up. I would. Tomorrow . . .

What do you mean tomorrow? You're kidding yourself.

Henry, I drink. I want someone to say it to. I drink. I mean that I am . . .

Say it. Go on.

I'm a . . .

Well? Go on.

Someone! Someone tough who can bear to hear what the other secret voice wants its whole life to declare. I want out. I want in or out. Want something . . . want . . .

What?

Nothing appears. Henry . . . I broke my arm. I have meningitis, migraine. Headaches all the time. I throw up. My heart is weak. . . .

You're in quite good health, Enid, considering the way you treat yourself. God! A woman with your . . .

It's a lie.

No. I'm serious. Your health seems perfect. It's nerves, dear.
That's all.
Oh, hush. Henry. Henry!
Who?
Father?
Who?
Mother? Mother! Mama!
There's the door. What do they *do* out so late? We petted in the
parlor. If Father had opened that door he'd have killed Jack.
Killed.
I killed Jack. Beasley is home, slamming the door like a shot
at one A.M. I killed your father Jack. Say killed don't say shot.
Your Honor I did not shoot I killed Jack Russell . . .

Do you remember these acts, Mrs. Russell?
Yes.
Do you regret these acts, Mrs. Russell?
Your Honor, I object! The Defense has pleaded guilty . . .
Objection sustained.

No. Let me tell! It was nothing. That's what you don't under-
stand. Any of you can do it. What's the difference if there's no
Jack Russell in the world? There's no loss. There's more peace.
Punish me and forget. I am free of him. Beas is free of him.

*And in all those years did you make any attempt to separate yourself from
a man you considered to be a threat to your life and to that of your son?*
We moved to my sister's house once for six months.
And you returned . . .
*He seemed to have changed. He seemed . . . penitent. He sold our house
without consulting me. Illegally. But he spent the money on us. He always
used money to . . .*

Oh, what's the use. You didn't elicit the truth. I did it out of . . .
What?
Hush. Hush. Swallow it deep. More. Take all you want. Your
health is perfectly good. Have to tell Swan to get me a better
brand. Quality. But the beautiful burn, slowly descending, like an
orb of slow fire, more than any knowledge, any caress, any word,
lies inside the body correctly.
I drink bootleg wine and whiskey, Your Honor. About two
fifths of wine a day sometimes. Less whiskey. I love it. Love myself
with it. I'm in excellent health and I love my bottle and my soft
rumpled me-smelling bed. My sheets are fine, clean every three
days. The room is aired twice a day. My house is cleaned once a
week by a colored girl who's strong as an ox. She works like a
nigger. I hear the news. Police calls. Send my son out for good
steak dinners. My hair is washed by Consuelo's Beauty Salon once
a week. I eat often. Oh . . . little things. Meat. I'm a meat-and-

potatoes person. Milk toast in the evening sometimes. Reminds me of my father on Sunday nights, his damp mustache, his grave gentle look, his love of daughters. How he cared for me when I was so sick as a child. I was once a child and it made me as I am.

Your Honor, my house is paid for. My son is a genius. Ward of the State and Pomeroy Russell, my father-in-law, financier, attorney, former oil broker and playboy husband of Lou Foray. You know—the actress?

My father was Kevin McCleod, City founder. My mother Adela Beasley, Washington, D.C. . . .

My husband was oil broker Jack Russell, son of Pomeroy and Lou. He died from a gunshot wound to the back of the head in August 1933. He deserved that death and he received it instantly. He did not suffer in dying. Neat and efficient, the way he liked things. His hand with its Third-Degree Masonic ring remained on the arm of the chair. He disappeared from life painlessly and forever.

Do you remember these acts, Mrs. Russell?

Remember. Was not, am not, never shall be Temporarily Insane.

Mr. Russell said Delicious! and set the plate down in that careful gentlemanly way of his—Pearl had noticed that in all his acts. Her pastry, he always said, was as fine as any of the great French pastries he had eaten in his time. That abstract—French pastry— had been her ghostly ideal for more than thirty years.

He moved to the back screen then as she quickly whisked away the plate, fingered over it with soap, held it under the tap and put it in the rack. She wiped vaguely across the top of the table feeling that curious pause when he was in the room. He tended to roam, tended to forget what they were saying. It was as if he had something dangerous or too serious to say to her and was delaying it. He stared now out into the backyard where half an hour ago he had parked the Stutz, hoping Wishbone would come on time to saddle soap it.

"Where the devil is that boy? It's almost ten o'clock. Those leaves are full of sap falling on that pigskin."

"He be here any minute, Mista Russell. I know he will. His cousin taken sick the other day and he muss be ova theah."

He stared at her. "Oh . . . Well . . . I didn't realize that. Well, we'll wait a little longer then."

"I'll let you know when he come. He be along pretty quick now, I know it."

She turned her back on him, opening a cabinet door. That was her sign to him to get out of her kitchen and it had always charmed and amused him. He lingered, fixing a cunning gaze on her splay of broad hips caught in the neat tight uniform. She had grown heavier in the past few years and was graying now around the hairline. They had that physical wealth sometimes. Irrefutable! He imagined her tossed out on a bed of tangled sheets suddenly. Her husband had died long ago and she had never taken another.

He went out then quickly and to his study. On the wall map was a line of black pins arced about Leningrad and the Kronstadt Fortress. A full black circle around Paris at which he stared in disbelief every morning and had for a year. Even that jealous romance of the Germans with Paris might not suffice to protect her. He slapped irritably at his thigh with the sash of his dressing gown. Germany reported that the drinking water supply in Odessa had been cut off. He fumbled with a few pins, sighed, jabbed them back in and went to the window. To save Europe again? For what? She seemed determined to perish. He brooded, wondering if a man his age ought not be somewhat ashamed to experience disillusionment yet again, and so late. Europe—France especially—had been a sort of general muse in his fantasy. As long as French culture existed, Pom had seemed to feel that he had a spiritual home. It shocked him to take a backward glance which revealed him as an alien in his own country. What then? Where? Lou, of course. His real land, his soul's country had been Lou. And France merely a culture that had seemed most natural to her. The glimmer of primitive passion in that notion of his own earth as a certain woman rattled him. Clearly one ought to contain it all oneself somehow. Maybe women could. But a man? He wasn't sure. His transparent reflection in the study window now alarmed him. Half-completed, maybe, he said to himself.

And all at once Jack loomed in his mind. Dead. Less fulfilled even than himself. And Beasley? Beas might well vindicate them all, the Russells.

Pom's own father had been a self-made man, rich on the exploitation of labor in his silver mines in Mexico and through his Latin American mining interests. A robber baron, hard-jawed. Jack had looked a lot like him. The old man had been a temperamental dandy, able to simulate the various aristocratic dispositions which were natural to Pom's mother, who must have married the man in a seizure of some sort, sexual probably, he mused. But he had always been his mother's son. He had plucked Lou, eight years his senior, out of the myriad implications in his mother's nature and her relations to him which had always been confidential, adoring, sensible, instructive, worldly, carrying a secret assumption of superiority, and the humility of a goddess.

What a pair of women! His earth, yes, original and adopted. He had never known life except on their heroic terms. By God, with them, through them, one was part of a heritage, a tradition of responsibility and courage! But how even to employ all that, ex-

cept privately, in this mad world of unheroic souls and circumstances? What besides war?

He shook his head. Disbelief came to him that way as if some
small ordinary colorless bird had arrived and planted itself on his
shoulder, persistently sure, awaiting recognition.

He turned to his desk to work. At eleven Miss Alice What's-her-
name would come to take dictation. She would settle herself tidily
into the wingback chair, cross her thick ankles seemingly without
the merest self-doubt and bend her flaky-scalped head over the
tablet. Most strange women infuriated Pom and that reduced him
to an almost maudlin courtesy with them. On the other hand, a
sexually attractive stenographer of the kind Abe Dietler seemed
to find would have been farcical somehow. He snorted. Ridiculous
preoccupation!

He plowed into his work, his notes on the regional petroleum
report to Ickes, who wanted a hundred more oil tankers for the
British. That meant drastic shortages for the East and gas rationing was inevitable in any case. Now was the time and only a few
sharp men were willing to say it. Abe Dietler had complained only
the day before—"I wish they'd drop a bomb on our periphery,
Pom. Drag us in. FDR can't do it. He thinks he'd be run out of
Washington, but I wonder."

"I wonder too," he had said. "The inevitability of it must be
reaching the hard-core resistance by now. But they may be fools
enough to let Britain collapse. These damned America Firsters.
What an ironic power."

This war and all the history he had once viewed hungrily as the
acme of theater now struck him as more importantly tragic and
personal—men driven through history like beasts through one
phase of the route to slaughter after another. Their patience after
the crash! There was still that look in many an eye. The ravening
gaze, a kind of static urge not for life but for mere survival. A
whole generation of them had been silenced. And now the draft.
And could there be any purge, any resurrection, any way to move
the herds through without violence? But he was done with all that.
Jack's death had ended his passion for history. Eight years ago this
month.

The phone rang. "Hullo, Pom. Abe here."

"Abe! How are you?" He welcomed the interruption.

"Fair enough."

"I hope you're not calling to back out of the meeting."

"Oh no. No no, Pom. Just feeling somewhat stymied. I just
heard Murray is pleading C.O.! *Without defense*, mind you, before
the courts! Political objection. Ha! Before a court that's bound to
have at least one fascist hanging around. I can't believe it, but I
know my son."

"Good Lord! That's pretty romantic at a time like this."

Abe growled. "Oh, it's perfect timing! Short of actual war he
couldn't be better primed for a slug in the brain or at least ten
years in a federal prison."

"Oh, Abe," Pom said, appalled, "they wouldn't give a boy that age federal prison. Reform school maybe, or some kind of strict parole, but . . ."

"Maybe, but in a way that's worse. I'm really feeling tied. I guess a man ought to be able to reason with his son no matter what, huh?"

"Well, it's very reckless of him, Abe. What's Helene saying?"

Abe laughed. "My wife's a mensch. Takes life like a meal she planned herself. You know that."

"He'll ask for your help at the last minute, Abe. He knows what you can do in court."

"Well, you're right, he's a romantic. And a romantic wants to make up the world as he goes along. Murray wants a chance to stand up and argue with a bunch of Army colonels and rednecks about the dignity of nonviolence yet! He's itching for it! And he'll mention Gandhi, you watch! To those idiots in the military, Gandhi is a *nigger*! He'll get mystical, Pom, I can feel it."

Pom laughed. Murray, like all true believers, was his own religion, he wanted to say, but didn't. A certain congenital surliness and secret despair seemed to define Abe's son. A leftist like a duck is in the water, Abe said of him. My son the hairy-old-man revolutionary by the time he was ten years old!

"The Party's used that kid shamelessly, Pom. That lousy Chicago outfit. It's a dirty shame."

"Well, it's just possible they're right and we will collapse according to Marxian prediction, right on schedule."

"Aaaahh!" Abe growled. "I'm trying to remember at what fatal hour I mentioned politics when I coulda bought him a box of Tinker Toys instead. If he wants a new world, better he should build it with his hands, not his head. Anyhow, if this is the decline of the West, couldn't he at least agree to apply a few bandages?"

They laughed together. The Second Fall of Man, said Abe, would at least be more interesting than the first. And Pom remarked silently how much he relished Abe's wry sensibility, that fused jolt of chronic misery and wit—all the Jewishness of him that seemed so alien and subtle to Pom. All my learning, Pom thought, was so *straight*, without proper irony. Does that mean then that I'll despair finally? Abe would never know utter despair, his would be only partial and chronic. That's better, Pom said to himself, wiser. Sometimes he wished to rush to Abe and pin him down for a real talk, more than man-to-man, more naked self to naked self or something alarming like that. But if that ever happened to him with anyone—and with Lou he had come close— it would happen with a woman, he knew. And with a woman it would be a different sort of confession, something tainted with his natural sense of greater freedom and superiority.

★

Wishbone Watson arrived, breathless, on his ancient rattling bicycle. "I'll get right on that Stuss fo you, Mista Russa. Have it rubbed up real fine fo you in no time."

Pom watched his nappy head disappear outside and saw him

dive into the garage for his rags. Make a good soldier, that boy, he told Pearl. But it pained him slightly to remember Wishbone only last year, just a kid running errands on that same bike, always pasting and cinching it together, pleasantly limping along with it.

"Private Wishbone Watson," he mused.

Pearl shook her head and suddenly dabbed at her eyes with a raised apron. "Oh . . . Mista Russell, I has this queer feelin Wishbone not going to come out of that Ahmy alive."

"Ah, Pearl!"

She quickly blew her nose and laughed at herself. He looked again at the gray in her thick wiry hair. No children. She had loved Jack for some odd reason; so few people had. Took his death hard. Sometimes her courtesy to Enid seemed fairly glazed with hatred. Couldn't pin it down, just a feeling.

"Don't you believe it for a minute. He's very intelligent and that's what it takes to stay alive in battle. Besides, we may be spared actual battle."

She shook her head, turning away. "The way they sinkin all those boats out theah in the ocean, you *know* somethin awful goin to happen. It jess seem like a matta of time. And these boys is jest chillrun. They not soldiers!"

His own phrase in her mouth mocked him—*a matter of time.* He might even have had Wishbone deferred some way if it had come to that, but the boy had enlisted before it had occurred to him. He mulled it, smitten with the notion of "these boys." Pearl must listen to the news. He wondered why.

"Well," he told her feebly, "it won't be the slaughter it was last time, even if we do go. Fewer men in the trenches and more in the air, likely."

Last time—Jack, rejected that day at the recruiting office— mastoid surgery on one side of the head . . . *not the side where the shot entered!* The shot! Eight years ago this month. It drove its old way through him and then he cast it off as he had learned to do.

He went to his study again and waited for Miss Alice. He'd send Sully Ketchum down to Texas to talk to them about tankers. A major pipeline would have solved all this and put a lot of idle men to work besides. It was archaic, this slow shipping to the East. Suddenly he wanted to do something right, to make a conclusive moral act. He felt uneasy, a shift of the soul's ground. .

Katie said once, "Why do you think humans are moral or always trying to be, Pom? I mean, seeing you don't believe in God. What's your answer?"

"Order," he had said. "Morality is order. First passion of the species."

A glib answer, maybe. Did he believe it? What would he tell her today and what would she ask? She asked little of him now. Seemed to think less seriously, in fact. Or had he merely turned her away, and if so who was her mentor now? She avoided him, whatever the reason, and his response had been a remorseful patience. He had failed her, probably because she could not compete with Beas for his deep concern. She was a survivor, a liver;

almost any milieu would do for her, it seemed. But did it have to be an either-or choice? Couldn't he have fathered them both? Beas, of course, was a special case. He'd surely end up in some future nuclear research program. But he missed Katie's questions and realized, suddenly, that Beas never asked an abstract question.

Pom would have been content now to retire completely and observe the unfolding of his grandson's life. Tyranny and fascism must be fought for Beasley. Civilization kept for him. It had to be done again. Yes, it would be in the air this time. And our tanks were safer. But it all sounded flat suddenly and he noted that Pearl had remained quietly resistant to his consolations. Certain boys, who were jess chillun, were going to be soldiers at war. She had made it real, putting it that way.

Nina's house was a palace, all shimmering chandeliers and sinky velvet couches, big ferns in Chinese vases, hanging lanterns, and a samovar. Really ritzy. She was lying down sipping something green. The maid let me in.

"I'm sorry I'm early. Shall I go away?"

"No, no. Come in. Sometimes I need someone to jar me out of that funk. I feel like Verlaine in prison." She gave her little belly laugh and shot me a jaded version of Sarah's apologetic look. Once you're overweight, I thought, you're always apologizing to the world. It was always as if you shared a little secret with Nina, though in those few short months of working for her I had never fathomed what it might be. She had a history almost as crazy and terrible as Enid's, but more exciting—parents dropping dead, sudden wealth, men—meaning Red Southwell—jilting her halfway down the aisle.

She rolled up off the couch and excused herself. She came back in a big sweeping flowered cotton number that was more tent than dress and handed me a glass of cold spumanti with a raspberry in it.

"There. That's more your sort of drink than this."

"What's yours?"

She shrugged. "Absinthe." She laughed. "Makes the heart grow fonder." We giggled like kids suddenly. God! She made you want to light a cigar of self-congratulation or something.

"Well, fonder of what?" I asked.

"Oh . . . Verlaine. I've decided breaking the law is the only way to live."

"Wow! Really? I've always thought that, but . . . you have to be careful not to do something ordinary about it."

"True, true! When you do it, do a real job."

"I wonder what's the best way?"

"The worst way is the best. Ha!" She sipped and laughed. Fools, maybe, but major fools is what we must be, she said.

We sat there and got drunk. The air conditioning felt stale and clammy to me. What a life! Imagine living in this big place alone, sweeping around in those gowns, lighting candles and sipping absinthe and champagne! She rolled back into the velvet couch, hefty and voluptuous. She swooned so easily it seemed she had no skeleton. And she sighed like a wave washing in. How did you get that way? I felt like a shaved hound. I tucked my feet under my chair. I regretted my muscles.

She said she would have to get up off her tuffet soon, no fooling, and get to work on some war aid. She felt guilty lying here dreaming when the world was being torn to shreds. Think of my Jewish kinsmen somewhere in the world, she said, in those camps. She shuddered.

"You look a little fractured yourself, Honey," she laughed. "You have fun with Eric?"

"Well . . . ha! We didn't quite make it."

"Oh, you will." She laughed a little. "Everybody makes it with Eric."

"Well, then I don't want to," I said.

"Oh, he's just young, like you. He's working his way through the female half of the human race. Nothing personal." She looked at me sharply then. "But maybe he'll fall for you and settle himself down. He ought to. You'd make a nice pair. You've got those gorgeous thick-tissued eyes like Enid."

"Oh, no. Her eyes are purple," I protested but was pleased to have my family traits and qualities recognized. Higgens be damned!

"How is Enid anyway? I haven't seen her since . . . oh, must be several years. I was at Pom's one night for dinner and she came by."

"Pom's? I didn't know you knew him that well."

She flushed a little. "We used to be friends."

I didn't ask what happened. My mind wrapped it up and stashed it away.

"Enid's the same, I guess. She never does anything."

"She still drinking?"

I nodded. I was beginning to think that real conversation just naturally demanded betrayal of some kind, of someone. "A lot. But . . ." It pained me but I told about Enid, about the Biography, and after another spumanti I even mentioned my passion for crime. She looked at me with queer surprise.

"Why a biography? Why not a novel or stories or something? Why all this crime business? Doesn't it depress you?"

I wondered how you knew if you were depressed. "Well . . . it's what I've been thinking about since . . . the murder, you know." She must be thinking I'm crazy, I told myself. Or mentally ill. Crazy was all right but mentally ill was dreary.

"Yes, I suppose all of you must think a lot about that, even now. It's hard to believe she really killed someone, isn't it?"

"Yeah. It isn't like a fact, you know? It's like something in her body or her nature. Like a disease."

"That's interesting. She carries something, it's true."

I was prickling all over. "It's the whole meaning of her life, I think. Do you think everybody has just one event and all the rest is just built around that?"

She looked at me, cagey. "Maybe. Maybe I do. No, I don't. I think some people have only one event. And the rest of us have a series of similar meaningless experiences."

Gee, how grim!

I told her I thought there was another kind of crime that nobody had ever discussed, or understood, except maybe women. But I couldn't articulate it for her. She had lost interest suddenly and I said maybe we ought to get to work.

She heaved up off the sofa and took me into the workroom off the kitchen. "Always remind me, will you, Honey? I'm fat and lazy and corrupt." And then it bubbled out again, yet again, the way Sarah's hovering laugh did, the tamed hysteria of it. I didn't have that. I was different from them.

I worked on files. She went over her phone list, calling women who had big houses. Her voice had authority, with intimate undertones and a cello sound. She seduced them into taking in a British waif. She made a point of intimate understanding and I decided that women like intimacy better than anything. But I felt remotely akin to the refugee children whom I could see standing in the train station being greeted by the clubwomen of Deliria. Stay home with the bombs, I wanted to warn them.

Later we had some little noshes, as she called them—some paté, kirsch cheese and cold grapes. More wine. How did she do it? Soporifics, I told myself. Necessary. Maybe she was alcoholic like Enid. I fumbled around, gorging and trying to think of something rare to say.

"You seeing Eric again?"

"I haven't heard from him."

"He'll call you eventually."

I cocked a sodden eye at her. "You sure seem to know him well."

"I do. I'm his mother confessor." She laughed then and patted my arm. "But he hasn't told me about your date."

I gave up all pretense, suddenly. "I was a mess. He found out I was . . . well . . . a virgin, and that did it. I kept getting weird feelings everywhere and he said I was like a bad wiring job!"

She laughed loudly. "Sounds like some struggle."

We giggled together over my dismal fate. *Stab her to the heart,* I thought, for laughing at me. Yet I handed myself over. My life, I told her, letting it all spill, was a vanilla pudding with lead sinkers in it. My life was a rabbit stew. The clients had branded me with initialed objects. I was a tattooed castaway. Sarah was too perfect, I was having sex dreams . . . truck drivers . . . I mentioned everything but Higgens and the downright who-am-I of it all.

She howled at me. What a card! I built on it.

Where You Goin, Girlie?
★
53

"But whatta you *do* about sex? I don't see why it can't be easy and just happen. To everybody who wants to. Look at Sarah and Enid. They haven't got anybody." I loaded her with every wilting blossom of our little nosegay—Hattie Finch, Iantha Abernathy . . .

"Iantha Abernathy! Oh my God! I thought that old crow was in the booby hatch by this time, Honey. Why does Sarah allow her out there? She's a menace."

"*Allowing*," I explained, laughing, "is what Sarah does. She doesn't know about the negative—you know, that little word *no*?" I waved a hand drunkenly. "She never heard of it."

I felt remote betrayal but squelched it.

"You know about Iantha and Henry Killeen, don't you?"

"No."

"Years ago she was crazy about him. She was so mad for him she went sort of insane. Really. One night she ran into him down at Piggie's Drive-In and he asked her to join him for dinner." She giggled tearfully. "Can you imagine an invitation to dinner at *Piggie's*? Heeee! Anyway, poor old Iantha got so excited she swallowed her tongue! She did! He had to lay her down in the parking lot and pull it out or she would have choked to death!"

We laughed ourselves silly. So there was old Iantha's heel at last! But I felt sorry about it even so.

"I wonder why women suffer so much and tear each other apart so much and . . ."

"Men are our grist and there ain't enough to go around, Sugar. That's all. Life really isn't as mysterious as you hope to make it."

"Well, it must be deeper than *that*."

"Why must it be? So you can get your sharp little teeth into it? You need bigger material. Woman is a farce."

That hit me. "Gee! You really think that?"

She sobered. "Oh—maybe it's a projection, something Freudian. I don't know." She spiked me a look. "I don't think I like women much. I like men. For company and . . . everything else."

I felt like running. Why had she laughed and talked with me then?

"I guess I *do* . . . like women, I mean. Or maybe I'm just so used to them that I . . . feel their life or something. You know?"

She smiled, rueful. "Yes. I know. You're more humane. I'm something of a spiritual cripple, Honey, I admit it. My mother was a slave to my father and instead of hating the wicked master, I learned to hate the capitulating slave. She even *contrived* to be subjugated, for all her talk of liberation."

She had a sort of chronic disgust. My head was whirling. But I had to admit I liked sufferers. When I had first read St. Julian the Hospitaler I thought I had found the secret of the world. St. Katherine the Hospitaler. I went around looking for lepers, never finding them. I decided finally that you had to be an aristocrat before you could become a saint. I'd never make it, thank you, Higgens.

She rattled on about keeping your best self to yourself, about making your life important and invisible to everyone. Invisible! I nearly laughed. She said make the Biography fiction, don't reveal so much. Tell it slant, Honey. Emily Dickinson. I hadn't read Emily Dickinson. I sat still as if a dentist had his fist in my mouth.

"Okay," I said finally, sighing. Nobody understands anybody else, I said to my creature. "I'll give up the Biography and turn it into a soap opera about a woman who lies on her bed all day twirling the dial of her radio and sipping bootleg wine she keeps in a blue satin lingerie case under her mattress because she killed her husband and was tried and acquitted. And her son is down in the basement making stink bombs in his homemade chemistry lab. Will he blow up the world? Will she die of guilt or boredom? Tune in next week. . . . Ha! I still think the truth is better than fiction because nobody has control over the truth."

She laughed. "You little anarchist! You're drunk, that's all. Get out of here before I get arrested for corrupting a minor with my expensive champagne."

At the car she invited me to a party Saturday night for the RAF boys who were out at the flight school. She must have been very drunk! Dozens of men, Honey, she said with a sort of smirk. I beamed. She said she'd never invited a woman before and I thought I'd fall down the front steps in gratitude and disbelief. I was now supposed to be a woman but I felt like giving a goat cry!

She said she'd send Eric after me but I protested.

"I don't want him to think . . ."

She shushed me and shoved me into the car. "I don't want you driving around alone in the middle of the night!"

Her propriety was thrilling if alarming. She obviously didn't know that part of my bloodhound life was driving around alone in the middle of the night, me and my electric mount. "I love this thing," she said of the electric. "Reminds me of Oscar Wilde."

She kissed both my cheeks and waved me away. I drove off half fainting, wondering if she might change her mind the next day or if she might try to make me over in her image, as they said. I saw myself scurrying across the lease after my own old dog self, my old me who had hounded her life alone so far. I didn't want anyone, even Nina Brosky, monkeying with my nature. I just wanted to *live*! And I wanted to find something hard and real and great outside of books and movies and other people's lives. Or some talisman of it, something in the hand. Or an act. Or if not sex then some crime that caused no damage. I imagined some huge agonizing act of riddance that would leave me standing on a horizon purified of all but my own true self. But who would have understood all that? I was crazy.

I passed the cracking plant and saw it as a castle of flaming light, something on the moon, an illumined future. There must be a way not to struggle and work and slave to get one's real life. Some sudden plunge that would turn on the light and move the wheel all at once. The first time I was on a merry-go-round, I remembered then, Pom had lifted Beas onto a pony beside mine and then signaled the man at the controls to start. It was at a local carnival, early in the day, few children around. Beas and I were almost alone on our frozen painted mounts. And when that grind up to full gallop first began and we curved through the shadow and around to the other side again, passing Pom who stood there waving, I realized something terrible about the world—that the trip was round and brought you back, whereas I had really believed for some queer reason that when I got on that wooden pony I would take off in a straight line and never see Deliria again, even though it would have killed me to leave. I had been ready to take the plunge even then. I was about seven, too old, I decided later, not to have known about the circle, the round and round of that marvelous trip.

And so I came back to the lease in the electric. Nothing natural would ever blast me out of Deliria. Look at Nina—money and civilization hadn't done it for her. Why did she stay here? Some violence, some catastrophe would be required. Bring it on, I said, but insincerely. The shot that killed Jack Russell had not sprung us from Deliria but curiously entrenched us there, had driven Enid into her boozy dream bed, and had driven us to her side with our plasma. Forever?

When you are only a little drunk, on alcohol or imagination, you know everything for an instant and your sadness is that your body cannot live out what you know.

Her party was a smash. Swarms of men and Nina in a black silk dress with a huge red collapsing flower pinned at the hip and red silk pumps with pompoms on them which supplied me with a pun about Pom, secret, and I used it the way I used other signs—to prove something quasi-illicit between them. The house glittered with a hundred candles and reeked of incense. Frankincense, Nina said, with her little harem belly-giggle, and I wondered if Iantha's story that Nina wore frankincense in her navel during Christmas season were ture.

The RAF was there in droves smelling faintly of sweat, clean and clammy, soaking through the cotton of their summer uniforms. Their arms were skinny and hard but white-skinned. They laughed a lot and said quick little subtle things that one missed. They admired Nina's crystal palace ever so much and said you Ameddicans have more style than one realized. For that compliment, nobody bowed. Nina swooped around introducing everybody. A Viennese Jew named Walter Lederer played the piano, sometimes weeping with nostalgia. "Time on My Hands" and "I Cover the Waterfront" and of course "Stardust," which he said was used as a code by some underground group in Europe.

A rabbit-mouthed rosy RAF danced with me several times, hopping mostly, and explaining to me that he had taken the opportunity to come to the flight school for two reasons: One, to get the special training; the other—well, frankly, to find an Ameddican oil heiress and meddy into our minerals that way.

"You're not an oil heiress by any chance, I suppose? I mean, you simply reek of petroleum. Spiritually, of coss! Heh . . ."

I laughed and lowered my eyes. "No. Uh, I'm in steel. Sorry."

He sparkled. "Oh! But that's splendid! Simply splendid. Steel will do, all right. But of coss you've got to be prepared for certain . . . uh . . . minor disasters. I mean I do need a charming woman like you who's brave and all that and wants to run the risk of having her lovely London flat blown off the side of the building and all that sort of thing, to beat the Hun, you see."

The other RAF were listening to him, snickering, and then they broke up into polite little hoots again. And the benefits of a party with two women and twenty men started to flow in after that. They passed me around, dancing stiffly, nothing like old Eric who was watching, seemingly more puzzled than annoyed. I liked it so much I began to shout everything I said. Eric kept drawing me back to the couch to force a new red whizzer on me. Five red whizzers later he practically threw me into those sinky down pillows and established some kind of homestead over my body. Then he said I was too drunk and pulled me up to take me onto the terrace for a walk. A few RAF were out there staring up. Safe skies, they said, softly, wonderingly. I wanted to observe and wonder about them but my head was swarming with wormy ideas. Eric pushed me against the stone chimney, in a kind of corner out of sight, and kissed me for hours.

Back inside they had begun to ravage a big buffet of paté and little sausages, little pies and rolls and raw cauliflower and artichoke hearts, hot sliced turkey and ham. Nina's colored girl and her husband served it, smilingly proud. Nina, I noticed, had a way of eating an enormous amount between sentences and breaths, vacuuming it down with fabulous ease so that it never seemed like gorging. Her big white teeth ground it all up so fast it took your breath away. It seemed to make everyone around her a little desperate.

Swan was there with his usual look of the frantic insect, his Adam's apple trembling, talking to some RAF about the dignity of certain suicides, Virginia Woolf's for instance. He'd cut his own throat, he claimed, before he'd be drafted into an army. But the general hush seemed to imply that that wouldn't be necessary. He got carried away, holding up a champagne glass and shouting above the din that *Death in Venice* was the greatest work of the twentieth century, Hun or no Hun.

I went upstairs to find a john. It was all silky and perfumy up there. The huge bed was covered with satin, including the sheets for which I felt under the pale-gold satin spread. There was a canopy with fringe.

By the bed were books of poems by Rimbaud and Baudelaire. I fell out flat on the bed, sailing, dazzled and queasy. Cary Grant, dimples, foxy eyes, loomed over me, only to be shot in the back by Sydney Greenstreet. I staggered up and went to the john. When I had flushed, I opened the medicine cabinet for further identifying evidence—pain relievers, valerian, Murine, Vaseline, the usual. A disappointment. On the table at the end of the tub were huge bottles of cologne and boxes of powder, however. I went back to the bed and rested for a moment, swaying and holding onto the sliding satin spread with a tight fist.

Nina had told me she lived on delicate little gourmet suppers, imported teas, champagne, a touch of Drambuie, "God Save the King" and *Gymnopédies*; long scented baths, a masseuse who came once a week. Nothing heavy, nothing ordinary. Limeflower water, hot, in the morning usually. Truffles. Thin Japanese soup. Marzipan? I did not ask. Surely marzipan. How else all that rich Persian fat?

Oh, how to cut through those little wizardries of another person's life and find the meat! Wow! What was she, really? Rich and living alone. All those men at parties. But what did she say to herself when she woke in the middle of the night?

I heard laughter below again and more music, a march. Swan's desperate cackle broke through. I sat up on the side of the bed and decided not to be sick. On the night table on a note pad was written E and a number. Eric's probably—29490. I memorized it. Then, I opened the top drawer of the night table and found lying there, neatly, faithfully, you might say, two candy bars—Snickers! My head flipped up. I laughed helplessly. *Snickers!* All the truffles and elixirs of her life spilled out into the sewers of the world suddenly. Everybody was a fake. I went down laughing. It made me fond of her then, merely fond.

"Seriously," Rabbit was saying to me, "you look like an intellekshull to me. Do you disdain the life of the mind?"

"Nope." I drank wine carefully and nibbled a sliver of ham. "Criminal law is my interest but I can't afford to go to law school."

Eric choked.

"Criminal law! How supah! I think you Ameddican gulls are splendid women. I mean it!"

He was so attentive I could have twisted his bunny nose off. I felt huge and spectacular, supah and splendid. This, I notified myself, is how a large Bermuda onion feels when admired by the king.

"What do you do," I asked him, "besides fly and look for an American wife with minerals?"

"Well, I'm quite keen on films. And a bit of spoht. But not now of coss. I'm quite busy in the air, ackshully. Heh!"

"I'm keen on films too!" I suddenly *loved* him.

We got onto George Raft and Peter Lorre and Sydney Greenstreet, Franchot Tone and Bette Davis, all very quickly. The

Ameddican dead pan was triumphant, he said, referring to Raft. Quite different from the British which had less horror in it, perhaps, more humor, but too much stiff upper and all that sort of thing. This was becoming a serious conversation. I produced goose bumps all over the back of my neck and arms. And then, in a lull, someone said quietly—

"But the Krauts didn't know a tank from a kiddy car till the French gave away their Skoda plans. One way or another . . ."

And the war lumbered into the room.

"No," said a solemn English wit, "it don't seem to be France's year exactly."

Everybody laughed politely. The RAF liked their own wit, after all. And then someone said the English could take a share of the blame, considering Chamberlain, and everybody twitched. Nina lowered her head modestly and poured some hot water out of the samovar. An RAF leaned over her, staring down into her cleavage, which must have been at least six inches deep. His eyes whirled like marbles in a bowl as he took a cup of tea from her.

Rabbit had stood up and was facing up close the man who had mentioned Chamberlain. "Yes, Old Man, and we're paying our debt for blundering in daily installments, don'tcha know."

More laughter. Code. Something about the war. Bombings, I supposed. The British insisted on laughing about the war. I looked for Eric, who stood transfixed behind me, watching them.

". . . finally decided he had to sign," someone said. "It kept the Germans off the Caucasian oil at least. He knew what he was doing." The voice was familiar. I looked over and saw Murray Dietler!

"He knew what he was doing all right," Swan bellowed out, terrified at the quick attention he got. "He was about to carve up Europe with Hitler and take his share of the loot. And look what he got for it. I don't trust him. I'll never be comfortable in bed with that Communist maniac."

And a big bellow of glee broke out at the idea of Swan in bed with Stalin. He giggled and camped around, successful as a rooster that survives the loss of all tail feathers. I turned to Nina to say that I was mad about her party but hated war talk.

"Well, Honey," she whispered, "our complacency must sometimes infuriate the British. I mean—here we sit while they're being pounded to pieces, and the Jews of Europe may be wiped out."

I hadn't known we were complacent. I had never been complacent about anything. I watched Murray Dietler then, surrounded by tall, cool RAF men, holding his temper and having to look up at them, he was so short.

"I hear he's pleading C.O.," Eric said to Nina.

She rolled her eyes and shook her head. I thought of the Snickers waiting up there. Did she eat them in bed?

"Our problems are different," Murray was saying. "We haven't that much in common now."

"Yaw problems," said Tommy, a pal of Rabbit's, "are identical.

Hitla and his Luftwaffe and his submarines. It's that simple. And if you think we can keep him off yaw shores indefinitely, then yaw greatly deceived."

Murray stood with his head bent a little and his eyebrows up. He asked something about Japan and the Pacific, about rubber and Japan's need for oil. Didn't Tommy think we were baiting Japan and didn't he think that it would be for control of the rubber and so on that we were hoping for war there. And what about the quinine and all that.

Japan, Tommy said with disgust, would do what Hitla told her to do even if it meant suicide. The sentiments of romantic leftists in Ameddicker, he declared, would come as close as anything else to letting the free world be destroyed. Ameddicans, bless their poor heads, had a hard time with the forces of evil. They tended to think of evil as something that goes on in bed.

Bed! said my head. Wow!

That broke it up, as if they had all come for the purpose of putting some Ameddicans in their places. I sighed, resigned, thinking of going out with Eric later, of leaping together with him. I stood up. Nina looked at Eric.

"Sure you're sober enough to drive her?"

He grinned. "Sober as a lemon."

Nina served another RAF who leaned over her seacoast bosom asking for tea. The word seemed to have gotten around that if you stood leaning over her you could see everything. Somehow ramming herself into clothes seemed to fail with Nina; there was always the feeling that she was temporarily restrained in them and would burst out any minute.

Walter was playing "God Save the King," eating bites of Viennese torte between times and weeping. So good-bye. I stood up reeling. I'm going out to be raped! I kissed several dozen British cheeks and lips. Rabbit said good-bye you splendid gull you, I hope to see you again. Then Walter played a waltz and Swan began to float about by himself, waving his arms, driving the alarmed RAF to the walls.

If only, I thought, it would all end up in one of those orgies people talked about. I wondered, when you got right down to it in so many arms and legs and nethers, what was so evil about sex in a group? It seemed safely familyish to me.

Eric dragged me away.

★

"You always smell like baby soap," he murmured at my ear.

"Castile. Some client paid us a hundred bars."

He let out a hoot and the car swerved. He was going to take off his clothes and my clothes and . . .

"A *client*? Paid in *soap*?"

"Yeah. My mother's a . . . psychologist, didn't you know?"

"Yeah, but I didn't know they paid in *soap*!"

I laughed. "They pay with what they've got, so they say. They don't pay cash, I know that. Since the crash, I mean."

"That's a long time. What else do you get?"

I gave him a rundown starting with the electric. I'd never quite told it in just so many doodads before and it was something of a relief. He laughed madly and pulled me across the seat toward him. I was terrified and still half drunk and so I babbled on, even telling him about Mrs. Truex giving us a lovely little antique velvet box that had her dead father's glass eye in it. He kept his arm around me and I shifted gears for him. We said nothing about our plans but I was about to see and know his big, his huge. We roared up the mountain to his spot. We spread out a blanket under the tree. He turned on the radio—"Chattanooga Choo Choo."

I asked him what he thought Murray Dietler was doing there.

"Oh, she offers hospitality to all types, you know. Used to be a Commie herself, did you know that? Probably feels sorry for them with all these black lists and everything. She's funny that way—she'd rather have stray cats and castoffs than ordinary people around."

My ears lit up and I coughed. Maybe she'd found her first female stray cat in me!

"Anyway, I've heard Murray's pretty smart. Graduated U of Chicago when he was seventeen, didn't he?"

"Yeah," I said, "but look what it did for him. He's still all mixed up and never seems to know how to talk to people without making them mad."

"Well," he sighed, "he's pleading C.O. That'll force him to talk a little. Pleading his own case! What a nut! Can you figure a thing like that when your old man is one of the best lawyers in the state?"

I couldn't and didn't want to. My hair was standing on end and I was palpitating, staring down over the lights of Idiotsville. I waited and finally he said, "Lie back," plaintively. And I did. Everything, it seemed, was choreographed correctly. We lay there on the Army blanket talking and he did it all so slowly, lacing it into our talk, telling about rescue drill in the Navy and all, ships and men and danger, that while my mind cruised around the world with him, my body slowly unfurled on the earth with him, both rhythms overtook me and I never lost a step.

"You talk to Nina?" he whispered.

"No. Yes . . . but . . ."

"It's okay. I've got something. I'll be careful. I won't hurt you."

And he did move with a sort of slow grace and gathering fire and drove me off into space. I did it all. It hurt me but I didn't care. My eyes rolled far back. We writhed up together like two crazy snakes to that high hot hard drive up *split!*

"Oh!"

that infallible surprise! Yes yes yes Baby, there there . . . he whined on, driving through me.

And then we fell like a tent, sighing and murmuring. And that was it and all of it. The first time I ever gave in to anything all the way.

"You all right?"

"Yes."

"It's never as good the first time. It gets better."

"I thought it was good," I said, not admitting I hardly felt finished.

He craned up to stare at me. "Yeah?"

"Yeah. I like it already."

He laughed like a jackal and squeezed me.

But there was nothing much to say. We lay there rippling in silence and looked up at the stars over mere Deliria. My body paused, throbbing, wondering where to go next, how to be. I lay there a long time slowly burning out, ruined and amazed. Later I saw my blood.

Renfro

Went to a phone booth just inside the Salvation Army entry and dialed the old number and when the ring broke over the earphone he tapped the hook down with his other hand. And then he hung up slowly with a sense of apology. Once he had been tempted to spy on Julia when she sat necking in an old battered canvas glider in the back yard with her drugstore delivery boy. It had been this same feeling of chastened solemnity, with the sudden sense for the first time that the bodies of his mother and sisters were not part his own, neither his charges nor his sustainers, nor even his to speculate upon. Without his father he had always felt guilty and lonely and fraudulent among the women of his home and never quite known before now what that long habit of feeling, like an old familiar garment, had been.

So he hung the receiver in the hook again with care and humility, knowing that if he forced them to answer, he must not refuse to speak to them.

And then a quick flash of destruction went through him. As if he'd had a glimpse of some catastrophe—a tornado or a fire in which they were all consumed. He was desperately lonely, he realized, and just now could bear to admit it for the first time. Their name and number were still in the book—Renfro, Alma, 1401 Cincinnati, 95807. Such magic in old names and numbers. And then it hit him—she had not married! And he felt worse. He started to look up Vic's number but changed his mind. Didn't want to know yet, if ever, what had happened to them all. He gained a perverse power by not even knowing if his own mother was still alive.

"I must be sick in the head," he said. But he felt more competent and at ease now. What was that occasional attack upon his senses—oh yes, *hope!* Yes. He was all right. He began to walk the town at dusk, searching out its old and new secrets. He began also to tell someone about his wanderings, these and the others. But in the abstract. The details would shock her. *Her!* Yeah. Some woman somewhere. A conversation with a confessional quality. She would sit facing him. They would drink something. She would nod, patient, knowing. He could not imagine her features, only her presence.

Enid

If I did, it would be to face her. Or something like that. I'd go to the mirror, just that one real definite time, and face her and say, Whoever you are you've got to show yourself here and now in total. Or else. And maybe she actually would. And then I could and would look away and never have to deal with her again.

But what am I thinking, really? Is nothing coming? Is no one going to come in and say, *Now!*

But what difference really how you live or don't live? All lives are stupid, meaningless, babbling, bungling, self-delusion.

Who's wise? If there were *one* wise man . . . I say *man* . . . yes . . . it would have to be a wise man.

Mother wasn't. Sweet and patient and neat, even intelligent. But not wise. Playing house. Tried to tease us into growing up, marrying. Look at Sarah! Yes. Isn't she divine! Isn't she a fantastic foolish saint of a thing!

If I were to turn on my side toward the wall and see the eye, the whole face, staring at me . . . So many times beside me in bed, waking to that head, that face . . .

If I were to see some real whole tangible head, nearby, waiting, pulsing . . . I would get up and . . .

Tomorrow maybe. But really really really—no one wants you to. No one cares a damn really really whether you do or not.

Two weeks. Eric had disappeared. I could hardly breathe although it was cooler. Indian summer, burning leaves and the dry dusty smell of the ground, the scurrying life of little animals everywhere. It was stupid even to consider staying indoors all day. I delayed applying at the plant a little longer. I hovered not far from the house, sitting in a pile of leaves I had raked to show Sarah and Ruby I was busy. And half listened from there for the phone which after a week I knew wouldn't ring again. Not for me. I burned up my days by breathing in and out and yielding up a little attention to Sarah and Ruby at teatime.

I am not a virgin, I almost said aloud to them each time. I stared at them to see if I could press it into their minds. I looked the same, it seemed, but I felt stunned and frozen. I waited to do it again. How about just going out to the highway and flagging down a truck? I conjured the driver's hard arms, his T shirt, his lunch pail on the floor. *Where you goin, Girlie?* And I would jump up to the seat beside him. *Anywhere you are, Mister.* Every man, I reminded myself, has one, don't forget that. *Every single man on earth!* Wow! Penis. PEE-NISS. I looked it up a dozen times but the definition—the male organ of copulation in higher vertebrates —didn't describe Eric's big number at all. I wanted to see his face again. I had lost a memory of it. And to get a look at the rest of him, and to feel that plunging drive again! I slugged around like a slow-growing wart.

I decided to improve my mind while trying to distract it and so I borrowed art history books from Pom, and also thoughts by someone called Pascal who said, "Theft, incest, infanticide, parricide, have all had a place among virtuous actions," which perked me up for a while. I decided to memorize a lot of lines like that, shocking phrases, and slap them out at the dinner table when things became dull or crazy. Pom at least would be impressed. And I could try a few out on Nina, too. I could memorize works by all the poets she liked, all those decadent French! But Pascal pleased me more than any of the rest—"Can anything be more ridiculous than that a man should have the right to kill me because he lives on the other side of the water, and because his ruler has a quarrel with mine, though I have none with him?" But Pom stayed away for ten days or so and I finally lost interest. Poetry was easier. I wanted to sit by Nina's fire and read poetry with her and tell her my vices, whatever they were. But then that freak known as my body flared up again like a fire under thinning coals and I threw down the books. I went out running for hours. I picked hard little green wild apples in the old abandoned orchard at the north end of the lease and brought them back to Ruby, and she made up a tart cobbler, but that was only an instant of pleasure. It seemed to be all I was worth.

I wondered what had been so bad about that night that Eric couldn't bear to call me back. Maybe he went back to Ann Coolidge who had a lot of cashmere sweaters and naturally curly hair.

One night Beas and I were in the lab in his basement. I had decided finally to go out a lot, drink a lot of beer and red whizzers and keep busy. I stayed away from Nina's for fear of seeing Eric there. In the Creole it didn't matter so much.

Beas was talking about atoms. I half heard it. He said that learning to smash the atom was the greatest moment in the history of science. "The world will never be the same," he said reverently. I wished I could believe anything with that kind of ardor. The very quality of it always made me resistant and skeptical.

"Oh, yeah?" I whined. "What about religion and the wheel and all that?"

"It's different when you find a key to the universe like this," he said. "It's a whole new concept of power too. They can do anything with it eventually." He stood in the middle of the lab in his khaki shorts, bare at the top, with a big ocherish stain on his cheek. "They'll even win the war by it if it lasts long enough."

He had a map now, on his wall in the basement, somewhat like Pom's map except that his pins were red and yellow. Yellow for the Nazi armies, he said sternly. I gazed listlessly. "Let's go get a beer," I said, wondering if it would ever mean anything to me to know that Hitler might fulfill his vow to reach the Volga by winter. The Volga might as well be in Orion, I felt.

"When did you start finding all this out? I mean about the war?" I asked him irritably. "You never used to read war news."

"Science is getting more and more important to the war," he said. Then he handed me a picture of some Russian people cut from *Time* magazine. "Hitler," he explained urgently, "is only two hundred miles from Moscow!" He took on an expression of what seemed to be mock horror that almost made me laugh. "Looky here! This whole part is under siege."

"Under *siege*?" I said scornfully.

"Yes. See this. That's the Donets Basin. All the central Ukraine is gone already. If they got the Donets Basin then they'd have all the Russian coal. . . . Its industry . . . oil would be cut off, see?"

I thought I was losing my mind. I stared at him. He had never talked about anything even remotely connected with geography or countries or war. I couldn't believe it.

"Well . . . so what? I mean, Roosevelt knows about that. Let them get in if they think it's so important."

He started to straighten up the lab.

"Come on, let's go," I said, sullen. But I heard the sulky child and hated myself for it. Nobody cared that I was going crazy. And then Beas said something quietly and my mouth fell open.

"*What*? You're *what*?"

"I mean it. I'm enlisting. Tomorrow. I made up my mind."

"*What*? Why, you can't do *that*! You must be *crazy*! Why . . ."

"Shhhh! Not so loud. I haven't told *her* yet." He stood there like a rubber doll, adamantly staring at me. He was holding Lucille now, a white rat from Dietler labs. Her tiny body curved over his fingers, docile or terrified, I wasn't sure. They were doing experiments on her, injecting her with some kind of serum.

"Beas . . . you must be *nuts*! You're not acting *normal*! Why, they won't even take you in the first place. You're not even eighteen yet. My God!"

He turned around, put Lucille in the cage carefully and shut the cage door. Then he washed his hands.

"But I will be in two months and by the time they've checked up on me and all, I'll be legit."

Legit! He never used that kind of language! He sounded like a kid playing gangster. I laughed sourly.

"You're crazy! I don't get it," I whispered loudly, furiously. "You don't have to go in at *all*. Pom's had you deferred. What's it all about anyway?"

"Oh, he says that, but they'll get everybody in the long run. Look at the way this war's going. Eric says . . ."

I waved a hand. "Oh, *Eric!*" and all my wrath at him for not calling me was dumped into the very name. "What does he know about it? He's not a chemist. You're important."

His yellow head was like a small whole sun giving off a maze of lemonish light. I had never shown Beas all or even half of my feeling for him. We took each other for granted. We hardly touched. I didn't know whether my impulse was to hit him or grab him into my arms. The very Beas of me! Even *thinking* of such a thing!

"If you go away, I'll just . . ."

"Well," he said quickly, "I'm telling you I think the draft would get me. We'll be in the war, that's all. Everybody knows it. If I get in now I won't have to interrupt my education."

"You're not even out of high school!"

"Shhhh!" He snickered at my fury. "That's not important." He turned out the light over his counter. Lucille squealed in her cage. He turned away toward the stairs.

"You're not a *soldier*, Beas. You're just not the type."

Maybe he had been planning to be a soldier all the time, since Foxe Hills, and had kept it secret.

When we went upstairs I smelled Enid's life in the house as usual. Dead flowers. In the car I said—

"It's just going to kill her if you go, Beas. Pom, too. Look at all the trouble he went to to get you on at Dietler's and all."

He nodded patiently. "Well, I can come back to Dietler's. I've made up my mind. A person has to make his own decisions."

I sighed.

The Creole. Fats Waller on the juke—"Feets Too Big"—Nina and her crowd. RAF swarming around. Rabbit and his same glee. Beas turned red and stiff like a just-picked tulip the minute he met them, and stayed that way. Rabbit applauded the fact of our being cousins, Beas and I. They passed around someone's flask of gin. I ordered a limeade and made a gin rickey. It was terrible. Nina handed me a little silver bottle of something else to add to it. That made it sweet and worse. I wanted to be drunk, to turn into Bette Davis and get into trouble with men. Beasley, I said, when Rabbit asked me his name. He thinks he's joining the Army tomorrow, I told him. That, like most things to Rabbit, was splendid. And then Rabbit confessed that it was his sisters, Janet and Claudia, even more than his cousin Yvonne, whom he really loved, desired even, and they were like little possible stars in the universe of his mother, the major sun. His mother, he said, was a dark sun, though, because of the death of his brother in a Lincoln Brigade hospital in Spain. But a veddy powerful sun, all the more powerful due to the inversion of light.

The RAF sang "Lili Marlene" several times, raising their glasses. "Secretly," Rabbit explained, "there's a brotherhood in our hatred of the German airmen." It was all veddy complex, he said. He said that of most things. Incest, though, he explained, was a kind of ultimate, and even cousins would do. My ears sprang open. My cash register mind rang up a sum. . . .

I said, "Pascal says that theft, incest, infanticide and parricide have all had a place among virtuous actions."

Rabbit applauded me with laughter and hugs. He called Tommy, of course, to share the discovery of Pascal delivered up in the heart of Ameddicker. Poignant! Pufectly ironic. I kept a stony face. Nina lifted an eyebrow at me. Who is Pascal, what is he, that I should score on the nose with him?

So we drowned a few hours.

★

Eric Firecracker Witcher did not show up.

And then Beas told someone quietly, "Well, I think they'll get all of us. . . ." and the war talk started.

There were too many bodies. I wanted air. Rabbit walked me. I was flying. Oh Dahling, he said. My life with him became: a baroness before the vast stone fireplace, dogs at my feet, Rabbit with a cane, drinking port among other crippled veterans. . . . My back was against a tree on Eighteenth Street not so far from the Bledsoe School for rich girls. Rabbit said Dahling again. His strange hands like soft ice bags. I melted down to my essential ores. Why not just go ahead and let Rabbit do it, now that I'd been dumped by Eric? He pushed his budlike whole-O mouth into mine and I think we fell down and lay in a pause, trying and trying, and he said suddenly on the other side of it—

"I'm sorry, Katie. I haven't been able to do it since the raids. I used to do it a lot before that. But now I always manage to . . . muck it up. I wouldn't be any good for you."

"That's okay. It's okay," I said, holding a strange body with its thick clothes and thin waist, its childlike clammy smell, its long bones. He felt young. "Do you have a parachute?" I asked him. My head cleared and I saw his face, now not like a rabbit's. We sat up against the tree, huddled close. It didn't seem like sex.

"Of coss, Dahling. I told you."

"Let's just sit right here for a while. If I move I'll be sick. Talk to me."

"Yaw shivering."

"I'm not cold. I'm burning. Rabbit, if you have to bail out, then what? Have you practiced?"

"Yes."

"If they shot you down . . ."

"I might jump but . . ."

"*Might?* You want to die in your plane or something crazy?"

"Well, I'd try, you see, to get huh back, or at least ova some border or something. My duty of coss is to go and return alive."

Duty. I felt like crying.

"Well, *my* duty," I said, "is to get up and move."

I walked away.

"Heah, Katie! Wait!"

"I don't care if you can't do it, Rabbit. I don't think you should worry. I mean I don't think you *should* do it." He had his arms around me loosely. He trembled.

"But sometimes," he whispered, "I want to awfully. Women are the only thing left in the wuld, you know."

We clung, swaying drunk.

"I'd like awfully to be yaw friend. I'll telephone you. I'm rally keen on the telephone. I can think of all sohts of things on the telephone I can't think of face to face, you know?"

"Yes."

I was beginning to see the plan of the gods—sex with a mute and talk with a rabbit who couldn't do it right now.

"I feel ratha shoddy," he said. I said I thought he was pufectly splendid.

Someone was in the yard when I got home. I plugged the electric into the battery and went through the gate trying not to weave as I walked. There was Ruby, and Wishbone in a uniform. It was ironed like a windowpane. The moonlight slid off the starchy surfaces like milk. I almost laughed with pleasure.

"Gee! Wishbone! How'd you get a uniform so fast?"

I imagined his penis. And Horace's. And Gifford's.

He laughed shyly, pleased with himself. "Oh, once they gets you name on that line, they snaps you up pretty fass."

Ruby twitched and camped around him, picking at his sleeve. She was dressed up herself in a new red blouse. Her friend Lucille had taken her shopping in the Willows.

"Look good on him, don't it?" she said.

"Yeah! It's really nice-looking." It was just the usual khaki number with all those pockets, and pants creased by a hot iron. He must have been standing up since he put them on.

"Miss Sarah feeling pohly," Rube said suddenly. "She turnt in early. Say all that heat finally jess laid her out."

"Oh yeah! Was Pom out?"

"No. But Miss Iantha were." She laughed when I groaned. "But she didn't stay long. Miss Sarah jess sent her off. I neva thought I see the day Miss Sarah send somebody walkin. Shhhttt! I had me some surprises today."

We laughed and Wishbone laid a casual arm around her waist. I felt like a kid. Gee, Rube had her life all arranged with Wishbone, it seemed. I forgot for a few minutes that I wasn't a virgin anymore.

★

Still no Eric. Pom called me every few days to talk about Beas.

"I'm trying to avoid pulling my rank, as they say, my Dear, but . . ."

"I don't think he'd ever forgive you, Pom, if you made him look silly at the induction center."

"But isn't there something you can do? He listens to you if he listens to anyone, Katie."

I sighed. "I'm trying," I would say. But I wondered if I was really trying. Beas was unapproachable somehow. He had always been preoccupied but this was like no other mood of his. He stared and wandered. Sometimes at the Creole I would discover halfway through a sentence that he hadn't listened to anything I had said. I had stopped talking about it finally. Once he said, "I got a card from Brad Finch. He's about to make a solo flight."

I shrugged. "He's tough. They'll never shoot him down."

Beas lowered his eyes knowing that I meant that he himself was not tough and probably wouldn't come out alive if they sent him to war. I wondered if I thought that or if I was only eager to keep Beas at home. Sometimes I asked myself why he shouldn't go if he wanted to, but I had, underneath, a creepy feeling that his reasons were wrong or confused, and not what he reported. I spent a lot of time with him and hoped that would bind him home. But home to Beas, I knew, was Enid, and there wasn't much reason I could see to want to stay with her.

I wrote in the Biography, pushing my imagination back to the days when Enid used to drive and would go shopping or take Beas and me to the wading pool in the park or drive Sarah to the country market. For a while after Enid came back from Menninger's she had lived, intermittently, a life like other women's lives. But women's lives confused me when I looked at the clients and at Enid. Sarah seemed to be the only woman on earth who liked her life. Maybe men were smart to go to war. At least it got them away from their Delirias, wherever they were.

Rabbit called and asked me to go to the Palm Lounge to dinner with him. I had never been out to dinner with a date. I thanked him profusely, feeling a little crazy and definitely fraudulent, and said no. I was busy. Then I whispered that my mother was sick. Maybe later. Then, when he hung up, I went into a queer frantic depression and took everything out of my room, cleaned it, covered the old brown wood floor with some wallpaper from a client, put the room together again and lay on my dais scribbling, reading the magazines Iantha brought out and waiting. Waiting. I hated myself for that. I wondered if my old dream that some exotic man was moving through his life toward me would ever be true. I pretended to myself that Eric wasn't my type and that he definitely didn't find me fascinating. I fumed and fussed.

When the nothing of nothing whatever on earth finally settled like a disease on my soul, I picked up the Biography again. I didn't know what to do, what to be, what to say. I wondered, hunting Higgensian ghosts in the mirror, if I was just naturally a watcher, like Pom, who said of himself, "I'm a born spectator. That's what theater meant to me—a grand spectacle laid out for my benefit. Every spectator is royal for a few hours in the theater."

I found myself desiring other people's dreams but I craved to be a dream myself.

The Biography brought me a kind of reality. I worked hard at it to render all the irony and cruelty and bitterness I saw in Enid's life.

The Biography
of Enid

Other people made her hysterical as they did her sister Sarah. Except that her laughter at them was always brassed with scorn. Those most soft pouty childlike lips could draw down into bitter scorn as quickly as a burn or a dye draws the flesh.

She dressed before and after the EVENT in three colors—champagne, French blue and black. Pongees and linens, voile and lawn, fine and sheer and flowing. Black wool as fine as hair, and black silk. Her own thick dull gold rope of hair like a fabric seemed to weigh her head down to that slight droop that on first glance appeared to be a considering nod of sorts but then, when examined, when lived with, proved to be a bowed head, not cowed but religiously bowed almost. And the body too, moved with a sort of cast to its style; it meditated even when in motion; it waited, it hesitated, not falteringly but with decision. Moral decision. That was it, her body was moral, not her mind. She did not pretend not to lie there and drink any more than she had pretended not to have shot Jack Russell. She had a criminal's honesty.

Even after the crime, Enid lived out her old rituals. Six months at Menninger's did little for her, it seemed. She would make her semiannual trip to the Boston Shop in a taxi to replenish her wardrobe. She would call for an appointment and go late in the afternoon midweek when the shop was not difficult to empty. Sometimes her niece Katie drove her there and waited for her inside the scented little chapellike shop, pacing, watching the ritual with the child's third eye, even at sixteen years of age. It was as if those women were together for some awful ceremony of destruction and not mere business.

Sometimes, for special clients, the two managers of the Boston Shop would deliberately close early, hire a model and in all cases but Enid's probably make more money in that two-hour private showing and fitting than they would make all week with the general public. But from Enid they rarely got more than three hundred dollars a year. Even before the crash.

Miss Gladys, her flat chest and her lorgnette, always in tidy black, waited at the door for her like a priestess. And Miss Martha, horsy and chic, waiting inside, her legs just a bit too heavy, her walk adamant therefore, would suck in her cheeks to control that queer hysteria that seemed to overcome her on this occasion. A rack of things waited too —a cashmere coat, sheer and light; a chiffon dress with a short train— very smart just now, they said, in a new shade called fawn, perfect for

Enid; a blue velvet suit. Well, Miss Martha knew it was a bit brighter than her classic blue but heavenly on Enid, good God look at those lines, wasn't it made for her flat hips and her good legs, what a shame, she thought, Enid didn't go out more. And inside their predatory heads, visions of Enid on a slab, sacrificed to some whimsical god who had made her in his image and not made them, Miss Martha, Miss Gladys, quite so . . . not quite . . . But rallying. They always rallied to her indifference, her ennui, her incontestable beauty and glamour, her *past*—God, the *nerve*! Imagine *killing* someone and walking around afterward! Even the pain she revealed had its beauty, its class. Look at Garbo. Same thing.

She always heard them—Try it over the shoulder like this, Enid. Look at that!—but didn't listen to them exactly. And the complex rhythm of approach and retreat necessary, the subtle bargaining with her was not, they knew, ever precisely over the clothes—Screw the clothes, thought Miss Martha in the rarely opened scullery of her mind—no, the bargaining was over some intangible and more dangerous issue which they could not name, either of them, and Miss Gladys was quicker than Miss Martha although Miss Martha had spent one year on a scholarship at Smith College before the Great War. No, the bargaining had something to do with Enid's decision to let them live *if*—and they were never certain just what that conditional meant but only that if they kept to their timing, not missing a step, as in some delicately designed minuet which they both seemed to have to learn over again each time, if they kept to that, countering with agreeable persuasions, they just might come off— not victorious, that, up against an adversary like Enid, was out of the question—but at least with their hides, *alive*! That, for them, was victory enough. Alive. And so it all came down to life or death again with them when they faced Enid and they harked back to the murder she had committed and the trial and saw in her the Arch-Acquitted, the Great Forgiven, someone chosen and beloved by chance, and saw the Arch-Sufferer there too, something in the restraint: She never camped, never laid it on, never bothered to impress *them*; no, at the most she might swat out at one of them, or at the model, poor girl, as if at an insect, with some quick irritable word.

"The ribbon isn't important, Gladys. Concentrate on the *hang* of it. Let me see how it hangs in back."

And then, as if she knew this to be the most ridiculous of all activity, giving it up suddenly and walking to the back of the shop idly to snoop for coffee—*Don't bother, I'll get it myself*—knowing it was ready and waiting, fresh for her. And then, without making a decision, leaving the coat, the fawn silk dress, hanging there, divested of the model and of her own perfect form again—suddenly looking up as if after round ten and a draw, a truce, to say—

"How's your mother, Martha? Is she still alive?" with utter available impartial interest that brought them up short and caused the model, who was by then frantically dressing behind the curtain, to peek out in amazement at the possibility that this infamous Russell woman might be human after all.

It took three, sometimes four, hours and she rarely left the shop with more than two garments. Once she was there until nine thirty in the evening, showing not the slightest fatigue and not the slightest interest in their—Gladys and Martha's—having been there since ten A.M. and now nearly eight hours away from lunch. The model had brought doughnuts that time which by seven thirty had begun to cast a cheap greasy-spoon aroma over the shop, driving Miss Gladys to a fury so that she flung them into the store room and slammed the door, experiencing a few moments of stern self-respect for not having stolen a bite. Her mother had been a sweet large Swedish seamstress who had loved pastry.

That, Miss Gladys had probably told Miss Martha, is how Enid kept that figure. She never ate, obviously. But, Miss Martha had reasoned, she didn't work either and in fact hardly moved all day, and furthermore took in plenty of calories through alcohol, probably. Or was it all a myth? They alternately hoped true and rejected as pure spiteful gossip the tales of booze and bootleggers and assignations with delivery boys and even something not quite natural in the frequent visits of Robert Swan, queer as Dick's hatband though he was, all of which made up Enid's reputation.

And sometimes Enid offered the same quick cool favor to Miss Gladys, whom she seemed to pity less than Miss Martha, possibly because of the legs, they both had privately reasoned—offered a word of inquiry—

"You still in that sweet little apartment over on Trenton Boulevard?" or "How's that dear little nev-you of yours, Gladys?" pronouncing it the way her actress mother-in-law, Lou Foray, had probably done years ago. And Miss Gladys might or might not, depending on the hour and the subtle intonations in the question, pull out a snapshot of the nev-you who by God was studying hotel management up at Cornell and not without plenty of help from aunty Gladys. But that was rare, that revelation of family pride. The slightest brassy note in the question was enough to restrain Miss Gladys's hand and to allow her only the modest, "Fine, everything's just fine." And the question itself was even more rare, in any case, than that put to Miss Martha.

And by the time she had risen to make her casual selection, touching the sleeve of the coat, then the suit, musing, putting the dress aside as if it contaminated the other more costly things, deliberating between the suit and the coat—that half hour of choice during which they knew she must be left entirely alone and surrounded by reverent quiet like some pasha choosing his annual supply of aphrodisiacs—in that half hour's time Miss G. and Miss M. would discreetly empty the cash box, put the cash in the safe, straighten the little Queen Anne table and seize quick glances at their less-than-possible shopworn faces in the mirror, dab at them, poke at their hairdos and run to the john.

And then she would choose. She would, after all, take the suit, a triumph for Miss G., who had underplayed it. The point was not the suit nor the blue which was not her favorite French blue, nor how she looked in it, no, the point was what she did to blue, what poignant importance and beauty Enid conjured from blue, this quicker stronger shade even more than the other. It was what a child did to an organdy bonnet all at once, resurrecting the pink of perfect little-girlhood. On Enid blue became heroic and pure again. And immediately the next day Miss G. would order it as her major seasonal color. How smart, how subtle of Enid never to wear white! How she could cause a pang of recognition by putting such a color as this next to that famous mat-brown skin and that heavy flaxen hair. What it did to those smoky eyes! They wondered at her, utterly lost to themselves for a while.

And then, if she had come alone, finally calling the taxi. Always at the end when they had survived, each of them secretly wished somehow to detain her for more simple women-together business, a moment of talk. They had been girls in the same town at the same time. Look what had become of them! And each secretly believed that she saw some similar faint desire cross Enid's countenance when she sat sighing at the front of the shop on the little mauve tufted silk settee waiting for the taxi. Yes, some lingering trace of simple familiarity, the old recognition which made the world comprehensible and tolerable to them—belonging to something together, even an evening. And each of them wondered at the silence that fell there. Miss Martha's scullery mind opened up brazenly before her inner eye one time and showed the three of them sitting in Rush's Department Store tearoom having a Gulf shrimp salad and chuckling over old school memories together. She imagined Enid's mouth opening very wide in a laugh that turned to howl suddenly, a wailing, bellowing cry so shocking that she turned off the dream and got busy with her raincoat, her keys.

And when the taxi came and she quickly, almost unimportantly vanished from the shop, from under the small coffee-colored marquis, hardly saying good-bye to them, and Miss Gladys called after her, "I'll get it out to you by Friday," they would close up soberly, exhausted and strangely disgusted and embarrassed with one another, like two choirboys who had hurled themselves with mock passion into their prayers, imitating some fervent priest, and they would not make their usual wry or stiffly affectionate good-nights. They would not stop for coffee together. They would go their ways like strangers.

That is what Enid Russell did to them, something to which they helplessly submitted twice a year, and not, they both knew, for the purpose of selling a one-hundred-dollar dress or a two-hundred-dollar suit. No, but for the sake of engaging again in some old inscrutable ritual that had to do with their being alive and relatively endured here upon the earth where Enid Russell did not merely live but reigned in some mysterious way and was sent to them as omen or accuser, passing upon them some strict judgment which they had always believed, even from childhood, they deserved.

Midnight. I caught the phone on the second ring, running through the dark, knowing.

"Katie. It's me. Eric."

"Oh! It's midnight! Where are you?"

"I just got back from St. Louis. I forgot to tell you I had to go up to see my grandparents."

I was shaking. I felt myself pouring into the phone.

"How are you, Kid?"

"Okay," I whispered. "Everybody's asleep around here."

He waited. "You sleep naked?"

I waited. "Sometimes."

And he laughed with terrible glee that made me want to stab him. "I like you, Kid," he said. "You're not coy."

We waited.

"Listen . . ."

"What?"

"Can I see you tomorrow night?"

"Okay."

"Eight o'clock?"

"Okay."

"Make it seven thirty."

I laughed. "Okay."

"I thought about you," he whispered, making a kind of mouthy sound.

"Me too," I said. And it struck me then suddenly how innocent everybody in the world was, having to fit bodies together no matter what. Not being able to resist. And having to lie down. And having to die.

"I'll come out there and get you."

I told him how to find the lease but told him to wait for me at the end of the lane so Rube wouldn't see him.

★

Sarah stayed in bed, sickish. It's nothing, Hon, she said, but she was white and breathless. I hovered. She consoled me. I stamped my foot alone in my room. I couldn't go out. But I would. Iantha, Pom, someone would come and watch her. Ruby could give up screwing for one night to watch her. Just for an hour.

Iantha came and I told her I wouldn't be long, I had an errand. And Sarah said, Aw, Hon, don't hurry. She had her supper in bed, nibbles of pears and cottage cheese. Wearily she laid it aside, saying that she didn't need food, she was too heavy already, Hon. And that was the first time I had ever heard her refer to herself, I believed. I stared at her in wonder. She had felt that same plunging into her of some man; Higgens, in fact, and maybe no other. Maybe only that one time! It seemed incredible to me that she had ever bled from such a thing, that her eyes had ever rolled back in her head that way. She would probably have laughed through it.

Her hands were still. Her smile was wan. I thought I wouldn't go. At seven twenty-nine I still thought I wouldn't go but I was bathed and smelling like Mrs. Kitteridge's recent payment of carnation soap. I was leaping at the gate like a horse before the race. My imponderable fluids were moving toward the sea. I had to go. She was already dozing under Iantha's squinty old gaze.

★

He grabbed me and I quaked against him. He drove into the center of the lease near the pecan grove and we leapt together, struggling. Our teeth clashed, wrecking our kiss. I wore nothing under my dress, knowing everything. I knew. I knew.

He started saying come on Baby, and I twisted up to a pitch of explosion and began to clamp and open like a fist and clamp shut, my eyes rolling back. Like the beginning of the world, thank you Adam and Eve!

Renfro

"Sure!" the neat little man told him, looking away and clearing his throat, "we're hiring. What can you do?"

Renfro had to laugh, suddenly homing in on a vision of the triumph of dispossession, of "nothing-to-lose." It made other men squirm, this security of the outcast. What a freaky world! It struck him quickly as a useless sort of power and a bitter wisdom, but nevertheless the little bastard who wore his gray-and-blue-striped tie as if he'd been born in it, this little tin cock had slipped through the Depression somehow like a slick little turd on its way out of an inhospitable gut, kept himself well oiled through those coarse dry times some way—Renfro could hear him buttering up, selling something discreetly, insidiously, insurance to old women, maybe, funerals to niggers—

"What can you do?"

He shrugged. "Anything you want," he said, tall and cool over the neat stumpy trussed-up little . . . Gee! How had he gotten so steamed up so fast by this little fart? Maybe he was half expecting to be turned down.

"I've knocked around garages and . . . railyards a lot," he said more humbly. "Done a little riveting. Can't say I'm a pro. . . ." He laughed drily, reaching for a cigarette butt in his pocket and stopping himself.

But the fellow, looking up half curious, half irritated, had seen his open smile and his teeth! Renfro sucked in his lips and cheeks. Christ! He'd forgotten. He thought of turning away but then he saw the eyes streak over with something else, just a flicker of respect maybe, and he stayed, holding his breath. And the fellow —Shoats was his name—said with infuriating kindness—

"Well, I'll give you a form. Just a routine thing." He waved an intimate hand, small, ringed with a gold wedding band. Two nice obedient sons in the Scouts, probably. "I'm sure there's plenty of work you can handle around here." He waddled before Renfro's loose, embarrassed stride toward the office. "Frankly," he said, just-between-us-men, "we can't find many trained or experienced men under forty. Service has most of 'em, I guess. And California shipyards have the rest."

Renfro took the form and went as directed to a room full of old school desks where half a dozen other men sat diligently doctoring up their histories for the same purpose. He sat down, his long legs plunged under another's seat. His hand shook. He wanted a weed badly but couldn't see himself firing up a dirty butt in their presence. He licked the tip of the pencil and carefully printed his name. And then it hit him again, this time with a smarting freshness, that there was work to be had and that he would have it. And money. Asking for it had that feeling of begging entrance to some sacred order—a pledgeship. All those sombre moments of boyhood when he had raised three fingers, crossed his heart and hoped to die, or bowed his head as a heavy male voice began, *Our Father . . .* somewhere, or swore in silence with ferocious conviction at the sight of the back of his mother's neck once to protect her to the death—all those and a dozen other forgotten oaths clamored up as if to drive his hand and voice again in that passionate way— *I, Weldon Renfro, do hereby swear—*

He stumbled up coughing, creating a vague curiosity in the room, and went out again into the hangar. The machines and hammers made a mad racket. Finally, leaning against the outside wall of Shoats's office, out of sight, he got hold of himself. A large Negro walked by him casually and, taking a second look, offered out of his white overall pocket a long clean whole straight cigarette which he forced easily with a flip of the pack to stick out beyond the others the way Renfro had forgotten.

"Thanks." He sucked in his lower lip and nodded shyly. That was a twist, taking a whole fag from a colored. His hand shook.

"Comin to work?"

He held the offered flame in a cupped hand. "Looks like I might." Then he met the large doleful murey eyes. "You like it here?" he asked.

The Negro grinned. "Well, it beat de street, Man, lemme tell ya." And he laughed easily, moving on.

Renfro hung on the laugh, signaling thanks. The taste of the cigarette, a Camel, nearly knocked him cold. His head soared. After all, it was true, he had handled the drills, worked in the yards. He could do a thing or two. It looked good here. Everybody working and nobody thinking, nobody staring into space, nobody nodding, drooling, puking, nobody with the shakes. Except himself. He'd get on here, he knew it. He went back and filled out the form.

"Well, you're even kinda blue around the mouth," I told her. "You look weak as a cat. I think I'd better call the doctor."

"No, Hon, now don't you worry. I'm just tuckered out a little. Law, I wouldn't get Henry all the way out here for the world. I'll just take a nap."

"Well, I don't know. I don't like it. . . ." I was actually almost at the point of confessing to her, or asking her for something. I wasn't sure what but felt driven toward her in a hard new way.

She and Iantha and I had looked at the snapshot albums the night before. Old Beas on the roof of Pom's pigskin Stutz; Sarah standing like an opera singer—her back straight and chin up—half profile, by the honeysuckle bush in the back yard of Grandfather McCleod's house before she and Enid sold it and we moved out here. And another of her when she was young (I probed that one until they took the book out of my hands—as if I'd never seen it before), taken down in Shreveport where I was supposedly conceived—oh, so young and pretty she was, not especially plump like now, more delicate and angelic, in a nice bodiced dress with narrow sleeves, ruffled at the wrists, and tiny buttons all down the front. Made of voile, they said. I loved and envied her, seeing that. It had a large soft middy collar. Sarah's hair was up in a knot but billowing wide at the temples. Her neck looked young and fragile in that picture and her expression was sweetly sad.

I wished we could talk about sex and life and men and moving into the world, but I knew we never would. She thought Deliria was the whole world. She didn't even care for Shreveport, and she hadn't been out of town since. And now here she was laid up. Had she ever gone around thinking of penises the way I was doing?

The clients came bearing soup and flowers and wounded looks. She was just a little under the weather, she told them with a promising tone. Exhaustion after those last hot days. Pom came, felt her pulse and said he was sending Henry Killeen out the next morning. She said no, he said yes, it's better, and she said Aw, Hon, such a fuss. But Pom won. I shivered with relief. Ruby said Shhhttt, I think he oughta come yestiday.

I hung around her door to intercept Iantha, who was curiously somewhat obedient and sat most of the time on the sun porch with her coffee, wrapped in a sagging rust-colored knit shawl, rocking, mumbling, breaking into babble the moment anybody entered the room, like an idling car motor that is suddenly gunned up.

Sarah dozed, wanting to be up on pillows. She breathed easier that way. Her arms were more marbled than ever. She looked pretty small in that big bed when she was under the covers. Iantha changed her sheets every other day, which kept Ruby working like a beast. I stood in the back yard holding one end of a rough fabulously clean sheet with Ruby at the other end and we pulled, tightened, snapped and folded together in the autumn sun. I was riddled with painful surprise. I thought of a dozen things at once that needed doing but never knew which was most important.

"We've gotta gather the pecans, Rube. It might rain and rot them."

She piled up the sheets in the basket and started on the pillow cases. When she bent over she kept her knees straight like an acrobat.

"We gots time. Anotha week at least."

Later I noticed certain things to be falling apart in the house. "How long's this hole been in the screen? No wonder the flies come in. My God!"

"That hole," she said wearily, "been theah fo two yeahs, Girl. Where you been fo two yeahs?"

"I've been in my counting house counting out my nothing," I said.

And naturally she spewed her Shhhttt! at me.

Sarah sighed a lot. Iantha gently sponged her face, adjusted the curtains to keep out the glare, and brought soup which Sarah rarely touched. I woke up crying in the night, having dreamed something awful and forgotten it. Ruby stood in the yard with Wishbone one night and said that if Iantha didn't git outa her kitchen she was gonna set fiah to the whole place. That woman, she said, growling in whispers, was gonna run Miss Sarah's intestines right out with all that soup. What she needed was solid food, she said, to git up her blood.

★

Eric called twice a day. Ruby gave me a big bald look and a dropped ironic jaw when I raced to answer the phone. He would drive to the edge of the lease and when Iantha was on guard, Ruby still in the house and Sarah napping, I would tear out to meet him. Eighteen days till I go, he would say, and grab me. If he saw Ann Coolidge, he'd have to be sleeping in her presence. But I didn't ask. He bit and nibbled and kissed me, lapping away my pain. I tried to tell him Sarah was ill but he wouldn't listen. He pinned me to the floor of the car, to the fender, to a tree, to the ground on a blanket. He drove me awake, he rammed me clear, he rolled me smooth again. And I went home all red and scratched and swollen, with a bite darkening on my neck or my arm, and dodged into my conspiring room before Ruby could comment. I waited in a throbbing suspense, bored and smitten, for the next time. I took two or three long, meditative baths a day.

"Hon," Sarah said one day, "look in that box in the bottom drawer there and see if there's a blue envelope."

Life insurance.

"What's that? I didn't know you had that. Whatta you want it for?"

"Why, Hon, where'd you get that awful bruise? My Stars!"

I turned away. *Eric bit me. If you knew what we're doing!*

"It's nothing. I hit myself on the door of the electric."

"Heh! On the neck, Hon?"

God! I felt like howling. She'd never even seen one of these bites before!

She sat up a little, breathing hard, looking whitish, and I quickly plumped up her pillow. I handed her her glasses and felt her damp hand take them. It was puffy and white. What was the matter with her? Heat prostration, Dr. Killeen said. He listened to her heart over and over. I would wait in the hall but he never told me what he was thinking. He would stroke me under the chin as if I were five and say, "Let's just keep her quiet for a while.

She'll be all right." He had listened to my own mother's heart and I never had. Her body was better known to him than to me. I was a spy.

"What's this for?" I asked her. "I didn't know you had this insurance. You never tell me a thing. I might as well be a dust roll under the couch."

She spasmed out a laugh. "Now, don't make me laugh, Hon. Law, it hurts my ribs!"

Her nightgown was shredding apart. There was a hole in the old linen sheet with Selma Rawlings's fraying initials monogrammed there. The blanket had shrunk. God! We were too poor! She'd never had a decent dress or a trip or a new coat or good gold fillings or a manicure like Enid, or a night at the country club. But —she hadn't wanted any of it. Or had she? I stared at her.

"Stand outa my light, Hon."

I raged and froze in my place. "You're in my light, Katie, Hon."

I moved. Her doughy little hand reached up with the glasses and bobbed them across her face vaguely. One arm of the glasses was held on by neat copper wire, a repair job by one Wishbone Watson who was good with his hands and would probably be a mechanic in the Army. Private Wesley Watson.

She read the policy. "Pom took it out for us a long time ago, Hon. I forgot about it till this week. I was wondering if that thing was up to date and all."

I wanted to fall on her bed and sob. She hadn't snored since she'd been sick. I missed it in the middle of our still afternoons, that old nap of hers, steady like the pulse of our life, even and sure under the mad works of this house.

"Can you tell what it says, Hon?"

I took it and read that she left to me one thousand dollars when she died, purchased by Pom. Her last gift to me financed by someone else!

She'd never done anything but praise and work for me and keep that promise of cash in her bottom drawer for me and here I was full of crime and sex, scorn for the clients, hating Iantha, bickering with Ruby. I couldn't say anything. I held the policy and tears pumped up into my eyes.

"Aw, Hon! Here, Sugar . . . set down here." She patted a place beside her. I sat, swallowing and nodding.

"I wish you weren't sick!" I wailed like an infant.

"Why, Sweetheart, I don't believe I've seen you cry"—she said it with scientific interest, totally objective—"since . . . nineteen thirty-six. When we went up to the Grand River with the Abernathys and you dropped that old iron thing on your foot. You remember that, Hon? Law!"

She pounded my hand now savagely, as if it were a piece of tough meat. I chuckled through my sobs. I sat with my back like a broomstick. We rarely looked into one another's eyes, rarely spoke of anything personal—bodies, love, death, pain—except for other people's. We were weeds, rough-edged. Look at her split nails! Look at her tattered life monogrammed with someone else's initials! I supposed someone rich would give her a tombstone with PDQ on it someday. Shhhttt! I let the fire of my anger and hatred heal me. She nodded and laughed as if teaching me. She was holding my hand, I noted with wonder. Lying there sunk in her pillows, she was consoling *me*. Not a client. I wanted to say *Listen I've had sex and I'm crazy about it, in fact it's driving me nuts*. But since I couldn't say that, I said nothing to her. I craved too, to tell her that she was perfect, more than any rich or saintly person. But it would all have sounded trashy.

We sat there and chuckled a little, our glances crisscrossing and falling shyly away. That's the most we can do so it must be enough, I told myself.

"I have a job starting in three weeks," I lied.

Pom

As he unpacked he moved several times to the window and observed, exhilarated by it, the quick changing play of autumn light through the poplars down by the fishpond. The mossy grass was still thick and green under them and all around the flagstone terrace and the pool. He regretted that he had not planted the grass, laid the flagstones himself, the way he had seen other men doing on their weekends. But for whom? He had built the house with some vague woman in mind, a creature realistically unlike Lou, a kind, intelligent, maybe somewhat blousy woman who might have walked these rooms and possessed them. He would have retreated slightly before her presence and given her a dominion over his life.

He had somehow become sixty-six years old, still strung, he knew, upon that long, devious, persistent, indestructible thread of life with Lou, life as defined by Lou—no other man-and-wife definition had ever seized his imagination. He twitched, ironic, looking out at the lawn. She had been his life. Died in the middle of it, that was all. Other women had been friends, sexual pursuits (not even desperate) lasting rarely more than a few months. And then—nothing, nobody. Sarah was different, a soul companion, family, her selflessness made her that way. A kind of shield, he thought. Classic virgin. And Nina? A holocaust who had tumbled too quickly. Good mind there but lazy. Her life-style made him uneasy. In bed she had frightened him. He had cut it out after a few exhausting months.

The langorous winsome light plagued him. They would have been on their way to the continent by this time—he and Lou—forgetting the war for the moment, of course. Lou would have had an opening in London, probably. No travel in that direction now. He was grateful she had not lived through these two wars, especially the occupation of Paris, the Fall of France. Incredible!

He brought himself up short then and turned to the bureau. He took up the silver hairbrush and roughly slammed it down. Often lately he would restrain himself from these sentimental musings the way one cuffed the side of a truant child's head, not too harshly but with that quick annoyance of efficient mothers. Efficient mothers—those who had a genius for living in the present, and probably living with others. Yes. And for a long time he had lived formally, alone with himself, rather as his own ward, the two of them in a peculiarly grave mute intimacy filled with rituals and unuttered dogma of which he was only dimly conscious.

Lou. Autumn travel. The last time in 1912, two years before her death. The slow killing, filling the deep purple hollows of her eyes with a sickly yellowish gunmetal color. He stared at the silver hairbrush and grunted, turning back to his unpacking. Her photograph, which he did not look at just then—not out of pain, that was long gone, but for the sake of good positive thinking, his old demand upon himself of uncomplainingness—was an early one taken at the height of her career and her beauty, the apologetic forgiving eyes, the flicker of humor near the almost strict mouth above a slightly cleft, youthful, *brave* chin. Lou. Reduced to essentials, ashes. Only intangibles survived. Mainly her courage, which he remembered as her essence. And then he thought of Jack and wondered what kind of man he would have been if Lou had not traveled so much in the boy's early years. He realized suddenly that he never thought of Jack as a man, only as "the boy." But if Jack had had a solid mother, more devoted, quiet, less interesting, not famous? And he himself? What if he had not been so totally devoted . . . no, *addicted* to Lou and her career? What then? He hadn't been a father in the old-fashioned sense, doing things with Jack, following his schoolwork or whatever it was that it now seemed natural to him to do with Beasley. There had been something between them, him and Jack, from the beginning that had kept him aloof. So many days and nights alone with Pearl. Lonely childhood. He rummaged after the motifs of his son's life and it had seemed inevitable, somehow, that Jack would die young. Violence . . .

The fact of the murder itself seemed to belong to another saga and to have nothing to do with his own upbringing of and relationship with Jack. As if it were an aftermath to Jack's failure.

No, I wasn't much of a father. He admitted it to some final judge who only nodded and absorbed the truth without judging the acts, the history.

Well, it was all redeemed by Beasley. Beasley had, perhaps, been spared a final defeat by the death of his father. He was suspicious of such metaphysics but had found himself more than once lately falling back on them.

Old age, he muttered. He decided to put it all out of his mind. Jack had had his lovable moments, even that bullying boy. He had gone on a fishing trip at camp one summer, Pom recalled, and caught a ten-pound bass which he had mailed back to Pom wrapped in wax paper, a bath towel and a dozen layers of brown wrapping paper. It had arrived smelling to high heaven and been delivered by a reeling postman who had said that only Pom's illustrious name had kept the postmaster from sending it off with the trash.

Pom smiled and got back to his unpacking. He put away three pairs of socks he had not used in Washington. Then he began to hum. The autumn air was wood-and-apple-scented, filling the room, stirring him. He began to whistle now, softly, hanging up two silk shirts and his bathrobe. He felt transcendent suddenly. The air made him drunk, roused in him a reckless feeling, lightly sifting into the room that way. The glass curtains moved faintly. This morning's triumphs, modest to be sure and very personal, had given him, rather than a giddiness of success, a particularly susceptible and emotional feeling, as if he had been to the departure of a train that carried away someone important whom he had yet been glad to see go.

How odd the mind was! He stood with the suitcase in his hand, held loosely, empty now and strapped closed. If he himself was turbulent and emotional then surely all men were, he being the coolest in a sense.

He had spent the morning on the tenth floor of the McCleod building in various oil offices—Liebes, Rolfe, Ketchum and Bledsoe. The congratulations—amid cigar smoke and the alarming early-morning smell of whiskey in those carpeted mahogany and leather rooms—had carried the veiled envy and the potency of that primitive urge to touch the hand that had touched and slain the lion. He had spent a few hours with Ickes in Washington and had actually gone in to meet the President.

"You couldn't have resisted him," he had told them. "He has a way of rousing those people up there to fantastic feats of work. And to risk, you might say. I sense the men close to him are keyed up all the time by his magnetism. He was full of ginger anyway over his meeting with Churchill."

But there had been moments when he could have retched, his own voice turning to babble in his ears. Personalities, anecdotes, quick analyses—that was what they wanted to hear and he had rattled it out for them, clichés that gagged him but he couldn't stop them. And he had done it all with the old debonair manner that they had come over the years to expect of Pom but which he had consciously attempted to destroy in himself lately, not liking the sound of himself anymore, his heartiness, his assurance. He had rattled on. He had had them gaga. It was the same old envy and taboo of his youth—Tillotson Russell's heir, Sheila Pomeroy Russell's princeling and finally Lou Foray's bridegroom—the same. What integrity he owned without that history, none of which he had actually earned, he had never until lately asked.

Liebes, Rolfe, Ketchum and Bledsoe invoked his star again— not wealth nor ancestry nor borrowed fame this time, though. Ten minutes with the President, whom some of them distrusted and even despised, had been sufficient.

Old Sully Ketchum even, with his bursting jowls, his flaming bald pate, his alcoholic blood pressure, his passion for fidelity to a winner, had been seduced that morning.

"I've given a lot of thought to this thing, Pom," he had said. "Not something I take lightly. I don't like the man, but I agree defense is the number one ishya. If he wants a hundred tankers, then let's get em for him. You can count me in and I can bring Texiz in with me." He had rocked back, lifting his chin, and regarded Pom through lowered scaly lids, cunning and stagey. The old snake!

Pom had squelched a bitter laugh. Well, to hell with them all. When this thing was over he was going to sell the house, retire Pearl West and wander away like Gauguin to some island. Not for women and mangoes, however, but for decency, a clear head, something that could not be upheld among men like these. Suddenly he saw from inside his vision a quick little move of his own head and the absurdity of his own character, his poses, his fits of fastidiousness and good taste. It made him laugh, not that it was possible to slip up on himself as on a stranger.

But ultimately he accepted these men. Pom's nature, if not to forgive, was to accept, confidently unavailable to the smear that attends compromise. Forgivingly he knew himself—a romantic who intended to cure himself of it. For the sake of the goal he accepted Ketchum's loaded support. And Liebes, a Jew who refused to admit it, would, through patient cajoling, pressure, even through plain con if necessary, support the fight against fascism; they would finally get Liebes's money, especially if they let him pretend it would in the long run make more for him.

Ketchum and his sidekick Coombs in Texas, sport and lackey, were millionaires by default of a thousand fallen small oil operators who had saved their necks (or broken them) in a drastic rummage sale of lease lands and mineral rights after the crash. And those two scavengers were now useful for the good of an industry they had exploited and a country they thought of as their private ranch, divided not quite down the middle but somewhat obliquely in Ketchum's favor.

Yes, he accepted them. He had not had to grub like Ketchum, nor hide, like Liebes, his origins. Rolfe and Bledsoe would follow suit. Pom had lathered them with fit slogans—"We'll win it by oil. Nothing more or less. The President said so himself." And their appetites for that truth, he observed with disgust, were actually sexual.

"We'll have to fight the Japs," Sully predicted, "if we're going to keep ourselves in rubber. They want the Philippines, Java and the whole shebang, and if they get em, oil ain't going to be enough."

If Japan went south for oil, Pom agreed, the U.S. and Britain would have to oppose her. But it was already almost a fact, wasn't it? Sully had offered his usual epithets about little yellow bastards and they had parted with a laugh that sickened Pom. Few men would want Ketchum as an ally but fewer would want him as an enemy.

★
**Where
You
Goin,
Girlie?**
★
83

Meantime, his clothes, full of the acrid scent of his morning's success—tobacco mainly—were put away, his suitcase flung into the closet. Yes, he would, when the war was over, get out. He'd be old but that didn't matter. Nothing like winning them over to sour the stomach permanently, these rich men. They had helped to make him fastidious. He nodded at himself, Rueful Countenance, in the mirror. He looked aside now at Lou's photograph, so familiar he hardly saw it anymore, and gave her a wink.

Goddammit! What was missing in the world was, of course, simply women. These men knew nothing whatever about that pure adventure—life with a great woman. They all seemed to have those awful done-up wives, those bridge and golf playing wives with hairdos and red mouths. Women like pressed meat, he thought. No commitment nor even any interest in the world.

He turned away from the window and found Beasley standing in the doorway. He started awkwardly, delighted but caught off-balance, caught moody.

"Beas! What a nice surprise! I was feeling distracted. Just got back. What brings you over this time of day?"

Beas stood stiffly and grinned, his body stashed in a hasty-looking way in brown corduroy pants and a soft beige sweater over his white shirt, the collar of which stood up awkwardly on one side. His flat ashy hair was blown. His cheeks flamed like those long, full, delicious apples of the first of the season.

"Hi, Grandfather. I'm on my way to the lab. I just thought I'd drop by."

"Good! Good! Stay for lunch. Let's tell Pearl." Pom maneuvered him down the hall. "I was just unpacking."

"How was your trip?"

Pom guided him into the sun-room, looking in through the swinging door to tell Pearl in the kitchen that they wanted lunch.

"Fine. Very successful, Beas. I met the President."

"Gee! That's swell! FDR! What'd he say?"

Pom smiled. "He said, 'Mr. Russell, Harold tells me you have influence with those Texas and Oklahoma oil barons out there and I hope you'll use it to capacity. The war in Europe will be won by oil. I expect you know that.' "

Beas laughed a little. "Gee, the President! What'd he say about nuclear physics, anything?"

"Well, no. We hardly had time. But he's a remarkable man, I feel. He has what I call the life genius."

Beas nodded. Genius was a familiar pursuit of his grandfather's. He wasn't sure what moment was best to break his own news so he waited until the meal was done, rushing through it chatting about work at the lab, the new electron microscope, molecules, atoms—a conversation through which Pom, unbeknownst to his grandson, had always sailed cleverly on the surface like an amateur skater holding an invisible wire for support, a puppet. He had read a bit on purpose for mere decency, intending by one means or another to keep the dialogue open between them, but in fact he knew little of what was mere A B C to Beasley.

And then, when his grandfather drew up the napkin in that neat way that used to bring Beas and Katie into fits of giggles, rubbing it in quick little push-pulls across his lips, Beasley said, "I . . . uh . . . I came over to tell you something."

He froze then, looking into Pom's face with what seemed to be a kind of shock. Pom raised his eyebrows silently. "I . . . uh . . . decided to . . . well . . . enlist in the Army. I mean I did it already."

Pom rose half out of his chair and hovered there over the table. "You *what?*"

"I did. I enlisted."

"Why . . . why, you can't be serious! Why, what on *earth* . . . ?" He sat down with a *flump*, his face utterly aghast.

Beas swallowed. "I did, though. I figured, well . . . they would get me anyway, and anyway all the fellows I've talked to . . ."

"What do you mean, 'get you'? I can't understand you. Why, I told you you'd be deferred. Permanently. That means forever! You'll *never* have to go into the service, Beas. You know that!"

Beasley shrugged and nodded, patiently pained. "I know you did but . . . Well, Eric Witcher and Josh and some of the other guys say that everybody'll go, and anyhow I . . ."

"Beasley," he slammed down his napkin, "what in the name of heaven has gotten *into* you? I can't understand it! Here you are perfectly safe in the lab, not even through school. . . . Why, they won't take you in the first place. My God! You're not even eighteen yet."

"But by the time they find out, I will be. See, I just think that with everybody else getting in and all . . ." He shrugged again, leaning back as if exhausted, and took a few polite sips from a tall glass of water like a child, carefully replacing the glass, licking his lips and looking guiltily at Pom and then away, fingering the corner of the linen place mat.

"You lied at the induction center?" Pom asked softly, incredulous and knowing now that he was into a bucket of worms. "They'll want your birth certificate, Beas. Didn't they ask for it?"

He shook his head. "They didn't ask anything. They're really anxious to get you. I passed my physical already. Perfect." He looked chagrined at having been found perfect. "Gee, Grandfather, you said it yourself—they'll get everybody. If you get in early you can choose your own job and all. I could get into science or pharmacy or . . ."

Pom exploded. "For God's sake, can't I make it clear to you that you're an exception and you don't have to go at *all, ever*? It doesn't matter *whom* they take or what happens, *you* are permanently deferred! It's arranged. The lab's been declared essential defense industry. That means by the time we're in this thing, if we ever are, you'll be established there, essential to research. It's a *natural* way to operate, Beas, if that's what's worrying you. Nothing fraudulent or . . . phony about it. It's a perfectly legitimate way to keep scientists and researchers at vital defense work! You couldn't be in a more valuable job."

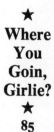

Beasley sat with his head lowered, nodding his little allowing nod that now touched Pom as entirely innocent, decent, blind and perhaps even a bit stupid. The first gesture, the first·hint even, of dullness he had ever perceived in the boy. He bit back his words, waiting for an answer.

"Well . . . I think they'd get me. I'm not a scientist. I'm not even in college yet. All I do around there is flunky work that anybody could do. Besides putting some serum in a rat, the most I've done is wash the beakers and mix a few chemicals. And I don't want to get into college, see, and then have to interrupt my work. I'd rather do it now. I've talked it over with a lot of fellows . . ."

"But those boys don't have your particular scientific bent, Beas. They surely will be drafted eventually and they may be wise to enlist early. But . . ." He threw up his hands and began to walk around the little sun-room where they had dined at a table against the window, the warm autumn light pouring over the surfaces like liquid. He swung his arms helplessly, moving about while Beasley just sat. "I can't figure this out, that you'd do a fool thing like this without my . . . advice or—or even telling me of your thinking about it in advance, Beas. I . . ." He swung around then and looked gently at Beasley, who seemed suddenly no more than twelve years old. Maybe he had panicked or something, all this news of the draft. Pom experienced a sudden quick pang of protectiveness.

"Do you *want* to go, Son? Is that it?"

"Well . . . I do know a lot about military life, remember. I spent quite a lot of time at Foxe Hills and that's just like the Army."

"Foxe Hills," Pom said carefully, "is nothing whatever like the Army. And nothing you ever saw or did there even remotely resembled *war*! Nothing!" He couldn't control it now, he let the frustration escape him in a kind of hiss. "Besides," he said, "you're not . . . real soldier material. You never will be. Good God! A boy with your talents . . ."

"Huh! That's what Katie said. I'm not soldier material."

"You've told her about this?"

"I told her I might."

"Well . . . " Pom sat down again. "Listen, Son—let's . . . not argue it now. You'll be late to work. There's no use for alarm. If you change your mind, and I think after some thought you will, then I can call the induction center—"

Beasley smacked him a look of determined fear. "I don't want you to call them. I can take care of everything myself. Just don't call up there, please, Grandfather. It's my . . . problem."

Pom stared, shook his head and dropped a hand to his side, aware of the dramatic gesture. He nodded acquiescence. Chances were Beas would regret it and come running for help. After all, the boy was still his ward and a ward of the State, since his father's death, and their power over him incontestable until his eighteenth birthday, not that he wanted to exert it to that point.

"You're almost of age, Beas. When you are I'll have no say in your life. I just urge you to think hard about yourself and your gifts . . . your life! You're not an ordinary young man, you know that, and that means something in this world. If there was ever a time to use your excellent intelligence, this is it."

They shook hands in their old affectionate, somewhat formal style and Pom was on the phone to Abe Dietler, to the lab and to Katie before Beas was halfway to work.

Beasley

He walked, distracted, to the corner and stood there with the benign sun cast over him like a confirmation. It had happened and he hadn't backed down but now his head was aswarm with ideas, needs, visions as if some huge laden pod had split open inside it, spewing a kind of saucy sperm there. Everything could happen now with Grandfather out of the way. He felt badly about that but had to ignore the feeling, he knew, to go on his own way.

He stood on the street. A dog went by intent upon dog business, paying him no attention, for which he was remotely glad. Yet he watched it with a sense of distant regret. He loved most animals with curiosity and protectiveness. Every time he put a needle into a rat or a rabbit, he apologized quietly. He walked on. He wouldn't hurry. Being late at the lab was no problem. He felt sure his grandfather wouldn't interfere, or maybe he would wait until he thought Beas was going to weaken and then he'd move in on it. But he wouldn't weaken. Now he could go. He could line up with hundreds of men and move with them into strange countries, on ships, in trucks, over rough ground, carrying nothing but a head full of thoughts—millions of stinging wasps of thought—a gun and a mess kit. He could *move*! His life at home and at the lab seemed like some tiny pet he kept in his pocket, whose protests could hardly be heard. He stroked and comforted it. His head exploded with the sense of freedom and mobility.

He had to tell *her*, of course. That was the worst thing and still to come. But later. At the last. She'd see his crew cut but he could say his head had been itchy and the barber had advised it. Then he'd have to tell Josh and Brad Finch, if that dumb guy would ever write him a letter. He walked along vaguely as he had when he was small, coming home from third grade, noodling along as Katie used to call it. Katie might end up being the problem.

He passed Harriet Semple's house and remembered how last year he had spent two or three weeks trying to see her undressing in her upstairs back bedroom at night, cruising around there on his bike for hours, wearing himself out. What a dumb thing, spending all that time! He had pumped himself up and waited for a long time and then when she came into the room and pulled the shade down, he just went ahead and let it go onto the ground, not enjoying it at all, leaning against a tree. He was tired of all that now.

Well, first the barber, then tell *her* and in the meantime get some girl to do it into and quit doing it outside. Cynthia Gillespie was the only one he knew for sure would do it with most people. It was just a matter of getting started, he knew that, just finding the right one and doing it once or twice. After that he'd know how to make them like it, using Brad's advice of course, and some other stuff he had read and some ideas of his own. His head sailed. His groin swelled. He went to Eighteenth Street and down the hill to the barbershop.

"Crew! You got a nice head of hair here. What're you doin, joinin up?"

He sucked in his lip. "Yeah. Next week they're shipping me out." He liked the terrible feeling of lies.

The barber nodded, twisting his mouth, soberly skeptical, slashing away at his top hair with a plundering indifference and whistling softly.

"Yeah, this hair lies neat. Kinda too bad to shave it all off. But a crew's clean. I like em on most heads. You young fellas look good this way."

Beas got a slight hard on under the big white apron and held it down with his concealed hands. He'd been doing it so much lately he wondered if it really might not be dangerous after all. It made you reckless, he knew that much. Maybe the thing to do was just call Cynthia Gillespie and invite her to a movie. But it seemed weird to do it that way, the movie not being the real reason and all. But in the movie he could feel her a little—Brad had talked about that—in the balcony. Oh, nuts! Why didn't girls cooperate better if they intended to do it all the time anyway? Why have to go through all that buildup? If he had a car. Borrow the electric maybe? But Katie would be curious or want to go along. Had she ever? Yeah. You couldn't go out with Eric Witcher more than once and not. Everybody knew about him. It was all he did.

The clippers zoomed over the top of his head now and goose bumps shot up on his arms and neck. His hard fell. It was a close crew. He looked, dazzled, at his egg head in the mirror. God! He hadn't thought to examine it first to see if it was knotty or anything. Powder, a flick of the cloth, a spin of the chair with a mirror thrust in his hand. His eyes spasmed and locked. He couldn't see himself. Never had been able to.

"Yeah. It's okay. It's okay." He satisfied the barber, paid and lurched out into the sunny street.

At the corner he called the lab and said he'd been delayed at the dentist. For two cents he would leave now, right this minute, and get on a train, a ship, go into space. He felt a little crazy and naked, as if this were his very huge hard lavender prick that was jutting right out instead of his same old public head.

He pretended on the bus to scratch his neck, running his hand up the bristling back of his head. He caught his reflection up close in the bus window. His head looked like a knob. He didn't know whether to laugh or cry. He was going through with the whole thing. Phase one now over. He gave himself three days to find a girl to ram it into.

When he entered the door of the lab he realized he had not told them and would have to. Dr. Zeisl's secretary stopped in her tracks when she saw him and said, "Beasley!" with what seemed like shocked admiration. Maybe even *she* would do. Maybe he'd just casually suggest that they have a Coke or something after work. She couldn't be more than twenty and he needed an older woman to start, Brad had said that was ideal. He hailed her with a grin and a little head-down nod, his usual, and she said—

"You look so . . . *different*! Gosh! What a difference hair makes! Makes you look a little older, now that you don't have the bangs."

She stared with a queer confused little smile—Andrea was her name—and he felt as if he could fall on her that moment and drag her to the floor with him, biting her, and squeezing her breasts, which were small and high up. *Don't go too fast at first*, Brad had said. *Knock it off a few times at home first so you won't be so eager.* All that preparation! It seemed awful.

Several people raised their eyebrows at him as he rushed down the hall to his own safe corner of the pleasantly smelly serum test lab. Sometimes he had even gone so far as to strap his penis to his stomach with a long band of double gauze stolen from the lab, to keep it under control, but that seemed to irritate it into an even more flaming hard.

"Beas! Hey, I'm glad you made it. I'm just about to try that last batch on Gloria. Here, give me a hand with her. Bring her over here, will you?"

Dr. Sandrew didn't even notice. Hair is for women. He took the soft quivering rabbit out of her cage—Gloria, who had had six babies two months ago. God! Even Gloria had been screwing. Did anybody ever do it to an animal? That dog once . . . if he had been big enough she would have let him. She had backed right up to him. But a *rabbit*? It would kill them. He took her gently to the table and held her down for her shot, his hands sunk tenderly in her fur against her quaking sides.

We were getting bold. We'd strike matches and look at each other. I still nearly went blind when I looked at that big long rod. It looked like a sentry standing in a helmet in the rain, so dumb and patient and faceless. It was plum-colored and very tall, the most naked thing I ever saw in my life. I felt kind of sorry for him having to carry it around yet I knew it was his favorite thing in the world.

Well, it looked like a cop, like an elongated desperate mushroom striving up. It looked like a shocked eel, a skinned mole, a slug, a cannon, or when finished like a shrunken old man in shantytown curled in a doorway. Like a miscarried animal, a rubber thumb, a fetal snake a neck a toy gun a giant's toe a creep's finger a helpless mutation—but then again up and like a tidy young naked kid boy standing up in the morning—behold! A rocket shooting at the sky, the dumb thing! Half a dumbbell!

And then we did and did and did it and I thought suddenly at a certain moment that *this* was correct and nothing else made any sense whatever.

Don't use that, I'd say, and he'd say You're crazy. He would use it then and the second time he wouldn't use it. Those little buggers, he would explain, were so weak by that time that they couldn't have made a baby.

But I didn't think I'd have a baby, anyway. I just didn't think so. I felt as if I were so propelled, so shot out into space, that my sheer momentum would by-pass pregnancy somehow. Not yet, I said to myself.

But all the time my body felt stubborn, swollen and expectant. It grew aimless. It withdrew from me. I stared at it for hours in the mirror until I felt myself go a little crazy. I felt often as if I'd break out of my clothes in public. When I looked at others I often saw through to their flesh and had to turn away.

★

It was chilly now. She was still sick or sick again. She never got quite back to normal before she came down again. The clients were faithful if restless, bringing over special dishes to strengthen Sarah, implying we didn't eat well. We had never had so much food, so rich and strange. I gorged it. "If this is the way Ada Barnett eats, no wonder her mind is confused," I told Ruby, and she slapped down a foot, bent over and let out a hoot. She loved a slam at another woman's cooking.

I sat with Sarah every evening and morning, reading to her from the newspaper, which she liked better than anything, it being full of the world's woes and wickedness, which she loved. Sally Rand, it seemed, had danced naked at a Harvard Smoker and urged the young men to take off their clothes too, an item to which Sarah responded with, "Law, Hon, with so many young men there at once, I suppose it was all just for fun."

"Yeah," said I, blushing.

" 'Napoleon Bonaparte's pickled intestinal tract,' " I read, " 'was blown to glory in a bombing of the Royal College of Surgeons in London last week.' Wow!"

"Mercy, it makes you wonder if that war isn't just some big prank they're all a-playin.' "

She didn't mean it, of course, and that was the important thing to know about Sarah—that she was smart as a tack and even a genius and part of her genius was in finding a way to sound like an idiot and in being a perfect idiot while she was about it.

We listened to "Are You the Missing Heir" on the radio and spent the imaginary money on a trip to Banff and Lake Louise for her and to a Chinese opium den for me. Just to see, I explained through her giddy desperate laughter.

Someday, I thought, I'm going to get up the courage to tell her everything I know and think and am.

Iantha took the afternoons, insisting on giving her a bath, a nice powdering. Not too much exercise, warned Dr. Killeen. Why? He wouldn't talk. Iantha trembled before him who had laid her down on the asphalt once and pulled her tongue out of her infatuated throat.

And every night, late, in the lease road, in the back of the car —Eric. I'll write you a lot, he had begun to say. I felt like a deaf mute. I couldn't imagine his going or anybody's going. I knew we'd never have a conversation. Once I asked him what he liked to read and he said the sports page and Sherlock Holmes. I tried to tell him about Sarah again, how worried I was, about how his war talk had influenced poor Beas to enlist and all, but though he pretended to be listening, I knew he was waiting it out until he could catch me off guard—the me below conversation, the beast me that was beating away under there—and pounce on her. I waited below my own talk for that myself.

We were getting so good at it we were going crazy. We could just look into each other's eyes and it started.

"You know the first time?" I said.

"Yeah?"

"I didn't make it all the way."

He laughed. "I know it. They never do."

I slapped him playfully. "*They?* Who's they? If you ever call me that again I'll run away and never see you. I'll stab you!" I liked stabbing better than shooting.

He howled. "You . . . you . . . you little red-hot!" He grabbed me then, as usual, and wrestled me.

He gave me a small gold basketball on a chain which I hung around my neck and left there though it became deeply tarnished and left a black smudge on my chest. He had won it as a senior in high school. He said he wanted to arrange to get me to his house when his folks were away some night but I didn't like the idea. The woods were hospitable to us. I knew of an old shack on the lease that was full of racoons by now probably, or skunks, which I had played in ages ago with Beas and which I hoped we could clear out. But time kept falling through our arms and legs. We never changed our quick habit of falling together wherever we were. I never knew what day it was anymore.

Renfro

"I feel like I oughta explain to ya a little," he said to the whore.

"Oh yeah?" she said.

He sat on the side of the sinking bed near the white iron foot of it, holding to it, his other hand poised on his shirt front delaying the unbuttoning. He looked at her and laughed sheepishly. She was leaning against a battered bureau (the idea of a whore having a bureau made him want to howl with pitying laughter but he kept himself sober) and smoked a cigarette and watched him, her tangly hair falling half into her face, her tricked-up eyes leveling on him, her knobbly feet kicked out of her pumps. She was skinny and knotty. He hated to look at her. They might even have gone to high school together. What was her name besides Mildred? Well . . .

"I lost these teeth bumming round the country, not eating right."

He stared into space and didn't see her look of boredom.

"Oh . . . I've had . . . women . . . in a few houses and all. Especially in Waco. Spent a lot of time there. Mexican women. I grew up here, though. This was my home."

He swallowed and lowered his head. Then he sighed and looked at her with a repentant grin. He bent over to appear to be preparing, and took off his shoes, tucking under his toes in their holey socks. She was a person. She sniffed and kept smoking and watching and listening. He could smell her.

"Graduated from Central High. My sister was a teacher here, may still be. But that's the thing, you see, I haven't called them at all. I just jumped off a freight out near the refinery a couple of weeks ago and came into town. Just . . . like that, without thinking about it. I'm staying too. Got a room . . . This is my home, after all. . . ."

"Yeah?" she said without interest. She moved and his back crawled. She smashed the cigarette in a broken glass ashtray and sniffed again. She seemed to have a cold.

He swallowed, sighed and looked at his narrow knees. And then she moved toward him and stood in front of him. Thank God she still had her clothes on. What was different in her, different from the ones in Waco or Denver or Los Angeles, he didn't know. But she seemed threatening. He oughtn't to have picked her up. Then he looked up at her and realized that she had a long sad bony face, and in that, and in some other subtler features which he almost grasped, she looked like someone he knew. His ears turned hot. Then he looked again and realized that she looked like *himself*! Jesus Christ! She did, she looked a lot like him, hound-dog and melancholy. He laughed quickly.

"What the shit's so funny?" she asked him.

He waved a hand, mortified, feeling himself disintegrate right in front of her. "Oh, me. Me. Not you. I'm—I'm a mess, I guess."

She sighed heavily. "Listen, Buster, it took two hours to git you up here. Now why don't you just lay down and shut up? I don't like talk. I only like action. I gotta eat, you know."

Everything in him seemed to stream down to his thighs all at once, all his fluids, his very saliva seemed drawn down and out of him. He stood up and cleared his throat. He nodded at her knowing he had to go through with it and began to loosen his clothes, taking them off agonizingly and folding them with care over the end of the chipped old bed frame.

She took off her dress in a flip over the head and was scrawny-naked before him, all dark nipples on small unanimated breasts, and a black hanging thatch. He goose-pimpled, puckering like a shaved animal. She jerked her head toward the bed and he lay down on his back. As she came toward him, over him, he let out a compulsive laugh that had no mirth in it.

He touched her almost kindly. "You realize . . . heh . . . Jesus . . . You realize that you and I . . ." His eyes spasmed shut with awful laughter.

"Yeah? What about you and I?" She hung over him, her little tits hanging like pockets in a wrongside-out shirt.

"We look alike. You see that, don't you? Jesus, it's very strange!" He laughed, his chin shaking. He wasn't sure whether this might not be a crazy kind of crying.

She gave a scornful horsy laugh that stopped his hysteria.

"Oh, we don't neither! You're just scairt! Whatsa matter with you? Look at that big thing. You got nothin to worry about, fer shit sakes. Lookit that!"

And she began to scratch and nick and bite him everywhere while he lay there wincing the way he had at the doctor's as a child, batting his eyes, shaking his head. He couldn't move. But then, when she became more serious and began to squirm close to him, dragging herself over his body, moving and hurting his rod, he found himself trying to sit up, to get on his feet. He felt choked by her hot vinegarlike odor and her rough handling. His head was beating.

"What's eating you now?" she said when he finally rolled away from her and off the side of the bed onto his feet.

"I'm nervous today. Nothing serious. Forget it. I just can't go through with it."

She shrugged and got up. She pulled her dress over her head again and began to comb her thick obstreperous hair in front of the bureau mirror.

He got into his clothes as quickly as possible. What a mess! He was about to weep!

"I'm . . . just preoccupied. Sorry to hold you up."

"So what's new about that? Half the guys I run into get the bends."

"I didn't get the bends!" he challenged her quickly, too personally. He looked at her long face with its punished expression. God!

As if he were gazing into a mirror at his own sorry mug. "We do look alike, though. We've got the same—"

"Oh, can it, Buddy! I'm not your sister, see?"

He buckled his belt quietly, standing by the bed. He wanted to break through the tough scab of her street style to the raw someone below it. But he wondered at the same time why he cared. He knew he was being sentimental and that she could see through him.

"Well . . . let's go get a cup of coffee. I'll buy you a—"

"No thanks. I gotta keep busy. How'd ya think I pay fer this place?"

He stared. The whole room smelled of her tartness. He wondered about her nights alone. Was she ever alone? There was a snapshot stuck in the side of the mirror. There was a knitted afghan on the back of the armchair; a pair of dirty satin mules by the closet curtain. Someone gave her a gift once in a while? The window shade was tattered and streaked, letting through fractured agonized slits of light. The maroon draperies were a touch of cheap desperate pride.

Maybe he had been offended by failure and poverty and desperation all his life and been too snobbishly covetous of his own sense of democracy to admit it.

"I ought to . . ."

She gave him a gritty look. "You're screwy!" she said.

Yes, he was a sick snob. He had loved but refused to drink with his bums so he could cure them. He had wanted to befriend whores, to kiss all his lepers. He had wanted to impose his own silly code upon them, to violate their tough self-knowledge. He turned to the door and held it open for her as if to escort her out. She had popped a piece of bubblegum into her mouth now and was chewing heavily. Finally, she blew a big thin rose-colored bubble almost in his face and exploded it in a loud pop.

"I'm sorry," he said, smiling faintly. "This must be a boring waste of time for you." But even the idea of boredom suggested to a whore showed him up to himself worse than ever. He got out his wallet standing in the open doorway. She reached across him and pulled the door to with a bang, shutting them in.

"Don't you have a brain in yer head? Sweet Jesus!"

He handed her two dollars which she snatched from him disgustedly, stuffing them into a drawer in the bureau. He looked at her sad jackal face, saw his own glowering visage there and imagined taking money that way, for almost nothing, yet for a supreme gesture of some sort. She said shit and they walked out the door, she flouncing ahead of him down the stairs to the street and quickly up the block while he stood in the falling autumn light wondering which way to go.

The next morning he moved out of that neighborhood to a sunny bedroom on the east side of town and that night at the plant he found a new ride through the car pool.

My old friend Di Finlayson called. "Why don't we see each other anymore?"

I did not say, Because I've turned into a sex maniac. It had been almost a year since we had had lunch together in the Plaza tearoom and talked about boys, not men, and sex which neither of us knew beans about. Di had a job at the plant, she said. Somebody's secretary. I gagged a little, quietly. I said I didn't want to work in an office. I wanted to work in one of those hangars where the men were. And she laughed in such a way that I knew she was still a virgin and wanted to talk about all that over a Coke again. She was getting into dangerous waters, she wanted to say. But then she said she could get me a job anywhere I wanted at the plant because of her boss and I wondered if maybe she wasn't having an affair with him. It all sounded like Lana Turner in a movie about a waitress, but actually Di looked like a country cousin of Hepburn, only taller, questionable skin; wry and a little mocking the way people are who feel invisible. A little clumsy but very memorable, very witty and willing to be desperate.

So I said I'd be out there soon to apply and I meant it now. I was waiting for Eric to leave.

And then on September thirteenth Beas told Enid. She had cried quickly when she saw his crew cut, but only over his loss of beauty. When she heard the reason for it she did not utter a sound. And I wrote in the Biography the only lines I had put there since going out with Eric the second time.

★

The Biography
of Enid

★

Her face after she learned her son Beasley had enlisted took on a knowing look, a look of having received finally her punishment, the sentence she must have expected at the end of the trial when she heard the verdict —acquitted.

The look—stern, wise, not bitter, not ironic—was one of recognition. Something painfully sternly acquiescent. Justice. It sentenced her life but the fact of its being just seemed to impress her.

She wore this look with a sort of clouded, mute pride as if these events had given her a new courage.

She got up.

She did not protest.

She seemed never to question Beasley's going as anything but an act justly taken against herself, addressed primarily to her, concerned with her salvation perhaps. Her yielding to it seemed to protect his innocence in doing what fate had arranged for him. But it also reduced the power of his act somehow.

She aided him in every way. She hired someone to help pack up his lab. She sewed his name on all his gear. *Enid!* They all watched her in amazement. Her head bent over the sewing completely unself-consciously as if doing penance while alone, sublimely unobserved no matter who witnessed it. And her niece Katie observed it with urgent preoccupation, seeing in that a slow development of sobriety. First came an end to all that scorn which had always tarnished her voice. And then a new sort of patience. She changed, simply that. It was as if the long-shaded underside of a half-buried leaf with all its molds and webs finally had turned to the light, the newborn vulnerable and fertile underside of her old bitter patience.

Beasley watched her too, uneasily, waiting for some show of anguish, some wrath or scorn, something resistant against which he could turn his cool back and go on with his plan. Or plot. No one was sure what moved Beasley. His grandfather, Pom, called Katie several times and whispered savagely into the phone, "Can't you *do* something about it, for God's sake? He trusts you if he trusts anyone."

Only Enid seemed to understand what he was doing, and to assume it as a pain preferable to her other old burden.

Her sister Sarah persuaded them to move out to the lease then, so that Enid would not be alone while her son was away, and she, Enid, seemed to take that too as some kind of divinely cast order which she obeyed and found reasonable and followed without rancor, without question, more than perfunctorily but with the same quiet acquiescence and perhaps even gratitude with which she prepared her son for his military life.

They moved in on us and Enid rented her "sweet little bungalow over on Madison Terrace" to a woman Iantha found who was leaving her husband.

Houses. We had houses in our imaginations, all of us, the way Pom had civilization and France and war and ships in his. There was a lot to say about our house on the lease, in fact, even that little ad hoc outfit.

Before we had moved there, Sarah and I had lived at home in town with my grandfather McCleod where she had grown up. Pom took Beasley and me out to that very lease and that very house one afternoon while he met with some oil men in the fields nearby. He explained to Mr. Willett, who lived at that time in that little house with his family, that we would wait there for him, Beas and I. He didn't ask Mr. Willett if we could wait, he merely explained that we would.

Beas and I played with Mr. Willett's three children, who were very solemn with scuffed and bitten little legs and drawn mouths with cracks at the corners, and green on their teeth. There was always dried mucus around their nostrils and a smell about them of the pee-soaked bed they slept in. They had a dog with no name that looked just like them. And they themselves had queer names —Wandalina and Boyboy and Coolie.

They were stern children but when they put their minds to it they could accomplish a lot of serious play. The big signboard on the east acre near the house which once had advertised Filer's Wholesale Feed and Grain was sturdier in those days and they used it like an exercise bar. They stared at Beas and me, making only a few tight comments—"This here doag don't bite. Don't be skeert of him." And "You folks fixing to spend the day?" Beas and I felt like a couple of zoo-fattened rattlers. But finally the oldest boy, Coolie, shot out across the lot and up the support post of the billboard like a spindly monkey and the other two followed. Beas and I joined them. They were all over that thing, shinnying up the posts, scampering across the narrow top beam; the sign swayed like a willow limb. But they seemed to have no fun in it; they were just wild and serious. "These children don't act like people," Beas, then six years old, whispered to me.

Finally we lured them up to the highway to Hubert's dairy store for ice cream. They scattered along the road, all sharp elbows and crusty noses, their mouths continually open to show those tiny teeth like pearls smashed in the dirt. We lined up at the counter, the Willetts with clenched fists, peering up at the list of flavors they couldn't read, open-mouthed and stern. Beas and I ordered.

"Can't you figure out which one?" Beas asked Coolie politely. "I think peach is best but maybe you oughta get chocolate or vanilla or strawberry or eggnog." He recited these flavors as if reading a primer aloud for the first time. He licked his cone, patient with the Willetts.

Finally they all chose chocolate by the look of it and Wandalina had dropped hers in the dust of the road a few minutes later. I was struck by the pain she displayed silently in grimaces and yet without tears. Coolie traded licks with her. Boyboy gave her the bottom half of his cone.

Ah, but they were so ragged and dull and dirty. What was there to like in them? They were like lessons. I was fascinated but with a kind of loathing and pity that confused me. I hated pity even then and wanted them to show some bravery or disdain to us— anything. I found a little hope in the statement from Coolie that he could wring a chicken's neck in the time it took you to say nuts. Beas stared with unabashed scientific interest at their crusty noses and watery eyes.

About dusk that afternoon I heard Beas sigh all at once and my own homesickness smote me. We had been standing around the back door submitting to gnat bites for over an hour after the ice cream adventure. I looked around for a sign of Pom, uselessly. Mrs. Willett came out finally and reported that Mr. Russell had said "youens orta stay here for supper" if he didn't get back from the Shellenburger lease in time. "They got them some big oil over there today," she said mysteriously, giving us a weary lift of the eyebrows which seemed to hope to cheer us but made me want to run to her and embrace or maybe hit her. I never knew what such violent urges toward others meant in myself. I could have cried at this news but I had to bluff it out because of Beas, who looked very bleak. We left the children to themselves and took a little walk out toward the woods to talk it over.

"Why didn't he take us with him? Why'd he leave us in this old puke place? I hate those children."

"He's on business, Beas," I consoled him. "He'll be back pretty soon. Maybe they'll have a good dinner."

What they served us was a kind of ham soup. There in the bottom of the pot, all pearly and slick, was the naked hambone. It looked like somebody. There were a few onion slices and little pieces of potato in it. The rest of supper was grits with syrup, called in this household seerup. Mrs. Willett had a garden but Pom said later that they had to save every last leaf of it to sell. They ate on broken and cracked plates, drank from tin cans and owned only three spoons. The children slurped their soup savagely out of old crocks and Beas and I were given two chipped bowls and two of the spoons. Flies fell in clots on the rims of our bowls and cans; the Willetts vaguely wiped them away. Beas fought them frantically with his left arm while spooning up his food with the right. He liked that old tank-smelling soup and, like Mr. Willett, sucked it in loudly. I dabbled with mine. The children picked their noses and swilled up their grits silently. The dog stood quivering at the door, his sides caved in. A hot wind swept through the house stirring the odors of stale grease and coffee. Their silence and their sharp-nosed sickly looks, their reddish eyes, terrified me. I thought Pom had done this for some awful grown-up reason. This kind of poor wasn't like our kind. We had our grandparents who owned a big house and no money. Not the same. And Pom, who was rich, was grandfather to Beas besides. Enid often said there were two kinds of poor: the poor people and the people who had no money. We were the latter and at that time not doing badly.

Beas was temporarily cheered by eating but an hour later he threw it all up on the back step. It made him angry to do that. He sat there sullen and quiet in the dark waiting for Pom until very late. I guarded him, pantomiming his pout. Without him I might have fallen into some cheap friendliness with the Willetts, as was my wont. Mrs. Willett came and sprinkled some sawdust on the vomit and left it, which horrified Beas. We languished there while the children caught a few fireflies and brought them to us in loosely closed filthy little palms as if to give us a peep into their empty, rarely lit lives, as if there were some subtle secret in the very barrenness of those lives. Finally they went inside to bed and when it was all quiet, Mr. Willett appeared at the back stoop where we sat huddled together in the moonlight and told us to come inside and lay down till Mr. Russell come back to git us because he and the missus had to git to bed. He had to git to town

the next morning with his truck of produce and that meant gittin
up at daybreak and he wasn't fixin to leave us two out here alone
like this in the night. We orta come in and lay down with the
children. Beasley gave a quick shudder. But we followed the poor
man with that creased and drawn look always on his face, never
a smile. I was sure by now that Pom had had some awful trouble;
that this, in any case, was my proper fate. We didn't know where
we were and the Willetts had no phone. I thought of Sarah and
wondered how many days it would take her to realize I wasn't
where I usually was—in a tree, on my bike, on a roof somewhere,
in someone's attic, riding the back of the icewagon. I trembled, but
for the sake of Beas and my pride I kept quiet.

There was a kerosene lamp on a broken chair in the hall, burning a yellow sallow light. Everything smelled of grease and heat
and weariness.

"We'll just sit in the kitchen," Beas said loudly. "Then we can
hear him come."

"Oh, no cause to set up thar and fall to sleep on the table, young
feller. We got a extry bed. We done put the kids together in the
big bed on the porch."

So we followed him into what later became Sarah's cubicle for
clients in that house, that little room off the kitchen. He gave us
a candle and told us to blow it out when we were in bed. He
wandered away leaving us there with one narrow iron cot, no
sheets, a broken chair and a climate of old imbedded pee. I
touched Beas.

"I'm gonna stand against the wall!" he whispered loudly.

I started to shake and gasp with a queer kind of laughter. I
looked around the room and quickly blew out the candle.

"Sit in the chair. I'll sit on the side of the bed."

Beas eased onto the chair and shot out of it like a burning cat.

"Oh, cow! Somebody wet on there!" He wiped madly at his rear
end.

I started to laugh again, softly, trying to hold it in. I could have
peed myself, an act which, for this family, customarily took place
in the woods. I used to ponder the probability (years later) that
the Willetts had fertilized our very lives—the little wild berry
bushes, the stray stalks of corn, the very pecan grove. I helped
Beas out of his pants and shorts, quickly wiped his behind, folded
them up, dropped them by the leg of the bed. He submitted to my
care gratefully.

I tested the bed—smelly but dry. I eased onto it and moved to
the wall at the other side and said, "It's okay. Come on. Lie
down."

Beas dived onto the cot and sank against me, his cool naked tiny
soft behind touched my legs, his hot strong dense body like a small
wrapped ham thrust into my arms. I had a doll that felt that way
and was mad about it. I was mad about Beas too, only Beas. I
intended to protect him for the rest of my life. I gripped him,
feeling a bleak wonder and power over everything. I was taking
care, I was being brave. That made me lonely. I listened for

tramps. The snap of a twig in the yard could be heard for a mile. I heard the distant grind of trucks on the highway and later the MKT midnight train.

Beas slept and grew hot and heavy against me; the deep stir of his breathing calmed me a little. Very late, when he was snoring lightly, I felt between his legs that ripe hard little snout like a rubbery acorn on a stem, and the two tight little lumps below it. I gave it all a thorough blind search till I had it memorized and then I let go of it and slept.

Pom came at three in the morning and took us, Beas asleep and half naked in his arms, to his house where Enid in her beaded crêpe dress and red silk pumps, and Uncle Jack Russell, Sarah, several Abernathy sisters, Abe Dietler, Pom's best friend, and a few other men, were already celebrating, with bootleg champagne, Pom and Abe's new oil well. Rose Abernathy, Iantha's youngest sister, was all wrapped up in lavender veils, sitting at the player piano pretending to be making music. She kept standing up suddenly, raising her glass and calling for a toast to The Sheik, Valentino.

"He's dead," Uncle Jack said, slapping her on the bottom much too hard. "Why don't you toast *me*? I'm alive and kicking." And nobody knew then, of course, that his own special death was hacking its way through the solids of the future to meet him. He did a little two-step around Rose which was very unusual for him and everybody laughed with a sort of relief the way they always did when he behaved with any friendliness. But Rose drank alone to the Sheik and later she went out to Pom's back garden by the grape arbor and danced in the moonlight. A few years later she gave up the world and became a nun.

Sarah, all rosy and jolly, hugged me and told me to lie on the couch in the study and come in to the party when I felt like it, thinking, maybe, that I'd just fall asleep. But I hovered like a crazed moth between the study and the living room the rest of the night listening to the chatter and the shattering sounds of champagne glasses hitting the fireplace with Pom's hearty approval.

They turned on the Victrola but kept forgetting to wind it. That seemed to me to be just like them—the grownups I knew—their lives droning down to a groan if they didn't keep winding them up. They played a favorite of Pom's which seemed to crack him up in embarrassed laughter—"Last Night on the Back Porch"—and something for Abe sung by Caruso which made tears come into Abe's big ugly eyes behind their thick lenses. He nodded and wiped his glasses with his necktie.

Everybody got drunk but Pom, Sarah and Abe. Enid became very waltzy and limp-eyed, sweeping around the room and sometimes crashing into a man, looking up into his eyes as if she were going to faint. They grew noisy. Uncle Jack stood in his derby, drunk as a frozen block of wood, and took the pins carefully out of Iantha Abernathy's red hair without her feeling it till too late when it collapsed down her shoulders, spilling like a clay bank in the rain, scaring her to death. She screamed and leaned over her lap, holding her hair up.

"That's all nachurl red," Uncle Jack said carefully. "And she can prove it, can't you, Antha?" His tongue was so thick it plugged his mouth. And Iantha slapped her hands over her ears and turned red enough to blow up.

I was delirious. I hoped they'd all go crazy. Pom stood around chuckling and pouring out champagne. Everybody laughed, threw glasses and shouted about being rich and taking ships, about Pom entertaining chorus girls in high style in New York, or shipping his pigskin Stutz to Paris to show them some real style. Uncle Jack smashed his fist into his other hand and said, "Man alive, Dad, you hit it!" But later he tried to sock somebody in the jaw and they pushed him against the wall in the hallway and said, "Jack, for the love of God! Get hold of yourself!"

I slept, finally, on the leather couch in Pom's study. By the time I woke up, Pearl West had the house cleaned and was cooking bacon in the kitchen. Pom and Beas were on the sun-porch eating breakfast, Pom in his dressing gown with the black satin lapels and his patent leather slippers. It looked as if he had even buffed his fingernails.

"They're terrible children," Beas was saying. "I never want to see them again. They're ugly and they smell and they won't talk. I'll never go out there again, Grandfather. Katie neither."

Pom smiled and tried to hide it. Beas waved his spoon—"They wet their pants anywhere they want. Right in a *chair*, even. I know 'cause I sat in it. They're terrible children, aren't they, Katie?"

"Yes. But . . . I guess they're poor and they can't help it." I looked to Pom for clarification.

"That's right, Beas," he said gently. "They have a very hard life and not enough to eat always, I suppose."

I winced. They had shared their not-enough with us. That old shiny hambone!

"Well," Beas said loudly, "if they weren't so terrible, people might give them something."

Pom cleared his throat. "But it's terrible to be poor, Beas. You become discouraged. You . . . forget your good habits and don't hand them on to your children. You lose hope."

"Yeah," I said, understanding it finally. "Well, Pom got rich last night so he can help them now, can'tcha, Pom?"

He shrugged. "Well, I didn't get *rich*. That's no gusher and Abe owns a lot more of it than I do. But let's finish up this breakfast now."

Beas gorged his cereal and drank his milk with big gulping noises, slamming down the glass and wiping his mouth on the back of his hand. He informed Pom then that nobody in the world had to let his nose run. You could wipe it on a leaf or an old rag if you didn't have a hankie. The Willetts were beyond excuse. And Pom said he'd see to it that Mr. Willett had a little help.

But the crash finally hit us all, like a tornado. Even Pom, with his roaring pigskin Stutz, lost a lot. Grandfather McCleod died and then a year after the crash, Grandmother died too. I couldn't remember much of it, only Sarah crying out and rushing to call the doctor. The doctor listening and listening at Grandmother's chest, then shaking his head. Sarah throwing up her hands and later kissing her mother's dead bare feet. Enid in the house, sobbing on a bed. Sarah crying silently in a corner. I tried sobbing a little, found it an excellent experience, worked on it. Once I even howled aloud and Sarah looked at me as if I had broken through a window with my fist. It felt good, though. I hung onto Sarah and when she came out of her mourning, I let her go.

The industry's dying, Pom said. They've got to stop closing down. And Abe Dietler would say, They can't compete with Texas, Pom. Prices are already down to two cents a barrel. You've got to work on the government for some price controls. That's the only hope.

The crash seemed to fell everyone. Pom talked and talked about Hoover who looked, on newsreels, like a big biscuit. "Hon," said Sarah to Pom, to Iantha, to anyone who would listen, "I feel sorry for the poor fellow. I just don't think he knows what to do." Pom said he oughtn't to have hid himself from the Bonus Marchers that way. I listened, uneasy, making nothing of it all. Pom talked with Abe about Commies and strikes.

Finally the Willetts packed up and left the lease house. They came by Pom's in an old truck stacked high with a teetering feeling to it, carrying all their old scrappy belongings that you wondered why they bothered to take along; and they said they were going to California to the bean fields. It gave me a harsh thrill. I was two years older by then and saw them differently. They brought me again that timid ecstasy of pity that I had learned for the first time with Sarah in her mourning. The Willett children were even sterner than before. Pom gave them money and the address of a man in California who might help them. He shook Mr. Willett's crusty hand.

"I never shoulda listened to them folks telling me to let go my pigs, Mr. Russell. Right there the trouble commenced. Them big farmers with crops is one thing, but for me, why my truckin never hardly paid me enough in *good* times."

His eyes were teary, with so beseeching and confused a look that Pom had to turn away. "God knows," Pom said later, "I told him he could stay on the place free. But I couldn't feed them, too."

But couldn't he have? Even we could have, I used to think, even we, if we'd really wanted to and tried.

They drove off, the children staring back, not waving. And others followed them. You could see them on the highways with their skinny dogs and children and their old bedding flapping. And sometimes when we took a ride with Pom out to his other property near the Panhandle and spent the night in a family inn, we would see them camped by the roads; they even had furniture right out in the fields. And Pom would say, "They'll never get to California. They'll stay right there till the county comes and moves them off the land. Look at that car, tires like paper." And shake his head. "Thousands! What good does it do to hand out ten bucks or a meal or a topcoat?"

But Beas and I said he was wrong—they'd make it to California someday. Because we both had a curious passion by then for those terrible travelers like the Willetts to get to the bean fields and eat well and start smiling for a change. Beas would sit on his little perch in the back seat of Pom's second car, the Pierce Arrow, and stare out grim-faced. "I don't like to go by in this pretty car," he'd say softly.

What are they, I thought, and what are we? They're Okies and Arkies, said Pom. And we were Sooners.

"At least they've got a few tents and packing cases in those Hoovervilles. Keep them out of the cold," he reasoned.

"Tents aren't warm!" cried Beas.

"Neither are piano boxes," said I, although I would have loved to set up housekeeping in one.

Every week caravans of colored people passed through, too, along the edge of town. And the begging increased all the time. Once they'd chalked your back door, you fed someone every night. Sarah never turned away a beggar, or anyone else that I know of, even when we were low on food and getting ready to sell Grandfather McCleod's house.

The gypsies were everywhere too, stealing and being thrown in jail. One of them, Gypsy Mary, would come by the house in spring, her hair half covering her face and a dirty black skirt on, her filthy feet bare. She'd knock and call out—"Don't eat tomatoes and beware of fungus!" And Sarah would say, "Aw, Hon, how about a cup of tea? My Stars! You're probably right. You folks know so much about those things." But Gypsy Mary wouldn't stay long. She'd drift through the house with her head bent low, swinging, and leave quickly with just a cracker, or a peach from our tree. Enid would laugh, showing her fangs.

"Oh, Sarah, for heaven's sake! You don't mean you still let that crazy thing in the house? She only knocks to see if anybody's there. She'd rob you blind if you weren't home!"

But Sarah trumped her with, "Oh, Hon, Law, I think she robbed me while I *was* there."

Jack Russell was hit by the crash too and moved his family to a smaller place, sold his big house and let his chauffeur go. Enid had left him and moved to our house with Beas for a while before that, when we still lived in town at Grandfather's house.

That was when Enid began to sell her treasures. If she made an especially good sale to Swan, she'd order a big spread from Schwartzkopf's Gourmet Grocery sent to our place and we'd all make ourselves marvelously sick on shrimp and smoked oysters and double cream cheese, artichoke hearts and stuffed olives, about three times a year.

But things grew shiftier every few months. We sold the old McCleod house where I was born and had lived those eleven years. Sarah and Enid divided the inheritance, of course, and then we had to begin a different life. Old Pom couldn't be expected to prop everybody up forever. But he managed to keep the Stutz and the Pierce Arrow too, so the Stutz—more a work of art, being pigskin inside and out, than a car—wouldn't wear out. And he kept his house and even Pearl West who cooked and did up for him. He kept some hold on his oil business, too, and a good temper the whole time. He and Abe Dietler celebrated everything—Repeal and Joe Louis kayoing everybody who came near him; NRA and WPA and FDR, our hockey team, win or lose. Pom was dandy and tidy. He always hummed and sang a little when he drove his Stutz around town—

> *My old flame*
> *I can't even think of her name . . .*

and then he would chuckle. Women fell in love with him but he had, as evaluated by Iantha, too much class for most of the local women. No woman would ever be to him what Lou had been. Pom wrote articles for the newspaper about world affairs which were answered by letters of protest from what he called the Local Ostrich Society.

So, suddenly we were maneuvered out there to the lease and that little shack of the Willetts'. The shock to me took a long time wearing away. It was as if that miserable night with the Willetts had been an omen. But why for me and not for Beas? And even with all our scrubbing, painting and bleaching, all the sanding and waxing, even years later, if I lay with my face close to that wall where those sad little snot-and-piss Willetts had once slept, I could detect their sorrowful presence. They were in the material of my very walls and I lived on top of their ruin.

We lived on Sarah's small inheritance and the clients. The decline set in inexorably—hand-me-down clothes from the Abernathys, mostly Rose's middy blouses and blue serge pleated skirts, now out of date, that she had worn at private school. I admired them and Rose, who had always smelled of mimosa and fresh air, just the opposite of old rank Iantha. But I stuck to my own old rags as long as possible. Sarah, gently and seemingly without care, went to seed and tatters.

We had a drastic cut in meat; the lights were turned off from time to time, and the phone too was cut off for a week at a time until Pom came blasting out in the Stutz to find out why. All those whispered discussions of which I grasped, customarily, the gist— that was always my talent, the gist.

"You know you needn't let this happen, Sarah," he'd say to her. "Good God! Your bill can't be more than three or four dollars a month!"

And her fond, "Well, Hon, don't fret. We didn't miss it. I was fixin to take care of it when Mabel made me a little payment she owes."

"You mean you don't have *five dollars*?"

"Well, they don't pay in cash anymore, Hon, you know that.

It's a little more like a trade. Mabel's one of the few . . ."

"But you've got *something* left of your inheritance, don't you?"

And she would bat her eyes and smile apologetically at him. Oh, I could have kicked Pom at those times! I wanted to hurl myself between them to protect her. But I was as feeble about that as about everything else.

Pom never got the clear truth about our state. Penniless to him meant that you couldn't get down to the bank yesterday. We'd never even used a bank. Sarah asked me when I was twelve where I thought we ought to keep our cash when we had any and I said in the ice bag, a gift we never used, payment for somebody's hour of consolation. It was still kept there when I was nineteen—our miserable stash.

Pom told me when I was about fifteen that he intended to will me the lease. I used to lie in the woods on my back dreaming of a huge garden I would plant there from which I would feed the poor, knowing them to be strangely different from myself who merely lacked enough of the right food from time to time, and lacked that famous other nourishment, hard cash.

I kept putting off work.

Eric's eighteen days were washing away. Indian summer burned across the lease in the oaks and maples, in the flaming sumac. The still dry chilly nights were whitened by that great low moon. It all seemed to say *This is everything there is* by that serene silence against which there was no argument. I asked Eric to walk and be quiet with me at least once and he did that, holding my hand, curious and moved maybe that I wanted a mere walk.

"Something is happening to the whole world," I said, knowing I did not mean what he meant by his answering yes.

"There's a snag in everything," I went on. "I mean, the very best most marvelous things are . . . flawed, I think. Every time." Why was I whining so?

Eric thought I meant that his leaving flawed our having found each other, but I didn't. I meant something I could not explain. I felt as if each separate value of the life I knew would soon fuse in my mind and reveal itself as part of a new whole. And that all of it would be flawed by timing, having happened too soon or too late. But he only believed I was falling in love with him. He got a crazy cock-eared look on his face and lowered his eyes like a girl for a moment.

"I can't wait any longer to get a job," I said, implying that he had detained me. "I made an appointment with Di Finlayson's boss for Thursday."

"What're you gonna do out at that place?"

"Drive a truck or something."

"You're crazy. Why don't you get a real job?"

"Such as what?"

He shrugged. "Oh, I don't know. Something in one of these oil offices. Can't Mr. Russell get you something?"

"He would, but I don't want to be in an office. I hate all that stuff. You're just somebody's flunky."

"Driving a truck isn't somebody's flunky?"

"No."

He laughed and looked at me. "Will you write to me?"

"Yes," I said. "If you will."

"I will. Say, that reminds me, when's Beas going? Is that kid really going in?"

"That's what he says. He's waiting for orders now."

"Shit! He's all mixed up. I think I'm gonna talk to him."

I laughed. "You're one of the reasons he's doing it in the first place."

"Yeah? How's that?"

I told him how Beas had conjured his name so often and he shook his head. "I'm gonna talk to him. Maybe I can influence him."

"That'd be swell. But he seems pretty bent on it already."

"Jeez, the first thing I knew he had his hair all cut off. You know, I bet that kid's never had a woman. I think I better have a talk with him."

I bristled. "Oh, he can take care of himself."

He looked at me amazed, "Are you kidding? He's nothing but a baby. I can't believe his grandfather hasn't stopped him by this time."

We argued it a little. I grew restless and irritable. I wanted all hands off Beas. And then he picked me up suddenly and rushed through the falling leaves to a spot under some low trees and laid me on the ground.

"I've only got a coupla weeks," he said. And for the first time I gave in to him without wanting to.

Their move happened too fast, as if they wanted no time to consider it. Sarah got up to help settle them and wore herself out again. Ruby and I whitewashed the basement walls for Beas, two rooms—one for his lab which he left packed in crates, and one for his bed and chest, his map and his pictures of great scientists all framed in narrow black wood, a gift from Pom.

Enid moved into the sun-room, which meant that Iantha now had to start rocking in the parlor, a room she despised for its heavy conglomerations of furniture, castoffs from someone's grandmother's house—mohair, oak, heavy rammed-in stuff that we had lived with so long we hardly saw its mothy and dolorous quality anymore. Enid seemed always to be pacing the floor, heating water for coffee, clicking her cigarette holder between her teeth. At night the house was haunted by the sound of her radio police calls. Sarah watched her with tender pain. And it was good to have Iantha around so much because in her envious way she occupied Enid. I nipped in and out feeling less guilt toward Sarah now that we had a big household. I gave them just enough of a look at my face to receive their dubious glances. Enid and Iantha had no doubt warned Sarah to keep an eye on me. I heard her assuring them with the craziest conviction that I was good, wise, clever and honest and would never let myself do wrong or get into trouble. That, I told myself one midnight, was why I wouldn't get pregnant —because Sarah wouldn't believe it.

Iantha had recently joined a group of Delirian women who were studying metaphysics with Serene Shandorf, a widow who in former times had given elocution lessons. She was said to be well educated in mysticism, metaphysics, parapsychology, astrology and a lot else. She always wore black silk, paisley headbands, bright glass rings, a bit of fringe here and there; and she chewed Sen-Sen. Enid laughed mercilessly at the mere mention of her. Her mother, after all, had been a seamstress and a pearl stringer. Sarah said she thought nothing could be nicer than a pearl stringer. And Enid shook her head in disgust.

Metaphysics, Iantha explained, was all about higher and lower animals and dimensions and all that. "It's not exactly science," she said; "it's more like spiritual science."

We were all in the parlor waiting for supper.

"What's spiritual science?" Enid asked her. "Isn't that just another name for religion?"

I cleared my throat and felt a pounding in my chest from expectation. I had looked up the word, memorized the definition, and was waiting for my moment, leafing through one of Enid's *Town and Country* magazines—long limousines and well-dressed people at country estates flipped by, and then at the back of the magazine, antiques, which looked curiously static and unreal. Back up front to cars—Hispano-Suiza, Rolls . . . I waited.

"Sometimes," Iantha was saying, "I write down one sentence from the whole lecture and think about it for *days*. It's deep stuff, *terribly* deep."

Enid swung her crossed leg and tapped on the arm of the chair with her cigarette holder. She had wound her braids around her head like a Dutchwoman but it only made her look more like a madonna. "But what's it *about*? What *kind* of a sentence?" She seemed to know but only to want to frustrate Iantha.

Pom paced the floor near the hallway and fiddled with the radio dials, waiting for the news.

"Well, for instance," Iantha plugged along, " 'Matter is a form of thinking.' Just think of that for a minute! *Matter is a form of thinking.* I wrote it on a card and taped it to the bathroom mirror. I say it over and over every day but . . ."

"Uspenskii," said Pom with a soft disdain.

"That's right! Uspenskii. *Tertium Organum.*"

Enid sighed. Sarah's chuckles fell like a lace mantle over the room. She was mending an apron. Pom lighted a cigar and turned on the radio but got only the last of "Orphan Annie." He glared at Iantha's back as if he might grab her in a minute and hold her head under some final water, or maybe just lift her and toss her out the window. It was hard to believe that Pom had a penis and had once done it to women.

I heard the pause and took my moment. "Metaphysics," I recited, "is the branch of philosophy that investigates the nature of first principles and the problems of ultimate reality." I let out a gasp.

Sarah turned her head, laughing. "Why, Hon, I didn't know you knew a thing about all that. My Stars!" And laughed as if I'd revealed the Grand Canyon as a mirage.

All eyebrows were up. Pom smiled. "She's right. But Uspenskii begins with Gurdjieff's idea that the human being uses only a very minimal part of his native forces. He defined matter as incorrectly perceived reality, by the way."

"That's it! Incorrectly perceived reality! Isn't that *fabulous!*" screamed Iantha. Pom threw his hands in the air and turned up the radio to blaring.

"Well," Enid said loudly, "it all sounds perfectly ridiculous to me."

I winked at a picture of the Duke of Windsor while Sarah laughed on and Ruby dropped a pan in the kitchen. Beas was as absent as peace. The news reporter said,

German Propaganda Minister Joseph Goebbels published this week a charter of anti-Semitism which proclaims:

"Every Jew is the sworn enemy of the German people."

And Sarah said, Well, My Stars, what did the Germans expect?

Enid rolled her thick brown eyes to the ceiling. I could have gouged them out.

Beas came in suddenly and sat by his mother on the couch, and Pom turned down the volume, hovering close to it while we talked.

"Serene says none of that is news really," said Iantha. "It's all just a sign of what's happening in men's souls. It's like when the animals see the sun coming up and they think it's something new. They can't remember that it came up every other day, that it's the same sun coming up."

"Huh!" said Beas. "That's interesting. I bet it's true even if Mrs. Shandorf did say it."

After the news Pom said it was an historical inevitability that fascism and communism should face each other over some piece of terrain in some mud somewhere in this century. German youth were still idealistic enough to die by the thousands in the Russian winter, he supposed. We would see. He felt the Russians would hold them finally, scorching the earth and God knows what else. They knew how to dig into their own country's gut and hang on. "That's it, you see, fighting on one's own land in an invasion. It takes a vast peasant population to do it on that reduced level. Defending a city is not defending one's own land. Let them come to Washington or New York. We'd run like rats. But get them onto the plains and we could hold them forever. Did you see that *March of Time* last week?" He asked it of all and none of us and it hit me how feeble we all were, descending in virtue and consciousness downward from Beas, I supposed. Defending Deliria was impossible to imagine but I supposed I would do it if it came down to that.

"I bet nobody here even knows what fascism really is," said Beas.

There was a dead silence. I thought I knew but wouldn't say because I never had. "Pure wickedness and a desire to lord it over others," said Iantha apologetically with a musical lilt of questioning at the end. Pom cleared his throat. The Atlantic Charter, he said, was a ritual gesture of reaffirmation of the rights of man, freedom of speech and all that. He hit no particular pay dirt there since we hardly knew of the Atlantic Charter. We sighed and leaned back. Something about the way he said these things, clear and emphatic, socked them to my brain and I didn't forget them. It tended to tie up my loosely housed random meaningless bits of knowledge which were like the doodads of this very dwelling, without a central theme, a vision. Leavings—that's what I owned and knew.

He talked about the conditions that fostered the growth of fascism. Deprivation, humiliation. I thought of the Willetts.

My mind wandered. Poverty was not as base as they were pretending.

Iantha said maybe the draft would keep the niggers from becoming Communists and rebelling.

Sarah said that we should give all the people, especially the colored folks, money now so that they wouldn't have to take all the time and trouble of rebellion, and Pom said that only a saint like her could be counted on to make such a recommendation. And Iantha said didn't he like the way Roosevelt (whom she hated because he was probably a Jew and had a mistress and was something of a pinko anyway)—didn't Pom like the way FDR was giving important posts to women. And Pom, in order to point up her usual faulty thinking, said that important posts were Secretary of State, Attorney General and so on and none of those were women that he knew of.

But about the poor, Sarah said, "Law, Hon, anything's better than starvation. You can't blame hungry people for following a reassuring kind of a leader, Hon."

Blame was not the point. Observe, he commanded us. Observe. Beas licked his chops. We nodded and swallowed—except for Enid—his gospel.

"I've always felt there was something wrong in believing that political problems could be solved," Enid said. "I don't think you can do much about history and cultures and all. Some people don't think slavery and cruelty are worth enduring just for food." Meaning that murder was a better answer?

"Law, Hon," Sarah said, "most people can't stand freedom."

What, I wanted to scream, are we *talking about*?

Pom said there was a metaphysical economics involved in the relations of people to their leaders and Iantha's eyes seemed to roll back in her head as if he'd thrown her on the ground and put his firecracker in her. Pom's firecracker was probably burnt out, however. I thought of all of their sex and came up with zero.

Sarah, giddy with the sense of our all being together and having a subject that obliterated Iantha's gossip and her bickering with Enid, laughed a little and got up to bring in our coffee.

★

The next day Enid was drunk all day. She got up swacked to meet Swan at the door but didn't let him stay. He hung at the door and she paid him. God! Our first bootlegged delivery! It infuriated me but I didn't tell Sarah, who was with a client. I watched them from the back of the hall. Enid's face was swollen and her eyes glassy, pinched, thickened it seemed but never bloodshot. I'd never seen her whites stained with the faintest red. You could smell her whole world of winy breath and perfume, the wisteria sachets that filled her lingerie drawers. Her special cold cream. She didn't like fresh air. Her cigarettes, too, clogged that air, and when she opened her door these remnants hung in the parlor for a long time. Her walk was wide-stepped for balance, her hand always out, her breathing was short and quick like that of a person concentrating. I began to learn the mechanics of the drunk body in a new way. My beer drunkenness had always been a quick falling to drowsy comfort, and then a short recovery the next day, stuffy head, a slowness in the limbs, but all gone by noon. Hers was never begun, never ended, had no clear-cut cycle. Her mouth, which had a curved innocence like Sarah's, only wider, hung at one corner when she was drunk. Her talk was dry-mouthed, sticky. She thirsted and always had coffee or carbonated water in her hand.

Beas, who usually did not see her at the peak of it, being away all day, saw her chastened phases and then those final discoveries of mine, the building agitation, the roving-eyed distracted look which was, even so, still in a hangover state, but looking now to renewal, and then that enlivened eager burning look of having had the first drink of the day, the efficiency which resembled that of a child gratefully punished and blessed, promising by silent deeds to be good from now on, from now on. . . . There was that queer quality about her at those times, usually at about eleven in the morning, of good-natured exaggerated intention. No depression.

Not much sarcasm. But even so, a hint of agitation which would build. A greedy monster in her was rather deftly managed. Until she moved in with us, it occurred to me, she had had no one to deal with at eleven in the morning. Her life was changing, too. I said no clear-cut cycle, except that one mood or condition might dominate the others like this for an hour or so. But I did not put any of this in the Biography. I restrained myself.

★

We settled into our routines together. Ruby resigned herself to Enid and even began to serve her in special little ways. A subtle understanding grew between them. I was going to have to stop prophesying, I could see that. Nobody was predictable anymore.

Enid watched me in a quiet conjecturing way, enough to alert me. I was always hiding now—my ideas, my moods, even my body, and not from Sarah, who had long ago accepted me without argument, but from Enid.

Beasley

He couldn't believe it. Eric grinned. "Here. Get in." He reached across and opened the door and Beas slid into the musty front seat shyly. He arched himself against the corner staring at Eric's profile.

"What're you doing in this part of town?"

They pulled away from the curb. "I came to get you, Man. Gee, they keep you a long time in that place. Whadda you do in there, anyway?"

Beas thought his head would fly off. "You came by to get *me*?"

"Yeah. Yeah. I wanta talk to you. Whadda you do in there?"

"I work in the serum test lab right now. We're inoculating some rabbits and stuff. But that's not the main lab. That's petroleum."

"You got time for a beer?"

Beas shrugged. "I guess so. It takes me so long to get out to the lease that I'm always late anyway. They save my supper. If I take the bus, I mean. Sometimes Katie comes for me."

"I'll drive you home," Eric offered. "I wanta see that dame for a minute anyway."

Beas had never seen the Creole at such an early hour nor had he ever sat at the bar there. It seemed like another place, duller, more serious, and menacingly half empty. Without Nina Brosky and her crowd it was hardly recognizable. He took the foaming glass up with a certain flourish of which he was aware all at once, knowing that Eric was watching him. The bartender didn't question him, thanks to his hair, he reasoned.

Eric ran his long swift tongue over his lip and laughed softly, kiddingly at Beas. He knuckled him lightly on the thigh.

"I hear you went down and offered your ass up to the Army."

Beas nodded. So that was it. Katie or someone had put Eric up to it. "That's right. I'm waiting to be called."

"How're they gonna take you under eighteen?"

Beas gave him a patient look, feeling shaken but only deeply, not where it showed. "I've got a birthday in a week."

"You going for officer's training?"

"I don't think so. Regular Army is good enough for me. I went to military school so I know something about it."

Eric nodded, gulping beer and making a loud studied belch that drew Beasley's jaws into a smile. Ah! He liked that sound and the presence of men-only. They drank. He ordered another beer.

"What's the matter?" he ventured. "You wanta talk me into joining the Navy instead?"

Eric looked at him and chuckled. "Oh no! Hoooo no! Nothin doin. I wouldn't talk anybody with a chance to stay out into enlisting. It's plain stupid."

Beas flushed and batted his eyes. Some people entered and he shrank from their passing at his back as if they might strike him. Eric knuckled him again.

"No offense meant. You've got your reasons, I'm sure. It's a man's own decision."

"That's what I told Katie."

"She against your going?"

Beas eyed him carefully. "Didn't she tell you?"

"Nope. Never said a word. I got it from some of the fellows."

Feeling his beer more pleasantly now, in the bellyish way that always satisfied him deeply, Beasley nodded, leaning on the bar, slowly turning the glass, man-to-man easy. "Most people don't understand it, especially women."

"Listen, Kid," Eric said all at once, close to his side. "I wanta tell you a couple things. One—ask a few questions. Not from me—" He put a hand on his chest and leaned back miming guiltlessness. "Get it from one of these guys who's been in a few months. Ask questions. About basic training to begin with. That already kills a few men and breaks a few more and just generally tears everybody up." He drank his remaining beer and went on. "That's number one." Beas nodded. "Two—" Eric laid a bony index finger on his arm. "Get a lot of screws in before you go. That's all, Buddy. Just screw till you're blind, Kid. Believe me."

He turned back to his beer as if two warnings were to be all. Beas sat swollen with terror. So that was what Eric was doing with Katie, getting a lot of screws in! He choked and coughed. He wanted to say it aloud but the presence of Katie in the idea stopped him. Screwing till he was blind, that's what he was doing all right. But it hit him hard even so, Katie or not; it thrilled him violently as if he himself had been screwed or something. Couldn't decide what that awful gutty good and bad feeling was. He coughed again and wiped his eyes slowly with the back of his hand. God! What was happening to him? He ordered another beer by knocking gently with the empty glass on the bar as all the fellows did.

"Yeah," he faltered, "I know what you mean."

"That's the ticket, Beas," Eric said.

Beas began to nod wisely. Eric drank, brooding, waiting. Beas downed the third one in quick gulps, silently. Suddenly a bird came in, fluttering around the ceiling over the bar, dashing itself against the mirror, going into a desperate swoop down in the shadows out of sight and then fluttering up and out again into the light. Beas felt it like thunder through his chest. "Well," he chirped much too loudly, his voice cracking the way it used to. "I don't know any . . . any . . . women I can get hold of . . . right now I mean."

Eric turned to him, moving in close. His manly beery breath reminded Beas of his dead father who sometimes had talked to him up close like this, connivingly. But his father had never really wanted to help him in any particular way, he hadn't really wanted him around. He saw that now, surprised. No, his dad had always had some strange secret business deal to work on someone, some trick against his mother. He smelled Eric's clean shirt, his cigarettes. His father's Old Golds! His hundreds of shirts hanging in a row, ironed by some colored woman. His socks with the fancy clocks up the sides! He ought to start smoking maybe. But it wasn't interesting, smoking. He felt like crying all at once. Gee! He never *cried*! What was it?

"That's what I wanted to ask you about," Eric said softly.

"Huh? What?"

"Women. You haven't got much time to waste. What if they called you this week? How much time could you spend with a woman? You given notice at the lab?"

"I'm giving it tomorrow," Beas said dutifully. Oh hell, he might as well, he thought, just give in and let Eric take care of his problems for him. Eric would find out soon enough about his being a virgin. "Well, it's pretty hard to find one, I'll tell you," he apologized. "Too many girls don't wanta do it." He poured down a huge swamping swallow of beer and belched in spite of himself.

"You need one who knows what she's doing, Beas; for the first time anyway. Not some dumb girl who's afraid to get pregnant."

Beasley's head began to hum. Maybe all that trouble with his flaming hards was going to be taken care of. He looked at Eric with smeared focus, knocking his glass again for a fill-up. He shook his head and smiled a little, resigned and affectionate. "I've just never been able to find one. I've really tried."

Eric laughed and gave him a shove. "Shit! Why didn't you tell me, Kid? I coulda had you fixed up six months ago. I'll tell you what, you call home and tell em you're out for the evening. We'll get a hamburger at Piggie's and then I'll take you around. You know? We'll find someone."

Some colored lady, maybe, he thought. Her bright pink crotch. Brad Finch had said it.

"You remember Brad Finch?"

Eric snorted. "Sure. That shithead! Talk about a screwer! He couldn't stop. He'd do it to a dog!"

Beas smiled. He hadn't heard that kind of talk since Foxe Hills.
In the showers. Giggling in bed at night. Then he laughed suddenly. "I used to be a member of the PYP Club," he told Eric
jovially. "Pound Your Pecker! I got it off first more times than
anyone in school since nineteen twenty-four. I set a record."

Eric laughed loudly and said shit.

"Brad told me a lot," said Beas. "He liked colored women."

Eric shrugged. "You gotta be careful. I don't even go to the
Willows after dark anymore. But I know a couple of maids over
on the south side."

Beas finished his fourth beer with a hard rising and fainting in
his lap like a struggling animal hoping to leap free of its cage,
wearing itself out. He wanted to ask something about Katie, hoping Eric would confess his using her to get in all the screws
possible. God! His head was whirling. He'd never been this drunk
on four beers before.

"I'm not eighteen, it's true," he said in a washy way to Eric,
"but I've seen a lot."

Eric poked him gently with an elbow. "I know, Kid. You need
a break. Come on."

★

In the car after Piggie's Eric gave him a drink from a whiskey
bottle. It put a hot jolt in his chest. "That's good whiskey," Eric
said. "My old man brings back a few cases every time we go up
to St. Louis."

Beas nodded, swilling it down. He thought, I don't want her to
be someone we all know. I don't want her to be colored either,
because of Ruby.

"I'm not particularly interested in colored," he said loudly.

Eric laughed. "Shoot! You kill me, Beas. You're nuts! What the
hell are you doin goin into the *Army*, for chrissake?" He careened
around the loop at the end of Boulder Terrace and parked halfway
down the other side, under a big tree away from the street light.
"I want you to tell me the truth now, Man. What's this Army crap
all about?" He turned off the ignition and leaned back into the
seat.

"What're we doing?" Beas asked. He was feeling drunker.

"We're talking a minute before we go get Cynthia."

"Cynthia *Gillespie*?"

Eric grinned at him in the dark. "That's right, Pal. She's waiting
for us."

"You call her from Piggie's?"

"Yep. She's a good kid. And does she love it! Wowee!" He
howled softly with his head back.

Beas snickered. "Jesus Christ! I've been wanting to get together
with her my whole entire *life*. God! Cynthia Gillespie!"

Eric was laughing hard now. Beas felt crazy.

"Okay. I'm enlisting," he said boldly, "because they'll get me
anyway. My grandfather's a dreamer to think he can keep me out.
I know what I'm doing and I'm gonna do it. I . . ." He faltered

against Eric's silent gaze. This wasn't it but wasn't it enough? He didn't know all of the why's of it. He had *felt* it out and knew he had to do it. That seemed like enough. But how to make it clear? And he was reeling a little now, urgent but careless.

"I thought you were working for Dietler's," Eric said. "That's essential industry. They wouldn't take you out of that if Dietler's said they needed you."

He shrugged, weary of it. "Well, why'd *you* go in?"

Eric laughed. "I told you, Man, I'm an opportunist! Ha! I'm gonna get the best deal I can outa the service before I get my ass shot off in some war. I'm gonna be an officer and give a few orders and stay off the deck if I can. And anyway, Beas . . . I've got a lotta respect for the Navy. It's—"

Beas stopped him. "But see, that's just it. I know they're gonna get me too. It's all so . . . big and everything. And anyway . . ." His throat seemed to close suddenly. He swallowed.

"Yeah, what?"

"Well, see . . . I think a person ought to . . . well, you know . . . go a few places and get away from—from the same old town and all. If they're gonna send you all over anyway. You might as well go and . . ."

Eric chuckled softly and snapped an arm across his chest. "Yeah, I know, I know. You wanta live a little and get you some big man buddies and all that. I know. Maybe you're right. But, if I was a specialist like you, Beas, I'd get into some kind of noncombatant work. I mean it. Enlist and make them put you in pharmacy or something. Be a medic. Don't get yourself shot up. It's nuts."

Beas sighed as if he were a spy and had passed a guard at a frontier. "Yeah," he said more easily now. "Katie's been saying the same thing over and over."

"Katie? What the hell's she know about it? She's a woman."

Beas lowered his head. He didn't want her name used meanly, no, nor used at all for that matter. "I grew up with her, see. I know her pretty well and we talk about a lotta stuff. She's really more like my sister, see." He stared across at Eric in the dim light and clamped his jaw. No monkey business about Katie. No insults.

"You don't have to worry about Katie," Eric said softly. "She's okay. She's a swell kid." He waited and Beas waited. "And she's nice," he said. Beas waited for more. Finally Eric looked him in the face. "I'm not playin around with her, Beas. She's my girl now. Okay?"

Beas nodded. "Okay." What the hell were they talking about?

"Well, what're we gonna do?"

Eric paused, staring at him. "You know—I thought you were just a kid. You know? With nothin on your mind but school and stuff." He whacked Beas across the chest again, seemingly drunk. "But you're okay, Beas. You're a good guy. I just wish to shit you wouldn't go get your head knocked off in the goddamn Army. You're too smart for it. We're gonna go to war, Man. You know what that means? It's the purpose of the enemy to shoot your balls off. Forget about all these tanks and airplanes. He's after your own balls and you gotta keep outa his way."

Beas softened. His groin lay still. Shoot! He had been fired up. He nodded, trying to take Eric seriously. He knew all that. "Okay," he said. "Okay."

Eric grinned. "Still feel like laying Cynthia?"

He said he did but he didn't.

★

They took her to Franklin Park. Eric had blankets. Beasley's hands shook the whole way with her sitting there in the front seat between them smelling like violets and hanging loose there inside her sweater, jiggling, and her hard rounding leg pressing his lightly. She giggled with Eric and smoked with him, marking her cigarette with bright red lipstick that in the dark looked black, and later offered them Doublemint and cracked it loudly herself. They turned on the car radio and sang "The Music Goes Round and Round." Her voice was like talking but he liked it.

They put down the blankets up by the fountain at the end of the long rose garden where Eric said the cops never came and couldn't see from the road anyway. Eric danced her around a little, laughing, falling into flower beds. He whipped her sweater up over her head and she let him. Beas stood by chuckling. Eric got her naked somehow and told her to do a little dance for Beas. He gave her a sip of whiskey. Beas felt ashamed before God. But he was thankful because she was going to let him put it in her after all this time, months that seemed like years, of wanting to so much. It was chilly but bright and much of the park still green. Cynthia's tits bounced. He began to go blind and a little crazy. The breezes passed across his face the heavy scents of autumn ground and of her violets, her warm soapy female body with flickers of other damp hot secret scents. Eric took off his own clothes and camped around with her. Then he fell down on the blankets with her and said Beas oughta watch, to get the idea. Don't be a prude about it, he said.

"We're doin it first so you'll get the idea," he said.

And Cynthia laughed as if she were being gouged in the ribs. "He'll get the idea all right. Silly! Oooo! Oh!" She giggled helplessly as Eric began to bite her. Beas tripped over a tree root and half fell down. He couldn't see. "Wait a little, Beas," Eric said.

Beas batted his eyes. "Yeah. Yeah. Okay." But he couldn't see. He stood there like a dog. He heard it as if it were coming to him through sleep.

Finally Eric fell on his back laughing, saying Oh Man, this girl is a lot of fun. Shit, he said, he never knew anybody who liked it as much as this girl did. Beas laughed softly, standing close over them now. Cynthia's entire seemingly swollen white body was sprawled under his gaze on the blanket. He fixed an eye on the dark V of hair that hid her crotch, her fattish legs and splayed-out feet. It all looked familiar but shocking. He sniffed. He loved the two of them. All that fast fun! He wished he could fold himself down into them in some way. He lowered himself tentatively on the edge of the blanket. Cynthia put out a hand to him.

"Come on down, Beasley" she said liltingly, tiredly sweet. Eric lay flayed out on his back. Cynthia pulled at Beas and he stretched out next to her on his side. She looked into what he felt must be his disintegrating face. He felt he had poured entirely out of himself toward them. "Whyn't ya take off your things and lay down here with us." She said it like someone's mother at nap time.

It didn't make sense but he started to take off his clothes, with her help. He was completely insane by this time and vaguely aware of a chuckling babbling sound that was coming out of his mouth; no feeling in his body below the waist. Cynthia's boobs bobbed near him and nearly knocked him out. But he loved her so much he could only pretend he didn't notice. He could have bitten into her cakey flesh with soft joy the way you bit into those slightly sweet muffins Ruby made.

"It's all fun, Beas," Eric said in a sloppy whisper. "Get the ticket?"

"Yeah, yeah," he whispered, pulling off his trousers.

And then Cynthia Gillespie touched his fainted hard and said, "Gee Whiz! What happened, Sugar?"

And he gasped, felt of himself, took the shorts off remembering something long ago with Katie, something about wet pants, and wiped himself. He lay down then pulling the edge of the blanket over him. They were laughing but he didn't mind.

"Plenty more where that comes from," Eric was saying. "Give him a little time. He just got carried away there, didn't you old man?"

"Yeah, yeah," he said, dazzled. What in hell was he doing? He was drunk and having the most amazing dream. But Cynthia's now sweaty violet smell, dense and lovable next to him, seemed intensely real. She began to pat him with her soft plump hand and he lay utterly collapsed on his back next to her. He doubted that he could do it with someone else around, Eric or anybody. But at least he had gotten this far. She was feeling him and he let her. After a short while he went to sleep. He couldn't help it, he just turned toward her and moved into her side, curled, hidden.

When he woke up he was cold. Cynthia was kissing his mouth with big soft fruity-tasting lips, almost drowning him. He had a big dangerous hard on and she was wagging it around! He looked around quickly. No Eric. He heard someone crashing around in the woods and then the sound of peeing on dry leaves. He pushed Cynthia away and rose up dutifully, looming over her, stiffening his whole body in a show of strength, pushing her onto her back. He poked patiently at her, feeling like a dog, and then her hand drove him deep into her. She made a little sound. Big bolts of easy lightning began to shake and blind him. He let out a raw howl in an unrecognizable voice, as if some other big terrible person lived in him and wanted out.

★

He kept his arm around her in the car and she let him, smoking and sighing. She was bigger than he was but he had always imagined it that way. When they let her out, he thanked her and she laughed a little and said, "Aw, Beasley, you're cute." He took her up to the door while Eric waited. He slept all the way out to the lease so he wouldn't have to talk. The depth of his gratitude to her stunned him. He felt as if he had hold of her still. He was swarming inside as if with hives of drowsy bees. Eric was quiet.

"I like her a lot," Beas said finally.

"She's a good kid."

"Why doesn't she have babies, with all that sex and all?"

"She's got a diaphragm," said Eric. He turned into the lease land and stopped. He turned out the car lights. "It's a rubber thing they put inside. Or get yourself some rubbers, Beas. In fact . . ." He opened the glove compartment and took out a small tin box which he slammed into Beasley's hands. "Here. Happy birthday. Sheiks. Use em when you aren't sure."

"Thanks." He pocketed them, having heard of them from Brad but never seen them. He didn't like to think of all that in Cynthia's case. It mattered not a penny to him that every fellow in town had probably done that to her since she got out of high school three years before, or maybe while she was still in. She was at least twenty-one. Twenty-one! He came to. It was late.

"It's too late to see Katie now," he whispered. "You'll wake everybody up."

Eric shoved him a little, playfully, as they went inside the back gate. "What're you talking about, Man?" he whispered loudly. "That's my girl in there. I wanta see her. She'll wake up for me. She'll come out."

He stood stiffly looking up at Eric. Suddenly he wanted to hit him. "No. It's not right."

Eric put out a hand and he hit out at it wildly, knocking it away. Eric said "What the . . . ?" and Beasley turned away. He felt shame that the two of them stood there sticky with sex about to see Katie and maybe Aunt Sarah and his mother. He had thrown away his shorts in the rose garden. He was messy and naked inside his rough cord pants. The night was calmly cold and silent now. But then suddenly he felt sorry about everything.

"You oughtn't to do that to her. It's a dirty trick," he said defeatedly. He knew Eric would do what he wanted, with Katie, with Cynthia, with himself even.

"Aw, Beas, Man—what's eatin you?"

"If you don't tell her what you did, I will. I mean it." His voice quaked. He turned away and went inside the kitchen door and down the basement steps, leaving Eric standing in the yard. He knew he'd wake Katie and get her out there. He was a wizard, Eric. With women anyway.

It was late October. Beas had not yet been called. He paced the basement rooms, unpacked a few chemicals, doodled around in the evenings. He was to graduate from high school in January but he hardly went anymore. It seemed like a dream. He spent most of his days at the lab. He was now forever talking of the world, civilization and war, whereas Pom talked less and less about it. They often went out for man-to-man dinners at the country club. And Beas seemed content otherwise to read in the evenings unless one of his favorite programs came on the radio. He pretended hardly to notice that I spent most of my time with Eric. He had suddenly begun to make secret phone calls, hiding in the hall closet for twenty minutes at a time. He asked me finally to show him again how to drive the electric. He borrowed it one day to take to school and didn't come back till ten P.M. But after that he never asked for it again. Pom, I learned, had decided to try to stop Beas's enlistment but Abe Dietler had talked him out of it.

Evenings being now full of family, crowded rooms, our expanded babble, gossip and metaphysics—it all pleased and excited Sarah. She was like some dazzled symphony conductor, plugging certain themes, repressing others, with an Aw Hon, a My Stars, a chuckle. It was her court by all our agreement. She gave her fondness to Enid by way of chuckles and patience. Sometimes she patted Enid's arm in that now-we're-not-a-gonna-worry way and I cringed. "But Enid," I wrote in the Biography, "in her suspicious reluctant fashion, began to flourish under it, putting out, if not blossoms, at least little buds." What if she got up? What if she never took another drop? What if she got something to do?

★

I was at Eric's house, in his bed. Actually in a bed! The luxury made us hysterical. His parents would be at the cemetery the whole afternoon, he said.

"We oughta be able to do it at least a dozen more times," he said.

I laughed. He bit my neck. His hard everlastingly famished fingers searched me with impudence. He ought to be a miner or a dentist, I thought. He was not just curious, he was nosy, but only about bodies and sex. His lips were cool but looked like those of a cherry-pop drinker. We had been at it every night for a week and some afternoons. I was sure everybody at home knew by this time. I looked like an alley cat. Enid would stare at me and let loose a faint smile, looking away. Ruby asked me why I couldn't take off that ball and chain around my neck long enough to wash off the smudge, and Sarah said Hon, when she was feeling better I ought to invite my young man to supper. But I made the excuses of a good spy.

I turned over against Eric and wrapped myself around him suddenly, wanting to throw away all doubt about everything. I got a sudden sense of abandon and a long stretched-out pleasant existence, easy and full of riches.

"I hate for you to go," I said, risking a lot. "Just when we're . . ."

"Oh, Kid! Shit, I never used to give a damn about anybody, you know that?" He swallowed. "I wouldn't want to hurt you or anything."

"You haven't."

He lifted his head off the pillow, craning at me. "How do you know I won't?"

"Well . . . I don't. But I can take care of myself."

He flopped back down, sighing. I pulled away and looked at our bellies, which glistened with sweat. A few tiny fine black curls lay on mine, torn from him. His firecracker was purple.

"It looks like it's choking to death," I said, feeling hysterical.

He lifted it, looked and let it drop. "Pooped," he said. "Let's rest a minute." He exhaled sublimely and lay on his back as if he had been thrown there. "Let's don't talk. Ha! You always did talk in the middle of it. Remember the first time?"

I laid a hand over his mouth and he laughed, jackal jaws, and bit the palm of it. I mugged him with it hard. He laughed more but turned his head down and shut his eyes. He shook the arm that lay under my neck. What if we lived in a house of our own, and had all this naked time together, all we could use? He would work. I would cook and iron. Well . . . no . . . no . . . maybe we'd both work and have a maid. Ruby. No . . . Maybe . . . Oh, forget it. I couldn't get a clear picture. I lay there feeling huge and faintly deranged. I wanted to look around his house a bit to get an idea of his life, examine the medicine chest and the bookshelves, but it would have bothered him. Even when I was exhausted, I was restless.

We dozed a while and finally woke at the same time wrapped vaguely around each other, hot and wet. The furnace was turned up high because Eric believed you couldn't have good sex if you were even slightly cool. You tensed up at the slightest drop in temperature, he said. That, he explained, was what was the matter with most women. Tension. It was the first I knew that there was something the matter with most women.

"Let's take a shower." He bounded up, dragging me across the bed. We tried it up against the tiles, our faces streaming under the hot water.

"Don't shut your eyes!"

"I have to."

"Naw. Keep em open," he said softly. "It's better. Come on."

"They'll come home. It's getting late."

"Naw! It's early. They stay out there for hours, till dark. We're on our last lap, Baby. Come on!"

I shut my eyes and turned into a vortex. I was too flaming sore to know what was happening but it happened anyway. I was so mad about it I didn't care if it killed us both. We writhed and soaped and writhed again. Finally, dripping and feeble, we got out. I leaned against the counter of the marble basin and he moved against me, twisting a little.

"Not again! I'm going insane!" I laughed in a spasm.

"Just one more. Look at that monkey! It won't stay down! Jesus Christ!"

I just let him, not even liking it anymore. I felt like a dog, the way they stared off into space when some other dog got stuck on their behind. We'd never have a conversation, I knew that now. He stopped and turned his hard tight fuzzy behind to me and put out a foot to drag the bathroom scales over. He stood on them for height, wobbling there like a puppet. We began to laugh. We went at it again laughing madly. He was so funny shaking away on those scales that we finally had to quit. He became serious then, looking right into my eyes with his big soul eyes and began to kiss me softly everywhere until my eyes rolled back again. Again!

We went back to the lumpy quilts of his big bed then, leaving the windows open. He kept some peanuts and raisins in the drawer of his night table. Wipe-out rations, he called them, and I wondered about his other girls, hundreds of them probably, here in this bed with him—wiped out. He lay there on his back giggling and popping peanuts into his jaws while I pretended to sleep.

"You don't realize," he said, chuckling, "how much sugar a man loses when he does all this screwing. You women don't lose a thing. You can go on all day and all night, but Man, we part with a lot of calories; half your brains can go flying out with that stuff. Here. Want some?" He held out the raisin box. "You look a little pale."

I laughed, shook my head and kept my eyes closed. I always got a feeling he was going to disown me in some way all of a sudden. Or just disappear. Finally we slept, Eric hot and heavy at my back, snoring gently and reeking of peanuts. The chain was pulling against my skin where his wrist lay on my chest, but I let it; I didn't want to stir and wake either of us.

The crash woke us at the same time. He was up and diving at the window, a towel held over his front, his legs bowed out as if in panic. I was paralyzed. He leaned out, took a look and lunged back in.

"It's them. Get dressed quick!"

I wrenched into my clothes, sluggish and half numb. My legs were weak. "God! What'll we *do*?"

The back door slammed. He was into his trousers like a shot, bare-chested though, and barefoot too. He thrust a knuckle into his mouth, figuring. Then he pulled me to the window and opened the screen.

"Climb out! Run fast and wait for me in the electric." I froze.

"Come on! I'll keep them in the kitchen. Hurry up!"

I balked. "This is a *rosebush*!" I whined.

"Get *out*, for shit sake!" he snarled. "You wanta get *caught* in here?" He gave me a hard boost from behind and I half fell, half leaped, through, arms and head grazing the thorny bush. My knees raked over it and then I was clear. Someone inside called, "Eric?" His mother! In a DAR kind of voice.

I ripped out of the bush and down the drive, crossed the street and pitched into the electric, ducking down. It was a cold, late afternoon, wide and serene. I cursed it. I slumped there watching the sky, shivering and wincing. Waiting. I should have kept myself to myself. I knew he would throw me out eventually. That *slob!* I waited a long time, hating myself for it. When it was full dark, I drove home. My hair was all matted and wild, my sweater was on backward, I smelled like a goat and was scratched all over. I had left my jacket back there and hoped they would find it and cut off his allowance or something.

In the garage at home I tried to put myself right. I crept indoors. But Ruby was there of course, finishing up her kitchen. She gave me her ultimate, rarely summoned, look of final horror.

"My God! You look like you been in some kinda wreck or somethin. Where you been all this time? We kep you out some suppa."

I asked about Sarah, nabbed a chicken leg from the plate, bit twice into a big cold biscuit and went to my room, followed by her Shhhttt and a few moans of disgusted amazement. Sarah was asleep. The house smelled fabulously of soup and biscuits. Enid and Beas were out to dinner with Pom. I locked myself in the bathroom and took a long bath, washed my hair and changed clothes.

★

The phone rang.

"If that's for me, I'm not here."

She raised her eyebrows. "Look to me like you plenty heah. Even if you is a little raggedy." She reached for it.

"Rube!" I grabbed her wrist. "I mean it. I'm not home."

She snorted and picked it up and said that this was Miz McCleod resident, with that cunning whine of hers. "No, she ain't back. I doan rightly know when she comin. No suh. Okay. I tell huh."

Very smooth, the great act of a high-class thief and liar. Wishbone one week and Horace the next and get one out the door before the other gets in, that's all. That was how to handle men.

"Shhhhttt! He very confuse, that boy. Po fella."

I lay in bed listening to Guy Lombardo in the dark, feeling ruined like Enid. And then Sarah was suddenly up and at the door of my room.

"Why, Hon, it's only nine o'clock. I've never heard of you a-goin without your supper."

"I thought you were asleep," I said feebly. "I'm just tired. I didn't sleep very well last night."

She gave me a long wise look, holding a hand at the bosom of her flowered robe like a woman in an ad for diamonds, and for a minute there I thought she was going to deal me the facts of life. Maybe she thought it was time. But I wondered again if she even knew them. She had probably become preoccupied with some old useless memory and Higgens had just slipped me in. Gee! I hated to think of her doing it at all. Yet I hated to think she'd never had any fun.

She fluffed up the blankets loosely over my feet the way I liked them.

"Maybe I oughta take your temperature, Hon."

I laughed harshly. "I'm not *sick*! Can't I even get tired once in a while?"

She laughed and went out quickly. "Well, Hon, you were never tired before. Seems kinda queer, that's all."

"Well," I called after her, "life is queer."

She chuckled and looked back at me from the hall.

"Are you better?" I asked fondly.

"Oh, yes. Law, I'm all right now."

★

Late. From my limbo, that slow fall where I had been for what seemed only seconds, drifting, the voice cut in like a conscience.

"Katie?"

"Huh?" I turned my head weakly. She was outside my window.

"Y'all gittin into some kinda trouble?"

"*What?* No! Go away! I was sleeping. My God!"

"Okay. Okay." She faded off through the yard with Wishbone or Horace or somebody. I heard the soft clank of the gate and their murmurs.

Why didn't they just say it—Do you need me? Just that. Not that I could have borne to hear it. It would have embarrassed me. But they could have said it and proven themselves honest at least. They weren't really honest, any of them—Rube, Enid, Pom, not even Sarah. If they could just have said simple things like: Enid's drunk today. Just that would have made all the difference. Imagine saying, Well, I've been out screwing! Wow! If we could have said, Ruby's out back screwing just now. She'll be in later. Shhhhttt! Tell it slant, said the poet.

★

The phone rang and rang before Enid and Beas came in and Sarah slept through it and I sweated through it. And then very late I woke up to find him banging on my window and my heart flipped over. I tore out of bed and tiptoed past Sarah's room to the back door, and out into the yard. Beas was home. I could smell him, sodalike, at the basement door. I ran to the quarters first and whispered to Ruby but she was still out. He came across the yard like an angry rooster.

"Goddammit, Katie! What the hell . . . ? I've been calling you . . ."

"Shhhh! Don't wake everybody up, for Pete's sake. You crazy—"

He grabbed me and dragged me to the quarters door, wrenched it open and shoved me inside. "What's this place? Who lives in here?"

"Ruby, you idiot! We can't stay in here."

He kissed me, shutting me up.

"Eric, not here . . . please!"

"You stupid little—I tried to call you seven times! I had to pay ten bucks to borrow a car . . ."

"Shhh! We gotta get outa here. This is Ruby's room. What time is it?"

"I don't know, midnight maybe. I have something to tell you."

"Tell me somewhere else." I was shaking. I smelled Ruby's life there: coffee and something fried and the vanilla she perfumed herself with. Her bed, her clothes.

He slammed me down on the bed suddenly. I sank and swayed, halfheartedly fighting him. He fell over me.

"I'm never gonna do it with you again, especially not in *here*! In somebody's *quarters*. Get *off*!" I shoved him but he went soft against me, nosing and breathing warm on my neck, stroking me, reaching up under my nightgown.

"I'm glad you sleep with my chain on," he whispered.

"I never take it off," I whispered.

"I thought you slept naked."

"In summer," I whispered.

"I'm going tomorrow," he said simply.

"Huh? *Tomorrow?* You said next week."

"They sent me a wire. Tomorrow. New York."

"New York? Gee! I thought you said Texas."

He slipped his trousers down. "I did, but now it's New York. Must be some emergency. I don't know . . . I wasn't quite ready . . ."

"Gee! New York!"

She looked down at the city twenty stories below. The lights . . . tiny distant people. George Raft kissing her neck, her peroxide hair. *It's all yours Baby.* She's his moll. . . . She'd shoot anybody down for him. He'll die in her arms. . . .

"Listen. Stop it! We've gotta get outa here before she comes home."

But it was too late. He was smoothly persistent, slowly driving me up to it again. Again! I couldn't believe it. I just did it. It was better every time we got together. Ruby's bed! God, I was totally crazy. We swayed through it, easy, like Rube maybe, with all that practice. Perfect. He kissed me so much afterward I nearly smothered.

"We're maniacs!" I said.

"Yeah!" he agreed.

I lunged up. "Come on. No arguments. We're going."

"Can I light a match?"

"Just for a minute."

The whole room burst into shady relief, so small, so narrow, Ruby's whole home! She *lived* here. There it all was—our ivory mirror, the silver silent butler, the antique needlework pillow. The walls were covered with brown peeling Sunday-supplement pictures, pasted there years ago by someone.

"Jesus! Look at this dump." He moved to the wall and held the match high. It burned his finger and he struck another.

"Come *on*! She'll catch us."

"Wait a minute. Look at this. *Albany to New York—Two and a Half Hours! Glen Curtis wins New York World Prize of Ten Thousand Dollars!* Wowee! That was 1910! Looky here! Look at this! Shoshone Dam in Wyoming. Looky here . . ."

I started out the door.

"Here. Wait a second! Mexican Revolution! Holy cow! This stuff is valuable."

The match burned his finger and he dropped it quickly. He lit another. "It's kinda nice in here all crowded up with this stuff. What's all this, these art objects?"

"It's our stuff . . . you know, from the clients. She totes a little. Come on."

"Why don't you take it back?"

I shrugged. "Oh . . . I don't know. Forget it. She doesn't own much. Look around. Come on. I'm leaving." I went out.

In the yard he whispered, "Aren't you cold, Baby?"

"Yes. I'm freezing."

"C'mere in the garage a minute. So we can say good-bye. Can't go in the house, I guess?" He asked it in a kind of agony of control.

"No, Silly. It's impossible." I led him into the garage and we piled into the electric and wrapped ourselves in the old patchwork quilt. He held me. We were quiet. Then he started again and I told him I was beginning to hate him but he said No, I was beginning to love him and I didn't argue.

"My folks didn't notice a thing," he whispered, feeling me. "I brought your jacket. It's in the car."

And when we got going again, I told him it was definitely hate and he laughed. After a quick one I said I hated him even more, for doing it so much, for going to war and just generally.

"My feet are all dirty on the bottom and I'm freezing. You maniac! I didn't even have time to get a sweater."

He moaned apology, seizing my foot in his hand and kissing the dirty bottom of it. I screamed under my breath and pulled it away but he grabbed it again.

"Holy cow! What a foot! This isn't a *foot*! This is a hand! How do you walk on this thing with this high arch?!"

I swooned, flattered.

Ruby came in the gate suddenly with someone. We listened, silent as wood. They shut the door and soon the bed began to creak. Eric crept out of the car and put his ear against the garage wall next to her room. He came back chuckling.

"Banging away in there. Think they know we were there?"

"No." I was still. He was going. He held me and got me warm. He still smelled faintly of peanuts.

"Sorry I dumped you out the window."

"It's okay."

"If I get some extra money I'll send you a ticket to New York."

"I'll be working."

"You always say that."

"I've just been waiting . . ."

"For me to go?"

He reached under my nightgown again and stroked my belly.

"If you get pregnant, call me collect."

"I won't get pregnant." I laughed. "Besides, how could you get a collect call on a ship?"

He kissed me deep and we went at it again, his monkey not so hard this time but hard enough. It was like breathing in and out and I realized that it was his way of not going crazy, this sex. He talked all the while he was driving me up to a pitch.

"I'll write. Every week. I write good letters. Oh, Kid! You like that? You cold? Come on, Baby . . ."

I began to cry from weariness which he thought was from sorrow. He took a long time at it, holding off, thinking I wanted him to.

"I don't want to leave you," he said. And then he fell flat on me, gasping. "I want to . . . leave something with you."

"It's okay," I said stupidly.

"Keep your legs around me."

"Okay."

Silence. An owl called in the yard. Eric looked at me through the dark.

"I love you," he said, resigned.

My body made a feeble leap to reply but I only nodded and sighed and didn't speak, pressing his head against me as in a movie with someone . . . with whom? I fell asleep.

I love you, I whispered to the wall. He had really said it. My innards sank. I wanted to run to him, fall on him, but I could hardly move my limbs. *I love you.* I wondered why I had just let him go off. I could have said it back but I didn't. Why not? Because I never had said it in the world. I wrote in my diary— *When a letter comes I'll know how I feel.*

His train left at seven A.M. They must have dragged him to it and thrown him on like baggage. Maybe he'd arrive in New York at the Navy Yards dead, smelling of peanuts.

Yet I knew immediately when I got up that day that I could start living now. I didn't want him to leave but I couldn't have stood it if he had stayed. Queer.

★

I went to the aircraft factory and filled out a form. I felt like some pulsating plant, Eric ripped like a branch off my side.

Di Finlayson's boss said okay, come in a week. Call one of the car pools listed on that bulletin board. Wear pants, coveralls or something. Ever use a screwdriver? Well, yes, I lied. He put me on a crew of men. Assistant mechanic. Swing shift. You may be outdoors a lot, he said. Wear a heavy jacket, maybe a cap. We'll get some ice on these runways in a few weeks. I smiled like a sailor getting my first ship. I wanted to write Eric as if to compare notes. I wanted to move into the part of our friendship that was talk, letters. I waited to hear from him. My body seemed pacified or drugged. It made no complaints.

Di had asked me to meet her at the Sunshine Café that day.

While I was waiting for her Murray Dietler came in, spied me and sat with me for a few minutes, ordering coffee and a sweet roll like a big city bum in a movie. He thanked the waitress with such mercy that I nearly gagged. Be kind to the workers of the world! His coming there reminded me of the few dates we had had two years before when he had tried to convert me. Now his pants were baggy, his hair longer, shaggier and dirty, and he seemed not to know which way to move.

"I hear you're pleading C.O."

He nodded.

"When?"

"I'll have a hearing sometime soon. In December maybe."

He smelled like ink.

"Why plead your own case? They'll get you for sure. They're smart."

He looked at me with those large pale naked gray eyes, wounded-like.

"It's a part of my political philosophy to defend my beliefs myself."

I shrugged. I feared he'd get into his philosophy again. Yet I felt differently about him now. Not exactly Sarah's world pity but something kind enough. Belief of any kind dazzled me. My own belief was so secret, so wild, so akin to my body's life in some way, if it existed at all, that his struck me as exotic. To what is your life dedicated? he would ask me in a minute. I always felt that Murray had some unfair mysterious God-given view into the rougher terrain of my soul (not into its cultivated areas), and that his mission was to invade that terrain. I shrank from his mournful wisdom, those patient knowing heavy Jewish looks he gave me. He was talking suddenly about disillusionment.

"You mean with the Communists?"

"It's not important," he said. "I mean about the Party. Oh, it takes guts to drop out. But the ideals aren't compromised in me, I know that. Politically I could support a fight against fascism. Especially as a Jew. But ideally, I can't lend my body to a war. That's all. And the Party doesn't know what it's doing anymore, I've decided. It takes a different stance every month or so."

I couldn't believe my ears! The Party at fault? Fantastic!

"It takes a lot to become disillusioned in life," he said quietly. "But if you're part of a cause, a big movement, even without actual membership in a party, then you can weather a lot. Know what I mean?"

"I dunno." I really tried to grasp the idea, the feeling of having such a concrete goal. "I guess my . . . ambitions or reasons to live are . . . more private or something."

"You've got to have a purpose in life. A purpose you can define and defend," he said. Then he took a big bite of his sweet roll and bleakly chewed it, looking straight ahead like a condemned man.

"What's yours?" I asked. "I mean really. Not your public purpose."

He arched his eyebrows, surprised. "My purpose?"

"Yeah. Really."

"To help promote a workers' revolution throughout the world. To support the struggle for a dictatorship of the proletariat." He said it as if I ought to have known it, like The Star-Spangled Banner.

I wanted to scream. It was enough to make you believe in God instead, which I sometimes took the risk of doing. "But I mean . . . something without that language. Something about life. What if you'd never heard of the proletariat or dictatorships or—you know. What if you were *them*? What if you were just an ignorant slob? Then what would your purpose be?"

He shrugged. "Well, I'm not just an ignorant slob," he reflected. He swallowed patiently, washing the roll down with milk. No wonder he was stopped up all the time, all that milk and starch. I saw suddenly what it was that defeated Murray—he was totally without a sense or any quality of beauty. Just beauty. I looked him over quickly. Where would it hide in him, beauty? In his white soft side somewhere, under the dirty shirt? Behind his knee? I shivered. Imagine his having a monkey like Eric's hanging there under his pants! I still had a not quite secret enough need to squash Murray like a bug, monkey or no.

"I would be the same," he was saying. "See, you've got a clouded view due to your background. People like my father and Pomeroy Russell have directed your education toward—"

"Oh, they haven't either!" I threw him a slap with my voice. "People like that haven't had anything real to do with me at all. I'm my own disaster!"

He laughed. "You're funny! You always were. Why do you think of yourself as a disaster?"

He kept the mirthless dough-plugged grin on me. Beauty, I quickly learned, turning away, must be fortified by at least one dash, just one, of self-consciousness. A human being can't sit there with chewed food on the teeth and smile openly, close up, at another, and expect to be received. A dog can and a little child can, but not a grown-up human. I wished Di would show up, whatever her latest problem might be.

"I didn't mean it that way," I told him patiently. "Where would you fit into the world, I mean, if you didn't know about the proletariat and all that stuff?"

"Oh. Well, I'd be a worker. And I hope I'd rise to leadership. If I was qualified, of course."

Oh, the modesty! You can't be so sure and rational about things, I wanted to shout at him. Somebody will throw a wrench into the middle of it. You've got to have a secret life. He finished eating and wiped his mouth vaguely, leaving some crumbs on his scratchy unshaven cheeks.

"Well, so what're you doing lately? You working?"

"I've just gotten a job at Douglas Aircraft."

His eyebrows went up. "Well! That's good. They have a union shop out there?"

"I don't know." I felt dumb all at once.

"You'll have to join if they do."

I shrugged. "So what?"

"A lot of colored being hired out there, I hear." He was baiting me.

"So what?"

Silence. And then he jumped up, fished a nickel out of his pocket and went to the juke box. "Something on here I want you to hear," he said.

It was Josh White singing "The House I Live In."

"You like it?"

I shrugged again. "No."

He was shocked. He had slid in beside me on my bench and I could smell his digesting sweet roll. "Why not? Don't you think . . . ?"

"It's sentimental," I said quietly. "What's he kidding himself for? He's never going to get that kind of living. They won't let him."

He stared up close to me. "But you're so cynical! How come you're so cynical? Don't you think he has the right . . . ?"

"Oh, what's the right have to do with it? Sure he does. All kinds of people have rights they never get. Why doesn't he admit it and—"

"And what? Revolt? That's just what I'm talking about."

I sighed. Then Di came in and I waved her back to our booth. She was dressed up in a new suit and brown patent-leather pumps, emergency clothes. She gave Murray a disappointed Hi and he stood up.

"You two are really slumming today, aren't you?" he mewed.

We gave him a couple of looks that drummed him out and he slopped away not insulting the waitress with anything crass like a tip.

"Good luck, Murray," I called. He would need it.

"I wonder if he'll shave and cut his hair before he goes to plead his case." Men! I had forgotten Eric for a whole half hour.

Di laughed. "How long have you been stuck with *that*?"

"I got here on time," I said, punishing her. I was always late but she was always later, just later enough for the fauna and flora of a moment or a place to be altered forever. Seeing her made me long to tell someone everything about me and Eric. But not Di. Nina then? Who if not Nina? He said *I love you.*

Di was wearing Tabu as usual, which always faintly nauseated me. It was too heavy for her tall thick-haired faintly toxic type, Hepburnish though she was. "Well, what's up? What're we doing in the Sunshine?"

"You'll never believe it," she said, whinnying out a little laugh.

The waitress came and Di ordered chili and a chocolate milk shake just to improve her questionable skin. "Aren't you eating?" she asked me.

"Nope. Dietler castor oil always spoils my appetite." I didn't want to say I was penniless as usual. I'd have to refuse a bite of chili and all that same old prideful business.

"I wanted to take you to lunch," she said.

I shrugged. "Okay, okay." I ordered a bacon-and-tomato and a glass of milk, which made her whine out another defeated laugh.

I used to have to sit through evenings at Piggie's Drive-In, movies, luncheons at the Palm Lounge or the Sooner Room where lots of businessmen ate, and a dozen high-school Friday nights of torture at Di's house, trying to fathom her virginity and the answer to it. I realized now that we had never really discussed mine. It had been as if mine, like all the rest I owned, were monogrammed with someone else's initials. And now, here, all that had passed. I no longer cruised the drive-ins with her in her father's old Studebaker, warning her not to be too bold but only visible, like some younger brother squiring his big art-nouveau sister through enemy territory. Her virginity and her despair over hanging onto it had been our mutual burden, and probably the real thing we had had in common all those months of our senior year. We had let it all pass somehow in this last year and seen one another only for occasional business like shoe shopping or going to the Little Theater to see *Charley's Aunt* with tickets paid by a client. Our friendship had become chancy, all the more reason not to accept the offer of lunch. But I did.

"This is where he had breakfast every morning," she said.

"Huh? Who?"

"Raymond."

I gritted my teeth. She was like Ruby, bargaining, building up to some red-hot useless news.

"You remember that time we went shoe shopping, last spring?"

"Oh no! Not that rhubarb-looking shoe salesman?"

She nodded. "Okay, okay. I know you didn't think much of him."

"Think much of him? How could I? I never even knew him."

She laughed, sick. "Well, I knew him."

"What'd he do?"

"He stole my bank, for one thing." She laughed, teary.

"Your *bank*? That glass kewpie?"

"Yes. Well, don't laugh. It had over forty dollars in it. And he took Dad's good camera, too."

"Oh, my God! How crappy! How'd he get away with it?"

"He drove out one evening when mother and I were in the kitchen fixing dinner and just came in and took them. I heard something and went in and there he was running down the front walk. I saw him drive off in some old red car."

"God! What a jerk!" I didn't remind her that slimy does as slimy is. "Well, so . . . forget it. You've got a job. You can earn it back."

"Well," she said, looking in my eyes with the flat truth. "That's not all."

"What else?"

"I think I'm pregnant."

"What? Pregnant?"

"Shhhh! Not so *loud*, Katie!"

I leaned across the table. "With *him*? With *Rhubarb*?" I whispered.

She nodded. The waitress cut in with the food. I sighed and collapsed against the back of the booth. Long live the idiots of Idiotsville! How did I know I wasn't in the same state myself? Well, I knew. Luck was familiar to me in some queer way. I had it instead of money, I believed.

Di was now crying into a wrinkled hankie with a butterfly in the corner. I didn't really understand her kind of mind. I wouldn't say that I might not have done it with someone as awful as Rhubarb, but I sure wouldn't admit it if I had. And I wouldn't cry! I'd swear or hit the wall or break something.

She shook her head and blew her nose. "I've got to find a doctor. I've heard there is one in town."

"You'd better tell your mother," I said stupidly, knowing perfectly well that Mrs. Finlayson worked in an insurance office and wore Red Cross shoes. She was hardly like Sarah, who would have considered it a windfall.

"And I'm broke, anyway," she whined, not failing nevertheless to attack the chili with lust. Chili is not good for babies, I thought. "I'm still paying for my phonograph."

"What're you going to do?"

"Think Ruby might know of somebody?" she whispered.

"Ruby? Only a colored," I whispered.

"Might be a colored midwife or something," she whispered, sucking the milk shake.

"That'd be dangerous," I whispered, collaborating. "You have to have a real doctor for that, I think."

I realized then that she was going to leave it up to me. I bit my lip, hating myself for taking it on. "I'll think of something. Give me a little time." I pitied Di because she insisted on it. I felt guilty for hating her while liking her and so I promised everything. "I'll find somebody. Just give me a little time."

"Well, there *isn't* much time, Katie," she said, as if I'd done it to her myself. "You've only got six weeks and then you've got to go through with the whole thing or it's too late."

"You sure?"

"Yes, Silly."

I wracked my head. Iantha? She'd tell it all over the state. I cogitated, watching Di with her chili, nibbling the edges of my sandwich. She lifted the spoon to her mouth with a little finger stuck straight out like a snail's horn.

"Well . . . someone I know knows a doctor. That's for sure. Gee . . . Oh! I know! Nina! Nina Brosky."

"Nina Brosky! Do you know *her*?"

"Yes," I said coolly. "I went to a party there a few weeks ago."

She laughed, looking at me as if I'd hit the jackpot and by birth didn't deserve it. "Well, get you, Cobina Wright!"

I snickered. "Well, I think she'll know. She's really sophisticated and all. I'll go up there and ask her. I'll let you know."

"That'd be marvelous," she said.

Finally she finished. I ate half my sandwich and bit into the other half. She started to watch me, noticing the chain around my neck. The basketball was out of sight.

"I hear you've been dating Eric Witcher."

"Yeah. He's not so bad." I swallowed a piece of bacon whole and coughed. I looked at her to keep from not looking at her and she smiled ruefully. We had done it, each on her own, and we knew we'd never compare notes, that was for kids, for virgins. What's the use? I thought. *Oh Baby, Oh Kid* . . .

"He's gone, anyway," I said. Oh dammit! I wanted to run out into the world. I wanted someone to say of me wistfully, She's gone.

She began to lecture me about being careful, getting a diaphragm, in soap-opera whispers. I sighed. Those men at the plant, she said, were hot after every girl who passed through the hangar. There was so much sex going on out there it would knock you cold. I began to feel like a lost Zeppelin roaming the sky. Here we were, helpless in Assinopolis, we two big sex talkers, our past full of Rhubarb who robbed the piggy bank and left the hardware owner's daughter pregnant, and Eric who threw girls out the window into rosebushes before he sailed off to war. I nodded, fallen. It would pay me, I told myself in Di's voice, to remember the rosebush plunge and blot out all the rest of the fun with Mr. Firecracker Witcher.

"But," I said, betraying him, "he's like all guys." And she laughed, glad of a fellow sufferer.

I called about the car pool and was told to be ready next Monday at three fifteen. Swing shift. That would take care of my nights. Incarcerated in a big hangar with nothing but men men men. But when I had it all arranged I felt depressed and stupid. Anybody with sense would have worked hard at flunky jobs and saved money for New York. Yet I had begun to wonder about the New York in my head. That sort of thing I had been yearning for all those years—something in movies, chic like Enid's infamy, Nina's glamour—all that had been slowly acquiring tarnish of late, what with Enid's move into our place and the revelation that she did not do something by doing nothing, but only did nothing; that her deep thoughts, whether interesting or not, were not available for scrutiny. She was only an irritant there. And the number of people continually present in the house grew without adding any quality to our lives except perhaps a bit for Sarah who loved a big family, though the cost to her was heavy—fatigue and a more rattled if no less pleasant behavior.

And the discovery of Nina's Snickers had disillusioned me too.

Sometimes I leaned against the wall of my room exhausted by confusion. What if I simply went out and forced myself to direct my life the way other girls had done—school, jobs, college scholarships, husbands? Di Finlayson seemed to have no trouble deciding what she wanted. But was she even aware that it was a *life* precisely that she had on her hands? I decided she did not distinguish between a *life* and a hoard of time. *Time.* It flayed me. I had to order it and I could not.

I saw less of Beas than when he first moved in. He seemed preoccupied and, having been forced by Enid to return to school, he found himself loaded with work to make up. He kept on making secret telephone calls, too. Maybe about the Army, I thought. Enid was back in bed a lot of the time and thick-tongued when she got up, or hung over, with that punished look of the person who has done herself wrong. She depressed me. Ruby complained that she could "never git in that messed-up room to clean."

Sarah breathed in gasps sometimes and sat down with a suddenness as if she had been pushed. But nobody seemed to notice it. I hated to leave her alone but I felt driven to get away, and so I shopped for work clothes and made a lot of unnecessary trips to Pom's house for books I never read. Pom came out often, watchful of Beas and of Enid and apparently blind to Sarah although he seemed as always to be in another sort of touch with her.

"When did you say your job starts, Katie?" Enid or Iantha would ask. But not Sarah.

All right, I whispered to the walls, I shall go forth. I shall slay it for you. And when I'm done with that, I'll run away and find the world.

I spent as much time at Nina's those last days before going to work as I felt I could safely request. She was always around, seemingly always glad to see me, which never failed to arouse my suprise and suspicion.

"All the deaths this past year," she said one day. Virginia Woolf and Joyce, Sherwood Anderson. Fitzgerald. End of an era. But who's on the cover of *Time* magazine? Joe Louis. That, she said, was the perfect comment on the American mind. A prize fighter.

But, I said, that was okay. Joyce and Virginia Woolf could afford it.

"Someday," she said, "they'll make a candy bar called the Joe Louis."

I laughed loudly. Would she, in that case, switch from Snickers? I couldn't ask, of course.

"Speaking of death," I said, finding an opening, "I've got a friend who has to have an abortion. You know of any doctor who does it?"

She heaved up out of the cushions and fixed me with a shocked look.

"Oh no! Not *me*. Honest." I laughed, swearing it was someone else, but with a quick little wave of envy that I couldn't understand.

She gave me Dr. Mackey's address.

"Well," she said, "don't go ruining *your* life."

"Ha! What life? And anyway, I don't even know how to ruin it. If I ruined it, then I'd be convinced I had a life at least."

"Honey!" She laughed at me the way Sarah sometimes did, as if such eruptions from me were out of character in some way.

"Even needing an abortion is having a life," I confessed.

"Don't kid yourself, Honey. It's having a death. Believe me."

"You had one?"

"Never mind."

"You *did*!"

She smiled, demurring. "All right. I did. Some time ago. It's—" She raised a futile arm. "—the worst thing you could wish on yourself. I wish now I'd had the baby."

"Gee! I wish you had too." I felt weak! Maybe it was Eric's. "I haven't heard from Eric. Not a thing."

She scrutinized me. "It wasn't Eric, Honey. I was his first but he didn't stay around here long. I did it as a favor."

I blushed and gagged. "I didn't know that."

"I thought he had told you. He was here one night and . . . you know. It just happened. He had to start somewhere. He told me before he left that he was crazy about you."

I went mute, blushing.

"He'll write you. Basic training or whatever it is is exhausting."

I laughed. "Ha! It's nothing compared to sex!"

We talked about men and love and sex, skirting the periphery. She had been reading Rimbaud. She was morose. Helping the British children seemed not to have cheered her. A large group of the RAF had been sent home. I couldn't believe Eric had done it to her. I wanted to hate her but couldn't. I hovered on the edge of my chair waiting, as usual, for some pearl to drop, but when it did it was only the confession that she had failed all her own dreams and that I ought to be sure not to fail mine. She had been in love twice and had lost both times, her world was too narrow for her and she was an alien in it anyway.

"I feel the same way. Why don't you leave? You've got the money at least."

"That's not all it takes," she said.

"That's all it would take for me."

"You sure?" She smiled a little doubt at me. "Well, maybe you're right. But whatever you do, don't try to make a man take you into the big bad world. Stay off their backs if you can. They always drop you at the wrong time."

I began to shiver with dread and excitement. She always did that to me.

"Who was the other one," I dared to ask her before I left, "besides Red Southwell?"

"None of your business." She laughed affectionately. She seemed to like to be teased.

It was cold. Ruby worked steadily, like a pump. She canned the last bushel of those sour little apples off the north acre of the lease, standing in the chilly back porch peeling and paring. Sarah sterilized her jars for her. The house smelled fabulous. In my own house someday I was going to have something brewing all day. Even Nina's incense couldn't compete with what rose on the kitchen steam of our lives.

Ruby wore an old sweater of Wishbone's that hardly wrapped her fat stomach. Wishbone was off to the Army for good. Horace's number had just come up and he was already training as an Army chef. She was left with Gifford, who wasn't dependable and wanted to be a boxer which she said was jess 'cause he liked to sock somebody in the jaw once in a while.

"Well, then, Hon," Sarah said, "I think he ought to be a boxer. A big fellow like that. It might keep him out of trouble."

Ruby scowled. "He doan *wanta* keep outa trouble. He *love* hit, that devil! He goan to hell so fass!"

"Well, good!" I shouted. "He can keep me company."

We laughed together, O circus of Deliria. Ruby made some hot mint tea for Sarah to take in to Mrs. Kitteridge, who was waiting to be consoled. Then she made herself a cup of what she called tough coffee, strong enough to rot a horseshoe, and sat down at the kitchen table with a big piece of brown wool cloth that she had come home with from the Willows recently. I didn't like it but it had a sturdy quality that seemed to give her great satisfaction. She yanked it around, spread it out and began to hem it. I'd never seen her sew before. She took large neat stitches, doing the whole thing with an adamant kind of concentration, tongue pushing through her huge carved lips, that fascinated me. She hemmed one edge, pulled a long piece of twine through the hem and stood up to wrap it around her waist.

"It's too big" I said disgustedly. "It's bulky. You should have cut it narrower at the waist."

"No, it ain't," she said quietly. "Hit's goan be jess right. I kin loose it in and out whin I wants to."

She gave me a kind of knowing patient look then and my ears began to hum. Oh! I got it! I looked away, my mouth open, not wanting to have been caught by surprise. I ought to have seen it before now. Ruby Steckle was going to have a *baby*! And she'd never said a thing about it! I stared at her. Well! She flicked water over the seam now on the other side of the skirt and began to iron it through an old bath towel right on the table.

I let out a little sound. She looked at me, drew down her jaw and made that crazy collapsing campy move of hers that always broke me up. She was making fun. She didn't have to tell her business. Ha!

Finally she said, "Lissen, Girl, git ova there an stir them apples. Make out like you wasn't the laziess thing alive. God, I be glad whin that Monday come and you gits you behine outa heah and brang in some money. Shhhtt! We needs cash."

"Okay, okay." I felt sublimely cheerful. A *baby*! Right in the middle of our life! I stirred the apples with the long wooden spoon carved by Wishbone. When? I wondered. And then I asked myself —Whose? But no matter. Ruby's, that's whose. Wow!

Everyone seemed to have known it before me. Enid said, after seeing the new skirt, "Well, it's about time. She's bursting out of her other clothes. She's big as a house already!"

Iantha said one night in the parlor, "Sometimes I think *they* have the right idea about it all. No fuss. God, they're as natural as children."

Children, Enid said, was what they were. I protested and they shooed me away as if I were a child myself. I was just prejudiced in Ruby's favor, no matter what, they said. You could count the dependable colored girls in town on one hand. Pearl West to begin with. I despised them for that, as if I didn't have a dozen other reasons.

Enid said of course you couldn't let the population go rampant like that forever, especially when too many of them were poor and hungry. Why bring more into the world? And Sarah said convincingly that Ruby's baby would never go hungry, Hon.

Enid gritted her teeth and said that wasn't what she meant.

Iantha said that from the point of view of metaphysics, it made no difference whatever whether Ruby had a baby or not, whose it was or whether or not it lived. And Sarah laughingly declared that that was communism.

I loved the idea of the baby and dwelt on it a lot. I dreamed one night that I myself was named America. I told Ruby the next day and she said, "That ain't a bad name." She was considering important-sounding names, she said.

"You could call it Meri for short," I ventured.

"*Mary?*" she said. "Nuthin doin. That the motha of Jesus. Name like that bring you nuthin but pain."

Oh well oh well. Call her what you want. America would be good, I said, for a boy or a girl.

"This goan be a girl," she said simply.

★

Rabbit called. They were being shipped home early. Something was up. He seemed like a dream, but I hated to say good-bye to him.

Enid joined the metaphysics group. She got up again and busied herself. I tried not to notice, having decided to broaden my life, to ignore the Biography and to forget about Eric whose firecracker had begun to ram itself into my dreams. I decided never to look at the past, where most people seemed caught and struggling. And in spite of metaphysics, Enid was irritable anyway, which dampened my interest. She even snapped at Beas and Sarah. She seemed less beautiful. Sometimes Iantha would snarl back at her and it thrilled me to think that she could summon that much courage with the one person she had always adored. Usually they bickered over the Meaning of Meaning or over kinds of consciousness. It seemed that Enid was now casting about for the language and the proof of her superiority whereas before she had merely sat there letting Iantha prove it by her own inferiority. That fascinated me. I decided it was the most metaphysical thing they could possibly do, but still I resisted their company in spite of interesting evidence that metaphysics had a grip on Enid. A trail of hairbrushes, hankies smeared with lipstick and the vapors of expensive perfume were left behind when she dressed to go to the group. Sarah got tears in her eyes once observing how long this ritual of preparation took Enid and how seriously she went about it—as if she were a crippled child struggling alone up a hill.

A copy of *Tertium Organum* came to her in the mail. She concentrated on it obsessively, her finger following the lines. I looked through it one day when she left it on a chair. She had underlined certain passages and words with a pen, marking the beautiful new pages with shocking boldness, something I had never been able to do to a book:

The Eternal Now cannot be expressed in language.

Alcohol—aha—creates the illusion of a communion of souls.

I made a note of that one in the Biography in spite of my vow not to look into it again.

A is not A. A is not not =A. Everything is either A or not =A.

Hmm.

Beas, after hiding in the closet for the third time, was now listening to Jack Benny. He sat on the couch with Enid and, wonder of wonders, she held his hand. I couldn't bear it. I wanted someone to touch me. All that sex and then nothing. Where was Eric by now? I had lost the peaceful shock that followed his leaving. My body now seemed to flaunt itself everywhere with deranged pride. I wondered if I were in love. Quit slammin doors, Ruby said sometimes. I looked irritably now at Sarah who lay on the chaise with pillows at her back laughing at Jack Benny as if the world were entirely credible and that this was all there was to it. But finally I laughed.

Later I made popcorn. Beas helped, carefully pouring butter from a chemical beaker he had given us. He was watchful of me and seemingly dubious about something. Very late I decided we should run in to the Creole and he agreed. Enid was furious. Sarah called me into her room and told me we had to be patient with Enid and Beas, that they were suffering. I sighed like the exhaust of a volcano.

"Okay. You want anything? I mean besides a million dollars?"

She laughed. "Aw, Hon. It's gonna be all right now. You'll see. You'll have so much money when you get that job, Law, you won't know what to do with it all. You can buy some pretty clothes." Oh, her quiet tender gaze! She had fewer clothes than I and, anyway, I had intended to give her all the money I made. What, otherwise, was the purpose of my working? Sometimes I couldn't grasp the logic of work and money anyway. And then she said, "It's a good thing too, Hon, with Ruby comin into her time. I think I'll start to send the laundry out. Law, I wonder what that would cost?"

"Gee," I said. "Everything's changing."

"That's the way life is, Hon. Just change."

She said it the way you'd say *small* change and I laughed. I'd never heard her mention *life* anyway. I felt as if I could do nothing for her short of yielding up my freedom or my very blood.

"Are you havin a good time, Hon?"

"Yeah. Sure. But . . . "

"You need something, Sugar?"

I turned roughly away. Pity pity pity. "No," I rapped.

"Did you hear from your young man, Hon?"

That was how things usually were—I hadn't even brought him into the house and yet she knew all about him. I couldn't ask her how, either.

"He's gone into the Navy." I started to go out.

A sailor, she announced consolingly, is awful busy.

And so I went to work one afternoon at three thirty in my recently purchased cotton coveralls with long johns underneath and a heavy jacket over. Ruby packed me a whopper of a lunch which she reminded me was really dinner, this being the swing shift. They all stood at the windows laughing at my weird silhouette as I waddled down the lane to the gate.

I got into a station wagon full of geezerish men—all but one, who kept his mouth shut and smoked his pipe, gazing out the window as if the Delirian outskirts were studded with gold. They told me their names, which I forgot, and made a few gruff comments to one another. I felt as if I were on the moon. What was I doing in these crazy clothes with these old coots in this rattly old station wagon? I entered the hangar and clocked into a new time and world at four P.M. It smelled of machines and canvas. It was noisy. Di, after a week's sick leave, was back at her job and just leaving for the day. She had waited to see me so I cavorted around swinging my lunch bag and kicking up my big work shoes.

"Did you get it done?" I asked her.

She nodded. "My boss loaned me the money so I didn't have to tell my folks. They thought I had the trots or something. It wasn't bad."

I nodded wisely. Her boss, I decided, was giving her his fire-cracker and maybe even thought it was his baby.

My crew of men were named Shorty, Smitty, Speedy, Slim and Mr. Fiveash, a fellow from the Ozark Mountains who was illiterate and who fell off the gas truck every few minutes, being so dazzled by the bombers out on the runway and all the people, the big buildings. His eyes bugged out and his mouth hung open all evening. Slim said he was being put up in a little hotel in town with his whole family, paid for by the company because he couldn't find housing and they needed him.

"Tell me what they need him fer, though. I hate to think who's gonna hafta fly these bombers after he gits his hands on em."

"Well," I said, "he can't do much to them with that broken arm. Did you see that cast?"

They all laughed. "He had one on the other arm a few weeks ago, Katie," said Smitty. "Busted both of em fallin outa that hotel bed. He ain't used to a bed, he says. Cain't stay in it!" They howled.

In three days I was head of the crew and did all the driving.

"Gimme yer kit," said Slim, reaching for my tool box. He carried it all the time after that like Tom Sawyer. He was the driver of my car pool, a skinny hard-boned kindly man who could have been good-looking except for a life which seemed to have gnarled and worn him down to his own grit.

Pom asked me a dozen questions about the plant. No union shop. Yes, there was a touch of camouflage. Planes lined up on the runways by the dozens. A B-24? I described it in detail. We rev up the engines to 2500 rpm's so the inspectors can check the instruments, I explained, knocking them all cold. Beas snickered, looking at me from under his blond brows, and was grateful for my having become the center of gripping interest, taking the heat off him. His crew-cut was sprouting up into a new field of haylike hair again. He hadn't been called up. He would wait up for me sometimes at night to hear my stories of the plant. Sometimes he fixed hot chocolate, which we would take down to his basement room. I would come in all icy-cheeked and find him there, beaming, waiting to serve me.

"I kinda like the place," I confessed to him. "Not the work especially but . . . just the men, you know. Sometimes the foreman makes us hide out in a plane for a few hours, when there's no work. They tell me the stories of their lives. You wouldn't believe it! They tell me everything!"

"Like what? Like what?" He hung on my words. It finally occurred to me that he was even more lonesome now that I was out five evenings a week and usually too tired to go to the Creole by the time I got home at one A.M.

"Whatta they say? What life stories?"

I laughed and told him about Kermit Slade being approached on a big boulevard in Mexico City one time by a gypsy woman who rammed a hand down into his trousers and snatched out a pubic hair! Beas howled. The gypsy had examined the hair and told Kermit he had big trouble ahead. Then she got him to go to a house with her where she shoved him into a room with a girl and they took all his money and all that. Beas beamed and blushed.

We were happy together with a hundred things to talk about. I could have broken his leg for him to keep him from going to the Army. I always felt lately that he was watching me warily, and it confused me. He would sober quickly, stare at me and then look away.

Well, I told myself, nothing stays the same in the world. Life is change. Nobody but Sarah seemed really happy with the way life was. The news was worse every day. Mere anarchy is loosed, said Pom of the Nazis. I checked an empty mailbox every day. I began to believe that I was definitely in love and that it was going to make me sick and ruin my life. I felt an expectant pain most of the time. He'll never write, I warned myself.

★

The guy with the pipe and the close mouth was named Renfro. He began to watch me the way I watched him, and it seemed to me, sitting in the front seat of the station wagon with Slim, that I could feel his listening behind me. Slim and I laughed and told silly jokes together. The Renfro fellow was as quiet as wood, but uncomfortably present. His thinking was like a peculiar drone in the distance, audible to special animals only. Like me. I *knew* I could hear it.

He had a neat head, rounder and smaller than Eric's. He was taller, lanky and slow-moving. He seemed speculative. There was a small book in his pocket all the time which he read at his break, standing outside Hangar B leaning against the wall and puffing on his pipe. He nodded and watched a lot. Nobody talked to him. He worked in blueprints, someone said. Moved up from drills. His pipe smoke smelled fabulous thickening in the tight car. Even when it made me choke, I liked it. But he only sat there with his static of thinking, and when we arrived he would punch in with quiet haste and disappear. I thought he must have someone who was taking all his money, or some sorrow, something that made him solitary.

My crew and I became rowdy friends. They pushed me down in the snow and rolled me along the runway edge like a log when we got our first storm. But they lifted me and brushed me off afterward, gave me a shot of whiskey and opened their lunch pails with offers of chicken or ham or homemade bread, pie, cornbread. I stopped bringing more than an apple and my thermos of milk, which made Ruby furious. "I doan keer what they bringin, hit ain't a suppa like I fixes." "Katie," one of them would growl shyly, "here's you a coupla ribs and some cornbread. My wife told me to fatten you up. I told her you look like a goddang wooden match."

★

They continued the stories of their lives—all that bumming around, working since childhood, the farm, night school or no school. Topeka, Lubbock, Denver, Salinas, Albuquerque, Needles, Phoenix, factories, the CCC, the WPA.

"Shit, if it wasn't for that war, lemme tellya, I'd be a dead duck. Why, I was ridin the rails oney a year and a half ago. I got off stone broke in Wichita, didn't have a cryin nickel, and some dang whore come along trying to pick me up. I told her I'd love it but I was cold broke and she tuk me home anyway to where all them other whores was, regular house right up the street not two blocks from a church, and set me up in a room a my own like they was my dang sisters or somethin. And by God I stayed in that goddang house for two whole dang weeks and not a one a them whores ever laid a hand on me. Not once! They brang me my breakfast in bed and set around there yakkin like kids. Tole me everythang that ever happened to em. Shoot, they was the nicest women you'd ever wanta meet. Why, when I went outa there them girls got up a pot and sent me off with twelve dang dollars and a new suit! That's the goddang truth!"

"Aw shit! Haaaaw! Don't listen to that pig mouth, Katie. He's jest talkin big. He never said boo to no whore in his life. He's a goddang virgin if I ever saw one."

"Shut up, Smit. Leave us be. Y'all go on and git lost somewheres. Me and Katie was talkin. It's the truth, Katie. I'm probably the only man alive ever lived two weeks in a whorehouse and come out a virgin. But that was back then. Jesus, I don't know what I'da done if it hadn't a been fer these *de*fense jobs."

Smitty said he fell for a woman in Lubbock one time till he found out she was doing some dirty trick in a carnival down there. Seemed to be nice at first, but then he found out she was settin up on a table seven nights a week lettin the men try to toss a silver dollar into her. And Slim said Cut out that kinda talk. Don't you know Katie's a lady? And dragged me away to walk in the snow. We hid out as much as we worked. When we worked it was because of an emergency and then we hardly had time for supper.

In the car riding home late and tired, Slim pressed his leg against mine. It brought me down to that hard heavy loaded feeling that I had almost forgotten. I knew sometime he would look at me or touch me and that I wouldn't say no. He was older, I didn't know how old. I seemed to have moved into a close sphere with him, familiar and natural, and seemed now to see below his lined leathery face to another, more fluid face that was all expres-

sion—the wise dog look, fatalistic and witty. His hands were thickened with work, full of old splinters and scars. And he smelled honest and clean. His wife, I imagined with pleasure, washed his work clothes by hand and didn't get all the soap out.

Renfro watched us flirting in the car. I watched him watching me and I waited but he did nothing. He smoked his pipe. His eyes were like deserts—flat, light, empty except of something vast and undefined. He kept his pipe in his mouth most of the time, it seemed, and his head ducked down a bit. He thought and thought until it made you feel peeled. Who was he?

Pom

"I'm considering a move to Washington for the next year or so," he said to Abe. "I've got an itch to get my finger into things up there. If we don't get some supplies to the Russians within the next month it looks bad. I've got a friend on Dies committee. I wonder if some of us with money and influence couldn't convince those idiots . . ."

"I kinda wish for winter in a hurry now, Pom," Abe said. "If the *Russians* can't hold up on those bad roads in the west, you know damn well the Krauts will never make it. I think Russia will hold them off. They've gotten used to the Blitz. In fact, I think they're slowing down anyway. But don't go to D.C. Don't give up the Petroleum Council for gosh sakes. You're the only liberal voice on it. Can you imagine Ketchum if he didn't have you around to impress him?"

They laughed. Pom's head cleared, his anxiety thinned. "You notice," he told Abe, "that some of those Republicans in the Senate are demanding actual repeal of the Neutrality Act? It takes fear to move some men."

"Most men," said Abe.

I, said Pom to himself, am afraid.

He wanted to act, something . . . something. . . . His head seemed to be exploding all the time lately. There were so many fronts now. China too. He felt that if he couldn't concentrate on one of them, he would begin to lose his perspective.

And his perspective, oddly, would return to him quickly when he was with Beas. No other way. He took him to dinner at the country club and made his final plea.

"You've still got time, Son. . . ." knowing it was futile. The boy seemed to be under a kind of hypnosis. His queer patience and intent alarmed Pom, but he himself was made impotent by it and the more obvious it became the less control Pom had over his own opposition to it. He had lately begun to think of visiting camp wherever they might send Beas. He imagined sending the boy books, magazines, food, toilet articles. He found himself making mental lists, pondering the essentials not of survival for the boy, but of comfort. Survival? He tended to shy away from that subject.

Finally one night Beas answered his timid urging for reconsideration simply by saying—

"Grandfather, it's my life. I hafta do what I think is best for me."

And in that he heard his own rational music and wondered how this boy had become in some ways manly and elusive, staunch, quiet. What was he? Pom suddenly let him go. He didn't know just when it happened. But one afternoon he was driving on the north side of town and it hit him. Beas was lost to him. He had to let Beas go to make his own errors and commit his own sins. He passed Nina's house without realizing he was on her street and it gave him a stark empty feeling to know that they did not speak, were not friends, that he himself had so easily left her; that people's lives could break away like that, in the same town; that she lived alone in that big house; that Enid would now be lonely and then that he himself lived alone and was lonely. And he wondered about the adventure of Beasley—his going out, his blind assurance that it was right. Maybe he was leaving Enid now with an instinct for survival that made war (or what little the boy could fathom of war) seem by comparison like life. It seemed too classic—the whole idea of the adventure in war as a life lure. Beasley didn't seem like that kind of male creature. No, he had a strange fatalism about him, Beasley did. And that was what worried Pom most. Not the going so much as the hint of some—what was it?—an almost *mad* reason. One that Beas kept hidden, maybe even from himself.

On his way home that evening he stopped, without invitation, by Abe's house, something he had never done in the long history of their friendship. Abe seemed to be moved by the visit.

They talked until late in the night.

"You know," Pom said, with a queasy feeling that he was revealing some soft spot, some idiocy in himself that he had not until now even remotely suspected, "I don't know why I ever even pretended to think of moving to Washington at a time like this. I think the war itch has caught up with me. Half these boys are enlisting just to get out of town. Or maybe to avoid getting dull jobs. You remember that old feeling? See the world . . . Heh . . ."

Abe nodded. "Yeah. I used to think I was a freak for not caring about it myself. I think I was too lazy, maybe."

"And *I* was spoiled by Lou, I guess. I lived her life without questioning it. My family had traveled so much before that, anyway. Imagine staying here though, Abe, when the hordes are moving out. Maybe it's a valid reason. The crash brought everything down to such a standstill."

"Movements get started," Abe said, "and everybody's got a private secret reason to get on the bandwagon. Come to think of it, Murray's taking a stand against a whole movement isn't so much different from my staying home. Aahhhh! Who knows what

moves these kids? Maybe Beasley's . . . been too much with women or something."

Pom blushed suddenly. "Well—one can hardly call his homelife normal."

Abe nodded, sucking on his cigar and holding it out to examine it with a thoughtful stare. "He has you, Pom. He'll come through. And he's got Katie. I think that girl's got a lot of guts and individuality. But Enid . . ." He shook his head. "How can she live it, will you tell me? Doesn't the woman need a man, for one thing? Well . . . excuse me, Pom—"

"Of course she does. Of course. But . . . I think she must despise us as a breed. And I've never known why—what . . ." He shook his head. "It's still a mystery to me. All I know is, she's weak in some way and she's my son's widow."

He went home more depressed than before. He thought again of Nina and felt shabby about her, even after all this time. A woman would somehow know the crucial thing about all this— letting go of one's progeny, even a grandson. Even Nina, who was childless, would know about that, he thought.

Beasley

"I've got to see you," he told Cynthia, whispering. Her fruit mouth sauced through the phone—"Well . . ." and he went on as if driving between her legs already, his hard pushing, blind, down doggy down! "I'm going. I got my orders to report. I could come tomorrow night."

"Well . . ." She was staying with the kids. Her mother was out playing Bingo. Her mother! Even her mother attracted his stuck-out, dry, desperate fever rod.

"Well, then you'll be there . . . ?"

Her gum cracked. He licked his lips.

"Well . . . okay . . . Gee, Beasley, I'm sorry you're going into the Army. I don't think it's right."

"I'll talk to you about it. I'll be there." He almost hung up on her.

"Okay."

He went down into the basement and rubbed and jerked but it wanted to wait for her so he swore at it and lay on his back waiting for it to go down. He didn't know how he/it could wait. He woke in the night having spilled, and patiently wiped himself up. His prick meant ruin. What did you do in the Army? Nurses? Maybe between now and then he could get the secretary at the lab if there was time. He dreamed of them, thrown on the floor, splitting open, halved peaches, before his burning eyes.

No letter. Things at home were touchy. Enid sighed, paced and glowered, trying to be sober, I supposed. Yet sometimes she drank late at night in bed and woke up savage and glazed looking. And of course we all waited and felt ourselves trapped by Beas and his supposed forthcoming orders. He got up early on Saturday mornings and went way out to the mailbox several times.

"Maybe we've still got time to talk him out of it," Pom said one night.

"Aw, Hon," Sarah said, "maybe he'll decide to forget about it. He's still got time."

To which Enid flashed—"Oh, for God's sake try to take somebody seriously for a change."

My face froze as if slapped. Sarah fell gently silent. Pom cleared his throat. Beas, Enid informed us, had a right to make his own decisions.

"But I remind you, my Dear, that he is my ward and a ward of the Court until he is eighteen years . . ."

She turned on him with dead burning eyes. "If you'd taken that seriously in the first place . . ."

He turned quickly away. That was below the belt! I was building up a rage. There was a silence, and then Pom said quietly—

"It's been a delicate situation. . . ." Faltering, and then he announced that he had an appointment with Dietler at nine, kissed Sarah's cheek and left.

I felt beaten and insulted. Why didn't anyone ever put Enid in her place?

"No one has his real interest at heart," Enid whined. "Spending his evenings in that cheap Creole . . . It's a wonder—"

I turned on her. "He didn't have to go. Nobody made him go. Maybe he *wanted* to go out once in a while."

"Now Hon—let's all just . . ."

Enid turned on her. "Oh Sarah, shut up!"

I moved toward her as she headed for the sun-room.

"Listen here!"

Sarah stood up. "Katie, Hon." The softest command. I turned back to her. Enid shut her door.

"Of all the nasty mean things!" I cried.

"Shhhh!" Sarah beckoned me into the hall where I reluctantly followed. Something clear as ice had fallen over my head.

"That bitchy thing! I hate her! I *hate* her . . . !" Saying it was fabulous.

"Katie, I want you to listen now, Hon." She drew me into her room. I was shaking with rage.

"She can't talk to you like that!" I howled. "Why'd she have to move into our house anyway and louse everything up? I hate . . ."

She put her hand on my arm and her other hand to her bosom. "Oh . . ." I moved close. "Here. Sit on the bed."

She did. "I'm all right, Hon. But you've got to stop that shouting at her, Sweetheart. Beasley got his orders today."

Like a shot. "His *orders*! He didn't tell *me* . . ."

"He told her while you were out. He's gone into town for something, Hon, I don't know what."

"I thought he was being taken to dinner by his boss."

"No. That was supposed to be next week. He's tending to something. Law, he's been on that phone . . ."

"I know it. I wondered. Gee . . ."

We looked at each other. Pity, her eyes seemed to say, as always. But I felt harder than that. Even love, thank God, was harder than pity. And fear was more fierce and better. And hatred? I hated Enid gratefully. How had I kept it from myself? *That* was what the Biography had sought—not her reason but my hatred!

When he came home Beas showed me the orders. To Camp Claiborne, Louisiana.

"Listen," he said. "Let's go to town. You let me off somewhere I have to go. Then I'll come back and meet you at the Creole."

"Yeah? What's up?"

He stared sternly. "I have a date."

"A *date*? It's ten o'clock. Who with?"

He kept his mouth shut. And so I shrugged and laughed a little, amazed. Beas had never had a date.

Enid's face seemed an agony of disbelief when we went out. And the irony was that this time he wasn't going to the Creole.

I let Beas off on a corner. He wouldn't tell me where he was going but he came back to the Creole for me at about one thirty in the morning looking like a dead cat.

★

The next day by two P.M. she was so drunk she couldn't walk. Ruby heard her fall against the phone table in the hall and ran to help her back to bed, Enid muttering Son of a bitch, pawing the air. I watched secretly, ashamedly, unable to bear contact with her. If we had been alone in the house I might have let her lie there.

Ruby shook her head. "What goan become of that woman when little Beasley go off is what I like to know. She tryin to die, that woman."

It sickened me. Sarah slept through it and we kept it from her. Enid's aromas were heavy in the house now. I recalled how pure we had been before her moving in. Well, it was good to have the hatred with which to squelch my pity.

Slim took the others home first and took me to a roadhouse where we drank beer. He kissed me with hard-man lips, a desperate kiss, rough and shy. When I got home at two A.M. I found it. They had laid it on my pillow so I wouldn't miss it.

Dear Katie,

I've been on deck the whole goddamn day freezing my ass learning to fire these big 4-inch guns, antisubmarine stuff. Beautiful guns. Lifting the damn shells alone is a job. Too tired at night to dream, but if I did it would be of you-know-who and what. Besides I'm just getting over the effects of some double-strength typhoid shots they gave us. I have a feeling we'll be sent to the Pacific before long.

Kid, I think of you as my Baby, numero uno, my red whizzer cannonball Kiddo. Don't forget it.

Listen Beas has probably told you about that night I took him out, but I want you to hear my side of it. I couldn't help it, I had to help him out. He would have lost his chance with Cynthia if I hadn't shown him how, you know, just a little. He would have felt like a dumb son of a bitch if he had gone off to the Army without doing it. But it was only to show him how, honest. I never would climb on CG for any other reason especially since you and me. I went off in the woods as soon as he got started. You ask him.

Baby you know you're my Baby. I hope you are. I want your letters. When a man on the ship gets mail and I don't I feel like knocking him flat. I can't forget all our fun and it will never be like that with anybody else for me. Maybe I'm crazy but I think you feel like that too.

I hafta get up at five thirty in this man's crazy Navy so good night.

I might as well have left the old monkey in the zoo for all the company he keeps me. Ha. If you know what I mean. Send me a picture so I won't have to put Betty Grable up on the wall like these guys here. They're all tit-happy for one thing and never heard of anything else it seems. How are you Kid? Miss me? Did you go to work? Write me.

Love, your lonesome sailor
Eric.

I lay stark awake all night. I felt as if the breath had been knocked out of me.

So. That was what Beas was doing in the closet with the phone. I, O dumbness, O Arch Assinopolite, O Delirian of Delirians, had thought he was talking about the *Army* with somebody all that time!

Cynthia Gillespie. She was fast. She was pretty. She laughed a lot and lived in a run-down neighborhood and had a lot of loud, tough brothers. Her mother did housework. She was supposed to like sex better than anyone alive.

So. Cynthia Gillespie.

I got up at six A.M. and looked in the mirror at his red whizzer cannonball Kiddo! I could see my pulse pounding in my neck. I looked different—stiller, thicker. Life was going to kill me before it let me live.

And then I realized that I had been falling hard for him all that time. That he was perfect for me and I hadn't quite awakened to him before he left. He had hurried me too much and then gone. And Beas was going off to the Army not a virgin. Very smart. Men were very smart.

I lost my appetite.

Enid

"Bob? Am I calling too early?"

"Enid! No, no. I opened up early today. I'm redoing the lobby and cocktail room at the Sooner. It's a bitch of a job trying to decide what those dirty old men want. Heeee! What's on you mind, Sweetheart, as if I didn't know."

"I think you're trying to kill me with this awful stuff you brought, that's what's on my mind."

"Sweetheart! That's a good brand. Really. I've got a dozen people who drink it."

"Pssss. That doesn't mean it's good. Can't you get me something else? What was that you used to bring, last summer early?"

"I'll try to get you something standard. I think there's a hole in the bottom of St. Louis. I can't get a *thing* up there anymore. And now it's so hard to get there at all. I'm not seeing that friend I told you about anymore and I have to stay in a hotel and they're all full of Army these days. Not that I mind *Army*! But try to find a place to lay your little *head* these days! I'm going up to the antique show on the sixteenth. I *think*. You want some wine too?"

"Try to get me something good. Yes, I'll take the wine. And don't bring it to the house anymore. You know. I'm going to have my hair done at Consuelo's that week. You can always leave it there for me. And don't put it in shoe boxes or anything like that, Bobby. Wrap it like a . . . You know, a hat box or something. Square maybe. Will you do that for me?"

"Oh, you kill me! You really do. Listen, Dear, how are you? You really oughta quit, if you want my humble opinion. Jesus Christ, Enid! A woman like you out of circulation! Breaks my heart. Give the world a break, Dear. Really!"

"Oh, be quiet! Don't forget now. How are you, Bobby, anyway?"

His high whiney swansong laugh. "Oh, God! Don't ask. I'm so lonesome sometimes I could just—fade out. You know? What a world for a man of my tastes! The streets are *swarming* with flesh. You *seen* it? How long since you've been downtown? My God, it drives me *mad*! It's all young and prime and here I sit working for Mavis and Annette. Mavis got me this job at the Sooner. Oh, I don't know. Have you seen her, by the way? Since her lift? Jesus! She looks at *least* thirty years younger. At *least*! Her rich sister paid for it . . . the old fart! It's about time she did something for Mavis. Mavis has knocked herself out for that old bitch and what does she have to . . ."

"I haven't seen her. Tell her hello. Don't forget, Bobby, leave it at Consuelo's. I won't keep you . . ."

" 'Bye, Sweetheart. Get up and come have a bite with me some night. If it wasn't for the Brosky and her parties, I'd be in my *grave.*"

★

She remembered one of the doctors, Wycoff maybe, asking, Why drink from a bottle? Don't you deserve a drink in a glass, among friends, like everybody else?

She couldn't remember going from the glass to the bottle. Jack used to drink rum, had that little flask in his hip pocket all the time. That heavy dense smell of it. Man smell. Too heavy. Fanchon Clark drank gin. Killed her. But from the glass to the bottle was going backward maybe. And imagine a woman with a flask. Well, was a flask a bottle? Yes, Jack had been on the bottle too, then, if a flask was a bottle. But he had never been down like this, never been in bed and lost and gone from them all. He had stayed on his feet and driven them crazy and ruined his life and their lives. He had never gone to bed. But she had brought him down off his feet finally and done it when they were both sober. But from the glass to the bottle was interesting. Wycoff had asked her that seven years ago, and it just now lately, here at Sarah's, had become interesting.

It was because . . . No, it was *when* . . . Something to do with Jack. She had seen the truth about him one night when they were dressing to go out. Her beaded dress lay on the bed. Jack had taken a risk on some drilling with that crooked friend of Pom's, Ketchum. Behind Pom's back. And lost. And had had to borrow from Pom to pay back the loan in a single sum. Loss was something so intolerable to Jack that it had gone to his system like a poison and festered there. His neck pulse vivid, clear across the room. His hard curled thumbs. Why hadn't she seen all that when they had first gotten together? The strangeness of a man other than Daddy. The queer surprise of the softness of Jack's hair, the black curls, on his hard round head. The blunt courting of her. *When can I come over? What's the matter with the old man? Doesn't he like me? Can't he let you out of his sight for five minutes?* The huge need that seemed to rise up under the surface and alter him before her eyes. She had never known a man except Daddy. It was all Jack—what they did together, what they were. She had waited. Jack had thought it was the *two* of them together, but it had been all him. She hadn't changed much. His struggles with life had been so pathetic and ridiculous, and dangerous. He hadn't known the right, real things. There was something he had never ever known.

That night, standing in her slip, watching him. All at once knowing that he had no future or no way out of himself. Something. The sudden horror. She had sat on the bed, fussed with her silk stockings. He had said, "I'll show that Ketchum bastard. What a crook!"

"You knew he was a crook before you got into that deal."

"Shut up." That was all he had said. Not even violently. And then he had put in his cuff links and gone into the pantry to fill his flask and had made a telephone call while she sat on the bed knowing something too huge to be moved against or avoided. She had sat and known that Jack wasn't doing anything or going anywhere or learning or changing. No movement but that wild circle like the whirlpool that sucked him down. That he was crazy. Yes, and incomplete.

She had let Humphrey Stebbins bring her home. Jack had been drunk and had gone out the back entrance of the Sooner Hotel, leaving her in the ballroom with a table of people—Humphrey and some others—and had beaten in the fender of someone's Packard. A stranger's car, beaten in for no reason except that Jack didn't know what to do with himself any more than an animal did. Humphrey took her home. Put his arms around her. Fixed her a drink. Another drink. She went to bed stark sober and was awakened by the police calling to say Jack was in jail, Pom out of town.

Keep him, she had said.

And then some strange sickness hit her and she stayed in bed a week. Found an old witch-hazel bottle and filled it with bourbon, put it under the mattress. From the glass to that. And then all the rest. Jack home. Defeated. Hitting Beasley that time. She had moved into her own bedroom. Then moved to Sarah's. Then moved home again. He sold the house, not telling her. Then the crash . . . the shot . . .

Wycoff had said at Menninger's, When you come to the crucial moments you stop. You see that now, don't you?

But the sorting out was too hard on her brain. She had told him so and told him to leave her alone.

I don't want to do all that work just to let you know what I already know. Confession doesn't do anything for me. I confess to you that I drink, that I killed my husband, that I am not much of a mother. What else do you want?

But since moving into the lease house now, with Sarah and Katie, having gone from the glass to the bottle seemed more complicated than that. What was it?

She lay very still and courted it. And then, looking across the room at the vague moving shapes in the mirror, reflections of some motion in the tree outside the window, she caught it and her heart began to race. It was being *seen*. Being seen in all stages, all aspects but not quite at dead-drunk center. Being seen on the way into the sweet terror of the heart of it, or on the way out. Being seen. Yes.

She sat up. She wanted to tell that to someone. She had never wanted to tell anything to anyone before. But it was interesting and nothing much had interested her before except Jack in the first year or two of their life together.

She thought she might be able to do it—to tell it and then to stop. Altogether. The shaking would be terrible, she had tried once or twice for a few days and had had that long dry spell at Menninger's. But if someone were seeing and knowing what it was, then maybe the shaking could be handled.

She thought of Serene. And of Wycoff. Of Menninger's. Back to Menninger's? No, never back. Never go back. Serene might help. But if she got up, to what world would she do it? For what? Beas was going. For the sake of writing him letters? Not enough.

She sat on the side of the bed anticipating the shaking. Starting *now*! If someone—Serene?—came into the room and said, *Now, Enid! Now!* she might. She had dreamed a few nights before of Serene who in the dream had a scooped-out place in her neck where one's head was placed when being carried across the river. Into another dimension?

She wanted to try. She lay back panting with the excitement. She settled, thinking nothing, waiting. And then she gave a little cry and snatched the bag out from under the mattress and held it against her chest, not opening it. Her heart pounded. Being seen was it, and if *all* of it were seen then she might be able to stop. Or to try. To get up. She was already up more than before. But Swan was already planning to bring her another order. She waited, her palpitations decreasing. And then she imagined that a hand swept lightly over her forehead. She let herself sink down. Sarah was waiting to give her a cup of coffee but she let herself sink back and down.

★

She was in the phaeton with Daddy. Along the road. Rosy prancing. The jingle.

Daddy's nod, his little fond chuckle—Sarah was born of his fond chuckle, resurrecting him in her laugh—Daddy saying, "I used to own all this, clear across to the mountain and down beyond the woods there to the line. Now it's Route 121. Bledsoe bought a third, after I built the building downtown. Needed a little cash and I let him have it. Buy land, Baby. Marry a man who has land and hang onto it. Locusts and people, dust, tramps, they all ruin land that's not watched out for."

At Hemmer's farm, stopping for springwater. Mr. Hemmer's grave squint. Mrs. Hemmer, clabber with raspberries. Leaning into Daddy's side as into forever.

Home late and tired. Mother's whine.

"Kevin, you oughtn't to keep her out of school this way."

Daddy. His chuckle, the slow radiance of confidence, a burning energy in his sides.

"She knows her Latin, now don't you, Baby? I want her with

me. She's my last baby. I want her to see how this country looked when I came out here. I want her to see the Cherokee Line. We saw Hemmer today. He's making out all right now. That's a gratifying thing—to help a man and see him thrive. Now where's my lunch, Mother? I want my chowder."

She hadn't known her Latin. He had never waited for her answer. She knew her math. Not her English. Not her history. Not her Latin. Daddy did her knowing for her.

Days like cards laid face down, all the same. Played out.

★

She reached for the strings, pulled open the little bag and the bottle slipped out onto the quilt. She opened it matter-of-factly and took a sip. Then she put it away and got up to drink her coffee with Sarah.

Pom had a birthday party for Beas at the country club. I went as if to a hanging. I waited for him to tell me about Cynthia, about that night, but he said nothing. I couldn't answer the letter. I went to work, forgot it for long minutes, and then was swamped with it again. I stared into space. They washed all Beasley's underwear and hung it out on the line. We got a freeze and Ruby brought it in all stiff, hung it around the kitchen to thaw, ironed it like parts of Beas reassembled for a new life. Ruby had begun to love Beas like everyone else did.

Cynthia Gillespie!

The letter didn't give details.

He didn't say I love you.

He did say My red whizzer cannonball Kiddo. You know you're my Baby.

I carried the letter around in my coveralls pocket and reread it in quick snatches. Slim saw me. In the dark of the car coming home, he pressed my leg as always. I shut my eyes pretending to sleep. He took everyone home first and then said, "Let's us go to the Rooster Hut and git a beer. I wanta hear what's eatin you."

I told him everything because he had told me so much, and he nodded quietly. But I couldn't make it sound real to him.

Beas and Cynthia Gillespie, Eric and Cynthia Gillespie. The Army. Enid. Sarah . . . I rattled it out and Slim, that skinny character, took it all very seriously.

"Sounds to me like you've got a good life. Don't sound so bad to me."

I couldn't answer Eric's letter. I tried, dozens of lines. I wanted to say the very thing to him, just what I felt and knew and was, but I couldn't do it.

He wrote several frantic letters of apology. I finally got an answer together that said—

I don't know how I feel about it. You're so far away. But I'll never forget about us.

I told him my news. But I couldn't make the connection between the Eric absent from Deliria and the recipient of letters somewhere out there, because somewhere out there was nowhere.

It came to me then that I had never written a letter except in secret. I couldn't really understand the thing that is said at one moment and heard or read several days or maybe weeks later. I could only understand now.

Aha! *The Eternal Now cannot be expressed in language.*

"Well," said Slim, "most men'll cheat a little. But at least he told ya about it."

So Slim. Maybe Higgens was this kind of man. We began to take everyone home first, clear into town, including the Renfro fellow who lived in a room on the north end of Deliria, an old decent run-down neighborhood as silent at night as a graveyard. Then we would get a beer and afterward go into the woods near the lease. He had a real mattress in the back of the station wagon, the nearest I had come to a sex bed except for that one time at Eric's and for Ruby's borrowed bed. And every time we did it I thought about Eric. I was more depressed over the fact that he might never come back than over Cynthia, but it was Cynthia who made me mute.

★

"Why me?" Slim said out of a cigarette.

"Why not?"

"I'm no kinda man fer you. You know that. And you've got that fella in the Navy."

"I like you," I said.

He shrugged, confused. And so I had to go on liking him to make him believe it. But I began to pity him for the dull routine he quickly made of it, as if that were the only spirit in which such things could take place, as if we had been married for years. So, queerly enough, although he insisted at first I was too good for him, once he was convinced that I really liked him, he started to act as if I were barely good enough. And that forced me to admit to myself that I was, after all, too good for him. Whatever that meant. And I began to strive to elevate him or stir him out of his lethargy of ordinariness. Making love didn't surprise him, that was it. It seemed to be the same for him as the boring and ordinary food he found in his lunch box every day—that cheap old cotton bread enclosing a piece of baloney and the apples she put in there, mushy or, if from their own tree, wormy. And the slices of Velveeta cheese with hard dry edges, the three-day-old cinnamon rolls that smelled slightly of lard. His fare had always been stale and uninspiring and that was how he took me—more of the same.

★
Where
You
Goin,
Girlie?
★
153

But he had something that made me yield and even at times pursue him—the mere manness of him and the fragile presence that loomed in him when he was beyond control in sex, something ghostly that was like a memory I briefly witnessed floating in his head's landscape, a memory of the further, other, unavailable Slim. The old Katie that I was—Eric's cannonball—had been put on ice.

I stayed with Slim for a while. He stirred new, more grown-up strivings after the mystery of Higgens in my soul and kept me from missing Eric so much. I told him about Higgens and he said I oughtn't to trouble about it, that a person was alone anyway and didn't need to know about his ancestry. My mother was enough, he said. So he dawned on me as a mere dull man. His old banter in the car fell apart after we got thick. And it had never been, I saw, anything unusual in the first place. He ruined himself with seriousness, mainly about himself. I asked him about his wife but he didn't want to talk about her.

"I ain't about to leave er, I kin tell you that. Jist keep that in mind."

"Who asked you to leave her?" I flared.

"Nobody. I jist thought I'd tell ya."

I stopped going with him finally and he didn't pursue it. I told him at the Rooster Hut, over a beer, my fourth, and weeping a little as if I were Ida Lupino giving up Gary Cooper.

I went out a few times with Bern Swayse, an inspector at the plant, and a few times with a foreman named Clifford who ate even the bones of his barbequed chicken, picked his teeth afterward with studied thoroughness and then burped softly into my ear when we danced. And sweated a lot besides but was a kind of stolid version of Robert Taylor and had been to college for six years which seemed to have taught him very little including how to kiss and wasn't too kissable anyway.

And then I had a period of unconversational activity with Smitty who just wanted to do the fox trot at a roadhouse and show me off, he said, to the bums there. He was thick and short, just my height, very solid, arcing his arm down my back with a hand just above my rear cleft when we danced. He said he wished he could afford a mistress and I said who'd want to be a mistress and he said almost every woman he'd ever met was who.

But he was a very good fancy dancer and he did have a way of looking at you with kind concern and understanding that made you tell him something as true as your nose. You had to like him. He took me to the auto races one Saturday and to play miniature golf at his cousin's course which was opened especially at two A.M. in our honor in the freezing weather. We played, nipping whiskey from Smitty's flask, and then later he said in the front seat of his Dodge with the heater wheezing loudly—

"Katie, I've just gotta take you someplace and neck you a little." And I laughed so hard he grabbed me there with his feet on the brake and the clutch and kissed me with one of those thick anonymous-man whiskey kisses that always hit me in the gizzard. Sex, I cannot get enough of you, O fiend from hell!

So we went to a motel where he knew the manager and if it hadn't been for his sweetness I would have cried and hated myself. But I knew now that this was a certain sad part of the world's stupidity—this motel business. Everyone understood about sex—that there was no place to do it. The room was all maroon and green and the gas was escaping from the little heater in the corner. It smelled like a bus station. In Joplin maybe. I thought of Eric and the first time he showed me the lights of Deliria and said I was a bad wiring job. I decided never to sleep with anyone again. I wanted Eric to come home and take me to the woods again.

But Smitty was solid and warm. He was happy. Since leaving his wife, he said. "Man, that was the first day of my real life! When I run off from that dame." But when he was naked beside me, his hard stomach and his powerful thick blunt rocket thrusting out, he said that *she* had left *him*. His watchband left a long red thin gash on my arm. And when we got going he said Oh God, if he'd known that this could happen between us he would have thrown all those bums out of the bomber and laid me down on the floor of it.

Eric's letters, they came every four or five days, seemed to be addressed to someone known enough to be loved, but he never said again that he loved me. I wrote terrible stilted letters that I knew must have infuriated him. That was not his Cannonball red whizzer Kiddo talking at all, not her arms and legs talking. Once I ventured, *Dear Eric, I miss you. I'm going out with a lot of dumb guys.* Because by that time I was. I had stopped with Smitty and given Kirby Parks a try, and Ron Somebody, and others. Into bed and out like a bedbug. I kept a vague count and liked it all in certain ways. But it did not occupy me. I was moving through them as one moves through traffic toward a certain place, more even than toward a certain person. Eric answered—

Dear Katie, those dumb guys would never appreciate you the way I do. Maybe I'll get home on leave after OCS. We'll have fun again like we used to. Don't forget, Kid.

I answered later, *I never forget.*

But the absent person was not real to me. Not even as real as George Raft or Cary Grant.

And then certain things happened, like blows, like armies moving in. Starting with the departure of Beas.

Pom didn't cry at the train, of course, but stamped a foot strangely. He did not hug but embraced Beas. His dandy suited body always embraced, a formality that could be indulged publicly. Oh shorn Beas! We wouldn't get him back! I was not prophesying but preparing. Preparedness, ah yes, I was getting the hang of it. There's only one thing to prepare for.

He smelled as always—soda, old buried experiments, indomitable health, rain on shoes and hair, boy. I did hug him, quick and stern. "Don't worry," he whispered, shaking. The train blew steam on us.

I tried to laugh a little, to cheer him. "Have fun with all those . . . Army characters and all." He smiled. "Write me a lot. Everything . . ." I kept talking.

Then he hoisted his suitcase up the steps and waved to us from the window. There was a soldier at the train and several sailors. With wonder I saw that I did not know everybody in Deliria.

The train crept out into the gray morning. I was glad Pom and I had come alone. Pom looked frozen, though, and about to break open. Maybe he'd go home, put on his dressing gown and patent slippers, pour out a sherry and then cry. Oh, men! Why didn't they admit anything?

He saw me to the electric. "Maybe," he said, "they'll have the sense to put him in the Intelligence Service."

"Gee, maybe so Pom. He'd make a good spy. He's so . . . unbiased and obscure."

"Beas . . . obscure? But he's highly—"

I laughed quickly. "I mean he wouldn't reveal himself. If he carried valuable papers nobody would believe it. Let Shirley Temple carry valuable papers. It's the same thing."

He laughed, holding my arm when I got into the car. "Ha! Well, Dear, you have an original way of looking at things."

His voice shook. "Tell Sarah I'll be out later," he said. "Tell Enid he's safely off."

"Oh, Pom . . ."

"God knows what they'll do with him! Let's hope they push him into an office or the Medical Corps. Well, we'll hear from him soon. And we'll call him every Sunday."

"Okay, Pom."

I drove with caution. I didn't want to live in Deliria without Beas. I was going to have to get out into the chancy world myself. Soon. Starting by saving my money tomorrow. The sleet nicked the windshield. I purred through it. I wouldn't go to the Creole anymore, either. I wondered, moving through town, what the Renfro fellow did on Sundays. I wanted some bleak celebration. But they were waiting for me at home. Maybe Rube would make something sweet with me. I hurried when I got to the lane, spinning and smearing through the icy mud. The house looked strange to me, hunkered down there, Hon, in its friendly desolation. Inside, Ruby, ah ha, had made a cake, using her own vanilla which had originally been our vanilla anyway.

Pom

His throat burned. Something about putting Beas on that train, about Beas alone in an anonymous world, yes, among thousands of youths, country boys, sons of plumbers—that noble boy! He felt a caving in at the middle of his body. He sat still in the car listening to the train. He would let it out in a minute, cry torrents. Surely he would. He put the key in the ignition but only sat, waiting.

I'm not doing the right thing, he prayed abstractly. I know I am all wrong. I've lost them both. I don't know what a father is supposed to do, say, feel, I don't know the *being* of it. I've only known the logic of it, moving their lives. I oughtn't to have moved their lives. I don't know who he is, not really.

I'm so solitary. So lonely. I am lonely for . . . I never had it. *Never!* Even with Lou. I belonged to Mother. I feared Father, hated him. I wanted his death. I don't understand. Please let him be all right. Let him learn fast. Let them see what he is among all those hundreds of others. Please . . .

He wiped his eyes, gasping and weeping. He blew his nose and then backed out and moved into the street, aware that the car was too big, he was too dressed, stuffed in himself somehow. Katie had said a good spy. The absurd cruelty of the young, trying to fathom the world. Oh, God! He had done nothing, *nothing* that could be said to be real. Why hadn't he swept them all up, made them strong and safe, made them know his affection? His power. He had been steadfast but that wasn't passionate. Real affection, he knew in a spasm of revelation, was passionate. Oh, God! It was perverse to feel *now*, to regret *now*. He had let Beas go as if letting some piece of self go to do a delayed chore. He felt it as a personal sacrifice.

He cruised up Main Street for three blocks before turning onto his short-cut route home. Christmas trees up, overhead decorations—great red bells with shimmering garlands strung between, lights would come on soon. It needed snow, the scene. Life was simply there somewhere under the horrors or they would not ceremonially put up these trappings. Salvation Army woman in a bonnet, tolling her bell.

He passed the hot-tamale wagon on Cincinnati, the long boulevard that led south to his neighborhood. Instead of going on, he turned left, went around the block and headed back to town past the wagon again, slowed, went on. The Mexican stood blowing on his hands and stamping his feet. Probably didn't make two dollars a day. He gave a greeting with a toss of his head, recognizing Pom's car. Pom waved. Enid wouldn't appreciate hot tamales today. Too therapeutic. He had once bought Lou a corned beef on rye filled with sauerkraut, a dripping garlicky sandwich he had found somewhere in Paris and carried up to the room the night after a performance to an unresponsive audience. They had laughed like children. "Perfect shock treatment, Darling," she had said, dividing into it. "Go get us some beer."

Something in that little moment, the marvelous crude taste, heavy and satisfying, had driven out the blues. He had felt a triumph in it. He had caught and momentarily tamed and fattened his fastidious flighty fringilla, Frau Finch, with pickled meat and cabbage. They had gone out later to walk in the Place Madeleine and had picked up a Herald Express. Barnum & Bailey were touring Europe. They took an express to Berlin, caught the last day of the circus and saw the Kaiser in his black-and-yellow motorcar inspecting the mechanics of the circus's packing up. Sometimes he thought Lou was secretly happier without a play in the works, happier traveling with him, running about like that on impulse, happening onto little scenes, spectating with him. The world was the real theater. He hadn't seen before now that he had been lonely with her, waiting always for the few moments she might spare him like that, most of them the result of some little failure of hers. And anyway, he said half aloud now, she was to die soon after. To die. Not to see this war, Jack a grown man. Beasley.

And then—he spun around, cheered a little—he had taken her to Seville for Holy Week, and up to Cordova where she had spent hours in the mosque, spinning silently through the tunnels of arches like a moth, like a dancer. That Christian nave, she had said, is like a shaft put into a heart.

He stopped at the little wagon and bought a dozen tamales after all, mainly for Enid. Sarah would eat one, Katie three maybe, if she was not too depressed. He would give her something now, too, Katie. The tamales smelled honky-tonk lying on the car seat on a newspaper, the bag quickly stained with grease. He missed cities, he thought. Real cities. He'd go to Europe again, if the war didn't destroy it. But his heart kept falling that way, not consoled by memories, plans, gestures.

The traffic he had attributed to Christmas was more probably defense vitality. The money was loose again. Five years ago the whole town—Katie's Deliria—had been somnolent, the life blown out of it by dust and the crash. And once, long before that, Kevin McCleod had stood at the line at noon on the day of the Cherokee Run and nipped over the border to stake out two thousand acres, part of which Pom now drove through from the heart of town to the county line. Skyscrapers in the making before all the streets were even paved. Oil. The wasteful boastful flambeaus in the fields. Now it had to get them through the war. What could Japan hope to do without oil from the West? Borneo. Philippine rubber. She'd have to make her move soon. Meantime she was counting on Hitler reaching the Caucasus, of course. Oh, well, war was inevitable for the Americans. Why trouble it? Wait till it happens.

But I mustn't despair, he told himself, turning into the lease lane. I mustn't remain passive. I must achieve something in the positive comparable to the relinquishing of Beas.

The departure of Beas. Something integral to us had hooked itself onto him and was drawn out with him, loosening us. Our world unwound. His basic training was almost over and he would be home on leave soon.

Enid's seesaw life was down again. Up for a while and then down. Down was more permanent and convincing. Sarah shooed the clients out the back door, through Ruby's kitchen where they sampled a little of this or that and asked her, on the sly, if she would like a new job. That had been going on for years but they seemed unusually adamant this season. Ruby lowered her eyes and said I be's very happy right heah. Thank you very much, Ma'am. And after they were out the door—Shhhhttt!—of course. But when they saw or were informed of her pregnancy, they quit asking her.

Sunday. Late breakfast. Enid had written Beas a letter, which lay on the sideboard. We were to call him as usual that evening. She smoked and looked out the windows at the scraps of snow that had fallen. Sarah rested and I listened to "University of Chicago Round Table." I had begun to enjoy my days off at home, hating Enid with less relish but more conviction maybe, and watching Sarah, reading to her, talking about my savings of six dollars a week. She laughed every time I gave her my paycheck. But oh I missed Beas and Eric and my red-whizzer life, and the Creole. I hadn't seen Nina since going to work.

Around noon that day the phone rang. The Renfro fellow made a little breathy sound with his pipe which I recognized. I tingled all over. Then he said, "How'm I ever going to get a chance to talk to you? You live out there in the sticks and I don't have a car."

I laughed. "We're talking right now."

He made that little sound, a prolonged little hum that was his laugh, and asked if I ever came into town, talking on the phone bothered him.

Daytimes, I said, wondering why I didn't say meet me at the Creole. I decided quickly that he was poor and supporting his mother or something. He had that look of not only absence of money but disdain for it. His voice was a soft low stirring in the throat. He cleared his throat a lot and hesitated, taking long breaths. I felt like a fly, skittering across a windowpane.

"You know the Sunshine Café?" he asked and I laughed aloud. "Well, what's so funny about the Sunshine Café?" he said, amused.

"Never mind. I know it. Shall I meet you there?"

"Yeah. I'll buy you lunch. Then we can ride out to the plant together."

Tommorow. A date. Like before. Calling on the phone, not just asking me at work. The Sunshine! Ha! *How'm I going to get a chance to talk to you?* He'd been watching. I'd been waiting.

And then it rang again and Pom's voice rasped out high and shocked, ruining my fantasy.

"What? Pearl *what*? What's *that*? Huh? Where is it? Is it American?"

It was American. It was being bombed by Japanese planes. Our Pacific Fleet was being cut down. Turn on your radio, he said. Let me speak to Sarah. No, don't call her, I'll just come out, he said.

Pearl Harbor.

My heart thudded like a great ominous knock on a thick door. Enid came into the hall.

"What is it? Is it Beasley?"

It was, ultimately, Beasley, I told myself. I knew what the fates were doing. She looked shattered.

"No. No . . . Pom's coming out. It's the Japanese. They're bombing some place called Pearl Harbor."

"Oh my God! My God!"

She wandered into the parlor. A dread excitement swamped me. Sarah got up then. The phone began to ring—clients. Iantha called, crying. Sarah said Come on out, Hon. I turned on the radio and the voice began and didn't stop, for days, weeks . . . months . . .

This is Burns. Eugene Burns. We're being bombed. They're over us now and the attack is still going on.

I never even heard of Pearl Harbor, I kept saying. And Sarah said that Daddy had taken Mama out there to Hawaii in 1904, in the winter, about this time of year. That beautiful harbor, those lovely people . . .

I turned the dial and got a fantasia of reports.

My flesh crawled. Enid sat holding the arm of her chair and sucking on her empty cigarette holder. I thought of them all— Beas, Eric, Brad Finch, Wishbone, Horace . . .

But Pom had to come before it was truly said, nailed down. He wore a velveteen jacket and silk shirt, he smelled of bay rum. "There's an extra on the street already. We're in it now for sure." He swept a hand through his hair and listened fixedly.

This is San Antonio. News of the bombing of Pearl Harbor has rocked this city on its heels. All men ordered to posts at Corpus Christi Naval Air

Filipinos in Dallas feared to go into the streets. Some of them put signs in their windows explaining that they were not Japanese. Recruiting offices opened and were swamped within an hour.

Pom scowled. "Opened on Sunday?"

Ships were sinking or being blown apart—the *Arizona*, the *Oklahoma*—as if they were states on a burning map.

Ruby came, fright-haired, and made coffee cake. We hung on the radio and she hung in the doorway. The radio was bedlam. Iantha drove out, seven miles, to report that the Japs were dirty little yellow cheats, pretending to be here on a peace mission, and Pom did not contradict her. This is it, he kept saying. What a tragedy!

My mind crept out into the horizon. What, at this very moment, was Beas doing and thinking? I forgot Eric. I tried to concentrate my beneficent thoughts on Beas. Some man from Chicago was saying—

Rightly or wrongly, people seem to believe all the so-called experts' claims that Japan has only two bathtubs in its navy, no money, no oil, and that all Japanese fliers are so cross-eyed they couldn't hit Lake Michigan with a bomb.

Ruby snickered. Pom snorted. "They're not doing bad for a starter." Iantha said that you couldn't believe a thing you heard from Chicago. It was full of Jews and Italians. Finally there was a break and a little music. Pom paced. This would mean, he explained, that all leaves would be canceled. *All* of them. They might have to ship those boys out with a minimum of basic training. Enid bit her lips. Sarah said softly, Law, Hon, there'll be so many, they'll have enough. Beas, Pom went on, might not get home for Christmas.

"But I'll drive us all down there to see him before they ship him out."

Enid went out of the room. Iantha said she would feel better if she knew what Serene had to say about it.

"What is there to say about it?" Pom asked her fastidiously. "We've been bombed! He'll make a formal declaration tomorrow. This is war, that's all."

All leaves were canceled.

We couldn't reach Beas. He didn't reach us. The Japanese attacked Malaya, Hong Kong and places I'd never heard of—Guam, Wake Island, Midway. And the Philippines.

Everyone called again Monday—clients, Iantha, Di. Di was going to quit the plant and become a Red Cross worker. She wanted to marry a man in the Service. Why? I didn't even ask. What she wanted to do was marry. I didn't even know whether or not I wanted to marry. It rarely crossed my mind. Eric's letters suddenly stopped for a while. I missed Beas and things as they had been, yet I breathed in a new air suddenly and wanted to do something important.

★

Hattie Finch had a kind of nervous collapse. I drove Sarah in to see her and left her there while I had lunch with Renfro. Iantha took her home. Renfro was waiting in a booth at the Sunshine, sitting very still and reading a little volume of Nietzsche.

"I'm always early," he said. "Don't worry about it."

We sat down facing one another and I liked it like crazy. I said I couldn't believe the news and he smiled. "You sound happy about it," he said, and then the waitress came and we ordered. He took out his pipe.

"Well, it's exciting," I said. "It's like the end of a big sleep or something. You know how dull this town is."

"It seems kinda lively to me," he said. "But then I've been on the move a long time. Now everything will change. Military. We'll have some rationing, I guess."

"Lucky I don't use gas, huh?" I said.

We began to exchange certain vital statistics, cautiously. He mused, you had to call it that, about everything. Nothing seemed to surprise him. I hadn't yet hit him with Sarah and the clients and all that, though. He smoked his pipe right through his lunch, laying it carefully in the ashtray and picking it up after a few bites, finding it had gone out, fussing, sucking and then laying it down again. He didn't seem to know he was doing it. He smiled with his mouth shut. This was the same character who had been sitting all those weeks in the back of the car watching me with Slim. But the Slim of Slim-and-me didn't seem to bother him at all.

He began to talk about his last ten years, bumming around. I loved it! He had lived in a couple of piano boxes once for a few months, like the ones in those Hoovervilles we used to see when we went traveling with Pom.

"God! I used to want to set up housekeeping in one of those things myself! When I was little. I thought they were the very last thing!"

He laughed slightly, his eyes burned with something near to cunning glee, I couldn't be sure, he kept his mouth so tight.

"They're the last thing all right. Heh. But it wasn't bad in the good weather."

"Why'd you move?"

He shrugged. That was the way of it then, moving on. There might be something worthwhile further on, a job, day work. He had gotten used to it. He read a lot and stopped worrying about food and all. He had library cards in thirty-one towns.

"Why'd you come here?"

"I was born here."

"Oh. Me too. We're both Delirians."

He chuckled. And then he changed the subject and talked about theories he was acquiring about war and history.

"It's possible in times of crisis to see everything on an entirely different basis," he said. "Crisis allows for a break-up of old forms. We'll be seeing a new world now. It's funny though how used you can get to an anonymous life. Has its virtues. You have a new, different importance that's more . . . oh . . . mystical, you might say. But bumming . . ." He shrugged it off, self-disgusted. "It makes a bum of you, I guess, no matter what."

"Oh. Really?" I thought of Ida Brady Foresman's initials on the cloth with which I had washed my face that morning, and I knew I could never tell him my own kind of importance and unimportance.

He studied me with those opaque eyes like Henry Fonda's. There was something raw about him. When we left he moved along as though I were a dog that could keep up by itself. No holding doors open or anything like that. He kept his lips puckered around the pipe and strolled along like a man in a western movie with the eyes of enemies on him from all sides.

We waited at his corner for the car to the plant. I left the electric in front of his landlady's house and wondered if that meant that he would ask me in after work, in the middle of the night. Probably not. Slim came honking and smashing to the curb, jealous, I supposed. I'd have to get a new ride, I thought. I got in front next to him as usual and Renfro took his place in back.

"Well," said Slim loudly, "saves me goin clear over by your place. You oughta come down here every day to get picked up."

I didn't say anything. The others were talking about the war.

"My brother called from San Francisco at three A.M. He's a fireman out there," Otis said. "They got one thousand telephone calls in twelve hours. Anybody with a fire didn't have a chance. People thought the whole coast was being bombed! Jesus, what a panic!" We laughed. Slim pressed my leg slightly and pretended it was an accident. He was quiet. Renfro chuckled over his pipe, appreciating the banter. Some fellow named Charlie said, "This is my last week. I'm gonna enlist if they'll have me."

"*Have* ya?" said Otis. "Lissen, they'd take a monkey with two heads if he walked by the door. You know what it's gonna take to fight a war on two oceans and Africa besides? Jesus Christ! A

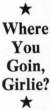

million men'll be killed before you can wipe your ass. 'Scuse me, Katie." The possibility of a million men killed seemed to satisfy him deeply.

It would be a different war, they said. More in the air, better tanks. Not so many foot soldiers exposed to open fire. Yeah, the air, that was the thing. These bombers could do the job of a dozen planes of the first war. How did they know?

The plant was electrified. Our schedule became tight, planes went out twice as fast; there were lines of men and women waiting to apply. They raked the Ozark hills again and came up with some characters like Fiveash who signed their names with an X. But some of them were plenty smart, said Smitty, don't be fooled. People started to talk about Americans and dirty little Japs and the Krauts. The loudspeaker brought the news twice each shift and Kate Smith sang "God Bless America" at least every two hours until we were drugged with it. But Eddie Cantor and Bob Hope and a lot of others sold bonds and made big donations. Mrs. Roosevelt was in the air like pollen.

Renfro and I got into a more civilized car pool with two drafts-men and a secretary, but I missed my geezers and felt embarrassed when I saw Slim arrive at the plant every afternoon walking bent-backed and slow with his tool kit and his big shoes. We worked quietly, avoiding each other when we could. Our car often stopped on the way home at the Rooster Hut or at a bootlegger's, and we all drank until we were barmy, except for Renfro, who drank like a priest, sipping, relishing beer but very little of it, deliberating over it, staring into his glass, brooding with a wry smile as if he were not quite there or perhaps had been there a hundred years before. I thought he must be saving his money for something or someone but he never mentioned it. I paid for my own beers and got no protest. It was a comradeship. I felt good and zinged up, and waited but he didn't start anything, not even a kiss. He always showed interest but no affection. I felt as if I were standing near a stove that contained all its heat for itself. But it drew me; I knew the fire was going somewhere in there.

I dreamed fragments of Eric and waited half-consciously to hear from him.

I met Renfro sometimes at the Sunshine or at his room across town when the landlady was out or in her parlor when she was in. I waited but it was all talk, always good talk, my conversation finally, and I consoled myself with that, but my hound was pawing the earth. Why didn't he even so much as touch my arm? I wanted to forget Eric or put him on ice or run and follow him to war.

His room was cruelly spare, its bed single. He had one armchair and one straight chair with part of its back missing. The whole house smelled of moth balls but was cheerful and light. He had some queer affection for the room and seemed to expand when he entered it, to become subtly animated. He made tea on a little hot plate and served graham crackers or Ritz crackers with nothing on them. That was enough. He wasn't interested in his body. Mine fumed under the neglect. And I waited. He must be saving his money or giving it away. Something, I kept thinking.

I read him all Beasley's letters and told him about Enid and Sarah, Ruby, Wishbone, Pom, everything but the murder. He loved the saga. And he smiled tightly, biting his pipe like a teething baby. I began to hunt slyly for a quick look at his teeth.

"Living at home with relatives of any kind would seem . . . oh . . . kind of queer to me now. I've been on my own so long." There was a fine thread of self-pity in it.

"What about your family?" I had begun to ask blunt questions since he offered little information about them. And he seemed to have wanted me to.

He told me then how he had left and how he hadn't written, hadn't told them where he was all those years, didn't know of their lives, nor even if his mother were still living.

"God!" I stared at him. It seemed like a kind of suicide. It bothered me. "Even if you don't *like* them . . ."

"That's not it. I didn't say I didn't like them!"

I shrugged.

"What do they need me for?" he said, suddenly grim. It was as if he had laid open his flesh. He didn't like himself or believe he had any value at all!

"Gee! Your own family? Why do you even wonder what they need you for?"

He smiled again, back in control, and carefully lit his pipe. "If you think of a family as an aesthetic form with a *reason* behind it, a concept based upon some emotional requirement, then I would have to say I think it is more or less a romantic idea and not valid *except* as an idea, you know? I've learned what I call the religion of asymmetry, but I *practice* it not as a religion but as a philosophical pursuit—I mean that the *reason* behind my being part of my family has disintegrated, whereas the *improbability* of it has grown in validity for me so that if I take them up again, I mean if I call them and take up some kind of life with them, it won't be a *logical* move but a part of the pursuit of something I think of as genuinely *natural*, more natural than our ideas of family and tribe and so forth are. I may or may not, you see what I mean? And that element of surprise or asymmetry is important to the whole nature of my view of things. I mean . . ."

"But do you think about calling them or think about not calling them and why *think* about it at all?"

He smiled again, hanging on to the pipe and sitting up quite straight in the broken chair, his legs crossed, his worn shoes drawn tightly toward the chair legs. Too neat, I thought.

"I think about it because I can't succumb to the false notion anymore that it is automatic and logical that I should call them after having stayed away from them for ten years and become someone—well—not defined by my association with them. I don't think about it a lot. I don't *know* whether or not I will call them. And the *not* knowing is just as important, I mean the fact that the

calling or not is still undecided and may remain undecided, is just as important and valid a fact as the act of calling or definitely deciding *not* to call would be. You see?"

"Well . . . I don't know. I just do what I feel, I guess." Somebody is crazy, I thought.

"And make a lot of mistakes and experience repeated pain and . . ."

"How can you live without making mistakes?" I shouted.

He laughed softly. "You can't. But you can see them differently and you can make different mistakes."

We fell silent. He offered me the plate of graham crackers. I thought of home and Ruby and her rabbit suppers and the feasts we used to have when we got our hands on a little loot. We had made ourselves sick but we had had fun. Was he talking about that too, maybe? I understood, but there was some trap door in it all.

"Let's take a walk," I said, wondering if he would ever just *do* something as asymmetrical as his thoughts.

He talked about Gandhi and Woodrow Wilson and Spengler. And Trotsky, a truly free man in spirit, because he had known banishment and understood it metaphysically.

I told him about Enid's metaphysics class, which he took very seriously. He had not read Gurdjieff and Uspenskii. He said, "I'd like to meet her," and I felt queerly threatened.

Renfro

Katie had lunch with him and then drove him to work, stopping at her house to change to her work clothes. He went inside with her.

Enid was a shock to him. They had no preliminary conversation, no sniffing. She merely said with a harsh irony, *I could offer you a drink,* and he knew that she knew from the sight of him of his saga that had never quite hung crucially upon booze of course but had made use of it knowingly as leitmotiv, that had it ever been quite literal and long pursued, booze would have become the fact, the logos of his peregrinations. She seemed to sense that. He said, *Thanks, I don't indulge,* so literally that her eyebrows lifted ever so slightly and her head capitulated faintly with a little nod. She had a raped look, he thought. There was something about her. She had instead of a sorry mug a stunned look, no yielding, and an old locked-in terror. Or some coldness that wasn't directed personally but just emanated like a vapor or a faint sound. She'd been through something, nothing present tense, he thought. He felt he knew something about her. A remote recognition stirred him.

And then Katie came into the room. He welcomed her with a leap in his chest. He reached for his pipe. The woman sized them up and something about it all made him hate to leave her alone. She was not old, not retiring, and she was alone.

And then on the way out she stopped Katie, something about the back of her work pants, something there. And then laughed and said Oh, only a shadow. He wondered. She had done it deliberately, to humiliate Katie. He decided not to say anything.

I got hold of an idea that gripped me for weeks—that everybody is writing an autobiography all the time, that there is some particular life that has more reality or intrigue for a person than anything else and that life becomes not a model, maybe a kind of occupation. And underneath it is your own life that you are writing, spinning as a tale through the other, and at the moment when a fact of one's own life is born or even conceived, the mind is already putting it into the record, recollecting and recording it as if it were history. Thus the Biography of Enid was the Autobiography of Katie and I didn't mind. I asked Renfro—

"What do you think the past really is, if you contain it all?"

"Cells piling up or something. The body becoming unfit for the future."

"Yeah!" I loved that. "If we didn't accumulate ourselves, we'd live forever maybe."

He smiled as if he were Socrates. "But without accumulating ourselves we would be too vulnerable. We wouldn't have learned anything."

That was something like what they were trying to say in Enid's metaphysics books, maybe. Maybe old Iantha might trip over a truth yet. But her genius for making gossip would diminish it into mere rumor probably, before she had a chance to see its flash.

So, Renfro. We began to take walks on Saturday afternoons, all over Deliria. We talked so much our bodies went to sleep. He didn't seem to think of sex at all and so I waited. And waited. And then I went out again with that guy named Kirby Parks and he might as well have been a dog. No, Renfro didn't touch me except sometimes my elbow when we went down a curb. We went down a lot of curbs walking his version of Deliria. But he was so intently with me that I couldn't imagine giving him up.

Finally, when I found myself hinting for some other kind of attention, we always got back to his teeth. He was saving up to have them fixed or get some expert to make him false teeth. It seemed to be very expensive. And then one night he told me he had been sending money orders to his family. He wouldn't have a bank and write checks and he didn't want them to know where he was yet, anyway. So he sent cash to the only friend he had, an old man on whose small ranch he had worked for a while, in

Arizona. He would send cash and a stamped envelope addressed to his sister Alda and a penny post card addressed to himself out to this old man, who would buy a postal money order and put it in the envelope to Alda and then scrawl off a note on the post card to Renfro to say that the job was done.

I told him I thought it was crazy but secretly I rather liked it. It seemed a little like crime and allowed Renfro to live like a spy. But I suspected that underneath the whole thing was a lake of sentimentality that was going to ruin his life if it hadn't already.

"Why don't you just walk up to the house one night and put it under the door in an envelope or something. Or drop it into the mailbox?"

"Because," he said with patient irritation "the whole point is to make them believe I'm still out of town. Or at least that their benefactor is."

"They know it's you."

"Then all the more reason to send it from another place."

Sometimes I got all mixed up trying to understand him and I told myself it was all his pride over the teeth. Other times I thought he was definitely crazy. And sometimes I decided that all of this huggermugger was taking the place of sex and I wondered if some other female wouldn't have just thrown him out of her life with a sniff. He seemed like some old cousin of our family, bearing remote similarities to the secret sides of a lot of us—Uncle Jack with his schemes, Enid with her self-preoccupation and solitude, Beas with his innocence, Pom with his information and knowledge.

But finally I decided that I would stick around with Renfro because he interested me and because I could say anything to him that came into my head, anything. I hadn't done that yet but I could. And the only thing that was interesting to me was talk and ideas. I was losing my animal, my old hound self. And then too I had a weird desire not to have sex anymore even though I was remotely dying for it all the time. And besides that I dreamed about Beas and Renfro as interchangeable people and decided that I was so insane that I had better not get mixed up with anybody at all, anyway.

And besides all that, Eric finally wrote me. He was in the South Pacific and said he had me on his mind and that my idea of sending him pages out of books and magazines a few at a time, which I had done once, was good, that he was tired and busy and the war was real. He had a buddy who had been on the *Arizona* in Pearl Harbor. Take care, Cannonball, he said. Which seemed to mean *wait around* but didn't say so.

Maybe Sarah and Enid talked about her drinking. I wasn't sure. But one day I heard Sarah say to her, You've got to do it, Hon. You've got to try. And I felt a huge weight rise off my chest.

So Enid was up. But down again. But up again. Pom invited us to dinner more often, strangely. Why hadn't he done it when Beas was home? He went to California to talk with other regional petroleum officials. He still had his maps of Europe. And now one of the Pacific and Asia. He kept up with every move the Japanese made. He showed me how they had taken the islands right after Pearl Harbor. It began to grip me, knowing that Eric and probably Beas and Wishbone would be there somewhere. How could they live through it? Pom had drawn in little pencil sketches of the Japanese fleet. I couldn't believe it. He knew the tonnage of every ship, it seemed.

Enid suddenly went off for a week with Iantha and Serene to hear a man talk about the fourth dimension. In St. Louis. Sarah and Ruby and I, alone again, had supper in the kitchen, babbling away like we used to, laughing at Hattie Finch who said she had heard there was a Jap spy in town. Ruby confessed, though, that she didn't know what a Jap was, and when I explained she said that was a Chinaman like Mr. Lee, who once fixed up a bunch of food for a benefit in the Willows. And being alone again, foolish as we wished to be and were, kept us there at the table until late, gabbing. That being the most fun I could think of, after Eric, I wondered why I had always wanted to leave, to get away from Deliria. If Sarah and Ruby would go too, I thought, then nothing would stand in the way of it. But the going fell into my head now as something slightly foreign, familiar but alien too, like a face that combined several old known faces, passed quickly in the street. The war seemed to make life more exciting but action less possible. And anyway, I was useless to the war. I didn't see myself as a nurse in an army or the Red Cross. If I saw myself in war it was as a soldier, a marine, or on the prow of a ship, or carrying a flag maybe but not a gun. Routing out the enemy. It seemed more truthful to me than merely tending the sick. Sarah's tending her clients had been enough for me. Not in my life, I thought. But then I thought of my life, or tried to, and came up with a fuzzy blob, not empty but undefined. Loaded but unclear, something unborn, in a big egg.

Wishbone

"Hello, Mista Russa, this Wesley Watson talkin."

"What? Who?"

"Private Wesley Watson. You know—Ruby friend? Out to Miss Sarah?"

He held a searching pause and then came awake and fumbled after the light switch. "Wishbone? Is that you Wishbone?"

"Yessuh! That's me. Wesley Watson."

"What the devil . . . it's after midnight! Is something the matter?"

"Yessuh. We can't wake Miss Sarah. 'Scuse me callin you, Mista Russa, but Miss Katie she ain't home an Ruby say call Mista Russa. We cain't wake Miss Sarah. She lyin' crost the baid an we cain't rouse huh."

He was up and reaching for his trousers, the phone cupped between his neck and shoulder.

"You can't wake her? Is she breathing?"

"Seem like she be breathin some but she don't look too good and look like she done fell out or somethin."

"All right, Wishbone, now listen carefully. I'll send the ambulance after her. If Miss Katie comes home tell her to follow the ambulance to St. Joseph's Hospital in town. You have that? St. Joseph's. Tell her to go there. You and Ruby stay and wait for her."

"Yessuh! We do that. St. Joseph. We'll wait fo Miss Katie." There was the snap of a salute in the boy's voice that made Pom jitter with an awful urgent laugh.

"And don't move Miss Sarah. Will she stay on the bed?"

"I think she be okay right theah. We ain't tetched huh one bit."

"All right. Hang up and wait for the ambulance. Send Miss Katie to St. Joseph's Hospital."

★

Wishbone turned back to Ruby in the dark hall. There was a sound at the back of the house. Lord God, he wanted to take Miss Sarah now, himself, they'd never get there in time and he could lift her as well as anybody.

"He say doan move huh," he whispered to Ruby, whose eyes rolled. "I wish that man tell me to take huh myseff. Now doan cry, Baby."

He had to take charge. He drew Ruby to the kitchen and told her to make coffee. What if they hadn't happened to come into the house? Katie would have found her. Better maybe. But what if Katie hadn't looked into the room? And what if—That noise in the back yard again. He looked at Ruby, who didn't hear it. The tap water ran and was shut off and she put on the pot. He wrung his hands.

"Goan take that ambilance half hour to git out heah. Shoot!"

Ruby was quiet. He moved into the hall and looked at her again stretched out across the bed. Without Ruby he wouldn't go into the room. He wanted to, but waited. Ruby got out the cups. He heard everything very loudly. And then there was a sound at the back door and Ruby said—

"Well, heah you be. Yo motha fell out an we cain't wake huh. Heah, Wishbo, git in heah!"

And there was Katie in a rush. Wishbone waited in the kitchen feeling like a splinter while Ruby ran in with Miss Katie.

He was alone. Maybe he should wipe up. No. Lord God, he hoped Miss Sarah wasn't dead with Ruby swole up the way she was now.

They came back in and Ruby heated up the coffee and made hot milk for Katie, who took it with her back into the room to watch. Wishbone's stomach hardened into a knot. Ruby went out and came back in and said, Wishbo come in here and tell this girl Mista Pom say doan move Miss Sarah, and he leaped out of the kitchen and into the hall. Miss Katie had packed up Miss Sarah's things in a little satchel.

"Honey, he say doan move that woman no matta what. That what he say."

Katie was crying. She took up Miss Sarah's legs anyway, very slow, and laid her up on the bed flat. "You can't let her stay that way. It's a strain on her. I knew it was something with her heart! I *knew* it."

And then the ambulance came, sweeping lights over the back of the house, and Wishbone directed them down the lane while Katie stayed by holding Miss Sarah's hand and Ruby came to the door. He felt raw. They lifted her very easy, he could have done it alone, and Katie said I'm going in the ambulance but Ruby said, Git on out theah like Mista Pom say and take that lectric. How you goan git home?

Katie said no. Ruby said, "Git on out theah and do what he say. You got no cause to go in that ambilance."

And then the ambulance men said she better take her own car and they went off and Katie fell against Ruby and gave out a loud cry. And then she commenced to telling them they had to go along. Lord God, all that fuss, he could have had that woman there by now.

"We ain't goan nowheres. Mista Pom say stay in the house an thass what we doin. You go on now and git down theah. She want you to be theah. What if she wake up an you ain't theah?"

"You've got to come, Rube. I'm not going if you don't. She wants you too. C'mon, Wishbone."

"Naw, Honey, he say . . ."

"Oh! Please! Please come!"

Lord, that child . . . He looked at Ruby. Ruby looked at Katie hard and then said okay, they would come. But what would they do there? he thought. Couldn't sit in the lectric in the middle of the night in town. The police weren't going to stand for that.

Maybe his uniform would help out. She stumbled out the door in her heavy work clothes—Lord she looked like some fat man or something from the back. But he took his eyes away and looked at Ruby, who had slammed a hat on her head and was moving herself and her belly out toward the porch. He picked up his cap and nipped out after them, fussing with the door. It don't lock, said Ruby.

Maybe they could stay in the basement or by the back entrance. He didn't know the hospital. Ruby didn't either but she didn't care. She was somebody's maid and that was okay. Shoot, what was he going to do? Mista Russa could ruin him in the Army. He hadn't even wanted to call him Private Wesley Watson.

In the back seat of the lectric holding his own hands till sweat sopped them. Ruby looked back and gave him the big eye. What you troublin? she seemed to ask. He kept quiet. Outside running along the edge of the ditch by the cracking plant a frost was pickling on the ground.

Maybe she would die, he thought, and let out a sigh. He didn't wish it but he felt better after thinking it.

Hushed voices. It was so swift. She was a body on a stretcher. Oxygen or something. Stroke. Spinal something. Pom and Dr. Killeen whispering. I hung at the door. A nurse came and said that colored couple at the service entrance . . . Ruby! I had thought she was with me.

"Why didn't you let them in? That's her *family*!" I cried.

"Well, Miss, I . . ."

"Goddammit!" I flung down the hall. Rubber shoe sounds of nurses. Oh God! Spinal something. I looked back at Pom going into a room.

Rube's big eyes. Her waiting. They were too patient!

"Why didn't you come on in? Come on!" I turned away.

"Wait a minna. They ain't goan let no . . ."

"Come *on*! She might *die*! Goddammit Rube. Goddammit!" I was crying hard and shouting.

"Shhhh! You goan wake the dead, Girl. I comin. You stay heah," she commanded Wishbone, who hung back among some trash cans.

I ran and she followed, slinking near the wall, covering her stomach with her arms. I waited, kept hold of her. She was coltish and wayward. I drove her like an animal. We got off the elevator. We walked ten steps. Pom came down the hall in a swift fall toward us, his face all bedazzled, his eyes . . . Ruby made a noise.

"Katie!" He grabbed my arms. He shook me as if blaming me. "She went. Just like that. She's gone. It's over."

I stopped still. Part of me stopped there forever. It's over.

Renfro

Decided he had probably made a mistake. She was distracted and slightly avaricious at the same time. She seemed to watch him like a thief and to steal confidence from him. She laughed a lot and he liked that. She wanted something from him. . . . Oh what was he kidding himself for? She wanted him to touch her and he couldn't. His teeth . . . the whore . . . Julia . . . his mother . . . and something else old and deep—he went through them and the past as through a deck of cards looking for the fifth ace. He had always thought of the fifth ace as the Ace of Loss, and of loss as freedom. He had that one straight. He had always seen a cracked heart in the center of the fifth ace, but it would have been a mistake to call it the Ace of Cracked Hearts. The Ace of Other Hearts, maybe. The animal heart? The Ace of Animal Hearts! You'd need a whole new deck—Ace of Animal Spades, etc. Katie had an animal ace up her sleeve, he told himself. He chuckled, looking into the smeary mirror over the dresser in Mrs. Peet's upstairs west/north front room. Twenty a month, linens laundered.

But he knew that if he held Katie off and handled it his own way he would not be false. He was a bog of nostalgia and confusion, he couldn't make a direct act of cutting through the morass in his mind and heart to the original sex of his body, as if his hand could not find a way into his pants. He remembered the bums then, hundreds, their hands in their pants at night. He had kept his hands out. No booze, no playing around. He had kept it. Had it atrophied in him? He could not imagine doing it again. Maybe trying with that whore had been the wrong thing for a beginning. Ah well, Ace of Asses Supreme! Jack, no, *Knave* of Cudgels. Deuce and Dunce of Pain. Whatever, he knew he had to wait and feel his way through, back to the touching that would always be finicky maybe, dubious maybe, but he trusted himself, the skeleton that had completed its circle, returning home like a sleepwalker. He knew his body lived there somewhere below. He would make Katie wait.

He imagined trying with her Aunt Enid. Her bitterness would have made it possible. But she was a little too old for him and too aristocratic and too sick, probably. But he suspected she knew everything that he knew. She seemed to have succumbed to all that he had survived by the skin of his teeth. His teeth! Maybe that was the whole thing. How ridiculous that a man can utter his soul only through the orifice which eats, which kisses, smokes. . . . He had enough money now. Why didn't he get them fixed?

He went to lie across the bed. He had to meet Katie in an hour. She said she would call and she hadn't. He slept, dreaming of a naked man walking toward him down a country road who had the beginnings or maybe the shreds of animal armour on his skin like pieces of armadillo hide, and when he came closer to him, carefully and fearfully, he saw that the man had actually tried to grow a suit of iron mail and that there were tears in his eyes and a face, tiny and repulsive, in his penis. It was frantically signaling him with its eyes, but so grotesque it frightened him. He looked into the face of the man himself and said, Well dammit, you shouldn't have done it. And heard himself ask the way to the lease house and then saw Katie's Enid standing in the middle of the dimly lit parlor the way he had first met her, waiting for him, like a shrew in a cave. He redreamed quickly a bat dream of some kind he had once had, kindled by a night he had spent in a cave. Knight of Caves. Then he heard bat wings and knew of black angels. Los Angeles. The books on divination in the Los Angeles Library in February 1938. A ten-cent book on the Tarot cards he had bought in that town. It rolled through his sleeping head, dream and memory. He had forgotten what he knew and searched for it in the dream. Divination. He saw a huge mushroom looming upside down in the sky. It was like a lurid heavenly hanging prick. The face on the armadillo man's prick was there. He woke up gasping.

He got up and washed his face quickly at the little corner bowl. He pocketed his money, bills and a little change, and struggled out. He was on time but just. He walked it, a long mile, and got to the Sunshine Café one minute late. He waited—three coffees, two pipes, the paper, some doodles, mainly wheels, on the napkin. She didn't come. One hour and ten minutes. Maybe she had tried to call just after he left. Before he got up to go he yielded to an impulse to draw the upside-down mushroom on a paper napkin. Without the face. Then he left a dime, paid his bill and went out. It was overcast and cold. He turned up his jacket collar and headed toward the secondhand book store. He would walk a little, buy a cinnamon roll, go to the library. He was after something. He would make Katie wait as she had made him wait today. All right then, Queen of Whimsies. He smiled and lit his pipe. But something was not right. It wasn't like her not to be there. He was growing an urgent fondness for her and her attempts to get him to call home and all that. Her staring at him. Her frankness. He liked her neat body too. Those arms, defenseless, like a small strong child's. There was a statue of David he had seen in an art book once—the power of defenselessness and courage in children. He wanted to get to the art books. He quickly designed his afternoon and evening with relish. He'd have a chili supper, alone, Knave of Silence and Circles.

But she was in it, simply missing. At the library he confirmed his vision—her arms *were* like those of the Donatello David. He would have traveled a long way to see that work. The hat, too. He ought to buy her a hat like that. Was it feminine or masculine? Queen, no, Princess of Dash and Jumble. Jesus Christ, he was probably falling for the girl.

When he got home there was a note on his dresser scrawled in pencil by Mrs. Peet—

The young lady called says death in family last night.

Our echoes roll from soul to soul . . .
I stand. In the woods. I want to fall but can't. I force her real *presence* there. I hear it—*Aw, Hon*—and take her abundant pity. But it is false. I created it.

My fists trouble the air near my sides. I am in my tottering frame. I am still here.

All the food, clients, phone calls, notes, tears, stillness of mock death reiterating real death—gone. Reality now. Its queer stall and tick. Ruby took off that black hat finally. Beas came on a twenty-four-hour pass, cried and left. He had a bruise on his lip and a sore shoulder from rifle practice. He was different. I couldn't find him. I knew the Army was awful but he wouldn't admit it. He shook his head at the grave, over and over. He talked guns with Pom, quietly, as if reporting on some terrible event. The Browning automatic was his favorite. If they weren't drilling or practicing on the range they were listening to lectures on venereal disease. There's a Negro battalion not far away but it's off limits. That, he says, is where Wishbone is now. How did he know? He left like Paul Revere. It froze my heart even more solid. Pom watched him, nodded, listened, winced. We sent him off again together, Pom and I. Without words this time.

Disconnected flotsam in my head: Wishbone, holding Ruby's arm, weeping into a khaki handkerchief at the graveside. Iantha coming into my room that night to give me a hard stingy bitter clutch, the bony chest. The honesty of it.

Enid up. Then down. All that time I had been believing she would finally get up, because of all the blows, that she'd try or be forced by shock. But she didn't. She'd get up and pretend that this was it, that this was up-for-good, but then she'd be down again, whether anything happened or not. It had nothing to do with events, with tragedies. Her tragedy was all in the past. Nothing

new could happen to her. She had no reasons for what she did.
Renfro moved out of Mrs. Peet's room and rented an apartment, second floor, a mohair sofa in muddy green. Trying to listen to Renfro, to let him lead me around Deliria a little. But the ruinous flashbacks! Ruby at the graveside standing against the late sun and casting a humped shadow over the fake grass, her bulge distorted. And later, in the kitchen "Ooops! This kid startin to kick!" To which the obvious answer, so sharply missing that we both paused and exchanged awful glances, was, Aw Hon. Of course. Of course.

"Maybe it's twins," I offered disinterestedly.

"Hush yo mouth, Girl. I ain't studyin no two babies."

Okay, call her America and let her kick her way out.

Finally my right hand swings out and hits the bark of a hickory tree in the woods, making a splitting sound that sickens me. Every time I close my eyes I see it crash against the bark. The reeling relief of that crude physical pain! I search the woods for a vision, my head wagging. And see that the woods can't absorb it, can't know it. The shrine of the woods is for animals. We are not heard there. We have made our own places. This is what and all we are.

★

Places. His new apartment, one room, Murphy bed, pullman kitchen, bath. It filled with library books like a tank with water. Inexorably they piled up. I saw him finding his own rhythm, that business he was always talking about—work, walking, smoking his pipe. He made lists and notes, sticking them in books. The history and philosophy of art. He seemed to begin to own the books. The library would never see them again and he'd never know that he was a thief. I took pride in that for him. But small anxieties gave me great pause lately. Would they find him? Sue him? I didn't know what to do with myself so I studied Renfro's little problems. He bought two sheets. A few more things taken care of, he would say, and he would find a car. I was dubious but agreeable to that dream. "But you'll have to teach me to drive," he said.

I laughed. "I can only drive electrics and trucks."

Renfro: Distract the eye. I'll take you on one of my more secret important walks. Did you know there used to be a button factory here, brought in the mussel shells from the Ozarks and made buttons out of them; and here, this is where the police had that shoot-out with Pretty Boy Floyd, right between those two doors. He ran out of the bank over there and down this way. . . .

Sedatives.

There were lots of soldiers on the streets now, mainly Army Air Force wandering in groups of six or eight or twenty even. Work, Renfro explained to a windy balloon head next to him, has a sacred aspect. You know the work songs of the Africans? The Negroes still sing them in the fields in certain places. . . .

The river. He was saving something he wanted to tell me before. About himself and the river. He fussed eternally with his pipe.

What do you do, I thought, when you are out like this and run out of matches? Stop someone? Is it worth wondering about? He makes the rattly sucking sound with the pipe.

★

Go. Move. Out in the electric humming around town.

"You goan wear out that thing in one mo week the way you goin in town all the time. Shhhttt! Then what you goan do with youseff?"

It was hunting with me. I wanted to rest somewhere. Hunting for the place. *The* place.

Beas looked stronger. Took my arm. It is done. Katie—her grief. Gives a person strength. Mothers. If I had been. If they had taught us *anything*. It is so still now, that room. Must empty it eventually. Katie will howl. Jittery as a cat. Henry gave Pom these pills. Not with alcohol, Enid. If Henry really felt that way about me he might have made a move. How did he know? I might have run off with him. Men never act at the right time.

She is gone. Can't believe it. Katie will never forgive my telling her to shut up.

Beas saying why didn't you answer my letter. I will. I will write two a week. I promise. *Don't make promises, Enid.* Guns and foxholes and venereal disease!

It is at suppertime that I can't. She meant to give me, all of us, life. She gave life . . . divine idiot. No more.

Katie's broken her hand. Love and hate of life will save her. If it could be loaned to Beas. Now how will she write him?

Sarah's little death smile. Her hands. Something never happened to her that makes a woman sorrow. Have to try for her sake. Have to try. Get back respect.

Try.

Iantha was always after me to go to the grave. I said no and don't ever ask me again. Enid said no. Ruby went a couple of times with flowers. If I ever went—not an impossibility—I'd go alone. Like Greer Garson. I could see it. And then I'd hate myself for imagining it that way and not let myself think about it anymore.

Sarah wasn't there in the ground, anyway. She ghosted through the house tormenting me. I tore the paisley curtain off the cubbyhole finally and there was the mere table, the two chairs, the hanging lamp, where clients had spilled out their pain all those years. Empty. I took away her trappings and left it there bare but nobody used it. Her bedroom was closed and unused.

It came to me finally what had happened. The sum of my life and the murder and the Biography, Sarah having a sister named Enid, a younger sister who in some other time or place might have been put to death for taking a life. All that. And it seemed like a plan that I should be here now alone with Enid. It seemed as if I had been driven through my life to this moment when she and I would stand opposite one another with no one in between. Starkly there. The decks seemed to have been cleared for us. But what was the point? I shuddered with disgust at the thought of what it meant. I was superstitious enough to believe it had a kind of logic to it. It was almost as if in writing the Biography I had created her out of thin air and now had to face her. I knew that was nuts but that was what I felt in my bones.

I couldn't remember what the house had smelled like before her dead-flower life had invaded it. A hint of the old Willetts, but only a hint. A whiff of Ruby's vanilla and her soda—yes, but something below all that, too, that seemed to have been obliterated. A flicker of Sarah's talcum, yes. And of course what had settled into our unsuspecting atmosphere from the old linen, marabou, wood, velvet, mohair and canvas of the clients' goods. But under that— what had been the original air? It now seemed to contain a most subtle decay.

My fate. I paced the rooms, nursing my broken hand. I started to struggle as if I were drowning.

The Boise
16 Hours
South Pacific

Dear Katie,

They flew me out here because they lost some men earlier. I'm an Ensign and this great old tub is a destroyer. I hope you get this. Still working on Fortresses? Cinch em up, Kid. Everything is needed. We're in rough seas and danger all the time. You heard about the Philippines of course. The men are so ass mad you can't keep them down. I wrote you about your mother. I was sure sorry about it. I know you thought a lot of her.

I feel fit and am working hard. When you see this fleet, even what was left of it after Pearl, you get a big kick. With men like Halsey and Nimitz and King giving the orders you feel like working your butt off. Anyway, if you don't, you'll get it blown off. It's beautiful in these seas. Someday I hope to come back in quieter times. Ha!

All the men aboard are swell. Lots of them have plenty of duty
behind them already.
   I can't tell you much. I'm a little scared at times but I feel like a
winner, Kid, and you know what that means. We'll chase these Japs
home in quick order. Just give us a few months. I think of my
Cannonball with pleasure lying there in the old bunk, tired as I am.
I'll send you a picture of Ensign Witcher in full dress soon.

Love,
Eric.

I tried to answer but my hand in its cast was useless. Secretly I
nourished its pain.

What's happened to the war? I would sometimes ask myself. And
then another letter would come.

Dear Folks,
   We are busy every minute from 5 A.M. till after supper. Then I'm
so sleepy I can hardly stay awake to get undressed. The old Army
guys here stay up half the night drinking or playing poker or
something, but not me. We drill at 7:45 A.M. till about 11:30 with a
little break where the Sarge tells us about first aid or breaks down a
rifle for us so we can learn the parts and put it back together. It's easy
but you have to be perfect. We get a lot of rice and some tamales
sometimes but not good like Mr. Delgadillo's.
   Then you have to hike with a pack and get into a lot of ice and
mud and swamps with the sling butting into your shoulder. You get
tough pretty fast. You have to practice falling and taking cover and
all. On the field at camp we have a wooden airplane on wires that we
fire at for practice while it goes gliding along in front of us. I have a
pretty good eye.

Enid grunted at that and the hair stood on end on the back of
my neck. Sometimes Beas wrote me privately, but not often. He
got a letter from Brad Finch from England, he met a fellow who
knew what a red whizzer is, he liked the fellows but the drills were
awful. He thought about me and hoped I would write letters to
Eric and not get out of touch with him because he was a good guy,
no matter what. Go down to my stuff in the basement and use
anything you want, he said. I always felt like crying when I got
his letters. But I trained myself to guard against it before opening
them.
   Enid read his letters carefully once but then tossed them aside
as if almost in disgust. These were not truths about Beasley's life,

not the things he ought to be doing. But she never said anything about it. Sometimes I turned to the imaginary Biography to make intangible notes. But then I would stop myself, force myself to see that she was real, that I had once hated her, that no biography could grasp her whole life and that it was trashy to try anyway. Sarah's dying had taught me that—that there is no way to seize another's life.

★

Wishbone was somewhere in the South Pacific. Pom said he thought it might be the Philippines. Ruby rolled her eyes, having heard what we had heard. But he always seemed to come through with a letter. Somebody helped her answer, I didn't.

Finally I began to write with my left hand. I sent letters to Beas and Eric every few days. It eased my grief and the sense of horrible emptiness I had at sundown every day.

I had not returned to work. I applied for workmen's compensation pay for my hand and got it by saying I hurt it on the job. It was barely enough to support Ruby and me but we managed. Enid had always paid her own way.

Enid went out sometimes with Iantha and Serene, to meetings. They were handling her sorrow for her, metaphysically. Sometimes she called me in to hear a radio program with her.

One day the letter came from the life insurance company and my one-thousand-dollar check floated down as if from some tongue-in-cheek god. A payoff.

I sat alone with it, crying and thinking. I could go now. To New York. And live at least six months on it. In that time I could find a job. There were jobs everywhere now. Everyone was necessary somewhere.

I opened a savings account at Pom's bank and let it brew there.

I could go, I kept reminding myself. But I was frozen in place, Enid at the periphery of all my thinking.

Every night I lay down forever.

Days. Fifteen of them. And then awake at three A.M. and knowing where. The place finally loomed. I got out the electric and went toward town. Deliria was empty, gray, a grave itself, but pure in some way that touched me. If towns could be emptied, or lives could, now and then, maybe the world could be purified, I thought.

The electric ticked up the long drive, passing the seven pines that Nina had said were all once Christmas trees. I was going to be healed. My heart pounded. At least I felt alive. At least I would be able to lay down my pain like a package there, like a stone. I rolled up to the house and came to a skid before I saw it—the Stutz! It was four A.M. The house was dark except for the low light she always kept in the hall and the garden lights. The Stutz! I laughed, sitting there in my mittens. Pom. Beat me to it. And then I felt ashamed that I hadn't been thinking or knowing about other people's lives and needs. Only my own. Pom had lost Sarah too and here he was. Gee! In Nina's bed? He must be in Nina's bed, I told myself. My head banged. I looked at the back of the Stutz.

It seemed to be sleeping like a dog there. The whole place seemed forbidding and tight. So, Nina and Pom. Maybe it had always been going on and we hadn't seen it. I felt shaky but I saw the sharp truth of it. What was I thinking? That I would just cry a little on her shoulder? Well, Pom. I sat and let it sink in. Pom was in Nina Brosky's satin bed. Here sat the Stutz.

I drove away. That's why we hadn't seen much of him lately. Gee, and only a month ago I had been unable to imagine his even possessing a firecracker.

It made me feel good, but afraid, bare and alone. I purred through Deliria exposing myself to the emptiness of it, forcing myself to drive through the run-down neighborhoods that Renfro said he haunted. I passed the Salvation Army hostel, the Cozy Hotel. There was a man, shuffling along. He turned into an alley and peed against the wall. I couldn't tell whether we were all alone in the world or all together. I cruised the dead town for an hour. What the hell, I told myself, I would only have gone to her for comfort and Pom at least can give her something back. Maybe they'll be happy. Everyone who can possibly be happy should be happy, no matter where or when or how. Whatever the moment is, just move into it as into a room. If you are alone in the gray dawn in Assinopolis cruising the empty streets, then do and be that and take its hard beauty. There was something beautiful about it that I accepted, as if I had had a crude object thrust to my chest.

Finally I went to Renfro's and threw a little rock against his window to wake him. I'd make him take me to the Sunshine for breakfast.

Pom

"I'm going to open one of those USO places," Nina told him. "I hope it won't embarrass you." She gave him a glittering look, surer of him. Yes, she was growing sure. He curbed his instinct to withdraw from her confidence and instead took pride in it, gave back, practicing. He wanted to be *there* with her, in the instant with her, always. To tolerate her utterly. He thought with a dim pain of Sarah. He may have learned all this from her, but by a sort of spiritual osmosis surely, not by instruction.

"I don't want to become idle and pampered and . . . fatter—ha! —with you, Pom."

The idea of *becoming* anything and talking so simply about it charmed him. His affection for affection and love made him giddy.

"I think it's a wonderful idea. Where will you have it?"

"You want to go looking for space with me? Give me your advice? I'm thinking of old storefront buildings downtown. You know, in the heart of things, a little seedy maybe?"

They laughed. He felt himself flush with pleasure and surprise at the continuance of it. He kept moving toward her, not driven but steadily propelled. He wondered if she were waiting to be asked to marry him. But it wasn't their style. She seemed to assume that it was not the point. Or did he only imagine that to protect himself at the final moment? Her being rich gave him confidence. They needed one another for other reasons. Nothing wrong with having a mistress, especially one who wasn't purchased.

Yet sometimes when he left her he felt as if it were all a dream and his life drastically empty. He would sit at his desk all morning writing to Beasley, carefully copying each letter, not content to dictate them to a secretary. It took him hours each time, yet he felt after each that there was something he ought to have said that he hadn't. And he would think of Jack then, away in prep school as a boy, writing home for money, for skis, begging for a car, a sailboat, and of his, Pom's, own failure to return more than just those things, his guilty sense of duty to Jack, his confusion in the boy's presence. He had never solved the problem of the evasions and formalities between them. Once Jack had called and said, I want to come home, Dad. Just that. But Pom hadn't let him. He had been preparing a trip and promised to visit Jack at school. It all seemed shamefully perfunctory now, a paltry show of mere paternal duty.

I didn't like him, he thought. Cared for him but didn't like him. He embarrassed me. He was so—so obvious and coarse.

And Beas? He took care in the letters not to burden Beas with advice, but failing advice he was not certain what he had to give his grandson. He always ended a letter with some word of praise. He wondered if there were men who wrote immediate loving intimate letters to their sons and grandsons. How did they manage it naturally?

"I'm too old to be playing the father," he told Abe one night on the phone. "That's one reason Beas didn't feel my having him deferred was valid, I suppose."

"Ah, Pom! The kid understands you. You've got a nice gentlemen's agreement going between you."

Pom laughed drily. "That's just the trouble. We're gentlemen toward one another."

He imagined then some deep terror that might invade Beasley's soul against which the boy would be unable to battle alone. And then he thought back to the murder and wondered where exactly it most influenced Beasley's life.

"It's going to be a little stiff, Katie," Dr Killeen said. "But it will improve. Do the exercises and the hydrotherapy and give it time. Might be a good idea later to take up piano or mandolin or something. Keep it in tune, eh? Articulate."

I smiled for him. I regarded the newborn whitish helpless hand, naked. A legacy. Crippled?

"Will it always be kind of . . . out-of-shape-looking like this?"

He chuckled. "It shouldn't. It'll never be all the way back to normal but it won't be noticeable. Take care of it. It's a fabulous instrument, the human hand." He mused. He examined it again as if there were nothing else to do with me there in the room. I felt as if I had brought him a bad dream in this hand. It hung on me. He spread it open and examined the palm. There was a red patch. Stigmata. That, he said, would go away.

Not really, I thought.

"Come back in a month," he said. And then, "Or come any time you want. For anything, Katie. I loved your mother."

Before I got out the door I suddenly said, "Well then, maybe you'd better give me one of those diaphragm things."

Their talk woke me. "I'll do this. Lemme carry this."

"No. It helps me to keep busy. Call Katie and get her in here to work."

I thought I was dreaming.

"What are you doing in this room? What are you doing with her things?" What vile wisdom lets a person be outlived by her *clothes*?

Enid with a little fine sweat on her brow and a flushed face. "Well, we can't leave it like this forever. Come on and give us a hand."

"I'll take care of this myself. I don't want anybody in here."

They stood, light and dark. Their cement patience. They stared. "I was waiting for my hand to get well."

"You've got to keep busy, even if your hand—"

"*I've* got to keep busy! You're a fine one to tell me *that*!"

"Never mind what I do," she said. "Just do a little better yourself. Don't use me as an example."

"Who's using you? You're the *last* person . . ."

"Oh, stop babying yourself and get to work. Here, take this to the back porch. This room has to be emptied and cleaned and you can help or not. Take your choice."

Ruby's eyes nearly fell out. I looked at her; I looked at Enid with fire, feeble fire, and took the bag in my left hand.

Hatred. It shored me up. Those flimsy dresses of Sarah's! I cried drily. Those shoes! Run-over on the sides. I was reeling. I threw it all out in a rage. I was afraid to see in her paltry belongings the absurdity of her life. I didn't want to see below her tatters, even though I already had long ago, in the beginning. Even the hatbox of old newspaper clippings on the trial came down lightly from the shelf into my hands finally, and before I could put it aside or hide it Enid had claimed it easily as if she knew what it was, and laid it in the middle of the bed. The bed! I didn't look. I ripped off the old shoe racks, hurting my hand. Ruby shook her head, carrying boxes to the back porch. Iantha came to take them away.

"Stay for supper," Enid commanded her. She reddened in the eyes, old Iantha, and pounded me lovingly on the back. Sarah was ripped and folded away. Ruby cleaned the closet floor on her hands and knees, a man's hankie around her head, her pink heels sticking out behind her skirt.

They had coffee. Enid looked wracked, her eyes in those big sockets were like purple cups. Later she took away the hatbox, which I had left there.

The next morning she got up and made her own breakfast—two fried eggs, toast and coffee. She changed her bed and made it up.

She made her bed.

I took note now of all her acts and stored them in my head instead of in the Biography. *Something* in her life was my business. I'd have to wait and watch for signs.

Yes, the imagined, no longer written Biography of Enid ran through my telegraph head—

Made her bed. Gave orders to Ruby and Katie. Planned supper. Said don't come today, come tomorrow, to Iantha. We're going to clean the room. Iantha, who took Sarah's soul from the house in limp cotton dresses, some of which she herself had made; that Iantha who had loved Sarah wasn't allowed to come out today.

Enid. Sober. Ordering groceries on the phone. Busy all day and at dusk a look of sudden doubt, staring around the room at places where Sarah might have sat, lingered, laughingly saying, *Aw Hon, such a lot of work.*

She stood at the mirror in the bathroom with the door open and braided her hair. *My mother bids me bind my hair. . . .* Mothers. Daughters. Maybe she remembered when Sarah had once said—

Law, Hon, when I was ten Mama quit braiding my hair and I

started the job of braiding hers, and she told me everything in the world, about Daddy and the Territory, about men and drinking whiskey and fast women. It put her in a trance, you might say. Law, she hardly seemed to realize she was a-talkin. . . .

★

Enid bound her hair. My hair had always hung loose, or was drawn back with a shoelace, a string. I watched Enid covertly. Sarah had braided Enid's hair too, until she was old enough to do it herself.

There was no peace in the house, but Enid said later, on a quiet day, Here. Can you do it? Braid it for me. Give it a try.

The famous heavy flaxen long hair lay in my hands . . . the good hand and the broken hand bare and just out of its cast. Behind her. She trusted me to separate it, three strands, saying, Hold the center. Left over, right over, draw it up, left over, right over.

"Is it evenly divided? Does it look even?"

"Yeah. Yeah. Be patient. I'm getting it." Was this my hatred talking?

I got the rhythm, binding it in. This was the hair of my mother's sister which I drew into place.

Pom

He found her more appealing intellectually than he remembered her, but then much could happen in those particular years. She was still only forty. Before, she had been caught up in the rhetoric of the Left and had belabored it a bit too heavily for his taste, although she had sometimes cut through to a titillating idea—her idea that the leftist movement had something to do with inequality between the sexes and all that. And he had brushed her off as a confused feminist and guilty capitalist or something just as academic as her own definitions were. He had never sat her down and asked her what she herself, in her own soul, thought of it all because he hadn't really taken her seriously. She had been too young, although she had always had that patina of the international hostess. And something more, an ennui, a natural sophistication. But he had brushed her aside as a starry-eyed romantic leftist, a mere girl with a woman's body and style who had happened to fall in love with him and flattered him enough by it to get him to bed a few times. How many times? He couldn't remember. It had seemed like a quick affair.

And hadn't it been convincing—the crash. No wonder the Marxists had been able to draw in the fringe types like Nina. They had predicted it when he and his ilk had had their heads in the sand. It *had* seemed like the possible beginning of an era of political change.

But now he cared nothing for all that and she had given up her flirtation with the Party and Marxism, and as a matter of fact lived in the most ostentatious style possible. And she had become beautiful, somewhat resigned, not exactly passive, and . . . what was it? Easy. She had an ease now with a man. She demanded nothing of him at first and so she seemed to be getting the best of him. He found that amusing and told her so. But then he would sigh it all away, looking into his invisible mirror or down at his wrinkled hand on his bony knee, and he would say, I'm too old for you. I'm too old! Putting into it all his wry amusement and self-forgiveness, his confident plea to woman, so old he hardly questioned it anymore.

"You're at least ten years younger than any man your age, Silly." She said it as to a school chum or little brother and then looked at him, seemed to recognize him, having taken him seriously, and blushed and laughed that bubbling Jewish-bride modest guilty laugh. Ah, she knew a lot! Some women did.

He wanted to talk about Sarah with her but restrained himself. She had befriended Katie, it seemed. He put off the subject for a while. They talked politics cautiously. They talked war. He knew he was compulsive. She was indulgent.

"I honestly thought it was anti-Communism at first. I really did," he told her. "I realized lately that I've always thought the Germans too absurd somehow to be menacing. They fool me every time."

"They don't fool me," she said flatly. "Just a hint that the Jews are to blame for anything is enough for me. It never fails to mean a big pogrom somewhere. Jesus Christ, Pom, three hundred thousand Polish Jews are dead. Aaaaah! I'm disgusted with the world." She looked at him. "Let's talk about something else."

He laughed. "I'm feeling awfully guilty," he said softly, "about a lot of things. Sarah. Beas. Mostly Beas. I have this ridiculous feeling that I've led him to slaughter myself. Look at Murray's son. He's standing up for his beliefs, whatever they are. Defending himself that way before the military. It's fantastic! You've got to admire him. But Beas went off as if he'd been hypnotized. You know, the day he told me he had had his physical and been found perfect I got a queer feeling that I had cooperated in some eerie way with a very negative force in the world—I can't explain it— that was working full force everywhere—you know—and I had been sucked right in, just like that, and handed over my perfect grandson." But he waved a hand at her. "Oh, don't listen to me. I'm a little foolish these days. I do miss Sarah a lot. She spoiled me."

"Were you and she . . ."

He took her hand. "No. Never, my Dear. It never seemed to . . . come up between us. I think the woman was some kind of . . . a visionary or something. She was quite an amazing person, very saintly but very earthy and practical too, in a way."

Nina had blushed again after asking reassurance. Suddenly his blood surged into his chest. He seized her and kissed her, blindly perishing in her passionate response.

Later he took her to see *The Great Dictator.* They laughed at Chaplin's Hitler but afterward at the private bar in the Oilers' Club, where he was uneasy about being seen with her and despised himself for it, he said he thought it was a bit previous, perversely previous, to caricature Hitler that way. It was dangerous, he said, to defuse him that way. Thank God, he said, we were in it now, one's sons notwithstanding.

"*My* sons," she said, "would have offended you by becoming guerillas or underground agents or . . ."

Her voice carried. He leaned near, wanting to force her to whisper. Yet he took pride in the sexual part of it. It must have been evident that they were lovers. He felt heady. He nodded several times to acquaintances. Few men brought women here to begin with, and none brought such an evident sexual partner.

"You mean they would have been something other than obedient bourgeois recruits fulfilling Daddy's expectations, is that it?"

She laughed. "Well . . . maybe. But the idea of *my sons* in any case . . . kind of . . . Oh, I don't know . . . torments me in a pleasant way."

She gave him a look of pleading but glazed it with humor, resigned humor. She had lost it all—marriage, children. He drew nearer and said softly, "Shall we go? I'm going away for a week. I want to be alone with you. . . ."

"Stay over with me," she said. They were creating an island around themselves, an antiworld. Exactly what he had wanted, always—a perspective on the world from some sure sanctuary. Lou had been part of a world pulse, allowing only moments, quick gestures, of privacy. And her power had been the power of illusion, whereas Nina had sat waiting for him in her too too solid flesh, and something in her modest trussed-up patience caught him at still center. It was an impact that stopped him cold and then propelled him in like a remote control device. She was waiting for him to yield all the way and he would do it now, with love and mirth, gratefully. I'm really much more passive than I knew, he thought. She's drowning me and I'm glad. God! The good fortune of some men! Why me? Life may be lived even now with a sensuous affection. Now or any time. War, peace, this was something else. But Beas would be in a battle somewhere in some jungle, while he himself was already half in Paradise!

Let him be safe and have his day, no matter when. Oh gods! He will have earned it far more than I.

On his night off Renfro fixed me a spaghetti dinner at his new apartment and then we went to the Creole for the first time. I felt uneasy, but the crowd seemed strange, lots of men in uniform. I scanned them for a glimpse of RAF, most of whom had been sent home, I had heard; and, idiotically, I looked for Eric. It was not impossible to be tricked that far by life, I told myself in a bitter whisper.

We sat back in the corner at my old table where I explained the doodles, most of them formulas, a carved biography of Beasley Russell, now Private Russell, Company B, 164th Infantry. Someone fed the juke nickels all evening. I was depressed and wished I hadn't come but tried to be gay. I began to stir and yearn for someone, some long body to move me around the floor, to jive me up, to ask in my ear, You like that, Baby? I tapped on the table and nodded my head to the beat. Renfro didn't dance. The logical time for him to become a dancer was about the time he had left home and begun to bum around. He had lost his youth, he said, wry but self-pitying.

"We're having Christmas dinner at Pom's and he asked me to invite you," I said.

He smiled over the pipe. "I'd like to. What do you want for Christmas, by the way?"

"Let's give each other intangibles," I said, flirting a little.

"All right. Give me some hints." He played along.

"Oh, you know—a whole day of what you want to do. A dozen driving lessons. Ha! On an electric. Or a two-hour reading or . . ."

"Oh! Okay. Fair enough. I know what I want already."

"What?"

"I'd like to read the Biography of Enid."

I shot him a look and he said quickly, "I mean, just to see how you write. Or anything else you've got that would give me a look." He blushed a little.

"Okay. Maybe I'll ask you to call your family. Or take me to meet them."

He looked as if I had hit him and I felt sorry. "Well," he said, "that's a different thing. Asking me to do something I have already explained . . ."

I waved it away, laughing a little. "I'm kidding." I began to mellow, like I used to do, nostalgic and sappy. I was thinking of Rabbit and that night we had fumbled together. Since the raids, he had said, he hadn't been able to do it. Renfro since the rods, I punned, and Rabbit since the raids. Maybe it wasn't so infallible as Firecracker Witcher had led me to believe. I decided to get drunk. Renfro drank as much as I did but didn't show it. But drinking only made me morose.

Back at the apartment he said, I don't know whether you ought to drive back full of beer. Maybe you'd better come in and wait awhile.

He didn't turn on the lights. I stood, my heart pounding. He seemed strange all at once. I made a sound and he moved near me. He said be careful wait till I find a lamp but he touched me and I fell against him. He half helped and half leaned on me, staggering toward the couch. We sank, quaking, onto it. His hands seemed terrified and frozen, struggling with me. His breathing roared. I looked at him in the almost dark and said, "Aren't you ever going to?"

He made a sound, hovering near my face.

"For Christmas. You have to," I whispered.

"Oh, Katie . . ."

"You have to," I whispered again. I put my arms around him and moved close. I liked it. Under the pipe smell I found his solitary neat-man smell, a little woody, very faint. Tentative Renfro. Someone. "You have to," I kept saying. I reached back and pulled the shoestring out of my hair. He gasped and moved, drily kissing my neck. He gripped me and then stalled there.

"You have to do it now." I lay back, pulling him down. There was no other way to get life back. I reached inside his shirt and touched his hot skin. He made scared sounds but gripped me. I took his hand and moved it over me. He kissed me everywhere but on my mouth. His teeth? I didn't care. I stood up and took off my clothes and fell back onto the couch. He began to crack finally. He knew how to do it all right. He took off his clothes. I *had* to have it now. He was hot. His firecracker was small and curved and hard like brass. He kissed me with dry closed lips. I lay back and pulled him onto me. All others packed together in him and I wrapped myself around them all, all of them, including Beas and Pom. Everyone. I didn't know Renfro at all and so I wrapped around them all. He tried and then faltered and tried again.

"You have to," I said.

"I can't right now. . . ."

"Yes you can. You have to. I need it and I want it."

And so he did.

Renfro

Boy did she ever move in on him! Man alive! He didn't understand her but he felt good. If shaky. Like a newborn babe, he thought. Well, that Queen, no, Princess—still a Princess of Whimsies and plenty more—had done it. Princess of Passions. She had used him against her own grief. Passion—a flower on a long shaft, noble, single, tough, perishable. Ought to be a Princess in the deck. Odd but correct, the triangle of King, Queen, Knave. Classic. A correct triangle excluding the Princess which may have meant that she was free. The old struggle between King and Knave, with Queen as subject and object, simply left out the Princess who ran away with the kingdom or something. She was usually sold off to a Knave who got half the kingdom with her, but . . . What was that man's name she said was her father? Higgens.

And the Ace? He felt a bit like the Ace just then. A very subtle card, indisputable, playing high or low, nothing in between. The

Ace—acme of Lucky Improbables. God and Devil combined. An ironic card. Man's only chance.

That time he had found a bum playing solitaire and gotten into a poker game with him. In a hut made of tin cans and Dr. Pepper signs. He had drawn two aces, asked for three cards and drawn two more. With a penniless bum in the middle of the Panhandle in an abandoned Okie shack, penniless himself. Betting imaginary feasts, cars, women. He had won a good cook in Kansas, a fine old Velie touring car and a pecan grove. An old affection washed his innards.

But what was he going to do with Katie now? Keep dreaming her out of his head with his old nostalgias? His hangovers?

He had watched her sleep. She was so young. He had never seen her still before. It struck him as profound, the idea of her stillness. But he didn't know what to do with her. Maybe he ought to tell her his nightmares. Having been inside her maybe now he could just fill her up with his soul, too. But the swill would contaminate her. But she was a survivor. She was not womanly but she was female. He thought of her legs, acrobatic. She was a monkey, thin and agile and hot and tidy. A little hairy. Soft, but good muscles. Sex! The mere idea of it made him weak.

She had gone off without breakfast. He imagined some other earthy woman standing at his sink after that night together, their first, washing last night's dishes or in some way picking up after him. Sometimes a streak, fine like a shooting star, of revulsion against women went through his brain, ignited his body.

I don't want to be the kind of man who has to spend his life keeping some woman pinned down on a bed and stoked with food. Just to be able to get inside her. Not to wear her on my back or hanging across me like a shield.

But he knew that if he went into a woman—more than in the biblical *in unto* sense—all the way, then he would open up into the strange tarnished flower he had kept in its aging tight bud too long. It might live only a day if let open now. But a day was better than nothing.

She was ideal. He might almost adopt instead of marry her. She was a waif. Always had been, mother or no. Higgens. The daughter of Higgens. Yes, the deck needed a few more figures, scrubby royalty, fillies, bums maybe. And heroes returned? Well . . .

He'd have to start telling her some truth now, and not just ideas.

I was sorry the minute he touched the Biography. He was too curious about Enid as it was. But I was purging and he had asked. I told him I hadn't read it in months but I gave it over anyway. In the Sunshine where we often had breakfast or met for lunch.

Since that night he had been tightly with me like a slightly worn spat, discreetly old-fashioned and firmly protective. It was as if he had made a decision to be that way. We made love in the daytime since he still worked the swing shift. He was quiet about it, neat and easy. Not wild like Eric. Not *with* me exactly. But Eric seemed like some fabulous dream of my childhood. He rarely wrote me now. He was in battle somewhere. I couldn't believe it, which was a way of not caring, maybe. Sometimes I sank in the middle and had to lie down. Sarah. Eric. Beas. Missing someone forever seemed intolerable. I had to forget one of them so I forgot Eric a little more each day. I couldn't care much about anything, in fact, except remotely about Beas.

Renfro spent one of his rare smiles on me. "Well, well. I'm looking forward to this." He laid the Biography on the seat beside him. "What're you going to do today?"

"I'm going down to the reform school to see Murray Dietler. With his father and Pom. I'm taking him some books I found in your shop."

He had discovered a good secondhand bookstore run by a First World War veteran who was giving all his profits to war bonds and had been written up in the newspaper.

"Oh, what do you think of old Max?"

"He's some character. It's a good store."

"I'm getting to know him. I realized the other day that I've known a dozen men pretty well, seen into their guts, and never had a real friend." He flicked his eyebrows as if he had just told on himself accidentally. "Well, I'm glad you're going to see *your* friend, Murray. I bet he needs company. That trial must have been something. He deserves credit."

"Abe says if he'd been a year older they'd have put him in federal prison with hardened criminals. Since Pearl Harbor. He won't even work in a hospital job. He's a pure pacifist."

"Well, let's hope they're doing something worthwhile with those kids down at that reform school. I remember what a bad name the place had before the crash. It beats war, I guess. You hear the news this morning? The Philippines definitely fell."

I thought of Eric. "Yeah." Everything, as far as I was concerned, had already fallen.

"How's the hand today?" Reverently asked, as if after my soul.

"Better. Doesn't hurt much anymore. It's just weak."

"How long does the compensation last?"

"As long as I'm disabled, I guess. Oh, that reminds me, I got my life insurance check. I put it in savings."

He approved. "The fellows still ask about you," he said of my crew. He pretended not to know that I'd never go back to work there. He stirred his coffee. He hadn't lit a pipe in thirty minutes.

The waitress delivered his waffle and my scrambled eggs. We traded halves and ate silently. I cooked up a little vision of us breakfasting here twenty years later, silent, knowing everything about one another and bored the way some couples were who came in together before work. Help! When he finished he took out the pipe. It no longer interested me that some people gorged and some minced their way through meals, or what they ate. But out of habit I still took note.

"When you read the Biography," I said, "try to forget who wrote it and just concentrate on the writing and . . . whatever else you wanted to see."

He puckered in a smile and I returned it. Without noticing it at first, I had begun to stroke his hand. I wondered if he really wanted to be making love with me or if he was doing it for me because I had said I needed it. He seemed sometimes not to be there when we were most together. He hadn't asked me if I were being careful not to get pregnant. He wasn't being careful. Maybe he just presumed.

"What're you brooding about?" he said.

"Us."

"It's been a long time . . . for me," he said.

"Don't be apologetic."

"I'm not. I wonder if you realize how—how questionable my life has been. These last ten years, I mean."

"But now it isn't questionable, is it?"

He stared. "I don't know for sure. Maybe less so. I've just lately figured out why I never killed myself."

"Why didn't you?"

"Something to do with work. I'll tell you about it sometime."

Visiting day. The families looked sober. Their clothes were poor, mainly black. The mothers and sisters were more sure of themselves, bringing gifts, crying or hugging the boys. One father stood in the yard and patiently threw a ball back and forth with his son, wondering what to do next, it seemed, and not saying anything.

I handed Murray the books and the cake Ruby and I had made him. He looked more interesting and sure in his new haircut and his work clothes. He was pale but tougher looking. He had chosen shoe repair as a trade but his corner of the room which he shared with three other boys was full of books and papers stacked neatly on the desk and in piles all around it. His real work was now the study of law. He gave me a quick quizzical look to see if I was surviving.

"I sure was sorry to hear . . ."

"Yeah. It was a bad thing."

He peeked into the cake box.

"She made it herself," Pom said eagerly. He looked like a dove sitting on a dung heap.

"With Ruby's help," I said.

"Gee!" Murray batted his watery eyes at me. His glasses slipped down a little. "That's swell. The boys will go crazy over it."

"I hope you get a piece yourself."

He smiled. "I'll get one. Maybe even two. But they all share with me." He laughed a little. "I get a lot of Mexican food."

We all laughed. Abe stood at the foot of Murray's bed nodding, studying him. Murray seemed, after much thrashing around, to have flipped over right-side up.

"What happened to your hand?" he asked me.

"I broke it. I'm living on workmen's compensation."

"Terrific! Think of the men who coulda used that a few years ago! You can thank the unions for that."

"That's right, Son," Abe said quietly.

"Yeah," I said. I liked him. He was more aware. His ugliness was a little bit beautiful.

"It's spectacular what Chicago has done for him," Abe had said on the way down in the car. "They're ready to give him a Master's degree right there in reform school if they can. They give him a little time off from work down there to study and Chicago sends down a faculty member to review him now and then. He may go through half his law studies that way. Can you believe it? You gotta hand it to him, he's not sitting in there moping. It beats carrying a gun and getting his guts shot out."

He froze, having hit Pom where he lived, but Pom said quickly, "You're damn right it does."

Murray, Abe explained, had a simple system of studying after lights out, and his roommates wouldn't welch on him.

"They're loyal as ants, these street kids. They've been through a lot by the time they end up in here. He turns out the light and gets in bed for five minutes every hour on the hour when the guard comes by. He says it's amazing how much it rests his back and his eyes. The kids call him the professor. Ha! He says there's one little hood in there who calls him Socketees! He's even teaching a class in government, for chrissakes! You gotta hand it to the kid, he's making the most of it."

"I have a feeling he won't be in long," Pom said.

"Yeah?" I said. "What'll they do when he takes the bar exams and becomes a lawyer? Keep a lawyer in reform school?"

"Well," Abe mused, "parole isn't usually a part of that package. Good behavior maybe. The warden wrote me he's making a contribution. He's a model. Well . . . we did a few things wrong. Maybe I shoulda laid on a little reform myself. It's my fault he's been slow."

But Pom protested that Murray had hardly been slow, graduating from college at seventeen!

Pom and I toured the shops and the barns while Abe visited with Murray. I liked it. It was safe. I wondered if girls' reform schools were as homey. They had a large dairy farm and a trade school. Life, I told my dreamer, could be orderly and simple.

Later Murray and I talked a few minutes in the big mess hall, alone, drinking Dr. Peppers. I felt a little bit alive. "It seems nice here," I told him.

He nodded gravely. "I learned a lot already. I like to have a trade. I shoulda had one a long time ago. It puts you in touch with the people. I'm not sorry I'm in here. The war's serious and everybody's paying some way."

I wondered about myself and the war but said nothing. There were still traces of Murray's old forlornness on his face, but he seemed sure. He moved his chair closer to mine and looked into my eyes. He had always been candid, I remembered. It seemed a long time since I had seen him.

"You know, I thought a lot about you. I appreciated that letter you sent me after my trial. Of all the people who didn't deserve to lose their mother, you were the one." He shook his head.

I lowered my eyes. *Careful, Careful.*

"I don't think life has anything to do with what people deserve, though," I said. "Besides, everybody's mother dies." There, I said it.

"Well, everybody dies. But we can change things a little in the world," he said. "More people can get what they deserve."

"But the whole idea of deserving," I said, roused ever so slightly as usual, "just doesn't work out. Life isn't logical or even . . ."

He nodded quickly. "You lean more toward anarchy. You really aren't the believing type. You think more like a poet or something. But I think we hafta try to have some principles that we really live by. And—" He waved a hand around the room— "try to apply them. To change the world. People get together over an issue and that starts them cooperating and understanding each other. Like the war. It's getting people together, you notice?"

"I know." I was submitting. The ice was cracking! "I broke my hand," I heard myself say, "because I hit it against a tree."

"Geee! You musta felt *terrible.*" He stared at me. "There's a kid here who does that. He's broken his hands a dozen times. But he's really a nice boy. These kids have all broken the law and got caught. They've got that in common. Usually they get along pretty well in here. There's a bond."

"Breaking the law . . . " I floundered. "It makes people smarter."

He nodded. "You ever break the law?"

I laughed a little and shrugged. "I feel like I'm breaking it all the time but I don't know exactly how."

"You're not a part of the people, the masses. Or a movement. Or . . . "

"Well, I'm . . . myself. I've got relatives and I live in a house and I've got friends." Why was I defending myself?

"Well, you're not exactly the bourgeoisie either. You take them —they obey laws that are outdated and crippling to society. Laws based on class or caste systems, and if you break one of their laws, you're in the soup."

"But people *are* of different classes, in some natural way," I whined.

"All the more reason to protect the weak and unlucky. It's a man's duty to . . . "

I sighed. "You still think you've got a duty and all that?"

He deliberated carefully, licking his thick red lips. He slowly knocked the empty bottle on the tabletop and the big room echoed it back. "Yeah. I think I do. I changed some of my thinking, but I still believe I have a duty to other men—to instruct them, make them aware of their historic mission, like Lenin says."

"What if your goal is wrong or not suitable for them? You'd be leading them astray."

"Well, we both have to be careful. They hafta be careful who they trust. See, that's why I'm going into law. That's where I've changed. Everything comes down to law in the end. I see people moving through the world of laws they've inherited from the past like crawling through a mine field. You've got to have a map or a plan or a leader who knows what he's doing. Where's free access? Where is it dangerous? The world's dangerous if you aren't educated. You have to keep up with it."

"But it's dangerous if you are educated, too."

"But more manageable, I think," he said patiently.

"You think?"

"Yeah, I think so."

"The world's just a symptom of what's going on in the souls of men," I said.

He looked at me forgivingly. "Well, it doesn't have to be one or the other—your truth or mine. Maybe you're more metaphysical. That's all."

Boy, had he changed!

"I am?"

"Yeah. I think so." He looked at me closely. "You oughta come down and visit my class some evening. Thursdays four to six P.M. It's neat. Some of these fellows never even knew there was such a thing as a Constitution." He smiled apologetically. "I do what I can."

"Well, I think it's nifty, what you do." I looked into his eyes too, not used to the same kind of candor. He was still as unabashed as a peeing dog.

"See, it's real nice for me here because they respect me. I hope you come back, Kid. They respect me even more for having a girl visit. Ha! And anyway . . . well . . . I'd like to see you. I sure like having company. People who . . . you know, you knew before."

★

I melted a lot. I thought if I was really metaphysical like he said, I wouldn't have problems or pain and finally I would glide out into some big marvel of a world where only terrible and true things needed doing. Learning shoe repair and humility like that still hit me as defeat. I knew I wasn't pure like Murray. Nor like Sarah McCleod, a woman buried under the ground of Rosewood Cemetery who once went to Shreveport and met a man named Higgens and so on. I couldn't get hold of that lifeline, that was all. I tried and I couldn't find it. Something was missing. And she could not now ever impart it to me, whatever it had been. Instead, I had the old clients' doodads and the one thousand dollars in the bank, the most unlikely inheritance from her who had never noticed the existence of cash in the world. Well, at least I was thinking again. I felt minutely restored after the trip.

I went out to the Rooster Hut and met him where his ride left him off. They didn't come in this time.

"Why don't you get on day shift?" I asked him.

He was smiling tightly, his eyes sparkling, the pipe rammed into very rosy lips.

"What's up your sleeve?" I laughed a little.

We sat down. He had the Biography with him. He laid it on the seat, signaled for two beers and then looked at me steadily for a minute.

"What's so . . . secret?"

Then he smiled, open, naked. His teeth! Marble white and even. I opened my mouth and let out a happy gasp.

"How do you like them? Pretty nice, huh?" He kept his lips back over them until he looked like an ad for Colgate. I laughed.

"Marvelous! They look wonderful. Makes you all different. But . . ." I shook my head. "How'd you get them so fast?"

"I was fitted for them two weeks ago. I had so much bare healed-over gum it wasn't much of a job. My gums won't shrink much, only where the new extractions were."

He always wanted to fill me in on the gory details. But he looked so happy! I had never seen Renfro look happy. It socked me in the middle.

"Gee! You must feel marvelous!"

"Just have to learn now to open my mouth." He laid the pipe down suddenly with a rap on the table. "Get rid of *that* damn thing. It's an affectation. You know that? I don't think I really like pipe smoke that much."

"I hope you quit." I realized you have to have access to the mouth of a person you care about. Caring about him, however, was complex.

"Well, Miss. You write very well sometimes, in my opinion."

"Oh, yeah? Only sometimes?"

He laughed. He was flourishing with authority. Wow! Just over a set of dentures that probably cost thirty-nine dollars.

"Where'd you get your teeth?"

"One of those bargain places. I shopped around. There's one good man. But look here, I didn't know you could write. You could write real fiction, maybe, if you put your mind to it. Of course this hasn't much form or anything. It just kind of opens up and moves without continuity. But you began to get the idea of a person in the flashback."

Are those teeth going to clack? I wondered. When we got into bed together would they stay in all right with all that thrashing around? Maybe he'd just take them out! I wished he hadn't put me through the life and death of his teeth.

"I'm glad you think so."

But, he said, the Biography was too psychoanalytical and it lacked a description of events. I said that Enid didn't have events and he said everybody had events and I thought of the round-and-round music of Sarah's life, and that similar in-the-negative round of Enid's, up–down, day–night. No, I said, Enid's were all psychological, couldn't he see that? That was the whole point and anti-meaning in her life. We argued. He said if I controlled myself and laid out a plan and outlined it and changed the names and all that, then it would be possible that I might even make a book out of it.

"But . . ." I shook my head, frustrated. "I'm not *doing* it to make a book. I wouldn't publish a book about her even if I could. God! And anyway, you don't see what I was doing. I was just making notes and . . . thinking . . . in words—you know."

"But without form and . . . intent, direction," he said, "a thing is meaningless."

"Ha! The Meaning of Meaning. Nothing is meaningless. To me it isn't meaningless, form or no form. There must be more than one way to look at form and all."

He was excited about Enid. That's what he really wanted to talk about and hear more of. I told him a little, reluctantly. It was spying, I thought—I, the prime Delirian spy! It went all wrong. The new teeth had made him bossy. He had a way of telling me I was good at something and showing me by that how I had failed. That was criticism. I didn't take it too well and was ashamed of myself and sorry I had shown him the Biography. It was a betrayal. I wondered if Judas realized what he was doing to Jesus. Maybe he was trying to save Jesus from doing something too risky. I'd have to read it again.

I took him home. He suddenly leaned toward me and said Thanks, Sweet, and gave me a quick little dry kiss on my surprised mouth.

He was more eager in bed but not exactly making love to *me*, or with *me*. I couldn't pin it down. He seemed to sail off into some dream as soon as we got going. But I liked his sides, his lightness, his patience. His sorrow? Yep, even that.

I heard Enid up. She was noisy. I remembered that Ruby was off with Lucille for the day. I turned over and slept again. When I got up something seemed wrong. Not a sound. I washed my face and put on a pair of blue jeans and a sweater. I went into the hall, the kitchen. Nobody. I took an apple from the kitchen. I looked around.

She was in the big armchair from Nadine Banks that Sarah had always preferred. Sarah's feet had hardly touched the floor but Enid's were flat on it. No crossed legs, no cigarette. Her hair was loose the way she slept; her peignoir, the champagne one with lace . . . I stared. She could have been dead. Bad news. Death? Death was all around her all the time.

"What're you doing up so early?"

"It isn't early," she said simply. Waiting.

"Did you have some news? Is Beas . . . ?"

"No. I didn't have news." She stared.

I shivered.

Then I saw the red ledger that was the Biography *in her lap!* I almost fainted.

"What're you doing with . . . that? That's mine."

"Some . . . *man*," she sneered, "from a place called the *Rooster Hut* brought this by on his way to town this morning. He said you left it there last night."

"Why . . . why I didn't either! That's not true." I saw Renfro get up from the booth, take his jacket . . .

"Then how did he get hold of it?"

I stared. I couldn't believe it.

She said, "You in the habit of carrying this . . . *thing* around with you?"

"No. I was just . . . I had it out because . . ."

"You were showing it to someone, isn't that it?" Her voice steady and dull as the minute after murder.

I was mute.

"Well, isn't that what you were doing? Showing it to someone? Who was it, your *boyfriend*?" As if he were the scum of the earth.

"Only a few sentences. He wanted to see how I write."

She snorted. She crossed her leg and started to swing her foot slightly. She didn't take her eyes off me. I sat down on the couch as if on nails. How could we have *forgotten* it? Silence.

"I haven't written in it for a long time," I said finally.

"Oh for God's sake stop lying! There's an entry here about Beas enlisting."

She had read every line! I hung my head.

The house was cold. We just sat there. I felt as if she had always wanted to punish me and that I had written the Biography so that she could find it and realize her desire. I had learned to hate her, not realizing that she might hate me. It made me a little stronger to consider that.

"Well," I said, sighing. "You didn't have to read it. It is *mine*, after all."

"Well, wouldn't you have?" she snapped. "With your own *name* on the front? My God! I was never so shocked in my life, a perfect stranger coming to the door with a thing like this in his hand."

Gus Streicher, the owner. He wouldn't have bothered to read it. He remembered I was sitting in that booth, was all.

"Oh, he probably can't even read," I said.

"That's hardly the point, is it?" She glared but her voice shook. I looked up at her quickly and she looked down, drumming a hand on it as if figuring what terrible thing could be done with it, or to it, or to me. Gee! Imagine reading all about yourself. It hit me harder.

"After all, your friend Renfrew read it, didn't he?"

"Ren*fro*. Yes, but just a few lines, like I told you."

She sighed. "You're lying. But what's the difference? It's that you would write . . . all that. A girl your age."

I was silent, waiting for the axe. She waited too. A long time. And then she said, "I just can't believe you could do anything so —so . . . vicious."

"It's not vicious!"

She was shaking her head. "And it's all—it's untrue. I'm not . . ." She stopped on a quaver. It had hit and hurt her!

I swallowed. If I cried, I'd kill myself. My whole life had been fattening me up for this and here it was.

"Well, I intend to burn it," she said.

"It's not yours!"

"It's mine now. By accident, but mine. You'd do the same."

I waited. She was falling somehow. After a long time she said in a normal, almost wistful voice—

"It's not true that I let the bird out of the cage." And then with a tremble. "And all that about my . . . 'my bitter scorn' and all. It's not true. Where did you get an idea like that?"

"Okay," I said softly. Gee! She cared about letting the bird out!

"I . . . must say I can't take much of Iantha's chatter—all that gossip of hers. That's true. But I don't feel scorn. People get into habits, ways of speaking, I guess. . . ."

I waited. My heart thudded. I didn't want to hear any of it. She lit a cigarette and blew a shaft of smoke toward the ceiling.

"You're all wrong about a lot of things. My . . . drinking. Before or after."

"You drink. That's enough of a comment." My heart pounded. That was the most dangerous thing I had ever said.

She stood up suddenly. "Well, there's no point in talking to you."

She went into her room. It seemed so silly and stupid, not just saying everything in the world, once you're caught. She was as caught as I was. Telling her she drank, just spelling it out, made my head spin. Even if it hurt her, it was fabulous. I sat a moment. I picked up my apple but couldn't eat it. Then I went to my room and threw a few things into a pillowcase and went out, leaving her the way Beas and I had always left her—alone. Her life, the whole burden and emptiness of it struck me, clear and hard—zero.

★

I stayed three nights at Renfro's. She knew where I was but she didn't call. I couldn't believe I had finally said it to her—*You drink.* I sat in Renfro's window looking down at the street. I saw the children come home from school. One of them hit another. It didn't matter at all. It happened every day, I told myself. And I saw a woman go down the street with packages. To some house somewhere, to some cooking. To some people, young and old. To cook and tell them everything was all right. Or to fight them. I saw a cat noodle around a bush and then skittle up a tree very near the window and lie on a limb forever. Like me.

I didn't fix Renfro's late supper. He woke me and gave me a cup of soup. He smoked his pipe and sat still in the chair. He ran a hot bath and lay in it a long time so that I went back to sleep in the Murphy bed.

When he came to bed finally, I stirred but couldn't wake fully. And didn't want to. On the third morning he said, Are you going to stay? And after about ten minutes of silence, I finally said, "No. I have to go back. Let's don't talk about it."

Enid

The nerve! The crass nerve, watching somebody that way. . . . *bowed head, cowed.* . . . Little spy. You never know. Never. If Sarah had known. Or Beas . . . Maybe he saw it.

Oh, burn it. Your Honor, I thought they had forgotten.
How could they?
I think Beas has buried it.
How could he?
All right all right then. I'll burn it.
Then burn it.
I can't. Yet. Don't ask me why. It is like having caught a hot coal in your hand. But I'll burn it. I'll tear out every page. This old leather won't burn.

In the Boston Shop, all that . . . that thinking . . . about those poor girls. D'you suppose they really see me like that? It's terrible what others really think. Terrible. Even a girl nineteen. If she knew what *I* think . . . all that running around, wild . . . getting a reputation.

All that talk about my bitter scorn. Do I? Am I? I stay out of their way.

Oh, but something in it is right, cruel but right. I am hurting myself. I'll burn the damn stupid thing. Why did I even tell her?

But we were there. Together. We had to eat together, we couldn't go off into our bedrooms to eat. You had to live. Ruby kept us surprised with all our favorite specialities, including some hot tamales she bought somewhere, not as good as the ones Pom usually brought and reminding me of the day Beas left. I felt sick. I was confused. I kept thinking Sarah would appear in a doorway or that I would hear her little sigh after sleep. I was waking up again to grief, as if—O dumb Delirian—it could have lasted so short a time.

I didn't go near Renfro, hardly went out at all except to walk in the woods and to take Ruby to the country market. I waited for the next axe, knowing I would have to talk to Enid again, or face her. I tried to fathom why I had written the Biography in the first place, why I hadn't thought of it as wrong, why I had let Renfro read it, why I had let him leave it somewhere. If I hadn't let him read it, no one would ever have known. It would have rotted away among my worn-out toys and child belongings maybe. Or I might one day have reread it and burned it. Showing it to Renfro had something to do with his having met her and of course his having met and seen her had something to do with his having seen and met *me*. . . . Well, my head fretted through it failing to find a single continuous thread back to the cause. I was the cause. Enid was the cause of murder and I was the cause of keeping the murder alive.

I would torture myself with regret and guilt and then wheel back on my old stance of suspicion and hatred of her. She *had* told Sarah to shut up and she *had* murdered Uncle Jack and she *had* let the bird out of the cage once. I knew she had, a thousand years ago but in my lifetime. She *had* moved into my house and she *did* drink. *You drink.* I doubled my broken fist, released it with slow deep pain, over and over. I couldn't read. I just walked the woods or slept or stared at the wall.

One night Ruby went out with Gifford. Enid was sitting in the parlor listening to "One Man's Family." I hung around the hall, nibbled things in the kitchen, lurking there. I was finally ready to forget the whole thing and go out in the electric. I saw that maybe I had deliberately waited for a night when Ruby was out so Enid would be left completely alone. At the table she hardly spoke to me and never looked at me. She was polite. Her whole face was wiped away. I couldn't see her.

"Katie? That you?" she called. "Don't you want to hear this? You haven't heard it for a month."

I went in. That's how it goes, one person makes a move. I wondered if she had thrown out the Biography but didn't ask. After the program, in which Ann telephoned Clifford and called his name over the phone in a distant whine and drove everybody in the Barber family crazy—after that Enid said she wanted some coffee, did I want some tea? I thought my head would fly off. Yes, I wanted some tea. She brought it on a tray. She was different. I tried not to look at her. She poured cream into her coffee. She sat back. And then she said—

"Beasley's missing."

I stood up, splashing hot tea on my hand. I could have laughed with the horror. It was a trick. "*What? Where? Missing?* How'd you hear?"

"Pom called me. Three days ago."

"Three *days*? Why didn't you tell me? Nobody ever tells me anything. My God!" I knew it. My heart froze. I *knew* it. I couldn't move.

"Pom has some friend in the Army. He's trying to find out the details. There was a mock battle in that camp they moved him to in California. He . . ." She swallowed as if her mouth were stuffed with cotton. "He got separated from the rest or something. He's lost. I don't know . . . I don't know. . . ."

I began to shake all over. They'd never tell us the truth. Somebody probably shot him. They probably buried him. My mind babbled on. I sat gingerly on the edge of the chair and took a swig of burning tea. If anything happened to Beas . . . Well, it *had* happened. I didn't think I could stand any more bad news. "He hardly got there," I said. "My God! Don't they even keep track of their men?" I started to cry a little, trying to force it back.

She waited. I gasped a little and got it under control. She was like some plant growing there, silent and immobile. Just waiting, dry and stiff.

Pom, she finally said, would be out tomorrow to take us to the club to dinner. He'd call the minute he had more news. I wiped my face with my sweater sleeve. I felt exhausted and wanted to lie down. I didn't even want to hit the wall.

"Why'd he go in the first place? I *knew* this would happen."

She sat with what seemed like a straight line drawn across her eyelids. A canceled-out look. Finally I said, "I'm sorry . . . about everything."

"He may be all right. The man said it wasn't unusual . . ."

"How can you *stand* it? Beas is all you've got. . . ."

"I don't have Beasley," she said flatly. "I lost him—a long time ago."

It thrilled me with terror to hear her refer to it.

"That's not true. He cares about you. . . . He—"

"Naturally. But he has all the freedom from me he wants or needs. He's Pom's ward, not mine. I wouldn't stop him, anyway, if I could . . . from anything, including going to war."

I made a noise and started to cry again silently. I felt like falling into a hole. I stared at the chair where Sarah should have been sitting, swinging her feet. I felt queerly as if I were doing it to make myself cry.

"I know," she said finally, quietly, "that you're . . . unhappy right now, Katie. Besides about Sarah. With me here in the house —and all. But . . ." She flicked a hand. "You shouldn't be here alone. Just you and Ruby. And besides . . . I—"

"I don't care if you live here," I said it in quick guilt, half whispered.

"I'm . . . I'm working on my life . . . and my problems." She had rehearsed it. "Just day by day. Serene's class is a help. I thought I might have the meeting here on Thursday night, if you don't mind."

She was going to go right on with living. I shrugged.

"You'd be surprised. . . . Metaphysics is— Well, it explains certain things." I couldn't believe my ears. "The ideas," she went on, "aren't personal. I'm so tired of personal . . . sentimental talk. Sarah—God knows she was a saint, but all that . . ."

She looked at me and I glared. "She wasn't sentimental," I said.

"I didn't say that. She offered so much protection. It was hard to . . . want to make your own decisions around her. You know that."

I knew it and didn't say anything. I wanted to hate her again but it wasn't full force anymore. Everything was shredding apart in me.

"I'm working on . . . things. My drinking. I don't care about the talk, all that gossip and all about my past. That doesn't mean a thing to me. That's not why I . . . drink. I'm not . . . miserable . . . like what you say in that silly thing you wrote. I *like* to be alone. I don't care much for people, really. I . . ." She waited. I was hypnotized. Then she sighed as if giving up. "Well, killing does terrible things to you." She said it in a raw whisper. "But I drank before. Before Jack's death. Jack didn't drink as much as I did, in fact."

This was going to be the real Biography, the Autobiography. I didn't want it. It terrified me. But I couldn't stop it. She was bent on it. She was folding and unfolding her hands, needing something to hold in them. She was breathing hard and looking at her lap, her eyebrows up slightly even so, with a quizzical and pained expression stuck there as if she had discovered a hole in herself.

I suddenly felt powerful and then disgusted, not with her exactly, but with people in pain, in quandary, memories of clients, pity—old pity!—death, crime, all of it. Goddammit! I didn't want to be sitting there in a room on an old lease outside the city limits with a murderer alcoholic sad beautiful woman. But I was. Here I was. I wanted to leap up and swab the place clean of everything that didn't belong to me alone, of everything that had been thought and done there. I wanted order and air in it. I watched her wring her hands and felt driven to grab her, yank her to her feet and shout, Just *do* it! *Do* it! *Act!* I waited. She waited. Finally I saw that she had handed me over the power I felt. She wanted me to drag it out of her. She couldn't do it. She couldn't. I let out a sigh. Finally I asked it—

"Why did you kill him?"

She gave a little sigh and a snort. "Well . . . it— Oh, Katie, there isn't a *reason* for everything. Maybe not for anything." Her voice rose and quickened. "It was— Oh, I killed him the way you'd . . . swat a fly, if you must know." She gave me a bitter disgusted look.

"A *fly?*"

"Yes. A fly. He was a nuisance and I swatted him. I'd been enduring and swatting at him for years and finally I . . . I just . . . " She raised her shoulders and held them there. "Well, I couldn't very well say *that* in a courtroom. I had to let them . . . rig up some logic to it. Something that satisfied them. *Temporary Insanity!* What in the name of God is temporary insanity?"

I controlled a little laugh. "I don't know. I never could figure it out."

She stayed in her flesh. I got a look, cold as brass, at her. It was because of what she was or wasn't that she had done it. Not because of something he had done to her, killable though he was. It was just natural to her to get rid of a problem that way. Could it have been? Natural?

"I had just suddenly come to the end of my rope with him. Jack wasn't—oh, he wasn't a whole person, really. Not that I am. I know. But he had no affection for anyone. Or for life. He hated life." Her mouth drew down.

"Don't you hate it, too?"

"Oh . . . I don't know. I don't know. I'm not even sure what it is."

"Life? I mean being alive. Feeling it. The world—"

"The world," she said with conviction, "is what is insane. I do hate the world. That I do. Life, I don't know. I've never really been alive, I suspect." She was deeply ironic. It was like a piece of metal shafted through her. "Except maybe for a few weeks after Beas was born. It was easy having him. It was . . . nice. He was such a neat little baby and—oh, I don't know—so complete."

Yes. Beas. Now lost!

"But . . ." She bent her head, pondering it, the way she did when she read her metaphysics books. She was looking for some clue in it all. I could hardly bear it. I was suddenly aware of the world. My rear end had gone to sleep. I was going to live! I was going to live in the world no matter what it was—real or not, stupid or not, war, murder or not, I saw that that was what I was going to do and it gave me a blast of queer joy.

"It wasn't possible to do much living when we were children," she was saying. "The Territory was so wild. Daddy had to follow us everywhere with a shotgun to keep the roustabouts and all those rough men and the Indian boys away from us. We weren't able to . . . run free, you know? Sarah didn't seem to mind that. But the way you've been free to run here on the lease. The way Beas . . . Well, he did a little of it, I think. On his bike."

"It's with your body," I said, in a trance. "You have to be able to move."

"You have to be able to move without reason," she said. That, she said, was what children needed.

"Yeah." My head was sparking.

"Having a baby is different. It's your own. No matter who the husband is. The reason behind it doesn't matter because it's such . . . a real thing." She laughed again, less bitterly. "Jack was jealous of Beas, and of me, I think, just because I gave birth to him, I guess. My having a baby. It drove him wild. He couldn't believe it was his for some crazy reason. Oh, he didn't suspect me of anything, he just felt left out or something. Serene says most men are like that. They feel left out of the birth of their children. I suppose it's so!" she said with wonder. "But Daddy wasn't like that. He believed we were born for his benefit entirely. God! It never occurred to him that we might prefer mother to him. And I didn't really—Sarah did, I guess. They were so much alike, she and Daddy, that . . ."

She rattled on. It would flash through me that she was talking about my mother, my grandmother, my grandfather, and then I would lose the connection. I remembered listening to family talk and tales when I was little, lying on the floor looking up into the mouths of adults—Sarah, Iantha, Pom—knowing they were doing this same thing and not needing to hear the content of it, just to know that it was going on. When Sarah had read to me when I was little, I had never listened to the words, the story—none of that mattered. What I had listened to was her reading, her music, her voice, her idea of it. I had been feeling her presence and listening to her music.

When she stopped, I said suddenly, "I think they'll find Beas."

"I think so too," she said, "but we don't know anything about all that. There is some kind of funny twist to the idea that he might be shot—like his father. Those mock battles are dangerous. . . ."

"Oh, it's too neat," I said. "It's like a bad movie."

She smiled bitterly. "Most of life, if you take a good look, is like a bad movie."

A fly! I felt a cold horror when I thought of Uncle Jack, or anyone, as a fly. I started to tell Renfro but decided to wait. And Enid and I waited, too, a kind of fractured communion of souls, for news of Beas. Pom's fury and impatience returned and he often reminded us of the stupidity of the Army's having put raw recruits into that kind of war game so soon. Enid reminded him that Beas had had a lot of training at Claiborne before California and that if they were going to send him to the Pacific she hoped he'd have all the rough training he could get.

I called Renfro, talked a long time, wanted to see him but liked something in the small pain of missing him. I had tea once with Nina. I told her I loved not working and never wanted to be employed again. "You can live so much when you don't work," I explained.

She laughed. "I think you'll live a lot, Honey, whether you work or not."

"God! You think? I hope so. I hope I get to. You know—big living!"

She seized my head and shook it between her hands. "Aaaaaa! You little pagan. You little con artist! You want everything and somehow you make a person want to give it to you."

I swooned. It was as if the winds were changing all over the world. But, I asked her, indulging in her affection, didn't she want everything too?

"I've got what I want now. Ha! A slightly mauled-over version of it, that is."

"You mean Pom?"

She blushed. "Pom. It just happened. I wonder if Sarah hadn't died . . ."

"But she did die," I said quietly.

"Well, I'm not questioning my good luck, Honey. We're both a little over the hill, Pom and I, but . . ."

I laughed. "*You're* not over the hill! You're only about forty, aren't you?"

"Honey, I was born old. I was wearing a thirty-four B by the time I was nine years old. My first day in kindergarten about five kids climbed on me and laid their heads on my bosom!" We laughed, she flushed up like a burnished peach. "Well, anyway, Sweetie, there's a war on. I'm going to open one of those clubs for soldiers. A USO. Want to work for me?"

"Gee! Sure. That's the least like work of anything I can think of. Thanks. I want to wait till my insurance runs out though."

"Oh, come on! I need you. The boys need you."

"What about me? If I need them it's just too bad, huh?"

She pinched my cheek. "Oh, stop feeling sorry for yourself. There's a war on!"

No news of Beas. No word from Eric. But things at home seemed to be shifting. Enid was up more or moved more, maybe that was it. I watched her in spite of myself.

We were to have Christmas dinner with Pom. I wanted to look especially nice or exotic, or memorable at least. I fussed around for two hours with my wardrobe, my hair. Enid merely put on something perfect. She had been shopping recently with Iantha, wonder of wonders. I had to fasten a few tiny covered silk buttons at the back of her new dress.

"I didn't know you'd ever been in the Boston Shop," she said casually.

The hair stood up on the back of my neck when she mentioned the Biography. I told her I had taken her to the Boston Shop once or twice. I remembered waiting for her there one time for two hours.

"Once was enough of that place, in fact," I said. "Hold still." I buttoned her up. Maybe she hadn't burned it. Maybe she was rereading it. I hated to think she might be.

"I'm going to look awful," I said feebly. "I don't have the right clothes and my hair's too long. I think I'll cut it."

She turned quickly. "You'll do no such thing! Don't you dare cut that hair. Pull it back, do it into a knot or something. I could curl it on the iron for you. Maybe I've got something you can wear. . . ." She wandered into her closet to look.

Why was she paying all this attention to me? It was irresistible. I turned into soft wax and was molded around by her whim all morning. She found an old pair of Chinese silk lounging pajamas and a quilted silk jacket with a dragon on it.

"There. You can take in the pants with pins for now. You ought to have a more severe hairdo for this."

She was behind me. She drew my hair back. I really didn't hate her anymore. She brushed and brushed. I nodded, blissful. "This is as heavy as mine! It's gotten so long. I'll braid it and you can let it hang down the back like a coolie or you can twist it around your head like Anna May Wong. What a mess! You ought to brush it more, Katie." I swooned. ". . . Olive oil treatments . . . Mother used to do ours every week. It's nice though—so straight!"

"I think," I offered by way of explanation, "that Higgens was an Indian."

"*Who?*" She yanked my head back into a straight-up.

"Higgens. You know. My father."

"Your *father?* Oh, yes. I keep forgetting about him. It seemed so unnecessary. With Sarah for a mother, I mean."

"Well, it must have been Higgens. Did you ever . . . did she . . . ?"

"I never saw him," she said softly. "But I know Sarah was happy about being pregnant. She . . . didn't try to keep it from us or anything. Iantha took her down there to their old place on the Gulf. For a little vacation. Sarah had had a terrible influenza. Of course, we all thought Iantha wanted to find a husband for Sarah, the old snoop. . . . Ha! She couldn't help it, I suppose . . ." The old brass had come into her voice.

Pulled down, left over, right over, weave it in. I held still. She took forever. She didn't seem worried over Beas. She was pleasantly preoccupied with my hair . . . *binds my hair* . . . weaving her talk into it.

"Did she . . . did Sarah and Higgens get married?"

"Oh, how would I know? I haven't the faintest *idea* what

happened. It might not have happened in Shreveport at *all* except that we all figured it back to the time of that visit. Sarah . . . It was typical, she just began to show, you know, and then finally someone asked her when she was expecting, Iantha probably, you know how *she* is, and Sarah said, Oh, sometime in June, Hon. God!" She spat a little affectionate and admiring scorn. "Daddy and Mother sailed through the whole thing like a pair of swans! And Sarah seemed so big!" She laughed.

I laughed myself, I had to laugh. But she seemed not to realize that it had been *me*, *me* in there, *me* coming in June, *me* making Sarah big. The marvel of my own birth hit me. One day at one certain moment I merely popped my head into the world! And Higgens, as I had always suspected but not wanted to know, was not relevant. A fly. A fly? It was pretty brutal but some sharp truth in it made me swallow it. Maybe Higgens had been another Jack Russell.

"Well, sometimes I wonder about him," I said.

She said that was natural, why in the world wouldn't I? Only Sarah would have been so casual about it. That was just part of the easy way she had with life that made people love her and not care what she did. Then, I thought, probably they *hadn't* married, hadn't bothered . . . or . . . I thought of my infant self.

"She never touched me hardly," I whispered.

"What?" She gave my hair a gentle yank to raise my head again.

"She never touched me much. Kind of like she'd forget or something that you were in the room."

Enid was still. She held the braid. She waited. I turned slightly. Then she put a rubber band on the braid and stood up quickly, letting the hair fall against my back. Done.

"Well, she was just that way. There you are. It looks quite pretty."

There I was. It was in the mirror, something I had been looking for. A certain person. There she was. I couldn't believe it. My face seemed to have assembled itself or something.

Renfro

Rushed into the store at the last minute to get something different. Wondering if the first gift weren't a little paltry. Something for a woman—perfume or something soft. Hankies? There were hundreds. Books weren't right, he ought to have known. Maybe he ought to take one of those fruitcakes from the bakery. He was confused. Too many people. A soldier at the jewelry counter was saying, "I don't know what size. She's little, that's all I can tell you. Gee! I didn't think . . . Lemme see your wrist, maybe . . ."

It made him want to laugh and cry. The place was so dazzlingly soft and fragrant, colorful, full. He must look, he thought, like a hound dog in a pansy bed.

He was looking at scarves when he heard the voice from the opposite side of the square of counters, at the glove side—

"Seven and a half, please. Not long. Not too dressy. She's an older woman."

His mouth ran with idiot slaver. His eyes pooled so suddenly he was blinded. He dodged quickly so that the big mirrored section of the pillar was between them. He hadn't gotten a look but Alda's voice was unique. The clipped, flat, unlyrical tone, no nonsense—a teacher—unmistakable. He went over to the umbrella counter by the door, half obscured by a display of scarves, and got a look from somewhat to the rear of her. She stood with slightly turned-out feet, slightly heavy legs, a nice coat—not smart, not like some of the others, but only nice, nice enough. Her hair had darkened. Her voice carried. It flattened the air as if an iron had fallen through space. He moved to the corner farther behind and about twenty-five feet from her. Crowds. He was in silver. Salt cellars and melon pattern pitchers.

"May I help you, Sir?"

"Uh, no. No. Thank you. I'm just looking and . . . waiting for someone. Thank you."

The only brave, decent, natural thing to do was go to her, follow her into the street and say *Alda,* behind her, softly, take her arm, sustain some of the shock. The only thing. But he was not decent, natural, human even. He swallowed and wiped vaguely at his cheek with his sleeve. Stouter too. He leaned on the counter. He couldn't do it. He watched her pay for the gloves, look around uneasily for a moment as if she felt she were being watched—never quite look fully in his direction, where he was frozen and stripped —and then go into the back of the store.

He turned around and saw a little silver bookmark on a velvet patch under the glass. He bought it for Katie. He picked out a bright silk scarf, too expensive but he felt reckless, not having spent on anyone but himself yet. He nipped out into the street quickly and toward the bakery. He didn't really want to go to the dinner party. He wasn't sure of himself yet, even down to eating with the new teeth in the dining room of Mr. Pomeroy Russell. He felt good at work, safe, deeply into the rhythm of it. And he felt cautiously good with Katie. But he had to go. He meandered toward his apartment.

It had begun to sleet. He held a newspaper over his head but couldn't quicken his steps. He saw Mother's solid short back as she stood at the stove, stirring gravy. Christmas. Julia and her husband, she must be married by now, coming for the day. Alda and Mother running the house. *Not too dressy, she's an older woman.* The myriad subtle definitions of women! He hated it. He didn't understand it. Alda had always had that keen dogged notion of the appropriate, the tasteful, the vulgar, the inexcusable, the *smart,* oh, God! The smart! He had forgotten her. The right

★
**Where
You
Goin,
Girlie?**
★
209

voice on the phone. The right tone to the laundry man, the bus driver. The propriety. Jelled in propriety. Her kindness itself had been a *proper* kindness.

He stormed along, his feet wet. At home he put on his robe and dry socks with his slippers. He sat with an unlit pipe and the paper. I am a bachelor, he said softly aloud.

He read, carefully, an account of the fall of the Philippines and the estimates of Japanese naval strength. He put away the paper and picked up an art book, flipping through.

I've got to explain to Katie why I can't come all the way, can't promise anything, can't protect, sustain, give, yield up, or become familiar even. Why I can't ever marry her or anyone.

Ace of Fractures. Ace of Scars.

But oddly, he knew he would forget himself and begin to unbend, exactly because Katie didn't *want* him to promise, protect, sustain.... Well, give maybe. But give in the moment, apparently, give the body. What the hell was she after, anyway? She'd slept with four or five guys he knew of, sorry characters most of them. And who else?

Alda . . .

Pom, Nina shimmering at the place to his right. Enid at the other end of the table, pleasant, quiet. The Dietlers there, gregarious effusions. And Renfro in a new black jacket and soft blue shirt and tie that made him look browner and his eyes more shocking flat blue, burnt-out desert versions of Beasley's eyes. Beas not there. Or anywhere? Ruby was in the kitchen with Pearl.

I was a smash. I was growing up. I was so unusually pretty that day. My hair that way. Why hadn't I done it before? What a stunning suit. Pom even raised up his glass and toasted me. There we were, pasted together, a kind of cinched-up clan, pieced-in, dubbed. Missing: Sarah McCleod, Beasley Russell and Murray Dietler.

I lived it in delirium, a proper Delirian, remembering that once on a stony Christmas after his father's death, killing—after the fly-smashing of Jack Russell—Beas had found a Christmas tree in the street that seemed to have fallen out of a truck. Pom had had Christmas ready for them at his house but Beas had wanted, without asking for it, his own tree. He had brought it in from the street and decorated it quietly, while *she* was asleep or drunk (on Christmas even)—decorated it with old trout flies from Uncle Jack's fishing gear, acorns, Enid's best pearls, yards of them strung across the branches, her earrings, pipe cleaners dipped in colored ink and tin foil off milk-bottle caps and gum wrappers. Pom had a picture of it somewhere. Remembering it, I wanted to hate her again but couldn't. But the fact that Sarah was dead and Enid alive tormented me. If you can kill a person the way you kill a fly, you can also die as a fly.

Beas and Sarah were so absent that we had to keep up the chatter constantly. I was glad of the Dietlers' presence. Renfro nibbled and kept his elbows close to his ribs as if someone were going to poke him there. He lifted his eyes to nab a quick look at Enid now and then—a guilty look—and of course I cringed. I hadn't told him she had seen the Biography. I thought enough was enough. And she managed with impressive serenity to ignore him completely. She hated men in general, I decided for the hundredth time. She had confessed herself to disliking most people but I got the feeling that meant men in her case. Maybe women weren't even people to her.

Pom was impressed with what Renfro knew about Deliria. They talked about its history, Renfro with his head ducked a little but in a listening way, not shyly exactly. When he spoke, he looked Pom or Abe in the eye as if it were required among men, with some cautious agony. I found myself swallowing my bites of food whole and feeling stuffed within five minutes.

When they discovered Renfro had been in the 1939 long-shoremen's strikes on the Gulf they fell on him. That, said Abe, was momentous, momentous. That gave the International its foothold. They came out of that with almost full control of the locals.

"But what were you doing there? I didn't know you were a longshoreman," Abe's wife asked him. She and Nina had both been Communists once, I remembered. And had drifted away from the Party for similar reasons, at the same time.

Renfro laughed a quick little dry coughing sound. "Oh, I was . . . roaming around with an old dockworker who was on the bum. They nabbed us up in a hurry. We were put up in an old warehouse in Corpus Christi. We were loading cotton bales for three cents apiece, by hand. When the strike was over, they were getting fifteen. I don't think anybody ever knew what they got out of us. Most of us would have worked for one meal a day, I guess. But there weren't enough of us. It was hard to believe, but even that early they were hard up for workers."

They talked about Texas. Oil. And of course about the war, but carefully. Renfro said he admired Murray and Abe beamed. I sat there on Enid's right and felt like a lady in waiting. She kept up a little repartee with Helene so as not to notice Renfro, I supposed, and finally I had to admit she had guts, sitting there with him, knowing he had read all those things about her. I felt as if I had been dressed and braided into the clan somehow, Higgens be damned and all that.

Afterward Pom showed Abe and Renfro his study, his maps, they had cigars there. Nina moved hesitantly around the house, in the hall, pretending to be admiring paintings—a portrait of Lou over the mantel, another in the front hall, staring at them as if hypnotized. It was pleasant and even a little thrilling to believe

★
Where You Goin, Girlie?
★
211

that Nina might become a part of us, whatever we were.

When we left, I lifted my silk pajama legs the way Enid did her skirt and walked behind her, my head bent the same way, indifferent to the scramble of six male feet to get me to the electric without damage. Renfro would be driven home by the Dietlers. I gave him a cool limp-eyed farewell and said softly, "Call me." An order from Queen to Page. He nodded with a little flicker in his eye that seemed to remember me naked on his Murphy bed.

The Boise
Way Far Off in the Blue

Dear Katie,

Why don't you write? I'm alive. Lotta action. This old tub will sail forever and so will yours truly, Baby. Think victory, Cannonball. Da-da-da dum*!*

Your lovin sailor,
Eric

Think victory? Eric was asking for something. Even that—*think victory*. Gee, maybe he just wanted to come home. I thought of him on the big seas, in the wind, the spray. Like a movie with Errol Flynn. But then I thought of the slightly murky backwater of Renfro and felt ashamed of myself. Renfro had a soul. He even had a firecracker but he just didn't seem to have much invested in it.

And anyway, *think victory* seemed like a desperate cry that week. Pom had just said a few days before that this was the worst week of the war and then *Time* magazine, which I read carefully to Renfro as if I were trying to get him to enlist, confirmed Pom's view. The *Lafayette* lay on its side, burned out, in New York Harbor. Singapore had fallen. I began to give an ominous thought or two to the world. Beas was still lost somewhere.

★

Enid hadn't had a drink for a week that I knew of, but I could see her eye stray, her hand clench open and shut loosely, as if she were looking for something momentarily lost, for the thing she came into the room for, and then she would go into her own room again, shut the door, be ever so silent for a minute and then come out. But she didn't smell like it and she seemed sober. So, I assumed—through trying not to think of it at all but being irresistibly drawn to watch her—I assumed that she was "working on it," as she had put it, and that all this indecisiveness was part of working on it.

One morning I heard her answer the phone early, while I was still in bed. She gave a little cry and I ran to the hall door. She was standing there with her hand over the mouthpiece.

"They've found him! He's alive!"

I rushed to share it with her. She held the receiver between us.

". . . in a hospital," Pom was saying. "On the base, apparently. No serious danger. Exposure and shock. He wandered off into some mountains or something during a mock battle. Seems to have gotten confused. I'm trying to reach a friend in the Army right now who'll be able to get me a more detailed report. But he's all right. He's safe. You girls just hang on now!" His voice rattled.

Alive! I made sounds of relief and Enid said simply, "Thank you, Pom" which sounded like Thank you for everything there is.

We stood in the hall near the phone, close to one another. I let out a little gasp and she laid a most casual long bony arm on my shoulder for a minute. She had lost everything and some had come back!

"It's all over. He'll come out of it. It's over now." She sounded like a sleepwalker. She walked into the living room and turned on the radio. She had begun to listen to war news too. She sat smoking, quietly, all morning, swinging her foot and pondering. Some days, like that day, she did not dress all day. She would wash her face and fix her hair again at evening and perhaps change her robe. She had dozens of them, some very formal. Staying-at-home clothes, like Nina's flowing robes. I wondered if I would ever become that kind of woman, sitting, lying around, pacing floors, wearing at-home clothes—flowing robes—beautifying myself for no particular audience. Its sullen desperate glamour frightened me. But it hypnotized me. I didn't know what was different in me from them. I couldn't imagine changing enough ever to end up that way and then it hit me that ending up was exactly what they had done and I could never ever do.

Beas was alive!

They invited me to the metaphysics group meeting and I stayed home for it to be polite. There were only five of them. I didn't listen much. I caught a statement now and then, usually one from Serene who did have a kind of grand manner, a sort of hysterical efficiency that made me want to laugh but which had to be taken seriously even so. She was intense and lofty. She did not know that her slip straps were showing. She did not know that sometimes in profile she looked like Dr. Fu Manchu with that fine silky black moustache of hers. She read from Uspenskii—"Christ driving the money-changers out of the temple was not entirely meek and mild; and there are cases wherein meekness and mildness are not virtues at all. Emotions of love, sympathy, pity, transform themselves very readily into sentimentality, into weakness. . . ."

I heard it. That was exactly what Enid wanted to hear, I knew. She sat with her head slightly bent, modestly intent and patient, considering and weighing it. She could not be bamboozled, I noted for the first time with wonder. She had hit the rocks and you could not kid her too much. She had, as I had always believed, a criminal's honesty. It made me want to suffer the most terrible thing possible and nearly die of it in order to become honest and on the other side of the world's manners.

Iantha, sitting on the chair edge, biting her lips and nodding, on the other hand, was a total pushover for almost any bold statement from anyone. She would hover there with her mouth open and then suddenly fall back dazzled into the chair, almost lying down in it, swooning. It was the same old swoon that she had taken in Piggie's Drive-In parking lot years ago, swallowing her tongue, over Henry Killeen.

But they were serious. One of the other women, Claire Shanklin, had a lot of knowledge and would quote it softly, relating it to something they were reading. I was faintly embarrassed around them, these women getting themselves a "subject of discussion." It seemed to me that they were doing it purposely in opposition to men, to what men could have and would have taught them. That even the kind of knowledge they were after was something that men would not hear of. But the master was a man—Uspenskii. I knew it would never lead them anywhere. I had a feeling about that. But I knew they needed to do it and that it was giving them all something comparable to what it gave Enid—another kind of world.

★

But all I could really lend my mind to for a while was Beas, his having been found alive. No serious damage, said Pom. Now it seemed to me that the war had ended. I always knew Beas wasn't soldier material. Eric wouldn't die, I thought. Not the type. No miracle in his coming out alive. But Beas seemed to have slipped through great danger somehow. Different. I tried to picture him lying in a hospital alone. Ruby was so pleased she shook her head for three days.

I began to go out again, finally. My hand was healed but weak and a little bent. I knew it would always be a little bent. I wrote Beas letters almost every night as always. Now I was using my right hand again. I told him I hoped he would realize he had made a mistake in enlisting and just come on home. I wanted to draw him into the awkward mix that was our family now. I felt that without my stitching it together, it would slip apart quite easily.

Beasley

He was back in the room with the doctor. He didn't know how many times. The doctor was not in white clothes.

"All right now, Private. Tell me again. What'd you do? You said someone yelled at you to drop and you fell down into the hole and then you fired your rifle."

"Yes."

"Okay. So far so good. Now. After you fired it, what? Did you hear it go off? Is that how you knew you had fired it? Let's talk about what you heard."

"I heard it. Then I opened the door and walked in the room."

"You walked in the room. What room?"

"Living room."

"All right. And then what?"

He tried to thrust it out. "She was in there. She had the gun. She shot it. I heard it. I opened the door and went in the room."

"What did she shoot?"

"Him . . . I—don't know."

"Did you shoot anybody?"

"Yes. I shot him."

"Who?"

"I don't know. The enemy. On the machine gun. In the room. After the shot." He had to keep remembering it—the head coming up and his shooting it.

"And then after you shot the man on the machine gun out there in the brush, what did you do? Did you turn around?"

"I opened the door."

"Which door?"

"Into the living room."

"All right. What did you do then?"

"I saw. They were in there."

"Who else? She was in there with the gun, right?"

"Yes. She had it. She laid it down."

His eyes. Something like a hawk flying in his eyes, swooping over, low. Watch out!

"Now, who else was in the living room besides her?"

"He was in the chair."

"He was in the chair. What did he do?"

He shook his head. "I don't know. I ran away. I don't know if I killed him or not but I shot his head when it came up out of the brush."

"I see. Well . . ." He waited a long time. Beasley could hear his own breathing and then the doctor said, "How do you feel today? Right now?"

"I feel okay. I don't feel like anything . . . in particular."

"I'm told you were going to study chemistry. Already worked in a lab. That right?"

He nodded. It seemed way back. Forgotten.

"You enlisted?"

He nodded.

"Why'd you enlist?"

He looked.

"Hm? Why'd you enlist? You want to shoot a gun?"

"I already did."

"You were at Camp Claiborne in basic. You get good training there? They prepare you for these maneuvers?"

He nodded. "We shot a lot. In the swamp. We did bazookas and . . ." He named them all.

"All right, Private. Get some chow and some rest and I'll see you later. By the way, where do your folks live?"

He was at the door. He turned back. Salute. He said—

"She lives out at the lease with Aunt Sarah and Katie now. She rented out our house."

"Oh. Okay. Dismissed."

Enid

It's the only thing to do but my hand holds it back. It's so real, all that thought about another person's life, and such a huge lie. But I made the lie myself. But it isn't me. I'm . . . Burn it, stop fooling. I'll say I burned it. No, burn it! Call Iantha. A weekend in town, shopping, dentist, Katie'll have time to think. Savage! Keep this anger, keep it! I don't want to let it go. I want to resist her. I want not to help, not to mother. Sarah, you left me too much. Beas writes Dear Mother. It could be Chinese. What is it? What am I? If Jack hadn't owned a gun . . . It's that simple and meaningless. Chance.

I am someone who has gone through . . . I have gone through . . . I have passed through something. I have been moving through and now I am here. Maybe I can because I have gone clear through and come out here.

Burn it. Tear the pages, a few at a time. Make sure they all burn. That's the end of it. That's all.

But I told her the truth. Why did I? To shut her up, or was it for myself?

Beasley

Yessir, I did kill him. He raised up his head and I shot him with the Springfield.

Yessir, the machine gunner. No sir, not in the room. No sir I was wrong. Outside. In the brush. I think. Yessir.

And then I ran away.

Yessir I did but she did too. She shot him but . . .

Yessir, I mean my mother.

Yessir, I mean my father.

No sir, I haven't stopped yet. I still wet it. But I think . . .

No sir, I don't know when I scream but they must be right. They told me I was screaming so they must be right but I can't hear it myself.

Yessir, that's the truth.

My Grandfather? You did?

Yessir, I feel a little better. If you say the machine gunner didn't die, Sir. But . . .

Yessir, I'm taking the pills.

Pom came out and sat in the chair with his knees apart, leaning over them, his hands clasped. So sober. He's in love, I thought, with a twinge. I couldn't tell whether I was happy or jealous or what. He seemed very perky these days.

"It seems he has some confusion over having shot at a machine gunner on the other side, in this mock battle. He seems to have taken a shot at the fellow and then dropped his gun and run away somewhere. He lived ten days in the mountains, wandering around!" He shook his head.

Enid was like a glacier. She didn't move. She stared at him. Pom couldn't quite look at us. We were all feeling Beas feeling lost, hungry, terrified. It was worse than anything, even Sarah maybe.

"Anyway, they've got him in the hospital. The Army hospitals are good out there. They've got rather sophisticated psychiatry, actually." Enid gave a sniff at that. "So many of these things happen, I suppose. They're treating him. They don't want him talking to any of us until his head clears. He's still confused."

He knew more than he told us but it was enough. Beas's body was safe. Somehow the idea of his confusion or mental pain didn't bother me as deeply. I knew him. I believed that when he came back I could inject him with cheer or joy, I could make him safe. Just send me home the living body.

"They'll patch him up in no time," Pom said, somewhat foolishly to cheer us.

"And send him back in," Enid said flatly.

No, Beas! No. Go crazy and make them let you out. I drove the thought out to him.

"Well," said Pom helplessly, "we can only wait and pray."

But Enid did not go get drunk the way I kept expecting her to. She studied her metaphysics books with mad concentration. I wondered if Uspenskii had anything to say about killing or about the meaning of being alive in another person's mind, and being no more than a fly there. I thought probably a person knew nothing whatever about life and death until after killing someone. Then you'd know the truth of all our value, having tested your own sense of it.

Do we know everything ourselves? I asked myself once. I liked fussing with such ideas for a short while but then they would begin to infuriate me and I would jump up and throw myself into some action, any action. Sex was the best action, I still believed, but I had almost given up finding anybody who understood it the way Eric had. He had no more questions about it than a monkey had. What was he doing for sex in the middle of the ocean, though?

Pom got ten cases of champagne from the country club for Nina's opening. Standing around G.I.'s. Haircuts and shined shoes. Insignia.

"Hi. Dance?"

"Okay. Are you at the flight school?"

"Yep. Mechanic. I'm staying on the ground. What's your name?"

What's yours? What's your rank? What's your company? Where's your home?

Whadda ya know? See that character over there with the beer bottle in his fist? I ran into him down at Randolph Field. Drunk as a skunk. Fought me and tried to tell me Pearl Harbor was a put-up job. Geez.

Be realistic, the Zeros are sensational. But the Navy's got this new Avenger, see?

Give me the bombers. Give me the Fortress any day, Kelly. You go out in one of those, you come home. You could knock her wings off and she'd walk in.

I got a buddy was in Bataan. Who the hell knows where he is? I wouldn't wanta be a prisoner to the Japs. Gimme the Krauts any day.

They've got New Guinea. They're after Australia. Aaaaahh! They'll never get the Aussies. But shit, forget the war. Let's take a walk. Let's have a beer. Come on, Katie. When do you get off work? What's your telephone number? Want a cigarette? Hold still a minute. Where can we go? You got an apartment? You got a car? I'm leavin in ten days.

Write me a letter sometime. I'll send you a souvenir.

Remember me.

Remember me.

Don't forget, Cannonball.

★

Is the world falling together or falling apart?

"Wow!" I told Nina. "They don't waste much time, these G.I.'s."

"Well," she said, "they don't have much. But you don't have to go to bed with them all, you know. Haaa!" She laughed as if I were a performing dog. "That's not part of our service."

I wasn't sleeping with them all. Just a lot of them. I didn't know why. It seemed like the only thing we had time for. I didn't tell Renfro. I didn't see him much. But sometimes I came crawling into his Murphy at two A.M. and clung to him. He was always there.

The USO caught my fancy, though. The smell of doughnuts, coffee, Old Spice, gum, cigarettes, shoes. The uniform, Nina observed, can do a lot for a country boy.

I think, among all those backs, those heads, I see Beas, Eric, Rabbit, Wishbone. . . . But then the body turns, the profile appears and is strange. I wander through them wondering. Pom was right —civilization was breaking up like a huge glacier. Even my own little fake piece of it was becoming unrecognizable.

I didn't tell you, Renfro says, but I saw my sister just before Christmas in a store downtown. How he didn't like her when he saw her. He sucks a pipe without tobacco now. He buys a sketch pad and sits by the river drawing old wrecked cars on the riverbank, broken trees, rusted cans among the brush and the rocks.

I think, he says, I'll get on the day shift after all. Can't leave you alone with that horde of soldiers every night.

★

Winter turning into false spring and then plunging cold with sleet and rain. Enid standing one day in the back yard at the burner. The smell of the Biography burning. The smoke. She stays, watching. That Enid is dead. Cremated.

When I think of Sarah, I touch my broken hand and wonder what I am supposed to do, to be.

★

Go crazy Beas, I say a dozen times a day. Make them send you home.

★

Nina and Pom on the society page—Seen Around Town.

★

An Indian scarf, long, silk, from Eric. My, says Enid, he has good taste. She moves in the house, sober, pacing the floor. Keeping hours. Saying, Ruby, take your rest now. Get off your feet. My God, look at her! She must be carrying twins.

Ruby's daughter America is raring to go!

Renfro working days. He buys a secondhand Essex.

"It has a few quaint limitations," he says through puckered lips, not to smile at his own jokey life. But to love it. Loves the pain of his past. "I may have to go up hills in reverse."

The story of his life?

Still talking about seeing his sister and not liking her much. Still not calling home. Confessing it, lying like a dry piece of wood, faintly fragant, in the Murphy bed.

In the night. "Were you in love before you met me?"

I don't think much of Eric anymore. But I still store him away in me. "Maybe I would have been. He went into the Navy. He's in the South Pacific."

"You hear from him?"

"Some. Not much anymore. The South Pacific seems to me the same as a thousand years ago. Out of my . . . understanding, you know?"

He laughs. "Yeah. You let the past go. Maybe that's good. I wish to God I could do it but something keeps me reliving it."

Walking by the river. "I used to stand here for hours at a time. When I first came back. I used to imagine myself drowned in this water and my body carried down to the Gulf and washed out to sea."

"But you *didn't* drown. You're *here*. You didn't do it. You *aren't* being carried out to sea."

"I had to learn to live again. I mean with meaning. It was work that did it. Or something I learned about work. When you can't get work and work is the only thing that can give you food, then you start a philosophy of work going, you understand its power. You see why men have to work and should get hold of a kind of work that they can stay with, get into the rhythm of—"

"Are you doing that in blueprints?"

"Not quite. I'll get into drafting some other way. I have a little ability with a pencil."

"Did you ever want to be a great artist? Like Leonardo or something? Something . . . miraculous?"

His puckering lips, eaten smiles. Then the learned smile of new teeth. "Well, not really. I'm more interested in the experience of work, the thing one is doing at the moment, the rhythm of it. You know, the mystery of . . . action. But what about you? What is work to you?"

I shrugged. "I don't know yet."

Deliria. More soldiers. More trains. Renfro has given up tobacco and we both stand in line to get our ration of cigarettes for Enid.

The Boise
South Pacific

Dear Cannonball,

I guess you heard about the Japs getting into Malaya. We're after them. Did you get the scarf I sent? Our bottom was laid open on some pinnacle rock near an island and we had to go to India for repairs. Missed a hell of a battle by doing it, too.

But we made up for it by getting a sub! At about 8 A.M. *GQ sounded. I got up on deck fast to try to find out what the hell was happening and then I heard it—whoom! Two depth charges off the stern. Then another eight more eggs were dropped and after a minute the oil began to surface. It's spooky as hell to see it, like the blood of a machine coming up, like a metal sea monster down there bleeding. Then the wreckage began to float up. It was a big hit but later you sometimes think about those Japs who have mothers and Cannonballs at home too. But Christ are they bastards!*

Sometimes we stay on GQ for 20 hours at a time and a lot of the men sleep in life jackets on the deck. The Captain's always parading around the bridge in his bedroom slippers. His Night Order Book is full of little quips and cautions like—Be vigilant, the enemy is. The enemy is combing the area. Relax and he'll have you. It's all true.

I've got a friend here, a JG you'll have to meet sometime. He likes your looks in that picture. I tell him you're a wildcat and he likes that. Write me a lot Kid, and keep your fingers crossed.

Love,
Eric

I wrote him more often, secretly. I didn't tell Renfro. I tried to tell Eric newsy things, to make it sound as if I were in touch with him and his ship and the war. Some people really were, I realized, in touch with the war, but I didn't know them. I was only beginning to enter the war. But sometimes my letters petered out. I couldn't conjure him. He had been about three fourths firecracker to me anyway. He said in one letter that he wished we had ham radios or wireless so we could talk. And I said yes, that was what was missing, the words and our sounds. Any words. *Cannonball calling Firecracker. Calling Firecracker. Come in, Firecracker. Go ahead, Firecracker.*

But what's to say, really? I asked my hound. If we did make connection—what's to say?

"I can't seem to get back into the world," Renfro says.

"Come on," I say. "I'm going to take you somewhere that will get you back into the world."

There's a circus in town in the Colosseum. Clowns, horses, elephants, everything. We eat peanuts and laugh together. Maybe he never played when he was little. I keep watch. He cracks a little. Afterward I make him take me to a beer joint in the middle of town, one I've never been to. I realize I'm hunting a place that can become our place, something in place of the Sunshine which is sad and cheesy. The lights are amber in the beer joint. It smells like the usual but it has a good juke and is not too crowded. We have several beers.

"It takes awhile," I tell him, sitting close. "You shouldn't hide away from the world. . . ."

"What's the *world*? It's all relative."

"But it's all there is, that's what."

Later he asks me questions about Enid, how she is, how it is to live with her. I hedge. And then still later, when he is feeling his beers, he says quietly—

"I've been thinking—we . . . we ought to get married."

"*Huh?*"

He laughs. "Don't say 'Huh' when somebody asks you to marry him. Marry me."

I can't look at him. "Well . . . I don't know. I'd have to think a long time about marrying somebody."

"I thought you believed in action, just . . ." He waved a hand, peeved, a little sarcastic, "plunge in."

I looked at him then. "I do. When it seems right."

"Well . . . take your time. I'll wait."

★

Back at his apartment sitting on the sagging sofa and staring down at that tacky wine-colored rug with the brownish worn center, the threads showing, I say, "I'll help you but I won't marry you."

His face clamps like a grate over a tunnel. "What do you mean, 'help me'? I asked you to marry me, not help me."

"But I think that's what you mean. Help you to . . . oh—cheer up and all."

He stands up and walks across the room and back. That means taking four steps, long ones but only four. But it isn't the small poor room that bothers me, it is something about its anonymity and his blindness to tangible things. Not that I want possessions —I would like dumping most of the possessions I have. It is that he is blind to anything that isn't in a book. I have the feeling that if he saw any of those great works of art he talks about, actually saw it in its marble or stone or wooden flesh, he'd pass it by as if it were a street sign.

Well, he's mad now. That's good. Renfro is angry a lot lately. It seems to be a good sign. But I feel the derangement of a left-out person, someone invisible.

Just live, Renfro, I want to say. But I really don't know what I mean by that. I doubt that I'm living myself.

Renfro

Drove by the house at nine o'clock at night and saw the amber light in the parlor. A figure moved behind the glass curtains. He stopped, the motor running, the heater buzzing. His muffler up around his chin, scratchy. He was sweating. He had been born in that house in a heavy stodgy bed, feather mattress. He had run home to leave his books before going on his paper route. He had stayed home with Julia one afternoon while they went out. He had made a little wooden tool box on the kitchen floor while taking care of Julia, whose tiny pink fingers picked among the nails, the pieces of wood. Finally he had sat her down nearby and nailed her dress to the floor to keep her still. Her obedience. Mother's rage when she saw the dress.

He went on. At home he opened out the little drop-leaf table and got out his sketch pad and the charcoal Katie had given him. And the sepia pencil. At about ten he went down to the corner and dialed the number again in the phone booth. The minute the ring stopped he hung up. He didn't want to hear the voice answering. He just wanted to know that they were there. He walked for an hour and went back to the sketch pad, opening a beer and setting it carefully on a napkin so it wouldn't wet the table. He intended to spend the evening sketching and refusing himself even one thought of Katie. He had a tendency to obsession, he decided. Kill it, he thought.

He remembered a dream he had had about a naked man coming toward him. . . .

"All right then," Renfro finally said. "Do it. Just help me. Find a way if you can. I don't know why I'm so . . . disconnected and impotent."

"*Impotent?* You're not impotent!"

"Oh, stop being so literal-minded, Katie. It's really just a defense. Did you ever examine it?"

I thought I'd fall off the bed. I had never heard him talk that way.

"I meant you can't be impotent in one way and not in all ways."

He sighed. I rubbed his back. I remembered Eric and all the action, not much talk. The inevitability of sex. Maybe it was all in there in Renfro somewhere. Or maybe he really was different. He was older, maybe that was it. I felt like a nurse wondering where the bleeding is coming from. I stroked his fine, smooth, thin back; his strange perfume under the sheets made me fond of him. Stroking someone seemed to cool my own fevers, as if I were being stroked. Funny.

"Okay," I said, "I'll help you. But I don't really know what you want me to do."

"Just do what you think of," he said, laying it in my lap.

We talked about his drawing. He had made a sketch of me. Also a cartoon of the electric with a monkey at the wheel inside it. Me. You're a monkey, he had said, laughing a little. He was looser. Maybe he was waking up. I rubbed and rubbed. The back of his neck too. He grunted with bliss. It had been so long since anybody had touched him.

"You ought to do some cartoons for the paper. You know, political things and stuff about the war. You see how many cartoons there are about Hitler these days?"

He nodded. "I know. But I don't think politically. You have to seize the absurd essence of a movement or something. I don't have that kind of mind."

"You got the absurd essence, or whatever it is, of me, didn't you?"

He laughed and looked up at me with a sharp eye. "Maybe I did. Aren't you something more than that monkey in the electric?"

We giggled suddenly. Wow! I started to tickle him and he went wild, tearing up the sheets and howling, kicking around, holding me off with powerful skinny arms. Finally we fell laughing and panting on our backs, the covers thrown off the side of the bed.

He stared up at the ceiling and grew sober again.

"You see, it's kinda symbolic, this business of where a person belongs. I sometimes think it's a matter of place. You can't go back to a home, for instance, that you knew in a certain way, even if it's right there, the same building and all, same furnishings, same people, if you've been away any length of time. Because it isn't that way anymore. The . . . forces have changed. The balances. The chemistry of its life has changed. And you'd be like some dangerous catalyst thrown into the middle of a working system if you returned. And you might be destroyed yourself, or lamed by it. You might—It really might be a big mistake. You see what I mean?"

"What could be dangerous about it? Except that it might bind you in or something. Part of what they're doing there is trying to make it work without you, maybe. You ever think of that?"

He shrugged with a dry sort of disgust. "They can make it fine without me. What do they need me for?"

"If you need them then maybe that makes them need you. To help you."

"I wish you'd quit talking about helping me! You sound as if I were some kind of cripple or something! I'm thinking it out. I'm trying to behave in a sensible way."

I sighed. I doubted, and he strengthened my doubt, that you could act sensibly very often. "I don't know . . ." I said. "I'd probably make the mistake of just going home and trying it out. Maybe messing it up. . . . I don't know."

Maybe I ought to leave the lease house, let Enid and Beas have it. Get out. Go. But where on earth did I belong but in that silly place? Maybe he was right and it *was where* and not with whom or how or when. I realized for the hundredth time that I loved the lease in some stupid way and now that Sarah was gone I felt queerly more driven to claim it.

"Well, you know what I'm going to do?" I said. "I'm going to clear all the clients' stuff out of our house. Every last damn thing. I'm not going to have one thing that has anybody else's initials on it in that house. I'm going to get my own stuff or have nothing."

He chuckled. "Good idea. I'll help you."

That was the first time I had ever changed the subject from him to me and gotten away with it.

"I'm sorry I bore you with my . . . idiotic troubles," he said later, humbly, his head lowered a little. Something in that lowered head sometimes reminded me of Enid. They were faintly alike or knew similar things. I shuddered. Sufferers! Sarah had taught me to care about them.! I felt a guilty smart to find myself blaming her.

"Well," he said later, while we were walking again by the river. He haunted the river as if to tempt it to tempt him again. Maybe he had to. "What're you going to do with your life, Katie? Aren't you going to find some work that suits you, a career, school or something?"

I thought quickly. "I'd like to write some things," I said. "But not for pay, I mean not in a job. But . . . I don't want to talk about it. I want to know what the world is like. That's the main thing."

He shrugged. "The world's being torn to pieces by war. That's what it's like."

"But," I said, "even so. I'm ready to live. And I want to see it. I want to do what I want to do."

"Someday," he said softly, "you'll settle down."

"Oh! Settling down isn't the only thing in the world to do. Why settle down?"

"And you'll marry me," he went on, ignoring me. He took hold of my hand as if to ground me.

Never! I said to myself, therefore. Therefore. You see Renfro, you made me say never!

A week later he got a job, all on his own, at an architect's office. He quit the plant.

"Being with you gives me a grip on things," he said. "You are the Queen of Wands."

I liked that. "And you," I said, learning his language, "are the Ace of Doubt."

He laughed and squeezed me.

He began to draw a lot. He kept his unlit pipe in his mouth and his little book of essays or art history in his pocket, a little tattered volume, somehow he always found them, and his sketchbook under his arm. He began a series of scrapbooks of Deliria, all the buildings, giving them a gauche magic, distorting them all until they looked like bodies. Look, he would say, at the Methodist church. With that spire it looks like a Klansman, doesn't it? I climbed to the top of that thing once when I was a kid and had a hell of a time getting down. I liked him when he did all that.

I'll remake Deliria for you, he said, so you'll never want to leave it. Maybe, I thought, I should start a biography of Renfro. But something soured instantly in my mind over that idea. Having committed some kind of sin in writing Enid's biography had left my hand stalled. Then I had broken it. And now it was bent. Maybe it all meant something. Maybe they were telling me not to use my right hand to learn the secrets of other lives. Maybe I ought to use my left.

Renfro

Dialed the number and let it ring. It rang eleven times. He slammed out of the booth. He hoped to become angry. He walked fast, pretending urgent business. His book was in his pocket. He passed the Cozy Hotel and plunged farther along, through the slushy streets, past the worn gray coats, the bodies, moving, every one of them a whole world! His mind sparking on and flicking off, past the shoeshine parlor, the little Chinese café—imagine that one Chinese family in the town alone! Who knew them? Cousins? There wasn't even a Chinese laundry. He blasted through the door of the cigarette stand and picked up a paper, dropping the coin in the man's little dish. Blind. Jesus, what a life what a world what the hell. Let it flare up, his anger. Why? Because they weren't home? He must be crazy. Or because he had called? Well, the hell with it. He was at the river again. Ice at the edges, muddy, clogged.

I want to do what I want to do. Katie had said it so quietly. He didn't know her but he had come in some weird way to know her. He didn't love her but he cared for her. But she had no right to climb in that Murphy with him unless . . . Oh, what was he saying? Who had what rights? He had no claim on her. No claim.

He walked back up to the main road and into the lower end of town again.

He went into a cheap little department store and suddenly bought himself a pair of gloves lined with rabbit fur. Just like that. He wanted to spend money all at once. All that crazy cover-up, sending money home. Why not, she was right, why not just leave it at the house or send a check or open an account for them? Why not just go up there? How long now since he'd come back? Almost seven months. The store was crowded, lively even. Well, Saturday. But town was booming again. He remembered the stores in 1931. This was different. Awake. When he had left town the stores had been empty and the clerks all gone, the owners—a woman or a seedy man—standing at the rear, staring out. An agony of surprise over the stillness. They had held on like leeches until the end. Those memories and visions were more real to him than anything in the present.

Two hours later he went home and stood by the window looking down. He made himself coffee and sat with it then, fingering the newspaper in his lap. Thinking. I think too much. I am too much in the past, hooked there. She's right. I am scarred with it. I am going to quit doing what that old Weldon did all that time, which was nothing. I am going to call Alma. Call Mother.

But he sat very still.

Enid

All these years, the Judge said, you haven't been seeing them. They've all been here, right under your nose, and you have not seen them for what they are. You haven't touched anyone. You finally took hold of her hair and braided it and now you know what the real crime was, don't you?

Yes.

But do you really know? Because if you stay up and stop the bottle, stop all the dreaming that comes out of the bottle, you'll have to see it very clearly, more clearly even than some of *them*. You'll have to tell and teach yourself every day. Little by little. As if you were your own child you will have to teach yourself to see and feel again, all the things you have let go to ruin. All the words you've thrown away, wounded with, cursed, all the faces that have looked out at you and not found you there.

What did they need of me? Nobody needed me. I was Daddy's . . . object. I was his toy.

But you know better. You cannot come up and out of that deadly peace of your bed and bottle and expect anything. Not a thing. You have to do it all, to give it all, whether or not they return it now. You'll have to start with your own body. What you have done to it. It was a full living thing. You'll have to start there.

It was nobody's object. It was your own, in your trust.

All right all right. I know all that.

But do you? What the crime really was, do you know that?

Yes. Now I know.

Who was it you killed?

Yes. I know. I know. I didn't know that then. If I had . . .

You *wouldn't* know.

But I've loved Beas. At least I've loved *him.*

But not enough. Not enough to save him.

She sighed. Is it all so simple as that, Your Honor? That's what I can't seem to get straight. Is this all there is and is it this simple and is there really a—something moral in the world? Does it matter, I mean? I mean in the broad sense?

What's the broad sense? What on earth would you know about the broad sense?

Yes. You see, I understand things. . . . About the past I mean. Daddy and all. Keeping me dependent like that. He humiliated me.

Who is not humiliated?

But I'm not talking about everyone. I'm trying to talk about me now. I was thinking of myself. . . .

I know.

All right all right. I know. I'll try. I'll really try now. Sarah too, I even thought Sarah was in my way somehow. I *don't* really understand, that was a lie. I really don't quite, but I will try anyway. I promise. . . .

Don't promise. Don't promise it. Do it.

I decided to start staying home. I watched Enid. She seemed to be trying to keep herself busy.

I rummaged the want ads. Ruby shook her head. "I neva knew *you* to read no paypah! Shhhhhttt! This worl comin to an end."

"I'm looking for something on sale. Secondhand."

"You already got plenty seconhan aroun heah." She dusted the newly sanded and waxed parlor floor, which, divested of its mothy old rug, a persuasion of Enid's, looked like light molasses. Ruby couldn't resist it. She was always at it, shoving the oil mop around, rubbing it up, as she explained it. I raised my feet automatically and she swiped under my chair quickly.

Enid came into the room. We were shy. I had been staying out so late or away so many nights that sometimes I felt a stab of guilt when I first saw her. But she was quiet, inattentive, patient. She and Ruby held down the fort. I began to get the feeling that they wanted me to be happy and it both embarrassed and touched me. I decided to stay home more.

"I'm going to buy a piano," I said casually.

"A piano? Well." Enid yawned.

Ruby shook her head. "What comin nex? Shhhhttt! I neva." She became disgustingly good-humored in Enid's presence.

"Yeah. A piano. It's one of the few ways I can get my fingers back in shape. Doctor Killeen said so. Besides, I want to make some noise."

They both laughed. Enid raised her eyebrows. "Well. I haven't touched a piano in twenty years. That'll be nice."

I looked at her. She was about to fire up a weed but seemed to hesitate. I had brought her Renfro's and my cigarette rations a few days before and she had decided to cut down, to save them. Just in case. She took advantage of small circumstances like that these days to curb her habits. Her other habit was nowhere in evidence and hadn't been since I had said those terrible two words to her — *You drink.* Or since Beas had been reported missing. What had done it? Probably Beas. I didn't want the credit, nor the blame. She was sober. I told myself not to question it. "I didn't know you played the piano," I said.

"Well, you could hardly call it playing. I learned from Iantha's mother, in fact. When I was about thirteen. She taught Sarah and me both."

Something in her easy references to herself as a child always hit me in the middle. It gave her a reality which gave her an excuse for everything, I felt. But she didn't excuse herself. Her having been a child, I saw, exonerated her of all crimes, her more than anyone. I thought of the arrival of Raskolnikov's mother and sister on the scene, after his crime. They gave him a past, a childhood, an innocence that was inviolable. We all have that, I told myself, a childhood with which to become pure again. I thought of the Biography and felt the old urge to write something about all that in it. I knew she had burned it that day out at the burner. She had decided to bury the old Enid all the way, I guessed. I imagined, therefore, writing something else. I felt the words and the energy of some as-yet-obscure lives begin to burn in me, to take fiery shape. It gave me goose bumps.

Ruby turned on the radio—Connie Boswell singing "The Talk of the Town." Ruby did that sometimes when Enid and I were in a room together, as if she thought we might suddenly dance together.

"Well," I told Enid, "maybe you could give me lessons."

She waved a hand. "Oh, I've forgotten how to play. But it would be nice to have a piano around. Are you serious?"

"Sure. I'd like to do it. I always wanted to, in fact, but the only music I ever had a chance at was on that old jew's-harp we got from somebody." *Clients!* I was losing a sense of their lives and their doodads, their yearning presence in the hall, their cars in the lane. *Aw, Hon!* Here we were, Enid, Ruby and I. A new society of Delirians. I could have cried.

Enid laughed, rueful, sudden. She asked if there were any ads of interest. I began to read certain crazy things aloud as I might

have to Sarah and she found it very funny. Ruby made coffee and brought it to Enid without being asked. I read an ad for two good milk cows.

"Now you talkin!" Rube cried, clapping her hands lightly. "You spen that money on a cow, I make you some butta an cotta cheese you nevah tasted befo. I make you some clabba that you cain't git aroun heah noplace. Awkinsaw the onliest place I knows where you kin git this kinda clabba I makes. It *really* good. We could use us a good cow roun heah, all right. We gots de lan jess goin to waste."

"Well, I'm not going to buy a cow. I'm going to by a piano. Or maybe an accordion or a xylophone."

Ruby said one phone in the house was bad enough and Enid said don't be silly a xylophone was a musical instrument, but it took up too much room and besides wouldn't give my fingers any exercise anyway. And an accordion was a stupid instrument that only the Germans liked.

And then she said, "You know, I'll bet Iantha would sell that old upright of hers. They never touch it. She's not musical and the old man is deaf anyway. It's just sitting there. I'll ask her. I'm having the meeting here again this week if it's all right with you and Ruby."

She said it casually. I had a comfortable sense of defeat—my house was hers. "Sure," I said, pretending not to feel my resigned pleasure.

"I'll make you up a nice spongecake," said Rube. Enid picked up a magazine and said there was an interesting recipe in that issue Ruby might try. Ruby, despising the printed word, scowled. We sighed. Like the old chorus of sighs of before. I heard it with my old sinking feeling. These days I was either wildly smitten with grief like this all at once, or thought only half consciously of Sarah. And Ruby must have heard it too. She said quietly, "In the old days, one of them womens woulda been ova heah with a free pie-anna fust thing you said you want it. Now you gots to pay fo every little thing you gits. Don't seem nachurl." She shook her head.

"Oh, who knows?" Enid said. "Maybe Iantha will give it to us. I'll see what she says."

Us. There it was—our old babble. Minus the founder of it, of course. It quickly fell flat, but it had been true there for a moment. My gizzard was wrenched, bleating under the sorrow. I sat and couldn't speak. This was not a decent version of our old niddly-noodling P.M. oddity and idiocy, but it was what we had and better than none P I supposed. Try to be cheerful, Hon, I told myself.

"Rube," I said finally, "I'm going to move into Sarah's room and give you mine. You'll need extra space for the baby. We can cut a door in the sleeping porch and you'll have an outside entrance."

"Cut a *doe*? How you goan cut you a doe in that wall? You needs Wishbo roun heah fo that kinda work."

"Well, we'll hire someone," I said.

"That's not much of a job," Enid said.

Ruby stood as dense as clay. "Well, I hope you ain't fixin to carry all that trash you lives with into Miss Sarah's room. You needs you some new stuff fo a room like that." That was her way of saying thanks. If she had said Shhhttt I would have believed she was really pleased. But come to think of it—why hadn't we always given Ruby an even fair third of the house? I wanted to make it over, to throw out all the junk and start new. She was right. And she probably wanted the stuff anyway. She'd been toting it for years.

Later Ruby walked out to the mailbox and brought back several letters for me.

"You got you some lettas heah from some o those po soljas you messin roun with. You gots them all thinkin the same thing, I bet on that. Them po fellas doan know what happen. I bet on that." She had begun to rag me again.

Pom

"They're still apathetic," Abe howled. "Geez, we coulda stopped it a dozen times and now that we're in it they're frozen. You read that stuff about the American Legion? Maybe that'll get some of these men off their duffs."

"It's fantastic to imagine defeat, Abe."

"They've got all that beautiful crude now coming up out of Borneo, Pom. They don't even have to refine that stuff. They're getting around *two million* tons of crude a year out of those wells!"

"I know, I know."

Pom tried to care, even about that, but something had seduced him away. He was learning to live out another self.

"I'll give it three years even so," said Abe. "If you work hard at it and your enemy is half asleep, you can wipe out all the Jews in Europe in three years. Because that's what's happening. When it's all over we'll build new cities. But the Jews will remember if there are even two of em left."

"I'd say two years, Abe. Even so. I think we'll see a turn quickly. My God, we bombed Tokyo yesterday."

"Yeah, but it's a gesture, a show of strength. What was the cost? Did they publish the cost yet?"

"Well," Pom philosophized, "they'll probably send Beas home and Murray's locked himself up. I suppose we could be called lucky men, Abe. Somebody else's boy is going to do it for us. Ironic, but there it is."

I guess love is a compromise, I said to myself. I saw myself float like a feather on the currents that circled around Renfro. I was learning something from everything. I was breaking out of a kind of nutshell, pushing through some membrane of the past myself. Maybe everyone was, always being born, always yielding up, sloughing the dead epidermis of the past. Even the quick past. Even Deliria was changing.

Renfro. When he wasn't watching me, I moved nearer and watched him, looked over the shoulder of his life and saw him gleefully sketching Deliria—a little boat on the river with an Indian in it, being tossed high on the rapids, smoking a big stogie; a huge cloud hanging over the National Bank building where I had my savings; a monkey hanging by its toes from a limb, counting money—more of me. Ha! A mushroom in the sky. He explained to me that he was a surrealist.

I took note and went about my business. I thought of Sarah. She would have been patient and kind with Renfro, I thought. She would have wanted me to be this way. She may even have wanted me to forget Eric. And her reason would have been that Eric wasn't here. That would have been all. Nothing complex or moral. Just practical.

I stayed at the USO and danced with the bodies there, up against a hundred khaki chests, a hundred shaven cheeks. But I floated back Renfro's way. His working all that time, his preoccupation, gave me freedom and drew me to him. He couldn't put his pencil down. He began to draw tree bark and animal hides. Parts. Draw *human* parts, I said, and he began to draw noses. Thousands of noses.

"Do you realize," he said with his old cramped wit, his puckered lips, "how many different types of noses there are? You can go all the way from Caesar to Bob Hope and not see the half of it."

And then he drew hands. And then feet. He spent three weeks on feet alone.

We had begun to listen to war news, to read *Time* magazine, to go to *The March of Time* newsreels. The war slowly dawned on me and sucked up my imagination. I felt my head and body and soul crammed with men, flying, sailing, slithering through mud, falling into foxholes, exploding into bits, diving on ships, drifting through eternal seas on life rafts, bailing out, sneaking up, attacking, retreating, surviving and dying. Being decorated. It struck me dumb and wrought me patient. Renfro bought a map like Pom's and tacked it up. Suddenly the world was stabbed with pins in almost every part.

"There goes Pom's civilization," I said, dazzled and horrified.

"He was right." I winced to see Renfro jab the pins in. Finally I began to move them myself—Bataan, Corregidor, Australia, the Coral Sea, India, the Hump. I followed. I couldn't resist.

★

I'll work here for the duration, I told Nina. And I told all the soldiers and sailors to come back when they were in town, I'd be there. I grew lavishly patient. I seemed to have fallen into the eye of time where nothing moved and where I was not battered about anymore. I was fattening with resignation. I yielded to them all, one way or another. I felt the same toward Pom when he said if I wouldn't let him send me to college (and I wouldn't now. It seemed too late for that) then he would put the money into my account instead. I thanked him and accepted.

And I waited. Without knowing for what, I waited.

When I saw the Stutz enter the lane I thought, Here it is. *Beas is dead. Beas has gone mad. They lied to us.* I began to shake.

Pom had Nina with him. I faltered. He came over the back lawn and I ran through the house to the back door to let them in. I suddenly wanted to praise Pom, to know him in a new way—what was in his heart and soul, beneath the war and oil and all that. His arm was lightly around Nina. I opened the door and he seized my arms the way he had at the hospital that night, shoving in ahead of Nina. He shook me and smiled tearfully.

"They're sending him home. They're releasing him. Medical discharge. Where's Enid?"

It was early, only about nine, and she was still in her room. Nina and I embraced and Pom dived toward the hall door to call Enid.

Then she came into the kitchen and looked at us all, her sleep-wounded face, her cloudy eyes, for a minute a touch of Sarah in her face. Pom told her and she fell into a chair. And then she let out a kind of howl, flat and terrible. And she started to cry. Her whole face broke. It was something else, not mere face. I couldn't believe it. Her whole body seemed to be breaking up. She couldn't get it out. She retched it up, bitter and coarse. We stood. Pom touched her. Then he almost lifted her out of the chair and took her to the other room, crooning to her below her wail. I stood with my mouth open.

"I'm sorry I came, Honey," Nina said. "But we were on our way out for breakfast when the night letter came for Pom."

I stared at her and couldn't speak. "Oh, Honey," she said, her eyes brimming. I fell on her then, or she on me. I knew, though, that I couldn't let go, not all the way, or I might start crying forever. I gasped and pulled away from her.

"It's okay. It's okay." There were a thousand things I wanted to say to her—that I had come to her house to be consoled over Sarah's death and found Pom's Stutz there, that I knew something new and wanted to explain it, that I saw that the war was real, that I believed Enid had stopped drinking, that I had hope—for something . . . something. . . . I turned away and went to the icebox to get out something for breakfast.

Ruby came in and when we told her she shouted *Thank you Jesus*! and raised up a foot, slammed it down, clapped her hands. She started slamming pans around, a sign she wanted to be left alone in the kitchen. She fixed us a huge breakfast.

Enid began to glow, a slow rise of some light in her very skin. "I'm glad you've finally come out," she said to Nina. "I've been meaning to invite you." I thought I'd fall off the chair. Pom smiled shyly. Nina was cautiously joyful. We laughed and planned a celebration for Beas, knowing it was all a dream. He might be wrecked in some way, I told myself, but I fell in with it.

"What a lucky break for Katie," Enid said all at once, looking at Nina with interest, "that place you've opened." She meant it!

"When's he coming, Pom?" I finally asked.

"As soon as the red tape can be handled." He wiped his mouth with a quick zigzag and chuckled fondly at us, casting a glance over us and then looking down with a shy smile, the most joy he could allow us to witness, I supposed. If Sarah had been there the world would have been perfect at that moment, I thought.

At the car Pom said to me quietly, "Don't talk much about it yet, Katie. He's had some real psychic damage, apparently. He may need some kind of help here. It's all related to . . . the shooting and all that, you know, Dear. We'll play it quietly for the time being. Enid seems—" He shook his head as if he had seen an eighth wonder. "—almost normal, wouldn't you say?"

★

Normal? Maybe she was. Whatever that meant. But it was because she had committed a crime. She had seen her husband as a fly and swatted him—meaning she had seen him as zero. And it had put her in hell.

It took me a long time to admit to myself that I had been in some way a part of her becoming what Pom called almost normal. I didn't want to admit it, I didn't want to know it. But finally I saw that it was true. She had confessed to me and I knew somehow that she had never told anybody else why she killed Jack. She either thought I would understand or . . . ? It troubled me for weeks—why she had selected me.

And then I saw again something about life that was so simple it was shocking. She confessed all that fly business to me, her motive or her nonmotive, whatever it was—she confessed it to me because I asked. That was all. Nobody had asked her. They had tried in the trial to get certain answers from her, I was sure of that; the kinds of statements I thought of as "world answers," meaty answers. And they never allowed her to say or asked her to say, *There isn't a reason for everything. He was a fly. I killed him the way you'd swat a fly.*

So maybe that meant she had hit bottom *before* she killed him and that killing him actually propelled her upward again. I tore into it for a while in my old way and then brought myself back to the facts again—mainly that the Biography was burned and that to have written it was to have entered where I didn't belong. Her mess is her own mess, I told myself again. And mine is mine. I remembered then that I had often in the past imagined some huge act of riddance as the only possible means of entering the real world. Maybe Enid would enter the real world, presuming there was such a thing.

Renfro drove me to work one evening, passing along a street crowded with soldiers. They were lined up outside the Majestic Theater for nearly a block. *The Little Foxes* was playing.

"We'll have to see it," Renfro said. "It's from the play. By Hellman. Really good, I hear."

"Look at that mob," I said. "It looks like Times Square."

He laughed. "When did you see Times Square?"

"In the movies," I said. And we laughed together.

"I wish," he said, "that I had had a little sketch pad with me all that time I was bumming. The things I saw! All the towns. All the faces! I wouldn't mind recapturing just the faces alone. Now they all look alike. It's hard to draw from memory."

"Well, do the faces you see now. Come to the club and do the soldiers."

"It isn't the same. The old look that I used to see is gone. I suppose if I went back to the Salvation Army I'd still see it."

"Yeah. It's always in the world somewhere, I guess." I looked out the window. Deliria looked different to me now, partly because of his drawings. I thought I felt a little life in it now. With that many soldiers in need of something, it *had* to perk up a little.

"Yes," he said, "that look is always in the world, I guess. I suppose I've missed it because it was so real to me for so long and it seemed as if those faces revealed real humanity more than any others. It's funny what the mind clings to. I hear that prisoners sometimes become dependent on and even infatuated with their guards. You ever read about that? Even when the guards are brutal. I can understand it. You make a world and a life out of what's most constantly there, or something like that."

Making do with what you had was no news to me but I didn't say so.

Renfro

When he let her off he told her he'd be back for her a little before one. The hours were killing him but somehow he found it worthwhile to hang onto her. He could have retched to remember what infantile things he had said to her, help me and all that. What a lot of crap. She had her hands full enough as it was with that Enid out there drunk and her cousin in a mental ward. But he was going to find the key to keeping her while letting her feel free. She sparked the right connections in him.

Just before he parked the car in front of his building, he realized that he had not called home that week. He sat letting the motor idle and thought about it. It had gone somehow from a compulsion to a duty. Jesus! He now felt *obliged* to do it! Crazy. He sat there and his heart began to pound. There *was* a way to break through with an act, a simple act, of course. Katie was right because her mind wasn't all screwed up like his. And the right or wrong of the act was not the point, but important only if it was destructive. Mistakes, mere mistakes, were inevitable. How stupid of him to think he could avoid mistakes. Going to that whore, for instance, had been a mistake and he had survived it.

He backed up, pulled away from the curb and went to the phone booth near the parking lot a few blocks away. He got out of the car, found a nickel in his pocket, dialed the number and waited. The third ring was cut in half.

His hair stood on end. It was not Alda.

"Hello?"

He hung there, speechless. The voice tried again, a woman. "Hello? Who is it?"

Then he said it. "Mother . . . ?"

They both gasped. And then before she had to try, he said again, "Mother, it's me. Weldon. It's me. . . . " His voice was breaking. "I'm back."

When I arrived Nina was dancing with some Air Force Captain who was hopelessly good-looking, something like Tyrone Power. I imagined she must be thinking how his firecracker would compare with Pom's. I imagined it in comparison to Renfro's. It was easy to see that the Captain loved women. He looked natural with Nina in his arms. She seemed giddy and was dancing very well, something I'd never seen her do. I could see the power of being in love draw people to her like arsonists back to the fires they had set, or wished they had. Love is everything, I said to myself. I didn't think I loved Renfro. I was only marking time with him. He just kept me from marking time with someone else. And who then? Or what? Eric? Ah, well. *What are you going to do with your life?* I asked myself in Renfro's voice. No answer.

I hung up my coat and went to refill the coffeepot and open some new packages of doughnuts. I smiled automatically into the G.I.s' faces. The place was mobbed that night. Usually I grazed the scene quickly with a cunning eye and saw who was possible and likely, who was not. I had gotten so I could tell from the very style of the walk, the line of the shoulders, the head, under a cap or not. It suddenly occurred to me that I knew quite a lot about men—what they would do, what they were about to say. I could sum them up. I thought back quickly to my geezers at the plant —Slim, Smitty—and to the others there I had known—ha!— meaning slept with! I wondered if it showed on me that there had been quite a few.

When the music stopped, Nina and the Captain stood near the table talking.

"I haven't danced since before I was born," she told him, laughing up into his face. He let his head fall back and laughed loudly. He was intrigued. I smiled on them as if they were my children. Wow! I had never felt before that anybody was my child, except Beas a little bit. And Beas was more me than mine.

Nina was telling the Captain about her hope to open a hostel where the men could rent rooms for a small sum. Something run on a high level, but simple.

"Do it," he said. "It'll be a long war." The Captain couldn't take his eyes off her glowing face.

Nina took over the table for me and I danced with someone named Corporal Delmas Frame from Alabama. His skin was bad. His hands were clammy but he had a tight grip on me when we danced and a thick tidy body like a fifteen-year-old's. Probably a desperate virgin, I thought. It was several seconds locked up against him before I realized that he was drunk. He was also terrified.

"Where are you stationed?" I asked him.

"At the fligh school. Preparin to be a mechanic but . . . " He burped. "Didn make it." He cocked an eye at me and shrugged a shoulder a little. "Sooo . . . well . . . lotta guys doan make it. Pretty stiff . . . Oh, sorry, Ma'am . . ." He had ground my foot under his heavy shoe. I was used to that. He smelled faintly mildewed.

"Gee," I said, "that's too bad. What're you going to do?"

He shrugged again. "Get a lil drunker, Ah think. Heh." His Southern accent was a little like Ruby's.

I broke away from his hard hold when the music stopped and excused myself. He wandered away and stood against the wall for a long time holding a doughnut in his hand, not biting into it. Finally he asked one of the girls from the Bledsoe School who came in to help us hostess to dance with him. She stumbled around the floor with him looking over his shoulder like a tired calf, her head wagging. She was at least a head taller than Delmas. Sometimes a lost and goony soldier like that came in and stayed for hours trying to get us alone to talk to us, but we were too busy for more than an occasional dance.

The club seemed stale to me that night. I worked the counter and let the others dance. I felt like going home and staying there more often. Evenings. I thought of Enid and guiltily put her out of my mind. She was alone almost every night now. I had begun to count on the metaphysics group to sustain her.

About midnight Pom came to pick Nina up. He waltzed with her, holding his arms out wide, in a kind of shaky sweep around the room. There were only a few soldiers, including Delmas Frame and the Captain, left. Several had come in drunk. Delmas stood around looking starved. Finally he disappeared. Pom and the Captain went to the corner of the room and sat in our leather chairs smoking and talking while Nina and I began to close up shop. Usually we kept the music going until one A.M. on Saturday nights but I could see Nina wanted to go. I went back to the john at about twelve thirty. When I passed the men's room door I heard someone gasping inside. It wasn't exactly a crying sound but one of pain. I knocked and called but it went on as if it were a record, a kind of sobbing gasping anguish. I ran for the Captain and Pom. They plunged in and in a few minutes came out leading Delmas Frame between them, holding his bleeding wrists up and out in front of him, squeezing his upper arms to stop the circulation.

I let out a cry.

"Call an ambulance," Pom said. But the Captain turned Delmas over to some soldiers and called the Army patrol.

Delmas Frame! Why just thirty minutes ago . . . ! He blubbered and collapsed in their arms. They put him down on a couch, made tourniquets for his arms out of two soldiers' belts and wrapped his wrists in our dish towels, stanching them first with paper. Nina was cool as a flower, tearing up tissue paper, rolling towels. I couldn't speak or move. It hit me hard and made me shaky. Finally I closed the door and pulled the shades. We stood around Delmas, watching his red contorted face, helplessly hovering there and trying to console him. He cried and swore feebly. *Who are you?* my mind kept asking him. Pom too was so shaky he had to sit down. Nina gave us all coffee, including Delmas who sipped a little between sobs and burned his mouth. He looked up into my eyes then and quickly looked away. He couldn't make sense but kept babbling "Leave me alone, I don't want to, I want to go, let me go." His cuts were deep. The dark red poured through. He had meant it. He looked like a stuck hog but he slowly turned pale, his lips blue. I stared.

Finally they came and took him away on a stretcher. I'll never see him again! I thought. I had moved around the floor with him and talked and then—bingo!—his whole life seemed to spill out.

"Poor kid," Nina said. "He looked about fourteen!"

"Probably is," the Captain said. "Most of the ones who crack are too young. They lie like hell to get in and then fall apart."

"He was turned down at the flight school," I said. "He wanted to be a mechanic."

The Captain shrugged. Pom shook his head. Beas loomed there between us.

Renfro came for me, helped us close up, and he and Pom and Nina and I walked through the springy night to the Creole for a beer. But it was a mournful feeling sitting there facing one another. I hated the Army and soldiers and war. And men. Goddamn you men! I thought.

When Renfro and I left he said, "I've got something to tell you."

"Tell me tomorrow," I said. I made him take me to the electric.

"I thought you were going to stay over," he said, peeved.

"I can't. I feel too sad."

He nodded. He sucked loudly on his empty pipe. We drove around a minute. "Did you know that kid?"

"No, but . . ."

I couldn't explain how it had made me want to get away from men for a while so I didn't try. I kissed Renfro good night and started for home. I felt driven toward my solitary bed.

The lights were on. Standing in the garage for a moment I heard Ruby's bed creak through the wall. With someone, or only turning in her sleep? I didn't really care.

Inside I found Enid up, sitting in the living room listening to the radio, late music, drinking some kind of fake coffee Serene had given her. Her lap was full of yellow yarn, her wrists wound with it, as with handcuffs.

"Hi. What're you doing up? What's that you're doing?"

She kept at it. "Oh, I'm crocheting a little sacque for Ruby's baby. It won't be long now. I wonder if she's got a thing for it to wear."

I sat down. I hadn't thought of it.

"That's swell," I said. "She'll be thrilled. I'll get some things too."

She seemed content. She could have called Iantha to come out. She could have called Serene. But she had stayed all alone and I knew she had been sober. She was up. Maybe she'd stay up. Maybe she'd fall again but a new fall would never be the same as the old. If I could have written in the Biography I would have said something about her bent chaste head looking as it had when she had sewed the labels into Beasley's clothes. I would have said that she seemed more real and interesting to me than all the people I spent my time with. Not because of the murder but because she was changing, coming out into the light. I would have said that for all its madness and evil, the murder she had done hadn't, after all, ruined her soul. It may even have cauterized and purified her. I would have said that being stuck with her was, after all, better than anything else I had to do or live out at the moment. I would have said that crime . . .

"How did things go at the club?" she asked.

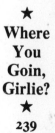

★
Where You Goin, Girlie?
★
239

"Oh, okay. Fine. Same as always. . . . You know . . . lots of guys." I didn't see any reason to tell her about the little Corporal.

She raised her eyes. I was on the edge of my chair. Her hands paused, enmeshed in yellow strands of yarn, bound lightly in her work there.

"I don't envy you," she said simply, "growing up in these times. Especially without . . . parents." I lowered my eyes. "But . . . you're not alone. Nobody's free of the war now, I guess."

"Nope," I said.

"There's a letter on your pillow," she said. Then she gave a little teasing laugh that had a flicker of the old brass in it. "He's a faithful letter writer. You'll have to say that for him."

I stood up. "Yeah. He is. But . . . there was a Captain at the club tonight who said it would be a long war."

"If you don't mind my saying so," she said quietly, "Renfro doesn't seem . . . oh—quite *lively* enough for you."

We both laughed quickly, catching each other's eyes.

I heard my own huge sigh. "No. I guess he's not. But he's *here*," I said.

She laughed again. "You're like Sarah. A realist. That's good. I think a realist is always happy."

"Gee, you think so?"

She thought so. It occurred to me that I *had* always been happy, she was right. Always. Miserable and crazy, but happy. I saved the letter for morning. I decided I would give all the clients' junk to Ruby, and half my money besides. *Follow the necessity of loss,* I said half aloud. But I didn't know what I meant.

I felt zinged up by our talk. I got into bed but couldn't sleep. Finally I realized that I still had my old dog self in there just as solid as ever. She seemed to give a remote yelp at my recognition.

Listen, I told her, lying there on my old bed, you just wait. When they get through with all this fighting and dying and burning up the world and get back home, get their civilization patched up again or buried—Renfro goes back to his folks and all, Beas is back in his lab making his bombs, Ruby's America is born— when it's all done—and I know it will be—there will be a right moment and I'll feel it, and then you watch. I'm going to let you run free. You don't need anything but that. I'm going to turn you loose and you're going to run free. I swear by god and damnation to hell that I'm going to let you go free.

You just wait.

★

That was the week when they lost Burma and all that area where that movie was set with Bette Davis and Franchot Tone— I couldn't remember the name. Or maybe Tyrone Power. I decided to buy my own map and pins and tack it up in my new room which had once been the room of a woman named Sarah McCleod, who had believed in forgiveness and patience and all.